ON SCOPE

ALSO BY JACK COUGHLIN

Shooter: The Autobiography of the Top Ranked Marine Sniper
(with Capt. Casey Kuhlman and Donald A. Davis)
Kill Zone (with Donald A. Davis)
Dead Shot (with Donald A. Davis)
Clean Kill (with Donald A. Davis)
An Act of Treason (with Donald A. Davis)
Running the Maze (with Donald A. Davis)
Time to Kill (with Donald A. Davis)

ALSO BY DONALD A. DAVIS

Lightning Strike
The Last Man on the Moon (with Gene Cernan)
Dark Waters (with Lee Vyborny)

ON SCOPE

GUNNERY SGT. **JACK COUGHLIN,**
USMC (RET.)

WITH **DONALD A. DAVIS**

ST. MARTIN'S PRESS NEW YORK

This is a work of fiction. All of the characters, organizations, and events portrayed in this novel are either products of the author's imagination or are used fictitiously.

Printed in the United States of America. For information, address St. Martin's Press, 175 Fifth Avenue, New York, N.Y. 10010.

www.stmartins.com

Library of Congress Cataloging-in-Publication Data

Coughlin, Jack, 1966–
On scope : a sniper novel / Gunnery Sgt. Jack Coughlin (USMC, Ret.), Donald A. Davis.—First edition.
pages cm
ISBN 978-1-250-03793-0 (hardcover)
ISBN 978-1-250-03792-3 (e-book)
1. Snipers—Fiction. 2. Special operations (Military science)—Fiction. 3. Banks and banking, International—Fiction. 4. Terrorism—Prevention—Fiction. I. Davis, Don, 1939– II. Title.
PS3603.O878O53 2013
813'.6—dc23
2013045678

St. Martin's Press books may be purchased for educational, business, or promotional use. For information on bulk purchases, please contact Macmillan Corporate and Premium Sales Department at 1-800-221-7945, extension 5442, or write specialmarkets@macmillan.com.

First Edition: May 2014

10 9 8 7 6 5 4 3 2 1

ON SCOPE

Prologue

FALLUJAH, IRAQ

THE AFTERNOON SUN was motionless in the scalding sky, and Staff Sergeant Kyle Swanson, wedged between the floorboards of a decapitated two-story house, cautiously wiped sweat from his eyes with a dirty handkerchief. A hundred and ten degrees out there, with more to come; heat merciless enough to bake a plate of cookies or sear a man's soul. He drank some warm water, then returned his aching eye to the telescopic sight of his 7.62 x 51 mm M-40 sniper rifle. Far away was gunfire. He had been in the hide since before daybreak, part of a deadly anvil on which a huge hammer was about to slam down as part of Operation Phantom Fury. If everything went right, the insurgent forces that controlled this dusty city beside the Euphrates River were about to receive a crippling body blow.

More than two hundred armored vehicles of the United States Marine Corps had just crossed the start line to the east, accompanied by some two thousand Marines and soldiers of other Coalition countries. Judging by the increasing volume of gunfire, the insurgents had been ready for them, but the bad guys in Fallujah were always ready for a fight. They were determined not to lose their ruthless grip on the people in Al Anbar Province.

"Blue Dog One. They're coming our way." The quiet voice in his earpiece was Blue Dog Two, Staff Sergeant Mike Dodge, whose own six-man team was entrenched a half block behind Swanson's. Each position supported the other.

"Ready here," he said, running through a mental checklist still again: squad automatic weapons, M-203 grenade launchers, M-16s, even two sniper rifles, plus Dodge's radio gear to call in roof-scraping Cobra helicopters and fast-moving fighter-bombers. They were the anvil. When the tanks and APCs and infantry struck hard from the front, the insurgents would roll back into the perceived safety of the city, smack into the waiting Marine force planted in the two buildings that dominated a broad street that was empty of traffic.

There was no doubt the enemy would put up a good scrap, for they owned the home field advantage in this stronghold forty miles west of Baghdad. Their deposed dictator, Saddam Hussein, was believed to be hiding somewhere in the stubborn region known as the Sunni Triangle, where he was protected by fanatic loyalists. The Iraqi force was comprised of members of Hussein's ruling Ba'ath Party political apparatus and government, elements of the Republican Guard, some remnants of the Iraqi Army, and a growing number of Sunni Muslim guerrillas and foreign fighters. They owed their allegiance, their very existence, to Saddam. If they lost, none of them had a bright future in a new Iraq that would be ruled by their religious rivals, the Shiites. The *burps* and *thumps* of automatic weapons fire rose in volume and came closer. Explosions popped on the horizon, and the usual thick haze of dust and dirt churned.

The Swanson and Dodge teams had inserted during the darkest hours, linked up, and made their way into the eerie stillness of the city before the sun rose. Mike had set up in a house beside a junk-littered field, while Kyle arranged his guys across the street and a half block up, but within sight of the other team.

Straight down the avenue was the broad entry plaza and main doorway of the Haj Musheen Abdul Aziz Az-Kubaysi mosque complex, a domed citadel that had surrendered its protected status as a religious site when it was turned into a base for the insurgency. Trashed by looters and air strikes, the remaining mountain of jagged rubble had become a fortress. That was the prime target today. Whoever controlled that palace and its underground bunkers had the city. From his strong position, Kyle

Swanson believed he held the keys to the front door. He watched gunmen pour out of the structure and up over the walls and head for the fighting. He reported the movement. The sniper teams were the eyes and ears of the assault force, gathering intelligence and picking targets, and only later would they exercise their trigger fingers. Let the big assault force do the heavy lifting and roll a couple of Abrams tanks up the main street in front of the old mosque, supported by a battalion of Marines. The bad guys would be concentrating so hard on the armor, they wouldn't even know the snipers were at their backs until it was too late. When the hammer closed the trap, the guns of the anvil would erupt to take out specific targets such as officers and radio operators.

The forces were almost fully engaged now. Kyle checked his team, all of whom were veterans who suppressed their eagerness with professionalism, and then he let his fingers wander over his big sniper rifle, wiping away dirt. *Ready.* He was happy that Mike Dodge was at his six. The Marine Corps is a large organization but a rather small family, and over years of service any one of them meets many others. He and Dodge had been friends since their miserable days of basic training at Parris Island and later during Scout/Sniper School. They had gone off on their own careers but stayed in touch. Both had served in the first Iraq War, and afterward, Kyle had been an usher at Mike's wedding two years ago. The bride's name was Becky.

Now it was November 2004, and they were back in the Sandbox with the 3rd Battalion/5th Marines for another round, this one called Operation Phantom Fury, with the goal of taming the wild city of Fallujah.

"Blue Dog One. Hear that?"

"Copy. Fire decreasing on the outskirts. What's going on, Two?" Dodge had the big radios. There was no answer. "Blue Dog Two?"

"Yeah. I was just over on the main freq. The attack has stopped. Repeat, the attack has stopped."

Kyle kept his eye on the scope. Insurgent fighters were flooding back into the city. "Blue Dog One to Blue Dog Two. They're coming our way. I don't see any of our guys chasing them."

Dodge's voice was calm but urgent. "Dog One, we are ordered to exfiltrate immediately. Something has fucked up, and the attack stopped at Phase Line Butler."

"They want us to leave a place that is filling up with enemy fighters in broad daylight? Let's just stay here and keep quiet until it gets dark." He wanted to know what had gone wrong, but shit happens in war, and he would think about that later. Staying alive was now the higher priority.

"Negative. Those bad guys are being flushed right toward us, and they will be in every building. We don't have until dark."

Kyle could see it unfolding. The attacking armored force had drawn up in a line outside the city and was laying down a massive barrage that was driving the insurgents back and making them hunt cover. The Marine infantry, however, was not in pursuit, although the enemy was scattering like a gaggle of scared cats. *Coming this way, fast.* "You're right, Blue Dog Two. This is untenable."

As if to make the point, a fighter seeking safety from the barrage threw open the booby-trapped door of their building, and the explosion shook the entire structure and drew the unwanted attention of other enemy elements in the area. They swung away from the stalled attack and opened fire on the sniper positions. Kyle's team answered with a hail of automatic weapons. Swanson squeezed off one shot that took down a dumb gunman standing in the middle of the street and spraying bullets from an AK-47 held hip-high. *You watched too many movies*, Kyle thought. Then he popped a second man on the plaza, who looked like he was giving orders.

"Blue Dog Two. You guys stay out of this. You haven't been compromised."

"Negative, One. We'll engage from here to take some of the pressure off, and you guys bound back to us. I've called air cover and the choppers for the extraction from the field next to our building. You control the fight, and I'll control the air."

Swanson clicked his microphone to let Dodge know the message was received, then let the fight talk to him. Bullets were crashing into the mud-and-clay building where they hid, and the Marines were answering with outgoing fire that was disciplined and deadly. "Corporal Burke! We're leaving. You and Ridgeway fall back to the Two position when they start firing." The two Marines slid from their hides and moved to the rear door, and when Mike Dodge and his crew opened up, the pair broke cover and pounded across the street and into the safety of the Blue Dog Two position.

That element of surprise was gone, and the gunmen would be ready for more Marines to make the dash. Swanson and his spotter, Corporal Boyd Scott, came down the broken stairs of the house with Kyle calling out, "Reynolds and Thomas! You're next. Stay low and move your asses when you see the smoke." Swanson, kneeling at a window, tracked an insurgent who was closing in and put a bullet in him. Scott fired smoke grenades with his M-203 launcher, and a soup of thick gray smoke bloomed in the street. Reynolds and Thomas took off running and made it to the house half a block away.

The firefight was getting serious as more insurgents joined in and the acrid smoke started to swirl away. "Now us, Scott. Shoot and scoot." Kyle slung his long sniper rifle over his back and brought up his own M-16A3, then followed Boyd out. The bad guys were firing blind, but with everything they had. Bullets whined off of buildings, skidded along walls, and kicked along the pavement. He could see Mike Dodge not far ahead, standing in the window, firing carefully over their heads and into the mob behind the smoke. *Movemovemove!*

Halfway across, Boyd Scott was hit. He spun left and crashed onto the ground. The corporal had been struck in both the neck and the head and was bleeding like a fountain. His helmet had been torn off and rolled away like a hubcap off a Plymouth. There was no time for emotion or emergency treatment, so Kyle dropped his weapon and grabbed the shoulders of the wounded man's armored vest and began staggering backward, pulling the bleeding man with him as more bullets sang around them. The possibility of being shot himself by slowing down to help a buddy did not enter his thoughts; Marines don't leave other Marines behind.

Then someone else was at his side, also grabbing the downed corporal and yelling something incomprehensible in the roar of the battle. Mike Dodge had left the safety of his building and leaped into harm's way to help, and the two of them stumbled into the shelter together while the other Marines laid a hurricane of fire up the road toward the palace. A corpsman hustled over to take charge of Scott.

"You were a fucking moron for coming out there, Staff Sergeant Dodge."

"Saved your slow ass, didn't I?"

"Shit you say. We were almost in the door before you even moved."

"Screw you, Staff Sergeant Swanson."

Kyle got busy placing the remaining Marines in tactical positions, and Mike went back to the radio. The incoming fire was growing, and two more Marines were wounded within the next three minutes. "Watch your rate of fire," Swanson called as he jumped from team to team. "Help's on the way. Don't let ammo become a problem."

The first Cobra helicopter gunship wheeled in and made a gun run straight down the boulevard, and another scoured the rooftops on the left side, where enemy shooters had gathered to get a better vantage point over their target. As the first team of snakes pulled out, another set of helicopters came down to continue the counterattack, and above the roar of the hellacious firefight, Kyle heard the deep-throated thudding of an approaching CH-53 helicopter, their big taxi out of there. Corporal Scott died before it landed.

On the way back to base camp, Swanson wiped his face and drank some water and thought about what had happened. No way was that a successful mission, not with one Marine KIA and two WIA. It wasn't an unsuccessful mission, either, because the insurgents had been battered pretty well. He might never know why the original plan had been changed. What was it they said about battle plans not surviving the first shot? This was Iraq. It was just another mission in a long and dirty war. He listened to the thunking rhythm of the helicopter blades and figured that he owed Mike Dodge a beer.

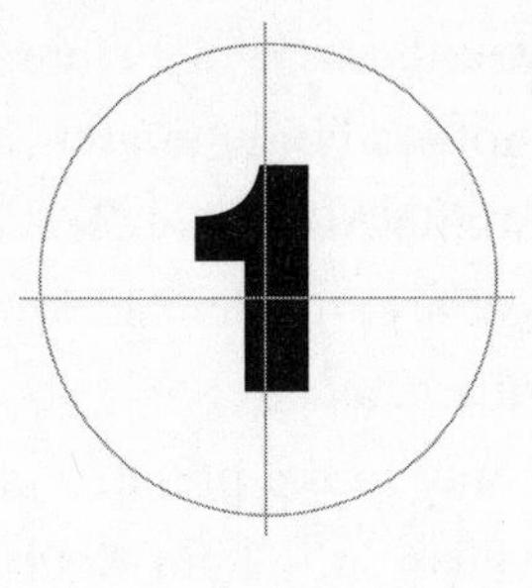

BARCELONA, SPAIN

THEIR CAREERS pushed Swanson and Dodge in different directions after that. Mike Dodge, with a wife, chose a more conventional path, while the single Kyle Swanson was swept up in special operations. Two years later, when Marine Corps Brigadier General Bradley Middleton was kidnapped by mercenaries and terrorists in Syria after the first Iraq War, Swanson went in and got him back but was mortally wounded in the fight, buried in Arlington, and posthumously awarded the Congressional Medal of Honor. It was huge news throughout the nation and the Corps, and Mike and Becky mourned the loss of their friend.

However, things are not always as they seem, and three years later, Mike was shocked one evening to answer the front door of his two-bedroom home in Oceanside and find Kyle standing there, alive and well, beer in hand, ready to regale Becky with wild stories. It had all really been a major league Pentagon paperwork mistake, he said, and they couldn't very well take back the medal, nor unbury him. Instead, they had bounced him around on special assignments until someone could figure out an appropriate job for a dead guy.

The surprise reunion became a party that continued at a seafood restaurant on the Coast Highway just south of Del Mar. Back home about midnight, Kyle got down to the business part of his resurrection and the surprise visit. First, he swore them both to secrecy, making them put their hands on the family Bible.

"Everything I told you earlier was bullshit," he admitted. "I'm sorry, but I had to see how you were both doing before I divulge the actual story. Tell no one what you are about to hear, not tomorrow or ever."

Swanson then confessed to Mike and Becky how he had been officially washed from the records to help create a totally black spec ops organization that was known as Task Force Trident. It was a handful of specialists who answered only to the president and was turning the War on Terror on its head by taking the fight right to the enemy's doorstep. Some really bad people had been learning there was no safe place to hide if they attacked America and its allies, and that there would be no martyrdom awaiting them, nothing but a bloody end. Trident could access any and all assets of the U.S. government to accomplish its missions; drones and SEALs and Delta Force and B-52s and computer geeks and federal agents and local cops and forensic psychologists could be called as needed for support. There were no paper trails to backtrack, and no punishment for carrying out the strikes, which were cleared personally by the president of the United States.

Kyle said that Trident had reached a stage where he really needed a partner he could trust out there in the boonies, and who was better at this game than Mike Dodge? Mike looked ready to sign up on the spot. Becky pulled back.

Think about it and talk it over, Swanson urged. Let me know tomorrow. Bumps could be expected in both pay grade and expenses. Big bumps, Kyle said. The Dodges talked all night before turning down the offer. It was the right move for them, Swanson admitted, but he at least had to try.

INSTEAD OF RUNNING and gunning in dangerous special operations, at the end of another five years, in 2014, Gunnery Sergeant Mike Dodge found himself in command of the Marine security detachment at the U.S. Consulate in the peaceful diplomatic backwater of Barcelona, Spain. He wore a coat and tie to work, commuting from the two-bedroom apartment where he lived with Becky and their one-year-old son, Timmy. The place was all the way to the Reina Elsinda station, last stop on the Metro's L-6 line, and it was a quiet life, a good life for a man with both a sense of duty and a family.

On a bright Monday morning, when Dodge stepped from the train station, he immediately had a prickly feeling along his arms and neck that sent him into a state of alert. He saw nothing out of the ordinary, but the gunny had often felt that special tingling just before trouble broke out back during his combat tours in Iraq and Afghanistan.

At least on the surface, everything seemed fine. A line of Spanish locals and citizens of other nations wanting to obtain visas and process business permits had been forming for the past hour at the main gate to the consulate. All were orderly, standing there for a specific purpose, reading newspapers and drinking coffee.

Four Spanish cops were in front at the barrier that controlled vehicle entry. Dodge walked over to exchange greetings, and they confirmed that there was just the usual morning traffic and pedestrians.

Dodge walked into the consulate through the heavy main door, crossed the polished stone lobby floor, and was greeted by the day-shift guy, Corporal J. V. Harris, in uniform at Post One behind the bulletproof glass wall. Dodge eyeballed him to be sure he was squared away. J. V. stood six-two, with a square chin and broad shoulders, and was an imposing figure although he was only twenty years old. Buttons on the short-sleeve khaki shirt and the buckle of the white web belt were in exact alignment. A holstered pistol rode on the hip of his dress blue trousers, and the white cover was perched firmly on a high-and-tight haircut. "Top of the morning, Gunny," Harris called out, buzzing him through the reinforced transparent entrance to the business area. "Another excellent damned day in our beloved Marine Corps. Sergeant Martinez is in the back." Rico Martinez had been the night man and would be changing into his civvies to go home.

"What's the threat assessment?" Dodge asked.

"Low. Martinez reports things were quiet all night. Nothing since I came aboard."

Dodge's eyes studied the young Marine. "Are you sober?"

"Of course, Gunny."

"And the guys at the House?"

"Absolutely. It was sort of a rough night in Barcelona, but if you want them, they can be on deck quick enough."

Dodge shook his head. That meant they were probably as hungover as sheets flapping on a clothesline. He couldn't shake the itchy warning feeling. "Matter of fact, I do want them. Call over there and get them up. And you stay sharp."

The big door hissed closed and locked. Harris added, "The RSO and the consul general are already back there." The RSO was the regional security officer for the Department of State's Diplomatic Security Service and technically in charge of overall consulate safety.

Dodge walked down the hallway, his eyes flicking to every door. Several consulate workers were at their computers at the front counter, getting ready to deal with the morning line. *I'll keep Martinez around for another hour,* he decided.

It was less than a minute before eight o'clock when J. V. Harris picked up a secure telephone and dialed the House. The telephone rang once, twice, three times, but no one answered. He hung up, planning to wait a few minutes and give them one more try before reporting to the gunny, who would rip them all a new one if they didn't answer. Corporal Harris hung up and buzzed the security lock again, to allow a consulate worker with a big ring of keys to exit through the barrier so he could open the heavy, bulletproof main door. The business day was about to begin.

THE MARINE HOUSE, a spacious Spanish-style structure of white stucco with a traditional red tile roof, was the official living quarters for five U.S. Marine Corps consulate guards in Barcelona. It was also a party place. When the large main room and manicured garden were not in use for diplomatic functions, it was one of the more popular nightlife addresses in the Sarrià/Sant Gervasi district. Off duty, the Marines knew how to have a good time.

Early on Monday morning, Sergeant John Dale was on his knees in the bathroom, paying due homage to the porcelain god after the latest Sunday night party. "I think my brain is broken," he moaned, then his stomach seized and he retched again into the toilet. The feast of paella, roast pig, beer, and red Rioja wine had tasted much better going down than it did coming up. He flushed and slumped back against the chill finish of the tub, awaiting the next upheaval from his protesting stomach.

The two other Marines in the House were Sergeant Pete Palmer and Corporal Chet Morrison, both sleeping off their own hangovers. Palmer had a girl with him. The large house was laid out along a central hallway, with a big living room and dining area flanking the curved entrance alcove. Kitchen, bedrooms, and two full baths were lined down a central hallway that emptied into the manicured backyard, which had an enclosed swimming pool. It was the best place that the twenty-year-old Dale had ever lived, far beyond his dreams growing up in his small town in Indiana. A hell of a lot nicer than his last posting in Afghanistan.

A dry and aching spasm clutched his stomach and he barfed again, and this time knew he was finally empty. *There just can't be anything left down there.* Sick as a skunk with an exploding skull, but finally empty. Staring into the mirror as he washed his face and brushed his teeth, Dale promised to pace himself next time. Someday. Maybe. Wearing just his boxer shorts, he headed barefoot for the kitchen and a big glass of water while the coffee brewed. The living room was a wreck, but by noon the maid would clean it, the gardener would fix the flower beds, and the handyman would repair any damage, all on the government dime.

Dale drank deeply and looked out through one of the broad windows in the rear and saw the fresh April sun rising, with its orange light glistening along the thick border of juniper bushes and tall blue-green Spanish fir trees. Things were a mess out there, too. It was about eight o'clock, but by evening it would all be squared away by the people who were paid to pick up after them and fix things. Like magic. This was his first embassy posting, and he liked the duty.

Had he been looking out of the front windows instead of the rear, Dale would have seen a small van coast to the curb, and five bearded men climb out and hurry through the front gate that opened without so much as a squeak. They all carried AK-47 submachine guns. With a low threat assessment throughout the area, all weapons in the Marine House were locked away in a safe. There was no local police security protection, for only an idiot would attack a group of Marines.

One of the men outside unspooled what looked like a long, narrow piece of weather stripping and snapped the prefabricated adhesive explosive around the edges of the heavy front door, then hustled for cover. A second one pressed the command detonator button, and a hard explosive charge smashed the quiet morning and blew the door to splinters. While the smoke was still thick, the five attackers rushed inside with their guns up and fingers on the triggers.

Sergeant John Dale was caught in the kitchen, where the blast of the door had left him sprawled on the floor beside the table, dazed and blinded by flying debris. The first burst of full-auto gunfire ripped his chest and stomach as the other gunmen hurried down the hallway, kicking in doors and shooting. Corporal Chet Morrison was leaping from his bed when he was knocked backward, stitched by a hail of AK-47 bullets. Sergeant Palmer and his girlfriend were still untangling themselves when a gunman stepped into the room and shot them both repeatedly.

The attack team, working from a map that had been carefully drawn by the maid, checked every room and closet, plus the garden and the tool shed, then hurried back to their car. As it sped away toward the harbor and a waiting fast boat to take them away from Spain, the Marine House telephone began to ring.

FOUR HUMPBACKED Volkswagen Eurovans were parked bumper to bumper and with engines idling along the Carrer del Doctor Francesc Darder, less than three hundred yards south of the consulate. Each vehicle contained five men and an assortment of serious weapons. When the man in the passenger seat of the lead vehicle, a brown-eyed veteran fighter named

Djahid Rebiane, received verbal confirmation that the Marine House raid was complete, he spoke one word softly to the driver, *"Vámonos." Let's go.*

They attacked just as the big front door of the consulate was swinging open. Gunmen in the lead car took out the Spanish police in the guard shack with quick bursts from automatic weapons; then Rebiane got out and lifted the boom-device barrier that blocked the road. The other four Eurovans sped through. Djahid Rebiane shouldered his AK-47 and walked calmly toward the consulate, opening fire on the startled civilians in the line outside. Three went down before they realized what was happening as panic grabbed the others. At the guardhouse, two terrorists established a defensive security position while two others began to assemble the tripod, tube, and aiming device of an 81 mm mortar.

The worker who had been opening the door saw the first shootings and moved to close it, but he was blown away by a pair of rocket-propelled grenades that demolished the entire entranceway. Almost simultaneously, another RPG team attacked the windows on the right side of the building, and the automatic weapons chattered in suppressing fire.

The three Marines inside the consulate, all battle-tested veterans, did not panic but moved with precision, although clearly on the defensive side of things. Gunny Dodge picked up an Uzi submachinegun. Martinez, wearing jeans and a blue T-shirt, came out of the back room fully armed and with a helmet and protective vest. Harris looked at the television monitors and saw civilians falling outside and a large attack team pressing in on all sides.

"No response from the Marine House, Gunny," he shouted.

Dodge also looked at the monitors. "We have to consider them dead. You guys hold in place while I get the RSO and consul general." Staff members were running down the central hallway to the safe rooms in the rear, putting Marine guns between themselves and the terrorists. Some of the secret squirrels began destroying sensitive equipment and shredding documents.

Dodge found the two State Department officials arguing. The RSO had his own weapon out and was telling Consul General Juanita Sandoval to get ready to move to an extraction point. She was refusing. Just then, the first mortar round hit the consulate roof and blew through the second floor, and the concussion knocked all of them to the carpet.

Up front, Harris and Martinez were hunkered into doorways as the first attackers charged into the destroyed lobby. Shooting would do no good because the thick glass that fronted the secure area was bulletproof on both sides. Djahid Rebiane knew that, and he brazenly strode through the lobby and slapped a small plastique charge against the inner door, then scrambled outside again. Martinez hollered a warning a split second before the detonation ripped the place apart. Harris loosed a volley into the opening, and then Martinez rolled into the hallway and opened fire, both ducking back to cover when a hand grenade came bouncing in.

Gunny Dodge and the RSO realized time was running out. The Spanish police would be on the way, but this was an orchestrated attack and would be over, one way or another, before any help could arrive. It was up to them to hold. The RSO ordered the consul general to get to the secure telephone in the safe room and call Washington immediately, but the woman hesitated.

"Maybe they only want to take us prisoner," she said. She had been a political appointee to the unimportant position of consul general in Barcelona, and her job was mainly to hold social functions. "Like in Tehran a long time ago. If we surrender, Washington will negotiate our release."

Dodge moved back toward the hallway, where the gunfire was increasing. "No, ma'am. Think Benghazi, not Tehran. These people want to kill us."

"But why?" Her eyes were wide in fear. "Let me just go talk to them. Maybe all they want is to give some demands, like the Basque separatists always do."

Dodge ignored her. It was up to the RSO to get her to an extraction point, if possible, and the gunny went crawling back up the hallway. Martinez and Harris were doing selective fire at a couple of terrorists in the lobby, who were doing the same thing back at them. There had been no general assault through the breach. Instead, indirect mortar fire was crashing into the right side of the building, opening still another gash. More gunmen outside found places in the rubble from which they could fire inside.

"How we doing, guys?" Dodge called out.

"Pretty good, Gunny. We've nailed a couple of the assholes, and they haven't come charging in." Martinez took a moment to change magazines. "Looks like they are just trying to hold us in place."

"Which means they are up to some other kind of shit," Dodge added. "So let's do a counterattack. Toss out a grenade, and we follow out to hit the front area and reclaim the outer doorway. The cops should be showing up soon."

"Or we can just hold the fort."

"I don't think that's an option. There has to be a reason for this to be going on for so long. They seem content that we are trapped in here, but they know a stalemate can't last forever." He slithered away back down the hall to alert the RSO and consul general as more RPGs and mortar rounds and automatic fire continued to smash into the building. Then within sixty seconds, it all was quiet again, as if someone were taking a deep breath. Everyone exchanged glances. *Is it over?*

Rebiane watched his men pull back and climb into the waiting Eurovans and head toward the open exit. His teams had used the time to place heavy crates of explosives at all four corners of the building, and he got out at the bullet-pocked guard facility and gently held the cell phone that would detonate the boxes all at the same time. Satisfied that all was ready, he ducked into a fetal position and thumbed the predialed number, which ignited a cataclysmic explosion that flattened the building. When the rocks stopped falling, Rebiane stood again and spent a moment watching a great fireball boil and curl and reach into the morning sky as walls and floors caved in. *Nobody could survive that.* Then he got into the van waiting for him, and it drove away.

BADEN-WÜRTTEMBERG, GERMANY

MARINE GUNNERY Sergeant Kyle Swanson burrowed deep into the muck of the Black Forest, covered head to boots in a ghillie suit layered with tangled twigs and brush. The Heckler & Koch MSG-90A1 sniper rifle was in a drag bag dummy-corded to his gear, and he was invisible in the gloom. This was only a war game, but he never mistook exercises for mere games when he had a chance to polish his deadly skills.

The woods were thick with big trees anchored in overgrowth, and although it was almost noon, it had an early morning feel. Fuzzy sunbeams filtered in columns through the low branches to stain the landscape with shadowed dullness. A stubborn mist still hung about, and a sporadic breeze was stirring every bush. It was prime stalking country.

He held his small Zeiss binos steady on a four-man team of German KSK Kommando Spezialkräfte that was moving as softly as a gaggle of ghosts; countersnipers, looking for him. Their backs were toward him, and he could take out all of them all right now, *right-to-left, four-three-two-one,* in a couple of seconds with the ten blank rounds in his box magazine. Swanson never entertained qualms about shooting the enemy in the back. That only made them easier targets. That wasn't his job today, so they could live a while longer.

Germany was to host the vital G-20 summit this summer, when the leaders of the world's most powerful economies would gather to attempt to resolve the stubborn global debt crisis. Security forces were in constant training to protect them, and the Black Forest was alive with war games testing their various abilities. The KSK special operations unit had specifically invited the Marines to send over Kyle Swanson to try an elite penetration; best against best.

Swanson had been running so many off-the-books missions that he welcomed the chance to slide back into his comfortable old skin as a scout/sniper for a while and recalibrate his basic skill set in some place out of a real danger zone.

His spotter was Corporal Harold Martin, a promising young scout/sniper from New Jersey who still had a lot to learn and was trying to pass a test of his own to qualify for future clandestine missions. Getting Swanson's approval on this job would be a big step in the right direction. Martin had already made a mistake because he was so nervous about partnering with the no-nonsense gunny. He had not emptied his bladder before the mission began, and now it was about to burst.

The exercise was to determine if an intruder could get within 400 yards of the Blue Force command center, a cluster of light military vehicles strung out along a valley road. Security patrols could only extend out beyond 350 yards, which created a no-man's land of 50 yards.

Swanson and Martin had helo-dropped in overnight three klicks away and spent the morning hours humping over the crest of a hill toward the grid coordinates of the target. Closer, and after freshening their ghillies with local vegetation, they began the low and slow work of moving without being seen. Poor visibility further hampered the hunters, and the sniper team easily oozed undetected to within 800 yards of the target. With Martin slithering alongside through the bountiful cover, they were at the 400-yard mark by the time dawn swam reluctantly through the trees. That meant that the exercise was technically over and Swanson had won. A shot from such a distance is nothing for a good sniper, so he could set up where he was and ruin the day of the generals in the command post below when one stepped outside the parked vans that bristled with radio antennae.

With that 50-yard cushion, the security patrol could not find them anyway. He had spotted two static observation posts supporting the four men on foot duty, and he admired the methodical KSK 5th Platoon troopers who were doing a solid job combing the countryside with a coordinated search. Blocked by the imaginary search boundary, it was nowhere near being an adequate test in such terrain. *Too easy. The Germans were looking for* X. *He would give them* Y. He never had much use for rules anyway, for reality always derailed plans made on paper. This was really unfair. He activated the small microphone at his throat and whispered, "We're going closer."

The response from Martin was the first unexpected thing Swanson had encountered all morning. "I have to pee."

"Hold it a little bit longer and shut up."

Swanson continued studying the area as well as the security patrol and soon found both things he needed for the next step. The patrol's pattern had a break in it, and just beyond that break stretched a long shadow that was darker than the surrounding ground and a safe zone that was further obscured by high brush. He would have a better chance in there of finding a clear opening through the trees to the command post.

Then life, the unexpected event, came visiting. "I've been holding it for an hour, Gunny. Now I really got to let it go."

There was nothing Swanson could do but deal with the situation. If Martin urinated, the smell could carry on the wind and might alert the patrol to their location. To lose this opportunity because of such a minor thing would be a crime. *The kid has to learn such things, but let him do it on somebody else's time. He ain't ready for prime time.* It was an even better reason to change their location.

"When I give the word, roll to your side and pee in the dirt, then be ready to move."

"Ah, man. You're going to mark me down for this when the exercise is over, aren't you?"

Swanson did not respond, but patiently waited as the corporal tended to his business. The smell seemed overpowering before the kid could cover it with dirt. They immediately moved out. Martin was right behind him. Once in the depression, the higher bushes provided enough cover to allow a high-crawl, and they scooted along bent at the waist rather than digging with elbows and toes. He stopped when they were only 200 yards from the command post, far behind the snooper perimeter and with a clear view down the slope to the vehicles. The little valley would mask the echo of any kill shot and confuse the searchers, who would not know where it came from. It was a perfect conclusion. He removed the H&K from its bag and checked it out, then put his binos on the backs of the patrol.

The leader stopped abruptly and held up his right hand in a fist. The rest froze but kept their eyes busy.

"Dammit, Martin, they smelled your piss." Swanson watched as the leader put his hand to his right ear, probably communicating with the command post. Then the German slung his rifle, removed his helmet, and put on the distinctive maroon beret with the wreathed-sword badge of the KSK. The other three followed his movement, dropping their wariness and standing in place.

"Gunny Swanson!" the team leader called out. "I am Oberfeldwebel Mausch. I have just been informed that this exercise is terminated and that you are needed immediately in our command post to answer an emergency call from Washington."

"Right here, Oberfeldwebel. We're coming in."

Mausch wheeled in surprise. The voice was *behind* him. A clump of underbrush stirred, then grew into the shape of a man as Swanson stood, shook off the hood of his ghillie, and raised his hand.

Martin also struggled to his feet, wondering how to cover the dark stain at his crotch.

"I think we would have found you," the German said with a reluctant smile as Kyle reached their group.

"But you didn't," the Marine replied. The two NCOs shook hands, then walked casually down to the command center, exchanging sniper shop talk.

"What's that awful stench?" asked another of the German soldiers as the rest of the team followed.

"I think the young American has wet his pants," mocked another one.

"My friends, that is the sweet smell of success," said Martin.

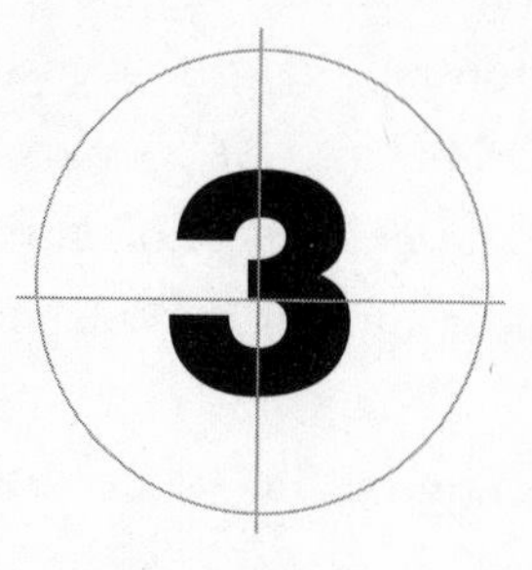

GERMANY

SWANSON WAS HUSTLED directly to the convoy's communication vehicle, a multiwheeled armored beast stacked with small satellite reception disks and aerials. Cables stretched to generators and subsidiary radio units that were hardlined into the vehicles serving the commander and his staff. Kyle stripped off the ghillie and dropped most of the gear, but camo grease still stained his face, and his uniform was caked with dirt. The call was said to be urgent, so soap and water would have to wait.

The door opened to show a frame of red light, and an enlisted man stepped out of the comm van. "Sound and camera have been tested, and the secure uplink is ready for you. Take the first seat," the soldier said, jumping to the ground. Kyle climbed up and in, pulling the door closed behind him. The soft red interior light automatically switched to regular lighting, and the whir of fans indicated a first-class climate control system that kept the guts of the electronics cool and provided temperate spaces for the human workers. Panels of lighted dials, knobs and switches, handsets, and a half-dozen small flat television display screens were lined precisely along both bulkheads. All were blank except one. Kyle sat down and swiveled toward the lighted unit. "Hey, Liz," he said to the face on the screen. "What's up?"

Navy Commander Benton Freedman was the technology chief of Task Force Trident. Marine Major General Bradley Middleton was the commander, Marine Lieutenant Colonel Sybelle Summers was operations officer, and Senior Master Sergeant O. O. Dawkins was the do-it-all administrator. Swanson was the field operator, the deadly triggerman for an organization that performed the sort of missions that would never be written about in the history books. Five people were the total complement of the unit. Trident itself did not appear on any military flow chart. It occupied a suite of offices deep inside the Pentagon, but from there, it had a worldwide reach.

Freedman was concentrating on whatever was happening, with his tousled black hair and big glasses giving him the look of a nerd on steroids. He had been called "the Wizard" by his college classmates because of his genius with electronics, but the Tridents changed that to "Lizard" and then chopped it again to "Liz." He glanced up but did not comment on Swanson's appearance. "Wait one for the general," he said, and with the stroke of a key, his face vanished and was replaced by the unsmiling grimace of General Middleton. As usual, the Trident commanding officer wasted no time with pleasantries. "Gunny, there was a terrorist event at our consulate in Barcelona, Spain, this morning. The entire six-man Marine guard detachment was wiped out, the consul general was KIA, and at least ten others are dead, including the RSO. Unknown number of wounded. Heavy local civilian casualty count."

"Yes, sir." Swanson just acknowledged the observation, since he had not been asked to comment. The general wasn't calling to tell him something that would be popping up soon on television news and Twitter.

"This is almost a real-time situation, Gunny, so we—the people we work for back here—want you to get in there right away and help the FBI do a tactical analysis and survey the area from a military attack standpoint. The Germans are laying on a helicopter to take you to a base large enough to handle a big plane, and you will fly directly to Rota. You will rendezvous with an officer who will give you a package of information, then get you down to Barcelona."

"Yes, sir." *Why do I sense that there is more to this than just me jumping into Spain in such a hurry to take a look at a crime scene?*

"We have six dead Marines, Gunny. I want you involved up to your neck. The frag orders at Rota will give you more details. Good luck." The screen went blank.

* * *

ONCE HE WAS CLEANED UP and had packed his gear, the Germans got Swanson over to Ramstein Air Base, where he had a seat waiting aboard a VIP C-20 of the 86th Airlift Wing, and the Gulfstream jet ferried him to the giant naval station on the coast of Rota, Spain. The other three passengers were an admiral and his aide and an Army brigadier general, so conversation was only polite small talk and kept mostly between the two flag officers. Swanson tuned them out and used the short time aloft to catch some sleep. He had learned long ago to sleep whenever he had a chance, and since he had been awake for almost forty-eight hours during the war game, he had a dreamless, deep rest. In fact, he snored. The plane had banked and touched down with a squeal of rubber tires on hard tarmac before Kyle blinked awake again.

It rolled to an easy stop, and the copilot, an Air Force major, came back into the cabin and popped the hatch. The admiral descended the steps first, followed by his aide, and they were greeted by other staff members in sharp Navy whites throwing crisp salutes. The general, a one-star, carried his own briefcase and walked toward a waiting car. The copilot raised his hand to stop Swanson in the aisle. "You might as well stay in your seat, Gunny. A messenger is coming aboard to deliver a packet for you; then we have orders to ferry you over to Barcelona. Plenty of fuel for that hop, and it won't take too long. Get yourself a drink out of the galley and be comfortable."

Swanson nodded. The job, whatever it was, seemed to be gathering speed, forcing him along like a stick on a rising tide, and he didn't know why. The supposed assignment of helping the FBI had to be bullshit, even though it had come straight from Middleton. By this time, whole teams of American investigators would be heading into Spain to tear the crime scene apart and map and photograph it to the inch. Middleton frequently left bread crumbs along the path to confuse anyone who might try to track what was really happening. Those trained forensic crews were much better equipped than Kyle for such work, for his own talent lay in killing people. The general was always testing him, and Swanson assumed that in the long run, Middleton would be satisfied that his prize shooter was still up to his unknown standard, had not mellowed out, and still had a sharp edge. Only then would he give the gunny a job and send Swanson out to take care of some violent business. Kyle got a chilled bottle of juice from the small refrigerator. *Middleton is such a pain in the butt. He doesn't do that measuring-stick thing with anybody else in Trident.*

A Marine second lieutenant wearing a sidearm ducked into the cabin and snapped, "Are you Gunnery Sergeant Swanson?"

"Yes, sir."

"I'm Lieutenant McDougal. Your ID." It was a youngster's order, and he should have known better than to go pecking around with a gunnery sergeant.

Kyle fished out his military identification card but held on to it. "May I see yours first, sir? Some of my information is classified. I have to see your security clearance."

The lieutenant was startled. *Classified? It's just a fuckin' ID card.* "Sure," he said, and pulled it from his wallet. After Swanson read it and matched the picture to the man, he handed McDougal both cards. Swanson's contained a color head-and-shoulders photo, his name and a serial number printed boldly over a gray Marine Corps eagle, ball, and anchor symbol, and a telephone number at the Pentagon that should be called if there were any other questions. Nothing more. The lieutenant had never seen anything like it.

The officer handed it back along with a tightly sealed box wrapped in dark paper. Red-ink letters declared it to be Top Secret. The lieutenant also had a clipboard to verify delivery, and Kyle signed the receipt.

Swanson put the package on the seat and laid his big .45 caliber Colt pistol on top of it. "Is there anything else, Lieutenant?"

"No, Gunny. That's all."

"Very well." Swanson called out through the open door of the cockpit,

"Major? If we're fueled up, let's get going." He stared blankly at the lieutenant.

McDougal, fighting the urge to say "sir" and salute, retreated up the aisle and out of the door, which was secured behind him. Back in his Humvee, he paused to watch the sleek jet take off. *So that's the famous Kyle Swanson, some kind of super spook and sniper. Not much to look at.* Swanson was only five feet nine inches tall, weighed 176 pounds, and wore his light brown hair short and neat. He looked like any ordinary Marine and had been militarily correct in their brief conversation. Those ghostly eyes were a great difference, though, for they had pierced the lieutenant like uncaring daggers, vacant of emotion, as if McDougal were nothing worth considering, much less worrying about.

After the C-20 settled in at altitude, Swanson used a thumbnail to pry up an edge of tape, then tore away the thick brown wrapping paper. In the box were six cream-colored folders—the personnel jackets of the slain Marines in Barcelona—and a short set of orders that directed him to identify and collect the half-dozen bodies and escort them all to Joint Base Andrews in Maryland, just outside of Washington. *Strange.* There were whole groups of specialists who performed this kind of duty; once you were dead, your remains entered into a realm of ritual in which every step had been preplanned with exactness. Just like with the investigators who were coming to Barcelona, this was not in Swanson's job description. *What the hell is Middleton up to?*

Whatever it was, the boss had gone to some trouble to route these folders to meet Kyle at Rota, so he must want him to know this information before reaching the next destination of the trip. Swanson opened the first one and began to read as the plane roared through the Spanish sky: Martinez, Ricardo D., Corporal, and his Social Security number. O-Positive blood type.

By the time the wheels of the VIP aircraft kissed the tarmac in Barcelona, Kyle had begun to understand, as if he were breaking out of a mental fog bank. The final folder had been that of Gunny Mike Dodge, who had been in command of the consulate security detail. It contained the official résumé, and Kyle already knew all of those details. Less than an hour after leaving the plushness of the plane, he was standing in a cold morgue in Barcelona, looking down at the scarred face of his old friend.

His driver, an FBI agent, took Kyle past the demolished Marine House and the collapsed ruin of the consulate to give him an idea of the ferocity of the attack, then ran him over to the city morgue, where the six bodies he had to identify were laid out beneath sheets on gurneys. The other victims were stored elsewhere. It wasn't the low temperature that made him shiver as he looked into the pale and empty faces of the recent dead, but a stirring of passion about how wrong this was, and growing outrage about the attack.

Then he broke investigative protocol and told the driver to take him over for what was sure to be a heartbreaking visit to the new widow. The apartment was located in a neat Barcelona suburb, and Becky Dodge flung open the door even before he rang the bell, launching herself into his arms. "Kyle! Come in! Get yourself in here!"

"Hey, Becky. How you doing?"

"Do you want some coffee? I just made some." The dark-haired beauty with the almond eyes fled back to the kitchen, calling over her shoulder, "Kyle, that's Dorothy in the living room, she's from the Red Cross. Wait a minute. I want to get Timmy. You haven't even met him."

Swanson looked at the Red Cross woman, a middle-aged brunette, who shook her head and whispered softly, "Total denial."

Becky was still emotionally at sea. She swept back into the small living room, hugging a sleepy child. "This is him. Say hello to the one and only Timothy Leland Dodge." She smiled. "Isn't he wonderful?"

"You better keep him. I don't do children very well." He smiled and guided her to the sofa.

She kept talking, as if silence were an enemy. "Now tell me, where have you been keeping yourself? Mike is always talking about the things you do, mostly rumors that you go out and do stuff that nobody really knows about. He loves this embassy work, though, and we're happy to leave the rough stuff to you." There was a break, her eyes misting. "He says there will be no more combat tours because he's a father now. I mean that in the past tense, of course. Mikey is dead, you know, but that's why you're here, isn't it?"

The Red Cross lady took Timmy into her lap, and Kyle put an arm around Becky, who finally broke into a fit of tears. "Damn the Marines," she burbled. "You goddammed Marines. He had a chance to get out and take a good job back in the States, but he wouldn't leave the Corps. He promised me no more combat, and that nothing ever happened in a place like Barcelona." She balled a fist and pounded Kyle on the chest.

"I came to take Mike home, Becky, and to see that you and Timmy were all right. Mike was killed by terrorists and died a hero, trying to save innocent lives. He will be treated accordingly. One of the best Marines I ever knew."

"And what do Timmy and I do now? Our child is going to grow up without a father, and I don't have any skills other than sewing buttons on uniforms!" He let her cry, and Dorothy from the Red Cross watched. It was a breakthrough moment, as the brave facade collapsed and Becky Dodge realized that she was no longer a wife but a widow.

He had no words for this, holding Becky and looking over at the gurgling Timmy after having just seen Mike Dodge flat on a slab in the morgue. He held her close and let the tears puddle the shoulder of his shirt.

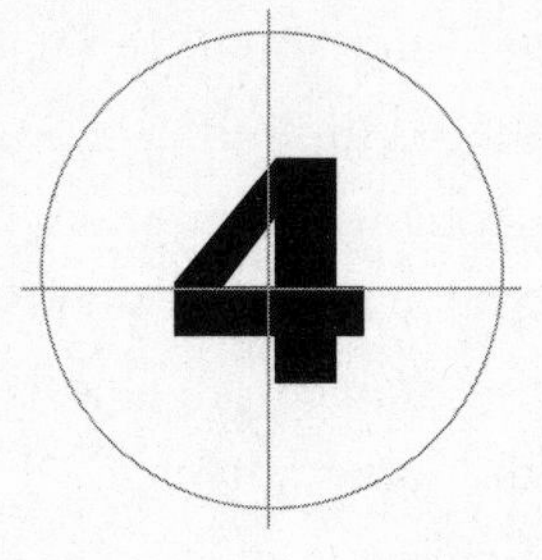

PALMA, MALLORCA, SPAIN

FORKS OF CHAIN LIGHTNING clawed the night, streaking sharp and blue beyond the verandah of the big villa, and bombs of thunder fought behind huge black clouds, as if the heavens were at war. The sea around the island sighed and heaved with waves that crested white and rolled high in the shipping lanes as the storm ravaged the western Mediterranean. Djahid Rebiane was content as he watched the turmoil, satisfied that he was not out in the weather; he and his element of the attack team had safely made the crossing from Spain before the low-pressure front caught up with them. The others had scattered into Italy and France and could be reached for future operations. The 130-mile boat trip had been rough, with the bad weather coming in, but manageable. Now he was stretched out in a comfortable lounger, watching the storm rage while he savored the fruity taste of sangria in the home of the renegade banker Cristobál Jose Bello.

Rebiane had showered and shaved his beard as soon as he arrived, and removed the contact lenses that had turned his sharp blue eyes brown. The thick black hair would be cut and styled tomorrow, and he would wear European clothing. The killer no longer looked anything like the thug who led the attack on the Barcelona consulate. If anyone asked for identification, he carried the passport and press credentials of a freelance writer and magazine photographer, but people seldom asked. Posing as a photojournalist allowed him relatively easy access anywhere he wanted to go. A gust of wind blew through the arches and puffed his new shirt. He was an imposing man, tall and strong through the chest, and at only thirty-one years of age believed himself to be immortal. Death was something he served to others, usually with a smile.

"Do you believe the Americans understood our message?" His father, Yanis, asked the question in Arabic from a nearby chair.

Djahid answered in the same language. "I think so. Our strike was delivered with force and finality."

"Enough to make them back off?"

"You know those things better than I, Father." He watched the rain fall. "This is a wicked storm."

Yanis made a dismissive face and lit another cigarette. "Washington has been taken by surprise and has not responded in any way, other than some rather common anger on television. Nothing has come through on the back channels of the diplomatic world."

"Give it a little time. We will know soon enough. We killed a diplomat and a lot of other people. They cannot just pretend it did not happen."

"And they cannot declare war on Spain." Yasim stopped speaking when a thunderclap seemed to shake the entire island, the largest of the Balearic Islands. "Señor Bello and I will fly to Algiers tomorrow for a meeting of the Group of Six to discuss how to best take advantage of your victory, my son. I believe we are now in a position from which we can impose a deadline on the Madrid government."

The Group of Six had stepped boldly onto the world stage a year earlier, when the European Banking Risk and Regulation Congress in London was shocked to learn that a special relationship was developing between Spain and a half-dozen investment bankers with Islamic links: a straight-up free-market business offer to the Madrid government as an alternative to the onerous economic rescue terms being presented by the European Central Bank. The five men and one woman identified as the core group represented international assets and credit worth billions of dollars, and contacts across the globe. Yanis Rebiane and Cristobál Jose Bello were two of its members.

Djahid closed his eyes. "Would Spain really do it? Drop out of the Eurozone?"

"The Spanish state is beyond the edge of economic crisis; it is now facing slow suicide if something is not done. We offer salvation and a chance to get out from under the greedy thumbs of the interfering Europeans who are telling them how to run their own country."

"By offering them thirty pieces of silver and Muslim rule."

"Yes," said his father. "The government was already under plenty of pressure to get its economy in order, and then the United States openly stepped in to help the Europeans. Washington abandoned neutrality and snubbed its old friend by coming publicly off the sidelines and getting in the game. That is the reason, as you know, that the Six decided during a meeting in Geneva to give them a stern warning of the consequences for such arrogant interference."

"You assume that the United States will abandon its opposition to any withdrawal by Spain from the European Union because of our single attack? That is a dangerous assumption, Father."

"Perhaps," said the older man. "Perhaps not. They probably will need some further persuasion."

ROTA, SPAIN

THE MARINE BODIES had been transferred from the civilian facilities in Barcelona to U.S. military jurisdiction in Rota to be readied for the long journey back to Washington in individual gunmetal gray caskets draped in American flags. Gunnery Sergeant Kyle Swanson, the official escort who signed the necessary papers, stayed to himself, a quiet man on a somber mission, stoic and enduring. Rain and wind pounded the big hangar that protected a mammoth C-5M of the U.S. Air Mobility Command that had been selected to fly the Atlantic with the grim cargo. The Super Galaxy was too much plane for such a small airlift, but was a token of respect. The bodies would be unloaded with utmost honors at Andrews.

Swanson had a quick dinner alone at the NCO club, a bland steak and tasteless vegetables, then locked himself away in the assigned guest quarters and read all of the personnel files again before putting the folders on a table and climbing into bed. The weather around the Med was to clear tomorrow, but it did not really matter, for the Super Galaxy would take off at 0900, storm or no storm. He felt hollow and empty inside, and after the visit with Becky, he had no emotions left for anyone else, particularly none for himself. He tossed in the bed and pounded the pillows in failed attempts to get comfortable enough to trap some sleep, only to awake in the darkness when a drum roll of thunder shook the thin walls of the building. He got out of bed, sat at a table, and stared through the window at blinding slashes of lightning and a sky that churned with clouds, and in the early morning hours, he saw a figure looking back at him while standing easily in a narrow little boat that was immobile in the tempest.

"I was wondering if you would show up," Swanson said.

The arms and grinning skull-like face were streaked with blood, and the dark robe flapped open in the wind, exposing the yellowed skeleton of the image Swanson's imagination seemed to always thrust forward when crises neared. He called him the Boatman. "And here I am."

There were six figures seated in the boat, and Kyle recognized the faces of the dead Marines. "I don't understand what is happening."

"You don't have to understand," replied the Boatman. "You just have to kill."

"But who? And why?"

The Boatman gestured easily at the half-dozen bodies. "Here are six good reasons why you must carry out your next mission. I do not have to explain everything to you. I just dropped by to pick up this lifeless cargo."

Behind the shimmering image, Kyle saw a break in the storm clouds, and through that he glimpsed a distant fiery shore. The foul reek of sulphur came to him. "Are you taking them to hell? They don't deserve that."

"No. I am just the ferry service. Others make those Doomsday decisions.

Do you want to come along tonight? I see the pistol on the table beside your milk. Were you thinking of it? Plenty of room."

"I always keep my weapon handy, so, no, I'm not going to commit suicide. Someday I might have to ride with you, but I will not make it easy."

The shrill laugh painted over the noise of a thunderclap. "Yes. Sooner or later, you must. Everybody does. But now to this vexatious uncertainty about what lies ahead for you. My six souls tonight represent a debt that you have been chosen to repay. It is a serious obligation, and you may not emerge from this experience as the same man you are tonight."

"I have been through a lot, but I am still here. I follow orders."

"Just my point," said the Boatman, showing the upper bridge of rotten teeth. "Suppose you must step beyond that safety point of being under the protective wing of your government? A very thin line separates defending your country from outright murder."

"Is that what they want me to do?"

The Boatman stirred his long oar, and the skiff began to move away. "Your enemies do not care about murdering innocent people. Do you?" He laughed again. "Of course you don't. You are my trusted stone killer, and I will be back soon to harvest your new victims."

"I'm no murderer. Fuck off!"

Continuing to look back at Kyle over his shoulder, the Boatman glided from sight as the storm closed tight, evil laughter trilling behind him.

WASHINGTON, D.C.

THE TRIP FROM SPAIN seemed the longest in Kyle Swanson's career, achingly alone in the giant cargo compartment of the C-5M with the flag-draped coffins strapped down in two rows of three each. He sat or he paced, drank coffee or rubbed a hand over the fields of white stars at the left-shoulder positions of the caskets, but he never dozed off, for he was keeping vigil, and the clock stood still. By the time the plane landed at Joint Base Andrews in Maryland, Swanson was furious with the people who had killed these men, and almost as angry at the man who had forced him on this terrible solitary assignment. He had never felt so alone and had worked himself into a black mood.

He stepped down when the ramp was dropped and blinked in the bright sunlight, facing an assembly of Marines drawn up at attention—the body-bearer teams from the Headquarters Barracks at Eighth and I in Washington. *Help at last.* Crisp in dress blues, with white covers and gloves, the ceremonial experts would transfer the remains into the military mortuary, where the victims would be officially identified through dental records and fingerprints and prepared for burial. He traded salutes with the officer in charge, who said, "Sorry for our loss." Kyle moved aside, and they filed aboard.

The voice of a woman cut through the fog in his head. "This was cruel, to make you do this. An entire honor guard should have pulled this duty. Our general can be such an asshole." The small figure pulled him to her and forced his head down to her shoulder with a gentle lock of her right arm, knocking his utility cover askew.

"Coastie," he said and managed a slight smile. He had not seen Beth Ledford since she had begun the rigorous training needed to qualify as a member of Task Force Trident. She had come out of nowhere as a low-level U.S. Coast Guard shooter and had been his unwanted partner on a tricky mission into a secret underground fortress in Pakistan. Although pint-sized and weighing only 115 pounds, Beth had proven herself to be the best natural shooter that Kyle had ever seen. She could be as mean as a Rottweiler with a sore tooth, and he had watched her kill terrorists without hesitation. Not to mention that she had saved his life. Swanson had a lot of time for Ledford, known as "Coastie" within Trident. Back in those days, she had been a petty officer second class, but now she wore the blue Air Force uniform, with the silver railroad tracks of a captain on her shoulders and the garrison cap tilted on her head.

She disengaged and straightened her jacket. "General Middleton sent me out to pick you up. The fake uniform is my cover to help things run smoothly around here; part of my training, you know, learn to lie like a thief? Get in the car and I'll take you in. It's good to see you back home, Kyle. Must have been a hell of a trip."

She drove the sedan with her seat all the way forward and raised high, and kept up a steady patter about her adventures as a little blonde trying to fit in among tough-guy warriors in the classroom and out on the training field. "I finished the explosives course, then they bumped me for a while into the Marine Corps Officer Candidates School at Quantico, which was boring. Running around the woods with the snake-eaters down at Benning in Ranger training was exhausting, but I didn't have to finish first, I just had to finish an abbreviated version, just like with the OCS."

"Sounds about right. Nobody can live long enough to go through all of the schools," Kyle said, leaning back, closing his eyes. "Our people just take the cream. On-the-job training is the best for us, but you have to learn the basics."

Once on the Beltway, she opened up the speed and charged into the fast lane. "The one thing that set me apart from making friends with the other troops was that I wasn't allowed to shoot with the rest of them. I put in some range time with private instructors, but never with others around. Caught a lot of crap from my classmates."

That brought a laugh from Swanson. "You are bad enough for morale among the hoo-ah boys just being in their midst, Coastie. They paint by numbers and you are an artist. Watching you shoot would have crushed too many egos. Anyway, you don't have to prove anything to anyone, and it's better for people *not* to know about your skill sets. You are a secret weapon, and those other guys don't yet have the clearance to learn anything about you. You have an official rank yet?"

She shrugged. "I don't know what I am anymore. I have a closet full of different uniforms and a box of insignia and another box of false identities, and they make me wear something different to pretend to be somebody else almost every day. Master Gunny Dawkins claims I should be a Marine second lieutenant because nothing is as useless and expendable as a butter-bar. I don't know what the pay scale is, but the checks are pretty generous, better than a lieutenant and much better than what I got in the Coast Guard. Right now I'm on office duty to learn what they do back here. Dawkins takes me shooting three times a week, and I enjoy hanging out with Sybelle, but I want some real field work, Kyle. I am not an office intern."

Kyle yawned and stretched. "Careful what you wish for, Coastie. This whole thing, with me bringing the bodies back? Something is coming up." He closed his eyes and fell asleep while Coastie charged on around the Interstate 495 loop, following a narrowing complex of routes until she was crossing the Key Bridge.

"Wake up, Gunny Swanson," she said quietly. She had seen how Swanson could go from sound asleep to a fighting posture in a blink. In the tripwire mood he was locked in right now, it would not be wise to make him even jumpier. "We're in Georgetown, and your place is two blocks ahead."

He came awake, and the eyes were still cold. "Yeah. Got it. What's the drill from here?"

"You rest up. A briefing is set for tomorrow morning at nine o'clock in the Trident office with the general and some other people."

"Who?"

"I dunno. I'm just a dumb lieutenant, or something."

"You are a spook now, Coastie, so you will be whatever we need you to be. Lose the attitude. You will get more than your share of action when the time is right."

A FIVE-MILE RUN shortly after getting up at seven helped burn away the cobwebs, but not the feeling of being used. At first, he ran at an easy pace, winding among other early birds, men jogging in baggy shorts, and women in colorful spandex with their hair up in ponytails that swished with the motion of their hips, everybody out getting healthy along the avenues where the cherry trees were in riotous bloom. It was another exciting day in which they could put plastic-coated credentials around their necks and go *be somebody* and pull the levers that operate the United States of America.

Kyle stepped up the stride, and his ankles and knees took the added pressure, making the burn. He didn't need this bureaucratic bullshit and thought that maybe it was the general's way of finally making him want out of Trident. Middleton had disliked him from the first day they had met, even before the Syria incident, and he had discovered Kyle's secret habit of decompressing after a firefight by going off on his own to endure a brief case of nervousness, thinking about the carnage he had wrought. Swanson had been known during his sniper days as "Shaky" by his friends, and Middleton tried to get him cashiered out of the Corps for being unfit to fight. It was one of the ultimate ironies that Kyle and Middleton had partnered to help create Trident. Swanson had thought they had become friends along the way. Tension knotted his shoulders as he ran.

So he thinks I'm over the hill? Can't handle the pressure anymore? Was the plane ride his way of breaking me by making me unable to separate my personal feelings from my professional job? Is Coastie the new go-to shooter?

Did I do something to piss off the Joint Chiefs and the White House? He can fire me from Trident, but not out of the Corps. I'll quit if he tries.

A long shower followed the run, then a slow breakfast and a careful reading of the *Washington Post*—very little space given to the deathly situation in Spain, yesterday's news—and Swanson decided to give the full treatment to the meeting and state his case boldly and defend himself with everything he had. Angrily, he gave his black shoes a buff, put on a fresh green-and-khaki service uniform, and clipped the rack of ribbons to his chest, including the pale blue Congressional Medal of Honor. There was no longer any need to be subtle.

He was out the door and once again into the scurrying crush of Washingtonians. Nobody noticed him as he sidestepped through GWU students texting as they walked blindly, then caught the Metro in the clean and cavernous bowels of the Foggy Bottom station and was hauled past the Rosslyn and Arlington Cemetery stops, rocking with the motion of the car and the synchronized lurching of passengers.

The best subway system in America never had to worry about funding, because almost every rider aboard lived on the dime of the federal taxpayer, in posts from the White House to Capitol Hill and the lobbyland of K Street. The result of having the influential commuters meant that the Metro was not only clean, cheap, safe, and convenient, eliminating the need to fight traffic and accomplish the almost impossible task of finding a parking place. *I don't have to worry about funding either. I have options other than being a pawn in some of Middleton's games. Boy, do I have options.*

All the way over, the feeling stayed with Swanson that he was among a lot of people but was not part of them. This time yesterday, he was alone in an airplane with a half-dozen bodies. These commuters were riding the subway to work, thinking nothing had changed in the world. *Get a grip,* Swanson demanded of himself. *Emotion is not your friend.*

He surfaced at the Pentagon and made his way into the section that was renovated after the 9/11 terrorist attack. The Trident office showed nothing unusual on the outside, but a retina scan was needed to get through the locked titanium door, and the whole place was encased in steel beams, with blast-resistant windows two inches thick that looked out onto the Rotary Road memorial park.

KYLE'S ARRIVAL in the offices of Task Force Trident was no cause for excitement, for Swanson did not work on a leash. He would go away for a while, then come back, again and again, sometimes little more than a visiting and somewhat menacing shadow. He gave brief hellos to the rest of the Trident team of Freedman, Summers, and Dawkins and saw Coastie working at a computer terminal. She was in the uniform of an Army Spec-5, the BDU sleeves rolled up, and she rolled her eyes with a look that said, "Don't even ask."

He knocked once, stepped into Middleton's private office and closed the door, and came to attention, but ready to jump all over his commanding general. "Permission to speak freely, sir." The voice was hard.

"Denied. Pull up a chair, Gunny, and tell me what you know about scrimshaw." The two-star general was totally relaxed in his own chair.

"Sir. If I may—"

"Denied, I said. Now listen up. Back in the day, much of the world was lit by fires fueled by whale oil. Those whaler-sailors would go out for months in frail ships, stick some harpoons in Moby-Dick, and boil the blubber to extract the oil. It was a big business at the time. Some of those old whale bones in museums still leak oil today."

Swanson's face was red with impatience. "I want to tell you, General—"

"Then some of the sailormen would take the teeth and spend months carving them with their knives, turning ordinary chunks of bone into incredible pieces of art. That's scrimshaw. It is expensive." He settled back in his chair. "You're all dressed up like you're going to a party. What's on your mind?"

"You want me out of Trident, don't you?"

Middleton dodged the question with a question of his own. "Do you trust me, Gunny?"

"Absolutely, sir."

"Do you like me?"

"That's different. You want honest or bullshit?"

"Do you believe I would give you an unlawful order?"

"The law is an awfully fuzzy area, sir, and can be bent like a twig. No, you wouldn't do that."

"My grandchildren like me. My wife still likes me."

"They don't know you like I do, and you didn't make them bring six dead Marines across the Atlantic. If you want to fire me, go ahead and quit playing around."

"And why did I do that, Gunny Swanson? Why did I get your sorry ass down from Germany and to the still-smoldering crime scene and then onto that plane?"

"You were testing me to see if I would do it. That's just like you, sir. The tests never stop."

"Wrong. Think about the scrimshaw, Kyle. I gave you this duty because I wanted to engrave it deep in your bones, down below the marrow where the DNA swims. Your next assignment may lead you to a moral crossroads, and if you have any doubts along the way, I want you to remember this trip, those flags, and our dead Marines."

"I didn't need that reminder, General. Mike Dodge and I were old friends, and I just left his widow and their son."

"You are about to venture into dubious territory, Gunny, and that's where the trust comes in. We don't have courtroom proof yet against the individual terrorists who murdered our people, but we have plenty of ancillary evidence coming from other sources about where the orders originated. U.S. intel has bugged houses and cars and computers to high heaven, collected miles of photographic footage from drones and stationary video, maybe even waterboarded a maid, I don't know the details of all of the surveillance, but I've examined the evidence and am personally convinced. It's international in scope."

Kyle shrugged. "I've never felt the need to match fingerprints before pulling the trigger, sir. If you say that it is not just speculation that the target is a threat to our national security, that's good enough for me. We work for the president, and I know Trident has already done all of the appropriate research. I have neither guilt nor pangs of conscience when I eliminate an apparent threat to our country."

The general, tall and muscular, walked over to the window and looked out, remembering the day the terrorists plunged an airliner into the building. "There has been a Green Light package issued for us by the big guy in the White House, and I want you to take it, with Coastie as your backup."

"I thought you were going to fire me."

"Just the opposite, Gunny. We are going to plow some new ground with this mission, because we are shit-tired of retaliating for an attack by knocking off an al Qaeda Number Two, and they respond by just promoting Number Three. We are going to change the game substantially today, with a lesson to remind them that nobody is off-limits. A conspirator and planner and paymaster will be just as open a target as a thug with a gun. It's going to be open season. Chop off the head of the snake and all that."

Middleton went to his safe, removed a dark green folder, and gave it to Swanson. "Here is a Spanish civilian by the name of Cristobál Jose Bello. We will do some background meetings first. Then I want you to go kill him."

"Aye, aye, sir."

"You thought I was going to fire you?"

"Yes, I did."

"You want out? Are you finally ready to take that big paycheck waiting over in the private sector?"

"No."

"So stop being paranoid and get back to work."

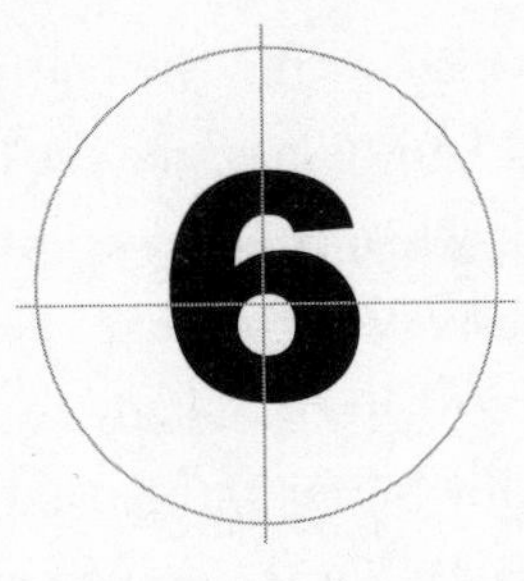

WASHINGTON, D.C.

"SPAIN IS A basket case," the gray man told the members of Task Force Trident during one of the briefings laid on before the mission was launched. He was an economist versed in both theory and a clear realism about the way money works. As a bright young engineer during the Cold War era, he had sailed as a technical representative aboard nuclear submarines, responsible for the intricate guidance systems that he had helped design. When he saw that computers had a future, he left the defense industry and started his own financial mutual fund, with a focus on technology. It currently held more than $100 billion in assets. Then he became secretary of the treasury. For Kyle Swanson, those credentials meant the man in gray knew what he was talking about.

"The country had enjoyed extraordinary growth until the financial bubble burst in 2008, and then it went into a downhill slide that was just as sharp. Employment is now over twenty-five percent, the separatist movement is gaining strength in Catalonia, the government is hamstrung because it's broke, and to stay afloat, the country is sucking billions of euros from Europe's central banks with no collateral. It has no wiggle room, no hope of a quick recovery. You can read all of that in the CIA fact sheets, and I did not come here today to bore you with numbers." He paused and looked around the table. The eyes were gray, just like the hair, suit, shirt, tie, socks, and shoes, as if fog had taken human form.

"If Spain were a corporation, it would be ripe for a hostile takeover. As an investor, I would look at that situation as an opportunity for a future turnaround under new management. The country has been run terribly for decades, the culture has grown lazy, and the European Commission is granting bailout funds only when coupled with firm demands for restructuring the economy. Thousands of jobs have been terminated, powerful labor unions have a crisis of their own, and severe austerity is the rule in Spain for today and tomorrow, as far as these old eyes can see."

Lieutenant Colonel Sybelle Summers pointed out that Spain was not a corporation but an independent nation, and therefore without a price tag.

"Ah," answered the man in gray. "Bear with me a moment longer. Suppose a way out of the mess suddenly appeared—the country could get the same sort of cash infusion to fuel a recovery but without all of the stringent terms. Madrid could turn away from the European Commission's demands for immediate change and go with an alternate Plan B, bailout help from a much less demanding source."

"Is that what is happening? You're talking billions of euros."

"We are seeing exactly that. A consortium of banks and financial interests in Muslim countries, that rich in petroleum resources and with nowhere else worthwhile to park their cash during the dark worldwide financial times, have entered talks with some Spanish leaders about the possibility of loans. They are led by the so-called Group of Six. The front man in those talks is a high-flying financial con artist named Cristobál Jose Bello."

Summers followed up. "The Muslims are trying to take over Spain? Is that what this is all about?"

The gray man answered, "Not in the sense of a military coup. Remember, the Muslims have been there for hundreds of years. The Moors ruled the entire Iberian Peninsula for some seven hundred and fifty years, until the fall of Granada in 1492. That seems like a long time ago to Americans, but it is only yesterday for the million Muslims who still live in Spain, and the Islamic religion is spreading as more immigrants come across from African nations. Their influence is undeniable, and it is growing. So this Group of Six offer is viewed merely as a gesture by old friends protecting Spain from being hammered about by the rest of Europe."

Sybelle shook her head in a combination of disbelief and disdain. "The other forty-six million Spaniards will not just stand by and watch a Muslim takeover."

"We can only wait and see," the briefer replied with a wave of his hand. "So far, Madrid seems to be welcoming the Islamic camel that is working its nose into their tent. A lot of money without visible strings attached makes for a pretty attractive camel."

After a coffee break, the Tridents were back at the conference table, this time facing a senior spook from the Central Intelligence Agency, a lady who had the pallor of an inside worker bee, for her days at Langley were spent as an analyst delving into reports and photographs and videos and radio intercepts. Fashion was an afterthought, if it was a thought at all. "The United States and the kingdom of Spain have a long history of friendship, which is a fancy way of saying that Spain is important to us." Her voice was without accent and dry, and she also spoke without notes.

"Until a few years ago, if you named almost any subject, from military to economic matters, Madrid and Washington probably saw eye to eye. That all began changing when the Spanish economy fell apart and they had to literally beg for help from the European Commission."

This time, Commander Benton Freedman questioned the speaker. "Begging? Asking for help from the richer nations seems to fall far short of begging."

"Not when almost every report of economic progress is either stagnant or negative. Off the record, of course, they asked Uncle Sam for loans, but we have problems of our own and not a lot of cash to donate to every failing old-world economy these days, so we decided instead to support the European Commission bailout. Then when we discovered the Muslims are trying to come in, we had to intervene more directly, so about two months ago, the major powers warned the Spanish bankers not to touch that tainted cash offered by the Group of Six."

The CIA woman adjusted the sweater around her thin shoulders, then steepled her fingers before continuing. "We are now certain that the attack on our consulate in Barcelona, with the deaths of so many people, was in direct retaliation for that intervention by Washington. Our sources say the Group of Six decided during a meeting in Geneva to show they were willing to fight for this lucrative prize, and that we should back off."

Master Gunnery Sergeant O. O. Dawkins grunted a dark laugh. "As if."

"Yes," the CIA briefer said. "Well put, Master Gunny. All they did was change the playing field. Instead of leaving it as bankers talking to bankers, they brought in a team of killers who destroyed our consulate, and that puts it into our ballpark. The Group of Six members themselves, of course, are not directly involved in the killings, but they authorized the attack. Somewhere beneath that benign-looking umbrella is a violent force. So far there has been no response from us beyond a normal diplomatic protest. That's about to change—CIA and Task Force Trident will be the ones carrying the message."

Kyle didn't like that. "I don't answer to any CIA case officer. My bosses are right here at this table. Them I trust; you I don't even know."

The woman gave a wintry smile. "Gunnery Sergeant Swanson, we all have our specialties. Trident will continue to control your assignments, but you will need outside assistance now and then as we accumulate information, and we will furnish those specialists. You have worked with us before."

Then the CIA representative turned to face Ledford, so there would be no doubt about her comment, although it was directed at General Middleton. Beth returned the sharp gaze. "We do worry, however, about having someone as inexperienced as Ms. Ledford running as your partner. Her training seems incomplete, her previous work is limited, and her physical size and strength may be liabilities."

Double-Oh Dawkins gave his deep bark of a laugh again and laid his big paw on the table. "If that's your opinion, then God help our enemies if Coastie ever really learns what she's doing. She drives me nuts, but she's been training for almost two years and has already won her spurs."

"We would prefer that Gunny Swanson pair with Lieutenant Colonel Summers or one of our best field agents."

"That's not going to happen," Summers responded. "You're looking at our team."

General Middleton gave his approval, then ended the briefing and thanked the CIA analyst. The Tridents took a break, then sat down again, this time without anyone else in the room.

"Our first move is to take out this guy Bello. Kyle, you and Coastie will do the wet work to open a path for a scraper team of CIA spooks who will go through his house for any useful information."

"He lives on an island. Do we go in by parachute?" asked Ledford.

"I'm thinking something a little more stylish, like a private yacht," said Swanson.

She grinned. "The *Vagabond*. Yeah!"

ABOARD THE *VAGABOND*

THE $100 MILLION YACHT, a gleaming 180 feet in length, was not only the favorite toy of billionaire businessman Sir Geoffrey Cornwell but also served as a floating laboratory for Excalibur Enterprises Ltd., the umbrella company for his various business interests. Once at sea, the *Vagabond* often assumed another role, assisting the special operations forces of the United States and Great Britain. It was not the sort of vessel normally associated with commando operations, which made it even more effective. The charming Lady Patricia Cornwell could host a luncheon party on deck for prying eyes to watch while combat swimmers exited through unseen hatches below the waterline.

Gunnery Sergeant Kyle Swanson was more at home aboard the immaculate vessel than he was almost anywhere else in the world: He was a part owner. In fact, much of his new life had started on that deck, when the U.S. Marine Corps had volunteered him to work closely with Sir Jeff to design, develop, and test a futuristic sniper rifle called the Excalibur. Jeff was a retired Oxford-educated warhorse colonel of the British Special Air Service, Lady Pat was a mother hen for elite soldiers, and Swanson was a lost and drifting soul when they had first met.

The following years saw Cornwell make a fortune in various fields, particularly with the Pentagon as his largest customer for new weapons. The Marines gladly gave Swanson temporary duty assignments to assist in those projects, and Jeff, Pat, and Kyle slowly became a family, something Swanson had never experienced as an orphaned kid who grew up on the tough streets of South Boston. When Kyle finished some deadly mission, he frequently ended up back aboard the *Vagabond* to recuperate while Pat ironed him out and Jeff listened to his stories. The relationship culminated when terrorists attacked the Cornwells at their castle in Scotland and Kyle became their protector, and Jeff and Pat adopted him as their son. Along the way, he became a vice president and major shareholder in Excalibur Enterprises, which technically owned the *Vagabond*. Someday, when he could no longer be a Marine and Jeff and Pat retired from business, Swanson would be put in charge. Knowing he had a family, and a future, might have turned Kyle into a better person, but there were still a lot of jagged edges.

"He needs a woman," Coastie told Lady Pat as they lunched at a small table that was dressed in white linen, china, and good silver beside the pool on the stern of the big boat. It was churning lazily out of the English Channel, destination Mallorca, and a light breeze north by east swept away the sun's heat. She was eating a cheeseburger and slices of deep-fried potatoes.

"That woman won't be you, child, if you continue eating like that. Your thighs will balloon." The burger did look good, but Pat picked dutifully at a shrimp salad.

"It won't be me anyway, Pat. Kyle treats me like a rock. Besides, I already have a boyfriend, one who knows how to treat a girl."

Pat arched an eyebrow. "Is that right?"

"Yes, ma'am. His name is Mickey, and he's a captain in the Mexican

Marines. Actually, I just love saying his name—Capitano Miguel Francisco Castillo, Infantería de Marina. Unfortunately, we can't get together much, but when we do, wowzee!"

"Ah, that's the boy who helped Kyle save you after that Pakistan secret fortress thing, right? Is it serious, Beth?"

Beth swallowed some tea and leaned back in the deck chair. "We want it to be, but it is hard, unless one of us quits our job. We are content to let things happen as they happen for now. We shall see, huh?"

Beth suddenly broke into a wild giggle. "I'll see if I can find a girlfriend for Kyle in Spain, some doe-eyed beach bunny that will curl his toes in bed."

"You be careful around him, Beth. Stay professional. Kyle is a perfect example of why special operators should never mix their personal and private lives."

Ledford slid a pair of big sunglasses that had been resting on her head down onto her nose. "Not to worry, Pat. I've got my Mickey, and besides, to Kyle, I'm just a trusted gun."

"Little Sure Shot."

"That's me."

SPAIN

POLICE WERE PUZZLED, but not exactly surprised or particularly dismayed, when the lifeless body of Cristobál Jose Bello was discovered in his elegant villa in the quiet island community of Palma de Mallorca. The shady financier had created many, many enemies during a long career of doing deals with dirty money from Russia, China, and Iran. His largest infamy was his role in crashing some of the biggest savings banks in Spain when the bubble burst. Thousands of investors went bankrupt, businesses were ruined, and the Spanish national economy was hurled into chaos. Bello had ruthlessly ridden the whirlwind and resigned just ahead of the sale of the vast Cajá de Ahorros del Mediterráneo for the price of a single euro to

Banco Sabadell. Bello came out of the debacle with a fortune in salary, spurious fees, and commissions.

The puzzle was not that Bello was dead but that his bodyguard had also been murdered. The banker was sprawled in his office; the guard lay outside on the columned plaza, with an unfired Uzi machine pistol with a full forty-round magazine underneath him. Each man had a large-caliber gunshot wound in the center of his chest. The house had been methodically ransacked.

The housekeeper who discovered the bodies when she reported for work that morning was more concerned about how to clean up the blood than about the death of her employer. The investigating officers of the Guardia Civil suggested that a strong mixture of ammonia and salt and hydrogen peroxide might be best, and agreed that it was fortunate that the bodyguard fell on the tiled floor of the verandah because scrubbing it would be much less work than doing the carpet that was beneath the banker's corpse. That blood had all dried, which would make her job even more difficult. Since her employer was now dead, she considered quitting, but leaving the house in such a mess was against her principles. The police said it did not really matter, for the whole place was now an active crime scene and would not be released until all evidence was collected. It would be at least a week.

Neighbors were equally unhelpful for the investigators, with one resident even spitting in disgust toward the home of the deceased. No strangers had been seen in the area, no tradesmen reported recent visits there, and the international delivery companies had made no deliveries. No gunshots had been heard, but there had been an automobile accident somewhere in the area with a lot of yelling. There were no brass cartridge casings, no broken branches on bushes surrounding the villa, no footprints, no signs of kidnappings or drugs. An antique safe with its open door hanging like a puppy's tongue stood empty in a beautiful wooden cabinet. A locksmith said it was collector junk, made before the turn of the last century, pretty but useless, and could have been popped open by a determined child with a chisel. Not a scrap of paper was left behind.

The computer equipment was gone, and the drawers of the big desk were also empty; likewise the night tables in the bedroom.

The police took photographs, filed thorough reports, and concluded that Bello and his luckless defender had fallen victim to an unknown party who had been scammed by the banker and had decided to settle the account by hiring some professional killers. The decision was made because Bello was so unpopular on so many fronts and the motives were revenge and robbery. The case was put aside to gather dust in the archives of a police building on the distant mainland. The bodies were disposed of by professional cremation, paid for by the Spanish taxpayers. The house was cleaned by a company that specialized in that sort of thing and was resold to a Canadian who had never heard of Cristobál Jose Bello. The fact that Bello was a member of the Group of Six was not considered important.

GIBRALTAR

COASTIE AND KYLE had retreated to the waiting *Vagabond* after the Mallorca hit, and Captain Michael Berryman had in hand all of the port clearances needed for the big yacht to cruise softly away from the island in the darkness. It dropped anchor in the shadow of the Rock by morning's first light, home again. For the next two days, while the CIA and the FBI in Washington churned through the information raked in by the intelligence sweepers who went through the Bello home, the white ship rode at anchor on the Med side of Gibraltar for protection against the usual stormy conditions that rolled in from the Atlantic Ocean. It was also protected from unwanted attention because it had every right to be there; it was registered in the United Kingdom to a permanent-resident Briton and flew the red ensign, and was therefore considered a little slice of London as it bobbed in the bay. Nevertheless, Captain Berryman posted watches around the clock, for his yacht was no ordinary pleasure craft, and trouble could come from any quarter at any time. British laws applied in Gibraltar, which meant gun laws were stringent. At home, private weapons had to be kept at a gun club, and if you fired ten rounds of .22 caliber long ammunition at a practice range, you had to hand back the ten spent brass cartridges. In contrast, the crew of the *Vagabond* was armed to the teeth, and the yacht, with the permission of the queen and her government, carried enough weapons to start a small war.

For two days, they relaxed aboard and played tourist in the town, batting away the thieving monkeys that were intent on stealing their lunches while ashore. Lady Pat guided Beth Ledford through the shops to gather art supplies and books to study for a future cover: They acquired a portable tripod and some blank canvas squares, and for a generous price they bought an unfinished work and the used paint tubes and jars, brushes, and palette from a street artist. The surprised artist, who had rarely managed to sell any of his work before, gave his generous patrons the paint-smeared smock for free. Then Beth Ledford went back aboard to learn a bit about art, since she couldn't draw much more than stick figures.

"You shall be an Impressionist, my dear," coached Lady Pat. "Slather on a lot of random color and say it's your impression of the palace at Versailles. Creative artists at work are given great license by people who think them crazy, for otherwise, why would they be artists at all? Hitler and Churchill both were artists, one crazier than the other. You can set up anywhere, for any length of time, with few or no questions asked."

Kyle suited up and trained her further in SCUBA diving, thinking that when she was underwater in her black wet suit and flippers, Coastie looked a lot like a baby seal. She did not look like a seal at all when she was sunning on the aft deck beside the pool in her blue bikini.

"Did it bother you, what we did in Mallorca?" he asked when they were alone. He was thinking, *The body on this girl.*

"Nope," she replied, eyes closed.

"Shooting an unarmed foreign civilian?"

"Nope."

"You're lying."

Her eyes popped open, startlingly blue against the tan on her face. More cover. People over here were not as ivory white as a kid from Iowa, and she needed to bronze up. "You and Sybelle and the master gunny have beaten it into me that I am not to consider myself as the judge and jury, particularly on this mission. You, *we,* are the sharp end of the stick, and these are targets, not people. Trust the others to make the ultimate decision. Anyway, you're the super sniper, so how many confirmed kills do you have?"

Swanson stretched his muscles, gripping his fists high above his head and pointing his toes downward, then relaxed back into the chair. He hated that question. "I don't know. I don't count, and 'confirmed kills' is a load of BS. It does not automatically translate into being really good at the craft. It has become popularized through the media as a way to identify tough guys. A single drone can kill more during one strike than any sniper over a career. What's it going to do, put notches on its tailfin to proclaim how badass a machine it is?"

Beth rolled onto her side and levered up on her left elbow, facing him. "I think I will remember all of mine, forever."

"No, you won't. Nobody can carry that load, so you will find some way to deal with it so you can get on with the job. Maybe you want to see a shrink?"

"You're my psychiatrist, old man. If this becomes a problem, you'll talk me through it. Right now, it just doesn't bother me." She unfastened her bikini top and lay down again, this time on her stomach.

Kyle got up, took two quick steps and dove into the warm waters of the pool, and stayed beneath the surface for a full minute.

NEW YORK

MANNIX DILLON had been a problem student as a child because she asked so many questions and took great delight when teachers could not answer. The professors at Harvard Law had no better luck in shutting her up than had the frustrated nuns at the Carondelet Catholic School in Minneapolis. Now she posed a question to one of her better clients, Yanis Rebiane, "Should I be concerned about the shooting of Señor Bello?"

They were in her carpeted office on Wall Street. Yanis was visiting the belly of the American money beast, and he was quiet while thinking, refusing to be rushed by Mannix, who was a frustrating person. She was an attractive woman of about forty, with light brown hair that brushed the collar of her tailored gray business suit, and long legs that ended in expensive high-heeled shoes. Without a veil, so really nothing but a whore. A whore with whom he must negotiate a price carefully, for she was managing partner of a powerful hedge fund that could slip millions of dollars around the world with the punch of a button on her computer. "No, I believe not," he replied. Her abilities had been very handy over the past year.

"Don't bullshit me, Yanis. His place was cleaned out after he was dead, which means my name is going to show up in his little electronic black book or on his computer."

"Mine, too. Along with hundreds of other names, if not thousands. Believe me, Mannix, we are in no danger. Bello was a peddler of influence and information but dealt with many unsavory characters. He did business with a wide range of people on an international front. If China wanted a license for mining bauxite in Sierra Leone, Bello could arrange it, for a price. Running some guns into the Balkans? Call Bello."

She gave one of her tight smiles that held no good news. "So who shot the bastard? Who's got that black book with all of our names and phone numbers? God knows what else is in it."

"No idea. It was a professional hit, but our best guess is that he double-crossed the wrong people in a deal. They would have emptied the place of information to prevent their own connection, and to find what else he was up to. Señor Bello was not above doing a little blackmail. It does not endanger the Group of Six, other than subtracting one from the number of members."

Mannix swept her right hand through her hair behind her left ear, then toyed with the diamond stud. The smile warmed only slightly as she remembered Sister Mary Margaret telling her that the devil is a natural liar who mixes his falsehoods with truth in order to sow confusion. She thought she might be sitting across from him right now. "I disagree. I think it is linked to the attack in Barcelona. That was stupid, Yanis. It brought us unwanted attention, and if Bello had information that can put the finger on us for sponsoring that event, Washington will throw my ass in the deep-fry."

There were times that Yanis did not understand the idioms she used, but that soon would no longer matter. "Let your mind be at peace. Think of your personal riches and future importance. Great rewards require great risks."

"No shit? How could I have worked on Wall Street all these years and not know that?"

Yanis Rebiane recoiled at the newest outburst from the vulgar woman, then swallowed and regained his calm. "I do not mean to insult your intelligence. We are all taking chances. I came to New York hoping to privately put to rest any concerns you may have, and to give you a gift as a sign of our appreciation for your work." He took a slip of paper from his pocket and handed it over.

Printed on it was the name of a small manufacturing company in Germany. She typed it into her computer and washed it through several financial programs, the brown eyes flashing on the numbers as she bit gently on her lower lip in concentration. "It's trading at fifty-four dollars a share today, and the fundamentals look normal. The price-earnings ratio may be too high. Beta is average. I am not impressed."

Rebiane gave her a steady stare. "The company will declare bankruptcy within two months. A class-action lawsuit is going to receive an unfavorable court ruling next week, accountants are finding irregularities, and when some loans are called by certain bankers, the chairman of the board will commit suicide. The shares will collapse at least thirty points. Anyone who sells the stocks short might make a little money and at the same time enhance their already enviable reputation for crystal ball predictions."

"Inside trading. Money laundering. Lying, cheating, and stealing? That I can do." Mannix had soared like a comet in the financial world, then bounced hard off the glass ceiling at the vice president level of an investment bank. She resigned before the real estate bubble burst and established BQM Private Advisers, a boutique company of her own that specialized in discovering unique opportunities unseen by other experts. She alone knew the initials stood for "Bloody Queen Mannix" and symbolized her contempt for rivals. Her clients considered the company's returns to be almost magical, particularly during the hard recovery years, but by then she had junked most normal financial rules and restraints and found that doing business was a lot easier and more lucrative over on the dark side of the street. Over there, there were no ceilings, just doors waiting to be opened. The Group of Six had been such a door, even if it had just become the Group of Five with the death of Bello—and she was smart enough to deal with anything Washington threw at her.

"So do you feel better now, Mannix? We can continue to count on you for the work in Spain?"

"Yes." Dillon stood behind her desk. This time the smile was genuine and the voice somewhat breathy, as part of her mind figured that if she played this right on the market, the profit on the German bet could be about five million dollars. "Yes."

The price agreed upon, Yanis returned the smile and said good-bye, thinking, *Whore.*

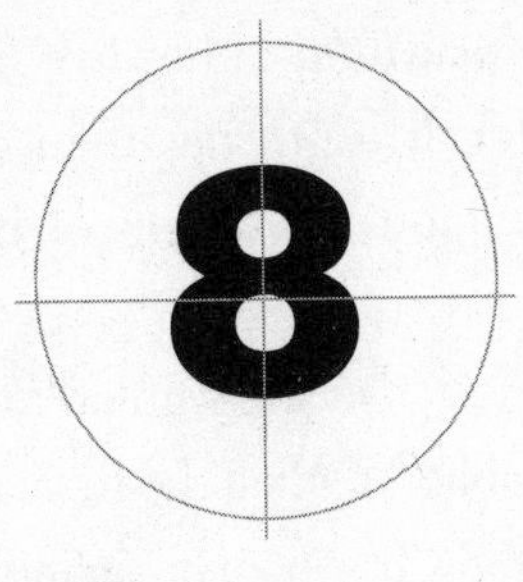

ABOARD THE *VAGABOND*

FINANCIER JUAN DE LARA was the next target. Kyle Swanson and Beth Ledford studied the photographs of a man who was no battle-hardened terrorist warrior but someone so soft that his idea of exercise would be a round of golf at an exclusive resort, where he could ride in an electric cart with his clubs jangling to the back. Violence was not de Lara's direct purpose in high-stakes business, but he did not object if casualties resulted, as had happened in Barcelona, to accomplish a higher goal. It was an unavoidable and legitimate by-product of his work.

The corpulent executive lived with his wife in a spacious villa with wide views of the Bay of Palma from their infinity pool, and he kept a beautiful mistress in a penthouse in downtown Madrid, not far from his office. Like the late Cristobál Bello, Juan de Lara had sidestepped personal disaster in the banking collapse and had been left perfectly positioned for continued success when the expected economic recovery kicked in. Rivals complained that he was propped up by secret oil money rerouted through mysterious channels, and he was raking in sizable fees from the European bailout.

"This man is a thoroughly political animal who paints himself as an ardent Spanish patriot," said Commander Benton Freedman, the wizard of Task Force Trident, who had delivered the folder and the decision that de Lara was to be eliminated. "He became such a player in opposing the European Commission's bailout conditions that he is now the go-to guy for journalists needing a quote or sound bite from that side of the fence.

De Lara says true Spaniards would rather live in an independent nation with ancient and honorable Muslim ties than in a state that is an economic cripple dependent upon the whims of Berlin, Brussels, London, and Washington."

"Did he order Barcelona?" Coastie wanted to know.

"He condemned it in public," replied the Lizard. "Fact is, he financed it."

The words jolted Kyle Swanson, who leaned back in his chair and closed his eyes. Memories flooded in of dead Marines in brushed aluminum coffins aboard a big airplane, of his friend Mike Dodge and his family, and a resolve took hold. "I want him," he said.

Freedman had seen that wolfish look before in the gray-green eyes and knew the final decision had been made. He adjusted his big glasses and continued as if nothing had changed. "The general sent me out here for a couple of reasons. I need to tweak the *Vagabond* communications suite to provide you guys with better secure contact with us back in Washington, so the general thought I might as well deliver the Green Light folder."

Swanson stared at the pictures again. So this was another paymaster who never got his hands dirty, a toad sunning himself on a gilded lily pad without a care in the world while innocents were slaughtered by his decisions. Swanson saw Juan de Lara as already dead and getting aboard the Boatman's skiff for a quick trip to hell. Then he snapped his attention back to the folder, which was thick with other information: layouts of his home and apartment, pictures of the wife and mistress, daily habits, overheads of surrounding neighborhoods, some media reports.

"Kyle, with this new secure computer and satellite gear now connected, I can walk you and Coastie through the decision-making process if you want. Part of it came from material taken from the house on Mallorca. Place yielded some really good intel on names, dates, locales, and amounts paid and collected."

Before Beth Ledford could speak, Kyle overrode any objection. "We were discussing that very thing a while ago, and we know that we are involved in something that is way bigger than ourselves. You don't need to justify anything to us, Liz. We are satisfied that you guys are making the right calls."

"Nevertheless, Kyle, the general wanted me to be very clear that this target is a Spanish national and a civilian. His death will demonstrate conclusively that the United States and its allies are rewriting the strategy of retribution. His fingerprints may be all over the money, but Señor de Lara did not directly kill those people nor destroy our consulate in Barcelona."

Coastie tapped the table with her trimmed and polished nails, which she had painted blue that morning. The little sequence sounded like the hoofbeats of a running horse. "Commander Lizard, sir, are you mistaking us for someone who gives a shit?"

Freeman chuckled. "No. I just had to deliver the information, and I wanted to get out of the office."

NEW YORK

MANNIX DILLON slipped an arm through the shoulder strap of her Louis Vuitton handbag and gave the long mirror on the wall behind her office bathroom door a final check. Her hair was fluffed out a bit today to get a windblown look, and she used a small soft brush to smooth out a blemish that she saw in the skin tone. A heavy antique bracelet encircled her right wrist, and she liked the way the tweed skirt and short-sleeved sweater caressed her figure. No doubt, the gym time was paying off. She closed the purse and walked out to the desk of her personal assistant, a nice young man who adored her.

"Perry, I'm going to a short lunch and will be back by one thirty. How about the reservations for tonight?" She thumbed through her electronic diary as she talked at him as if he were a lamp.

"Three places are reserved at the Four Seasons at nine o'clock, Ms. Dillon," he responded efficiently. "A driver will pick you up at eight thirty. His name is Harold."

She said, "OK," and turned away, still not looking at him and asking herself silently, *Lunch with Joanie and Patrice, and then clubbing tonight with the same two?* She liked them as friends, but really, wasn't this too much? Patrice, with her crazy hair that drooped over one eye, was vice president of a publishing company and always filled with tidbits of gossip. Joanie had lost her job in the downsizing when the bear stomped through Wall Street and was only now coming back into the marketplace, recently landing an executive position that paid $150,000 a year. They would all bitch over lunch about how *anybody* could live on such a salary.

The restaurant was a Japanese affair three blocks from her office on Fifth Avenue, and they sat at a table slightly raised on a platform near the back, so they could watch the chefs chopping up ingredients at the sushi bar and shouting greetings to arriving customers. A round of drinks started the lunch; then came tea and some raw things and rice and finally a dessert that bore a vague resemblance to a pudgy rat. It was a good hour, and Patrice was enthusiastic in describing a sex scandal that was about to break involving a mover-shaker type and two pregnant mistresses, one of whom was filing a lawsuit against the other. "Someday," Patrice said, "the idiots will realize that there is no such thing as privacy in the digital world. The photographs are delightfully grotesque!" They laughed, split their bill three ways with a 15 percent tip, fumbled for exact change, and went back to work.

The April sunshine was warm on her shoulders as Mannix fell into her stride, matching that of the postlunchtime crowd, hundreds of people on the same street, heading in both directions and illegally crossing between cars as taxi horns blared. A hawker selling fake Rolex watches had set up his open briefcase beside a parking meter, and a boxy kiosk newsstand overflowing with newspapers and magazines squatted on the corner. A subway rumbled by underfoot, shaking the metal sidewalk grate. She flowed through the crowd, never so much as brushing a shoulder or an elbow. Moving alone in a sullen crowd was a special New York thing; she loved it.

Her rhythm was suddenly broken when a tall, clean-shaven man with dark hair and bright blue eyes zigged when he should have zagged, and they were doing the foot-to-foot sidestep dance before he actually bumped hard into her. He grabbed her right shoulder, as if to steady himself, smiled, and muttered, "Excuse me. Sorry." Djahid Rebiane hurried on. No one had noticed the bump, and she was ready to give the automatic glare and maybe a shouted curse—*Fucking moron!*—but the words didn't come. Her momentum kept her moving forward; then a pain like none she had ever felt tore at her insides and her steps faltered and slowed and she grabbed her expensive purse hard as she sank to the pavement on her knees, and bright colors mingled in her swirling vision and *I'm hurt, I'm hurt, I'm hurt somebody help me* screamed in her head, but no words came from her mouth, only gurgling blood. She hit the sidewalk on her right side and rolled onto her back in a spasm of pain, and the moving crowd opened to accept the newly occupied space and kept moving, texting and talking on their cell phones.

The last thing Mannix Dillon ever saw was a beautiful canopy of light over the towers of lower Manhattan.

UPTOWN in the West Seventies, Yanis Rebiane was sharing a Central Park bench alongside an ambitious young investment banker, handing him a business card and finishing the pitch. "As a token of my goodwill, allow me to give you the name of a German company that is facing disaster. It's trading somewhere in the fifties right now but is going to nosedive about thirty points."

Peter McNamara had curly brown hair and big teeth and was itching to close this deal to become the money transfer point for a slice of that outside money being pumped into Spain. Two years out of Wharton, as an anonymous Wall Street drone, he was paid well enough for him to wear this blue suit from last year's end-of-summer discount rack at Barney's, but Peter thought of himself as more of a tailored Brooks Brothers kind of guy, with a pair of handcrafted J. M. Westons on his feet. He had no family money, but he was smart and willing to work harder than anybody else, and cut a few corners, for the right price. Arab money spent as well as American money. *Show confidence!*

He read the card, then stuck it in an inside pocket. "You know that one of my specialties is midcap internationals, Mr. Blanco, and I am always looking for undervalued companies that show growth potential. So I'm familiar with this one. From what I remember of the latest quarterlies, it is not in any trouble at all."

Yanis had not been entirely truthful with Mannix Dillon. He indeed was quite concerned about the possible material that had been scooped out of the villa belonging to Cristobál Jose Bello. The strike showed the tradecraft of professionals, not some waterfront toughs. Only Allah, praise be unto his name, knew what secrets Bello had memorialized on his hard drives, all of which were gone. Yanis had to assume the worst case, that they were being unraveled somewhere, possibly by intelligence agencies—American most likely, but the special forces from the U.K. and Spain were also possibilities. Nothing had leaked to the press, indicating it was a tightly run operation.

Certainly there would have been some record of transactions with Dillon's BQM Private Advisers. That was why Rebiane's son, Djahid, had just bumped into her on Wall Street and shoved an eight-inch blade between her ribs, digging around to cause maximum damage and leaving her staggering to die on the busy sidewalk. BQM had been a handy and efficient contact, but Yanis was confident that the avaricious Peter McNamara, with his country-boy smile and big-city tastes, could take her place. It had been a mistake to allow Mannix to know his real name, a mistake he would not repeat.

To McNamara, Yanis Rebiane would be Carlos Blanco, and he looked around the sidewalk for people who seemed out of place before speaking again. "The roof is caving in on them, due to a class-action lawsuit that is as good as lost even before it has been filed. Loans are already being called, and the company is hiding the troubling data. Bankruptcy in two months at the outside, and the chairman yesterday failed in a suicide attempt."

"They've been cooking their books?" McNamara's smile grew to include a large expanse of healthy pink gums above the teeth.

"A short sale might be a good investment."

Peter McNamara was thinking the same thing. With such access, he could reap a fortune. Making the biggest deal of his life, he agreed to Mr. Blanco's terms for a future relationship.

9

MADRID, SPAIN

THE FIRST MORNING of surveillance broke with a serene sky that polished the streets of the old city with the glow of promise for still another new day. They could only hope it would last. It rained a lot in April, when a downpour seemed always just over the horizon.

When Juan de Lara, still in his pajamas, opened the French doors that led onto the little balcony of his apartment, he stepped outside for a moment to enjoy the view of the capital and breathe deeply, huffing fresh air deep into his lungs. Marta was still sprawled on the creamy silk sheets with her dark hair fanned on the pillow, but de Lara had to go to work. He was eager to get out and about, for today he was to collect another wire transfer for a hundred thousand U.S. dollars for his personal account from Mannix Dillon at BQM to spread around Spain like a political lubricant.

He noticed that he was not the only early bird this morning, for a petite woman down the block was wrestling with a tripod, a large sketchbook, and a small valise of her paints and brushes. She was facing away from him, probably setting up to catch the morning light on the dome of the Almudena Cathedral over on Calle Bailén. Artists seemed to love the massive architecture of the cathedral, which took more than a century to build and had not been consecrated until 1993, but de Lara thought the bulky gray building was somewhat grotesque, a new pretender in a land of antiquity. The Muslims might have something to say about that in the future, for beneath the ornate cathedral were the ruins of a mosque.

He was dressed and out of the front door in thirty minutes, strolling briskly, his big stomach rocking back and forth with each step. The fat man took his usual table at a sidewalk café and sat alone for fifteen minutes to read both *El País* and *El Mundo del Siglo Veintiuno* while enjoying a thick coffee-and-milk mixture with sugar around the rim and a shot of brandy. The *carajillo* tasted so good that he had two more. He read that police had been forced to fire rubber bullets into a crowd of demonstrators yesterday, which he considered even better news than the 3–nil soccer score, Real Madrid over AC Milan. When finished with his liquid breakfast, he walked to his office.

Kyle Swanson followed.

AT ONE O'CLOCK, the city began to shut down for siesta, and de Lara made his leisurely way back to the apartment, taking a taxi all the way to the door. The little artist was still at her tripod, proving that she was not a native. Nobody but sub-Britons and Americans avoided the time-honored habit of the siesta, taking a break during the long day. He noticed that the woman was young and pretty, with blond hair pinned up beneath a bright green kerchief, and wondered what she was painting. Artists were strange people, he thought. They didn't necessarily draw what other people saw. He went inside and found Marta waiting, eager for his return. She had not even gotten out of her bedclothes from the morning, and he put on his pajamas and crawled in beside her, nuzzling the midnight hair before falling asleep.

"He's down for the count." Swanson's voice came to Coastie through a flesh-colored earbud hidden beneath the bright scarf. "I'm on deck, so you go ahead and break down your stuff and get out of here. We don't want you getting too much of his attention."

Beth Ledford took out her cell phone for a quick call, and by the time she was packed up, a hired car pulled to the side and Lady Pat opened the door. She slid inside while the driver, part of her security guard, stashed the art gear. "I did great work today," Coastie said. "I smeared some blue paint on the canvas, along with red paint and yellow paint, and drew circles and stuff. A nice lady stopped and asked what I was painting, and I said I was an impressionist."

"Let's get some lunch and continue your education, child," said Pat. "I'm taking you through the Prado this afternoon, where you will see the works of El Greco, Goya, Velázquez, and other Spanish artists. Everything from monsters and lunatics to court portraits and naked ladies."

"Our target appears totally unconcerned," Coastie said, scrubbing her fingers with some damp wipes.

"Wealth does that to some people, Beth. They view themselves as undefeatable sharks in the money sea, creatures with no natural enemies."

"I mean, he's trying to overthrow the government, but first he's going home for nappies with his babe? What kind of crazy is that?"

Lady Pat recognized the tone. Coastie was working through the mechanics without knowing it. "These things never fly in a straight line. You just do your part of the job and don't get sidetracked with conflicting thoughts."

"Should we go pick up Kyle?"

"Leave Kyle alone. He's at work, almost like a snake coiling in a corner and getting ready to strike. You and I have to do the Prado now."

AT THREE O'CLOCK, de Lara awoke and once again padded to the balcony in his slippers and pajamas, leaving Marta still snoring slightly. He threw the doors apart with a grand flourish and stepped outside again, smiling. The city was still there, beckoning him. The little artist was gone. He stretched, opening both arms wide, and thought about the cash that had come in that morning. There was a new source, not Dillon, along with a note that the new contact was another American, Peter McNamara.

DAY TWO was a repeat of Day One, for Juan de Lara was a thorough creature of habit, and they tracked him with ease from morning until after siesta.

The young artist was back at her easel on the street below early that morning, again facing the cathedral dome, and the mogul crossed over to walk by her on his way to the coffee and newspapers. She was cute, no doubt, and he said hello to her in English. She glanced up and briefly smiled but said nothing in return. Her canvas looked like a mishmash of colors, but what did he know about art? Later, when he returned for siesta, he wondered if he should make a more direct approach. Artists never had any money, and maybe a generous amount might lure her into bed with him and Marta for an afternoon. By the time he stepped onto the balcony right at three o'clock, she was gone again.

While Beth and Pat went to the Centro de Arte Reina Sofía to view the Picasso and Dalí collections, Swanson roamed the blocks around the apartment with a Canon camera around his neck, snapping photos like a tourist, and was in position at three to snap de Lara in his sleepwear. He also had a laser range finder, a GPS locator, and a wind meter, and he carefully measured and drew up a sniper range card.

De Lara had no security whatsoever. It would have been easy just to walk up and shoot him, but getting away after that might be impossible. The police of Madrid and Spanish security forces had stepped up their defensive posture since Islamic terrorists in 2004 killed 191 people on four trains, and Kyle had seen numerous cops cruising the avenues at random, while security cameras hung everywhere. An escape and evasion route had to be planned as well as the hit.

Swanson was not arrogant enough to think that such increased vigilance might not have spotted him. Having done such countersurveillance himself, he spent a lot of time that afternoon watching for watchers. A broad window in a jewelry store mirrored the opposite side of the street; sudden stops and reversing his route would make any tail duck for cover; going into a store and stopping behind a counter just inside would force a follower to hesitate long enough to be noticed; and changing lines on the Madrid Metro or swapping taxis made it almost impossible for only one or two people to keep him in view. He saw no suspicious people or cars behind him.

The street was a broad hive of buildings, mostly residential apartments and many ground-level shops. Windows and doorways galore offered opportunities which he bypassed. Swanson had decided to take down de Lara at three o'clock the following afternoon, so he was looking for a secure platform with a direct line of sight to the balcony. There was no hope of anything from a window directly across the street unless they risked breaking into a private apartment or a store, which heightened the odds of a police response. The possibility of taking a position on the rooftop of the opposite building was also discarded; sloping red tiles almost guaranteed failure.

He walked along straight for a while to create a channel that would stretch out any surveillance, then made a sharp left turn, a right at the next corner, and left again. No familiar faces or automobiles were tracking him.

A final wide detour brought him up the next street over from the de Lara place. The value of the property in such an exclusive area had overcome the depression, and an old building was being renovated. Kyle saw the opportunity. Checking his map, he counted his steps from the west corner until he was standing at exactly the distance from the west corner of de Lara's street to the front door of his apartment. The construction area was precisely on the needed spot.

During siesta, the workers had left the site unattended, and Kyle slipped beneath a yellow tape that cordoned off the building and went inside. He stood still, taking in the sights and smells and sounds. Empty. A staircase led from the ground floor all the way to the top, and he went up, his eyes searching everywhere for potential risk. A door frame beckoned at the top floor and he went in, pulling out a small pair of binos. Standing at the window, he had a clear and direct view of the balcony of Juan de Lara.

Turning around, he examined the far wall of the room in which he stood. It was back far enough to be in shadow from the midday sun, and carpentry debris littered the floor. He liked it. This would do. He used a broom to give the area a quick sweep and brush away his footprints.

There would be no time to loiter after the shot, because the Madrid residents would be on the move again, showing up for their afternoon shifts, but he counted on the laborers on this job to milk their siestas for as long as possible. He and Beth would not need much time to break down their gear and go down the stairs after taking the shot. The entire ground floor was wide open except for machinery and tools, wallboard, and paint, with multiple points of egress. He made a note to arrange for his CIA contact to park a 4x4 truck two blocks from the site, so they could get over to the M-30 and out of town.

It should work. Then the rain started, a few gentle drops that increased steadily in strength before he waved down a cab. It was slashing at the rooftops and flooding the streets by the time he reached their hotel. Night came early, preceded by thick and rolling storm clouds and curtains of falling water.

MADRID, SPAIN

KYLE SWANSON rapped on the door of the hotel room, and when Beth Ledford opened it, he stepped inside. She closed and locked it behind him and put her pistol back on the little table beside a vase of flowers. "This rain looks like it will be hanging around for a while," he said.

Beth's face was flushed, she had her hair swept back in a ponytail and was in a cutoff T-shirt that exposed her tight midriff, above cotton Victoria's Secret pajama bottoms, gray with PINK in big letters across the butt. No bra, and her chest heaved from hard breathing. *Damned near naked,* he thought.

She stretched, ignoring his disdainful look. The usual man-woman sexual tension was there, but neither acknowledged it, knowing it wasn't going to happen, not tonight or any other night. There would be no "friends with benefits" between the two predators. Coastie said, "I was watching the Weather Channel while I exercised. The forecast is for more rain over the next two days. De Lara may change his routine."

Swanson went straight to the big window and looked out at the downpour that was sweeping over Madrid. "I found a good site for a hide," he said. "A direct line of sight to his balcony. If this weather holds sour, then we need to be ready in case the target decides to run up to his sunny villa and play golf instead of waiting here. I want to get set things up tonight. Tomorrow may be too late."

She walked up beside him and looked out, crossing her arms. Lightning bolts split the sky to the west. "Kinda dirty weather for a precision shot, Kyle."

"It's only about two hundred yards, Coastie. I've made up a good range card, and we'll adjust for conditions once we are in position." There was no discussion about who would take the shot; that belonged to Swanson. "OK. I'm going to get cleaned up and pack my gear, and you do the same. Boots and jeans, and be ready to stay there all night. Meet you at the truck in thirty mikes."

They left the hotel by different doors at different times, pulling dark rain-cape hoods over their heads and with backpacks dangling from their shoulders. The few other pedestrians outside were all carrying wide umbrellas and hurrying to shelter, their faces down in the blowing rain, and no one gave them a second look. Kyle was waiting behind the wheel of the stubby black Renault Koleos SUV when Beth threw her pack in the rear and climbed into the passenger's seat.

They were already mentally in the mode of special operators in unfriendly territory, although downtown Madrid was not at all similar to Pakistan or Afghanistan. To be discovered, arrested, and exposed would be a major diplomatic setback that Washington could ill afford. They put on latex gloves, which would prevent leaving fingerprints, and black wool beanies, which they would pull down to become masks with eye and mouth holes once they reached the building. In addition to the long waterproof capes and hoods, the extra gear would make them little more than shadows in the storm.

Swanson keyed the ignition, switched on the lights and wipers, and dropped the Renault into low gear. No cars coming. He drove away, following the map he had memorized. No more than fifteen minutes of safe driving within the speed limits.

"I saw something at the Reina Sofía Museum today that bothered me," Coastie said.

"What?" Kyle thought she might have spotted someone on their tail.

"*Guernica.*"

"The Picasso painting? This is no time to be thinking about abstract art from the Spanish Civil War, Beth. Get your mind in the game here, and keep it there."

"I couldn't help it, Kyle. I studied that mural for fifteen minutes, and the longer I did, the more I saw, and the more it got to me."

He flicked his eyes over and caught her staring at him.

"It's about what happens to civilians in war, Kyle. Civilians. Like our targets. Are we really the bad guys in this?"

"No. The Group of Six is the enemy. No question." He lowered his voice and slowed the vehicle, pulling to the curb and stopping to glare at her. "Am I going to have to replace you? I won't let you screw up my mission."

Beth waved both hands in front of her. "Of course not. I'm ready. I was just thinking about the painting, that's all."

"Think instead about these targets as being the people who are responsible for the attack on our consulate in Barcelona. They are noncombatants only in the sense that they don't wear uniforms. Those assholes don't care who gets butchered in the process of their financial and political schemes. Personally, I'm thinking about six dead Marines and the others who were killed and injured."

"God, I'm sorry I brought it up. Let's get on with this."

"You picked a hell of a time to start getting philosophical," he said. "Just remember that Picasso was depicting the slaughter caused by Nazi bombing raids. I intend to stop another Guernica before it starts. Are you my partner or not?"

"You and me until the wheels fall off the wagon, bubba." Beth Ledford returned his stare with a black frown of her own. "Drive."

They rode the rest of the way in stony silence, trying to regain that quiet place in the zone, although both of their minds still buzzed with the brief altercation. There was plenty of vacant parking, and Kyle nosed into an empty spot more than a block away. They still didn't speak as they got out, rolled down the masks, fixed the rain hoods, and hauled out their bags. Kyle locked the SUV by pushing a button and led off, Beth tracking right behind him as hard rain blew horizontally.

Getting into the building brought welcome relief from the downpour, and no one was at the construction site. Kyle headed straight for the stairs and up at a fast clip, not having to worry about creaking boards because the old stairway was made of heavy stone into which thousands of passing feet had carved grooves over the last century and a half. The walls seemed to shudder beneath the onslaught of the gale winds outside, and rain seeped through the many cracks. On the top floor, he motioned Coastie to come through and close the door.

She walked to the window, and all doubt vanished. The little balcony of Juan de Lara was in plain sight across two streets, flanked by lights that sparkled in the falling water. *Kyle is right. This puppet master is overdue for getting his ticket punched.* Ledford stepped back, unslung the shoulder bag and gave Swanson a thumbs-up sign.

KYLE SWANSON had been here a thousand times. Lying on his belly behind a loaded, scoped rifle, ready to shoot. Most guys would prefer being on a couch watching football on television, but a sniper hide was Swanson's real home, the place he felt most comfortable. His weapon tonight was a Heckler & Koch HK-416 variant of the trusty M-4 carbine, with a magazine of standard 5.56 mm rounds, the identical combination that he had used earlier to take down the target and bodyguard in Mallorca. It was almost like giving Spanish forensic investigators an autograph if they tested the bullets found in both places. The cops were sure to figure out the connection. The real message was intended for the remaining members of the Group of Six.

The pair of snipers made quick work of piling construction material, stained tarps, and old furniture about seven feet from the rear wall. Kyle would take the shot from beneath a small table on which lay a haphazard collection of old books and trash. At his left, Beth lay with a small pair of Zeiss binos at her face, focused on the door of the de Lara penthouse. Throughout the night, one of them would always have that door under observation.

He had dismissed Coastie's earlier outburst, realizing that she was still coming to grips with the basic sniper dilemma of sorting through how to handle the bodies of those she killed. Swanson's own mind had created the spectral Boatman to cart away the memories. Before that, he had endured the awful nickname of "Shaky" due to his postbattle habit of finding a quiet spot for a quick nervous breakdown. Since he'd met the Boatman, the big shakes had vanished. Ledford was dealing with it in her own fashion, still getting used to being the sharp end of the spear. Everybody in Task Force Trident knew the kid had talent, Kyle had seen her at work in Pakistan, and she had since been trained to be even sharper. He had no worries about Coastie.

The tempest raged throughout the night, and they were constantly reading the instruments and calculating the effects on the coming shot. The distance, gravity, and the added weight of the raindrops meant the bullet would be forced downward during flight, even over such a short distance, and the stiff wind was going to push it to the right. A soggy flag atop the target's building was snapping like a whip. As dawn approached, they decided to compensate for a 12-mile-per-hour gust of wind and a two-inch drop, and Kyle dialed in the final aim point. The snipers remained hidden, unseen and silent, watching de Lara's door and listening to the brash rhythm of the deluge. At dawn, a mist hugged the low ground.

JUAN DE LARA had been unable to sleep, wrestling with the rumpled bedsheets throughout the dark hours and drawing complaints from Marta. He had never liked the unrelenting overnight storms, because they made him recall his childhood fears of monsters in the closet and death creatures lurking under the bed. He finally quit trying when daylight began washing the room clear of such dread, and at six thirty he rolled his bulk to the side and heaved upright. Marta made a small sound as the bed bounced when he lifted his great weight from it. He turned on the bathroom light, did his business in the toilet, and moved on to the kitchen, where he opened the refrigerator and found a cold bottle of juice. *Maybe the weather isn't so bad by now,* he thought. *Maybe just a noisy drizzle. I'll take a look and decide about going to work.*

"Lights," Beth whispered, pulling the binos tight to her eyes. "Somebody's up."

Swanson had been resting on his back, wide awake, and he rolled over easily to the stock of the rifle and got on scope. The door was still closed, the wind and rain continuing at the same intensity. A light came on in the main room, and Kyle eased the slack out of the trigger. The door opened.

De Lara wore a plush white bathrobe that hung untied over white pajamas, and his hair was mussed. He had a hand on each door and pulled them inward, thus framing himself in the portal, although he did not move onto the balcony. The rain was splashing hard on the tiles, and he did not want to get wet.

Kyle fired at the middle of the meaty chest, accepted the recoil of the M-4, and fired again at the same spot. De Lara winced in surprise with the first hit and looked down at the crimson bullet hole and the blossom of blood on the whiteness of the robe. The Spaniard crumpled to his knees, still holding the doors, and then the second shot struck and he collapsed. Kyle changed the aiming point slightly and carefully put a third round in the target's head, shattering the skull.

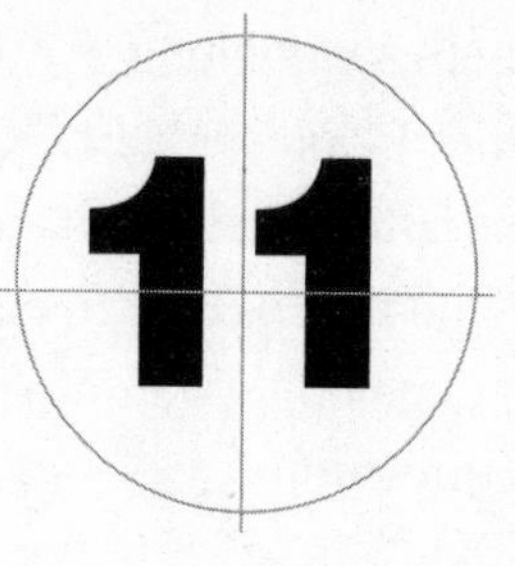

WASHINGTON, D.C.

YANIS REBIANE and his son, Djahid, could see the towering spire of the Washington Monument straight ahead as they strolled on the Mall. Much of the towering marble obelisk, some 555 feet tall, was cradled in a web of construction scaffolding and canvas, under repair after being damaged by an earthquake. Yanis believed in his heart that it had been the hand of Allah, whose name be praised, that shook the earth's crust and maimed one of the most cherished symbols in America, to remind these people and their unholy government that no person nor place nor thing was exempt from the wrath of the Almighty One.

The National Cherry Blossom Festival had ended on Sunday, and most of the tourists had gone home, so the two Algerian men could now conduct their business and enjoy the astonishing beauty of the flowering pink and white trees without being swarmed by thousands of sightseers. This warm April day was perfect for the leisurely stroll, and they spoke without concern that anyone might be recording the conversation. The White House, the very heart of America, was within a mile of where they stood.

"The Spanish police say they have no leads in the murder of our partner Juan de Lara," said Yasim. "Just as they had nothing after the death of Cristobál Bello on Mallorca. I do not know what is holding them back from officially declaring the rather obvious connection."

The sharp blue eyes of Djahid Rebiane swept over the people passing around them, heading both ways along the broad concrete sidewalks. "They were both sniper hits. Good work, too."

"Too good," replied his father, nodding in agreement.

"I looked at the shots, and they were extremely precise. Along with the planning required, and the stealth of getting into position and safely out without being detected—this was the work of professionals, Father."

"Yes. But who?"

Djahid could only shrug. "The world is full to the brim with well-trained snipers these days. They are a needed specialty in urban combat. For the Americans, the training of snipers has moved to a higher level than most, and that field was expanded during the years of fighting in Iraq and Afghanistan."

"I believe the Americans are hitting back in retaliation for the attack in Barcelona. There has been very little indication that they are pursuing our actual strike team, so it seems that instead they are going quietly after individual civilians, the Six. That is most unlike Washington."

"I absolutely agree," said Djahid, unwavering in his conclusion. He could not shake the uncomfortable feeling of an unknown presence out there, someone as cold-blooded as himself. "I would think the most likely suspects would be SEAL Team Six or Delta Force, but they are not the ones. Those people leave big after-action support footprints because they commonly employ helicopters, planes, and ships and a bright digital track. The de Lara and Bello shots were very smooth, conducted in secret, and no clues were left behind other than the Mallorca house being cleaned out. That part indicates the CIA could be responsible. They have great shooters, too, usually on loan from the military. Absolutely nothing is being said, not a word. Spain would see it as U.S. meddling in its affairs."

"The truth is that we don't know who is behind this," Yasim told his son.

"No. Whoever it is, however, is going after the Group." Djahid said, and they stopped. "First the fixer, now a banker. Since you are a member of the Group, Father, eventually you are likely to be targeted. I do not like the way you move around without protection."

Yasim never felt personal fear, for what was he, or anyone, but a pawn to be used as Allah had ordained? Dying was something that everyone would eventually do. "Yes. I am probably being hunted, but I am not helpless, am I?"

"No, Father, you are not. You have me, and I will lay down my own life if I see that it is required to keep you alive. But I would like to have a good security screen around you."

They resumed walking, making a slow turn to head in the opposite direction, where the shining white dome of the Capitol loomed at the other end of the Mall. Yasim pointed at it. "A beautiful building, is it not? This is where we begin hunting the hunters."

Djahid's face broke from its normal implacable setting of sharp planes and shadows and showed a trace of surprise. "We are going into Senator Monroe's office? The Capitol Police will never even let us in the building."

His father laughed. "Why, the Americans call it the 'People's House,' and we are people, are we not? I have documents that prove we own an import-export company that is expanding our international agricultural interests into Missouri, the senator's home state. It's just a front, of course, and operates out of a Kansas City mail-drop business. We have been regularly donating to his campaigns since political spies identified him about ten years ago as being willing to take a bribe. In the last election, we even set up an anonymous and secret political action committee that increased his treasury. His office has confirmed that he would be delighted to meet with us today."

"He just wants more money? What a sucking dog."

"The senator is corrupt but can be useful, for he sits on the Senate Armed Services Committee. He can find out who is responsible for what is going on behind the scenes with these shootings, if given the right motivation. Having you along will help remind him that he may have a motive even more important than a monetary donation. Fear works wonders, don't you think?"

"What do you want me to do?"

"Nothing. Just be yourself."

They stepped to the curb when the approaching black hulk of a Lincoln Town Car with tinted windows blinked its lights on and off twice and whispered to a purring halt beside them. The rear passenger door was pushed open, and Senator Monroe slid back across the leather seats to make room.

Senator Jordan Monroe was halfway through his second term in the U.S. Senate after having served five terms of two years each in the House of Representatives, and he had learned the truism that staying in office was expensive. His most recent election, which he won by less than 1 percent of the statewide vote, had cost almost $20 million. That wouldn't be enough in the next cycle, which meant the most important part of his job was raising funds, and this Rebiane fellow seemed made of ready money. The senator always made time for major cash cows, even ones who brought along muscle like this silent and menacing bodyguard. Well-invested donations to Monroe could translate to influence in the centers of power.

THE MAN they sought—the hunter—was much closer than they could have imagined. Marine Gunnery Sergeant Kyle Swanson at that moment was relaxing in a small conference room with the rest of Task Force Trident, just over the bridge at the Pentagon, and planning another attack on the Group of Six, which had shrunk to the Group of Four. The sniper hits had served several purposes, including forcing the remaining financiers bankrolling the Spanish overthrow attempt to hire more guards, while also making those guards spread out to cover a wider area, hunting for potential shooting lairs.

"I want to change tactics for this one," Swanson said. "No use making it easy for them to defend these people." He remembered the stricken widow of Mike Dodge crying in his arms, and he wanted to get just as up close and personal. *Six dead Marines on a plane, taking them home in coffins for six grieving families.*

The next target identified in Commander Freedman's folder was Mercedes Sarra Bourihane, the only woman on the list. Her picture was a head-and-shoulders photo of a woman perhaps in her fifties with a pleasant smile, dressed in a red designer jacket and discreet, but expensive, jewelry. The sandy hair had been styled by a professional, and the white teeth were the work of an artist, not some common dentist.

"Don't be fooled by that sweet 'I'm just your average grandma who shops at consignment stores' look. This woman is a hardboiled player." The Lizard ran through her French-Algerian background, her pampered childhood, her graduation from college with honors in economics, and her entry into the international banking arena, where she had made her name. Other photos showed Bourihane wearing a scarf over her head, for she was devout in her worship of Islam. It was virtually impossible for any woman to be recognized and excel in either banking or religion in Algeria, but she had shredded those odds by becoming a person with whom the men of central banks around the world liked to deal. She was not seen as a threat in those circles, and she considered the men to be the usual run of sexist fools.

"Bourihane is the person guaranteeing that the Islamist banks across the region will allow Spain to retain its political independence without the economic restructuring demanded by the EU and the United States. She can back her play with billions of dollars in assets, and Spain knows it."

General Middleton, the Trident commander, asked, "And you're certain she is one of the Six? No doubt on that?"

"Not a shred of doubt, sir. In fact, she is their poster girl. Watch." He tapped his keyboard a few times, and a video came on the big flat-screen embedded in a wall. A confident Mercedes Bourihane was addressing the European Banking Risk and Regulation Congress the previous year, doing the initial introductory roll-out of the Islamist banking effort. She said, "I am honored to be one of the 'Group of Six,' as we call ourselves, because being very smart people, we could not come up with anything better." A smile, a round of laughter. "This is a serious and open offer to help rescue Spain, my friends, and details will be made available . . ." The Lizard turned it off. "She *confirms* being one of them."

Master Gunny Double-Oh Dawkins grumped, "Hard to believe."

"Why? Because she's a woman?" Coastie almost barked in his face.

"No. Calm yourself, my child. I think it is hard to believe because she put this group out in the open way back then and nobody picked up on it as being anything more than an elaborate money scheme. After Barcelona, she is fair game."

Lieutenant Colonel Sybelle Summers rapped on the table. "Coastie has a good point, however. No matter how important Bourihane may be, she's not one of the boys over there. I think we might use that to get at her." She paused and looked around the table. "Let Coastie and me take a run on this one, since we can likely get closer. Kyle can do another one at about the same time. That will shock the hell out of any borderline supporters, change the attack pattern, and increase both the pace and the pressure on the opposition."

A broad grin spread on the general's face. "Surprise. I like it. Who else you got, Lizard?"

Freedman fiddled with the keys, and in thirty seconds the broad screen divided into four quadrants, with photos of Bourihane and three men. "Pick one and I will work up the details. Meanwhile, I have something else." Juan de Lara had received a cash infusion the day before his death, the Lizard said, and the payment had been routed through a New York broker.

"What's strange about that?"

"Well, for starters, the broker didn't have the money to make that kind of transaction. In fact, he doesn't have much money at all and is maxed out on his cards. I'm still digging."

"Suggestion?" Middleton wanted answers, not vague comments.

"Since you guys are all getting out and about, I think that Master Gunny Dawkins and I should go up to New York and have a talk with that broker."

"Yeah, I'm tired of sitting around while Swanson and my baby-faced assassin here have all the fun." Dawkins patted Coastie fondly on the shoulder. "I'll demonstrate for her that it is not always necessary to kill someone to accomplish a mission."

"Shut up, you Godzilla freak of nature," she snapped.

"Go," said the general. "Sybelle, I will clear a Green Light for you and Beth on Bourihane. Kyle, you review those remaining targets and make a plan with a timeline. Bring in a couple of MARSOC operators for backup if you need them, but it's your call."

NEW YORK

PETER McNAMARA loped along the interior of Central Park at six fifteen in the morning, counting his money in his mind as he jogged the usual three miles wearing brand-new red Nike Air Max shoes while his Garmin Forerunner 910XT combination GPS, watch, and heart rate monitor, purchased yesterday, clocked off his times. A chic black Reebok reversible runner's headband soaked up the sweat beading on his forehead. The ribbon of sidewalk stretched out before him, pointing like a solid path toward further success. It was an exhilarating time, marked by bass notes hammering in the sharp pop music of his iPod.

He had bet almost everything his clients had, and then had borrowed on margin to bet even more, on a short sale against the embattled German company on which he had received the tip from the enigmatic Carlos Blanco. He now held fifty thousand shares, and the price had already fallen two full points in two days, putting 100K in his pockets for following the tip. In return for the favor, Blanco had sent a messenger with an encoded list of money transfers, plus his fee, and it had taken Peter less than an hour to shovel the cash around the globe. He had the rest of the day to concentrate on growing his company, maybe reel in another client, and then get in some shopping before happy hour. He was on his way to the top, away from the trading floor, and the rest of the world could bite his ass.

Then a runner behind him closed too fast and stepped on Peter's left red Nike, making McNamara stumble. A big hand caught him by the arm and steadied him. Peter at first thought it might be a clumsy mugging attempt, which didn't worry him because martial arts were a regular part of his fitness regimen. Then he saw the huge man holding his arm and grinning at him with a face that indicated he wasn't really grinning at all, and he wasn't letting go but propelling Peter forward. "See that guy on the bench right before the tunnel? Go sit by him."

"I have a black belt," McNamara snarled, trying to jerk his arm free.

"And I have a Glock. Anyway, I can kick your skinny ass so quick that you'll ring like a tenpenny finishing nail hit with a greasy ball-peen hammer, as Brother Dave Gardner used to say. Go. Sit down and have a listen." Master Gunnery Sergeant O. O. Dawkins squeezed the man's bicep a little harder, and they moved toward the bench.

Commander Benton Freedman, the electronics wizard of Task Force Trident, did not get up but watched with large, intense eyes that seemed to burrow into McNamara's DNA.

"Who are you people?" demanded McNamara. "I'll call a cop!"

"The cops won't help you, because we have better badges than they do," said Freedman. "So, Mr. McNamara, allow me to summarize this situation: You are in a world of hurt. If you raise any kind of ruckus, my large friend here will reduce you to a puddle of piss in about three seconds flat. You run, he will shoot you dead. In the unlikely event that you somehow get away, a sniper in the bushes up on that rise will put a bullet in your head. Clear on that?"

McNamara's eyes widened as the Lizard continued in his calm voice.

"The first choice you have to make right now is whether you prefer living or dying. Second choice is whether you would prefer living or dying in Guantánamo Bay, the Supermax federal prison in Colorado, or a very sad place in Romania, where you can be going by nightfall if you do not cooperate. Do you understand me?"

McNamara took a seat beside the smaller man, and the giant sat down, too, so close to Peter that their thighs touched. He looked incredibly strong, but the little guy doing the talking seemed to be the more vicious.

"I haven't done anything wrong!"

"Oh, just shut the fuck up, kid, until I ask you a question. Keep thinking about Romania. We know everything about you, and spent most of last night going through your shit in the office of your so-called boutique hedge fund. Jesus, you don't even have a secretary. What is that about?"

"I handle everything personally. Instant access on my phones for my clients is one of my company's strengths. You need to move into the Internet age, old dude."

The big man threw back his head and laughed hard. Freedman was perhaps one of the top ten hackers in the world, and his rich Uncle Sam bought him any electronic toys he wanted. The Lizard worked with the designers of cutting-edge next-generation everything long before it hit the commercial shelves.

"I try to keep up," Freedman replied. "In reality, you have a cheapo answering service in Queens that picks up the calls. Did you know Mannix Dillon of BQM, another lone ranger in your business? Never mind. Of course you knew her. You exchanged e-mails several times in the past year. Some of it very personal stuff."

"Only from around the bar scene after work. We were fuck-buddies for a few weeks a long time ago, that's all. I never did any business with her. How are you reading my e-mails?"

"She's dead now, murdered right here in New York."

"I saw that in *The Wall Street Journal.* It was horrible."

Freedman popped open his Apple laptop and leafed through a couple of screens. "A few days before her death, she transferred a tidy sum to a gentleman named Cristobál Jose Bello in Mallorca, who was a person of great interest to us. Then Mr. Bello was killed. For those keeping score, you are tied to Dillon, and through her, you link to Bello. That makes two murders, three if we also count Bello's bodyguard, who went down with him."

McNamara gulped. "I don't know anything about it. Never heard of anyone named Bello."

Freedman readjusted his thick glasses and tickled the keyboard again.

"Ah. So next, a gentleman in Madrid, Juan de Lara, suddenly gets a hundred thousand dollars sent by you. He was also a person of interest to us, but alas, he, too, has been murdered. In the past, de Lara had received similar transfers from Dillon. That's four murders now, and you are connected to all of them. What are the odds? The cops will figure it out soon enough and will come see you. If they don't, I will personally make a call to the NYPD and throw you under the bus. You see where I'm going with this?"

McNamara felt walls closing in. "I want to speak to my attorney."

"He can come see you in Romania. Now I have learned that you are making a bundle off of a collapsing company in Germany, the short-selling that Mannix Dillon had done right before she was gutted. That's a lot of coincidences in one story, young man." He closed the laptop and looked McNamara square in the face. "So you, Mr. McNamara, are now also a person of interest to us."

"But who the hell are you?"

"Your new owners," replied the Lizard. "If you want to be able to continue to trot along the sunny fields of Central Park in coming days, then you will tell me who instructed you to send the money to Juan de Lara, and who told you about the Kraut company that's going belly-up."

The big guy shoved closer to McNamara, jarring him off balance, even seated.

"A man I had never heard of called me for a meeting, gave me the tip, and hired me to do some of the transfer work that Mannix had been handling. His name is Carlos Blanco."

"And you did no due diligence or background check, like ask to see his passport or driver's license?"

"No."

"Do you recognize any of these faces?" The Lizard turned his laptop screen so Peter could view the head-and-shoulders snaps of five men and one woman.

McNamara put his finger on one immediately. "Yeah. That's the guy. How did you get that?"

Freedman ignored the question. McNamara had just confirmed the identity of Yanis Rebiane, who had originated the Dillon transfers. Now Rebiane had chosen a new broker and had changed his business name to Carlos Blanco. "You stole her client, this Mr. Blanco, and that has resulted in a nice reversal of fortune for you. Any response?"

"As soon as we all learned that Mannix was dead, everybody on the street was scrambling for her client list, me included."

"You just took the money."

"Yes, I took the money. If I didn't take it, someone else would have. It is all properly reported, if you're from the IRS."

"We're not."

"CIA, then. The CIA cannot operate within the U.S."

"Wrong again. Can you contact your new client Mr. Blanco?"

"Maybe. We only had one meeting, right here in the park, and after that, he sent my instructions via bike messenger. I have a number to call in case something goes wrong. I'll give it to you."

"Don't bother. We already have it from your file." Both of the men stood up, leaving Peter on the bench. The smaller one tucked the laptop into a shoulder bag. "Do you ever want to see either of us again?"

"No," said the bewildered McNamara.

"And you won't, if you do as you are told. You can communicate with me through a phony e-mail account that I have installed on your office computer. You will write messages there in draft form, saved but not sent. I will access them and reply, if needed. Don't try to outsmart me, because this isn't a game of checkers. We are the only people standing between you and thorough investigations by the FBI and the Securities and Exchange Commission, with resulting prison time. That will be my call, son. I suggest you cooperate."

"But I haven't done anything wrong!" McNamara protested. His face was flushing red in despair and tears were gathering in the corners of his eyes as he saw his life, which was so beautiful only a few minutes ago, falling to ruin.

"I don't care. You get in touch with Blanco and I might make the government pressure go away. Once that happens, I strongly recommend that you take a two-week vacation from your job and never come back." The men walked up over the hill and out of sight.

NEW YORK

"I WARNED YOU." Mercedes Sarra Bourihane was not a person for small talk, and her sharp words fell like lashes on the sensitivities of Yanis Rebiane. Despite being a devout Muslim, the woman seldom knew her place. He bristled at her criticism and fought to keep his voice down, his outward manner unruffled. She had been in Morocco and he was in New York, a distance that Rebiane deemed adequate, but now here she was in his downtown Manhattan hotel suite, barking at him like a common bitch dog. *She should have stayed over there!*

Bourihane was seated comfortably on the long sofa with her legs tucked beneath her, and a glass of lemonade in her hand reflected the brilliant sunlight coming in from outside. "We were making good progress until Barcelona," she said. "Making concrete proposals to help them restructure their economy is complex, but we were winning converts within the government by forcing the European Commission to take an even harder line."

He said, "The Americans needed to be shown that we are serious and will not be intimidated in reaching our goal, Mercedes. Even you agreed to that." Yanis had a vodka over ice. He was somewhat loose with religious rules: Sharia law was a tool to control the masses, not the elite.

"It was to be done in a civilized manner with diplomatic and financial pressure, Yanis. Spain is not Afghanistan, but you decided to turn your thug son loose and attack America directly." The woman snorted, a sound that reminded Yanis of a grunting horse.

"When we all met in Geneva, I was given a unanimous vote to take forceful action to put pressure on Washington. You did not object at the time."

"None of us agreed to a full military-style attack on the consulate and that massive loss of life—none of us!" Her voice was harsh; then she took a deep breath and calmed herself. Mercedes Bourihane was famous for her unwavering charm throughout intricate financial negotiations at the highest levels, and here she was lowering herself to scold a man who was steering the opportunity of a generation toward the rocks of failure. "We told you then that there were limits and not to take it too far. You made the decision on your own."

Yanis rose and walked to the line of windows looking down on Manhattan. "Do not call Djahid a thug. My son is a hero who has fought the infidel Crusaders all of his life. His military skills are invaluable to our cause." Thirty floors below, he could see lines of automobiles, trucks, and taxis swarming through the city streets, and he knew that somewhere among the traffic was Djahid, truly risking his life by pretending to be a bicycle messenger.

She did not apologize. "What happened in Barcelona also guaranteed a violent retaliation. Two of our number are now dead. Why didn't you foresee that?"

"Every time they strike back, they mobilize more support for our cause," Yasim replied. *I just did not anticipate their choice of targets; instead of going after the low-level gunmen, they are aiming higher.*

Mercedes put down the glass and unwrapped her legs, sliding her toes into stylish high heels. "You must understand, my friend, that Juan de Lara was much too valuable to be expended as one of your car-bomb martyrs."

Ah, he thought. *She's finally getting to the point. She is afraid.*

He pressed onward, bringing up another sore subject. "We do not know for certain that the Americans killed them. Men of such huge appetites for wealth and power as Bello and de Lara have many enemies."

"Of course they did it," she said. "Now the rest of us are at risk."

"I agree that the United States is the most likely party, Mercedes, but we have a whole field of opponents. The U.K. and NATO are perfectly capable of doing such operations, and who would benefit more than Washington if the current regime is left in place? The Spanish government itself may be at the front of the line in order to squash the very idea of an Islamic takeover, no matter how it is camouflaged, and tens of millions of ordinary Spaniards would not lift a finger to help us. Last, but not least, are our brothers in Allah, the Shia. They were already unhappy that the Six are controlled by the Sunni, and they are always ready to shed blood. That is why there are no anti-American riots right now; nobody knows exactly who to blame."

"No matter," she replied. "It's the Americans, and you know it."

"I urge everyone else to be cautious and make their personal security as tight as possible."

"We might have drones circling our heads right now because of your stupidity. You are guarded by your Rottweiler son and can disappear at will, but I cannot." Another deep breath and a faraway look. "I spoke to the others before I flew over last night, Yasim. We cannot continue our work very well if we are dead, and although we willingly sacrifice our bodies, our brains and positions make us irreplaceable in this task to reconquer Spain in the name of the Prophet."

Rebiane wanted to slap her impudent face. "I am pursuing those responsible, Mercedes. If the Americans are the ones, we will find out soon. A United States senator is already badgering the White House and the State Department to solve that puzzle. We will discover and deal with them."

WASHINGTON, D.C.

PICK ONE. Kyle Swanson had the three color photographs lined up on the table before him, each atop a file folder containing the subject's history. Three human beings: Pick one. Who would be allowed to live a little bit longer; which would die at his hand first? He stacked them one atop another, then rearranged them into a new line and studied them some more. Nothing jumped out. *Eenie-meenie-miney-mo.* Did it make a difference? Trident was going to kill them all anyway. If they had been wearing military uniforms or carrying weapons, or if they even looked threatening, the choice might be easier, but the result would be the same.

He got up and walked to the coffeepot and poured a refill, then stood before a map of the world. There sat Spain, hanging off the southwestern end of Europe, buffered along the Atlantic by Portugal. Gibraltar guarded the choke point for the Mediterranean and was just across the watery street from Africa. The country's strategic position was undeniable, and it was over that strait that the Moorish Muslim armies invaded and conquered in the eighth century, holding power until the thirteenth century. *Five hundred years is a long time,* Kyle thought. *The United States hasn't even been around for three hundred.*

Spain was only about the size of Oregon, and while that state contained only four million people, the Spain of today was crowded with a population of more than forty-seven million. The economic collapses of the past thirty years had left many of them distrusting their government and doubtful of a secure economic future. Change was hurting, and the thinly disguised Islamist rescue package seemed attractive when looked at solely as a business deal with favorable basis points and almost nonexistent interest rates, unaccompanied by harsh demands to change their accustomed way of life. The obvious power grab was unseen by the public.

Wars have been fought over less, Swanson thought as he drifted back to his chair. Left unchecked, within a few years, Spain might become the first domino in Europe to fall to Islam. It would be like allowing al Qaeda a vote in NATO military planning and EU economic policies. That's what the Group of Six had in mind, and it was why the guy on Mallorca was popped and the fat banker was taken out in Madrid and why the woman financier was on the chopping block and why the other three men had to die. He was cool with that.

A sniper prefers not to know the name of his target, for that anonymity drains emotion from the shooter. In a combat situation, that is easy, for it is a rough-and-tumble business that spreads over a wide front and you engage targets of opportunity. Then comes the stalk attack, in which you are after one specific target, such as a colonel in a headquarters area, and a personality is unnecessary. As for Kyle the victims he would be harvesting over the next few weeks, he knew their names, their histories, and much more about them. The Lizard was amazing in compiling information.

He leaned back, both hands around the thick porcelain coffee mug. If security teams for the bankers were any good at all, they would now be anticipating another sniper hit and spreading out the protective perimeter. Kyle would lay aside the rifle this time in favor of collapsing the security pocket like an offensive line in football trying to prevent the vulnerable quarterback from being sacked.

Instead of working his next target by himself, or with Coastie as his only backup, this time he would overwhelm that offensive line by employing a full fourteen-man MSOP, a Marine Special Operations Team, from Camp Lejeune.

That meant planning for more of a footprint and better logistics than just sneaking into a construction site as he had done on the previous one. The target had to be convenient, so they could get in and get back out in a hurry. They needed distraction. He shuffled through the stack, pushing aside two folders.

Winner: Daniel Ferran Torreblanca, chairman of the Spanish holdings of the Islamic Progress Bank, based in Riyadh, Saudi Arabia, and run in accordance with Sharia law. Where: Seville, home of his wife and parents. When: Next week, during the Feria de Abril, the April fair. How: Slash his throat.

NEW YORK

DJAHID REBIANE was happy to safely dismount from the SquareBuilt fixed-gear bike when he reached Union Square West. He had ridden only a few blocks from Eighteenth Street, with the alleycat race cards whirring in the rear spokes, just far enough to establish some authenticity as a bicycle messenger and more than enough to make him pray to Allah for protection, particularly after almost getting doored by some man getting out of a yellow cab. He got off at the edge of the open park and walked the bike the rest of the way to the building on Fourth Avenue.

For only a few hundred dollars, a bald, skinny kid named Bobby had given him a quick lesson and the use of the scarred bike for an hour. Bobby said bike messengers were a dying breed, and Djahid believed it, not because of the influence of faxes and the Internet, but because he felt that no one could survive long on the streets of Manhattan. Bobby made more money in that moment than he would make all day hauling garment bags around the fashion district uptown, and asked few questions.

Rebiane pedaled downtown anyway to see a money-grubber named Peter McNamara. The office was on the tenth floor of an address that had been prestigious in the boom times, then slipped to third-rate status with the banking crisis. He locked the bike with a chain to a lamppost. Bobby would retrieve the bicycle in one hour. Djahid removed his plastic helmet, shifted the one-strap bag on his shoulder, and did a little squat. He thought the narrow bike seat might have crushed his testicles. He wore old running shoes, a pair of cargo shorts, and a brown, forgettable T-shirt.

The elevator was claustrophobic as it clanked up the shaft, shifting from side to side along the way as if being blown by the wind. Finally the door opened, and he stepped onto the cracked linoleum squares of the tenth floor. Two doors were on each side, and he knocked on the one that had the name McNAMARA GLOBAL INVESTMENTS in gold paint on a pane of frosted glass.

"Come in," called an impatient voice, and Djahid walked through. There was a smell of fear in the room that was as overpowering as a bowl of rotten fruit. The skin of the man inside was pale.

"I got a delivery for a Mr. McNamara. That you? Somebody gotta sign this receipt." Rebiane was trying for a Brooklyn accent. He held out a pad on which was written: *You called Mr. Blanco. Why?*

McNamara's eyes flicked up at the tall biker. "Yeah. That's me." He took the pad, which trembled a bit in his hand. "I want to see the man who sent this package."

"I don't know nothin' about none of that," said Rebiane. He tugged at his ear and raised an eyebrow. McNamara shook his head. No listening devices? Hard to believe. "I got a call to pick up this package and bring it here. I hustled my ass through heavy traffic for you, man. A tip would be good."

Being face-to-face with the messenger sent by Carlos Blanco scared him. This guy didn't have the usual vacant slacker look of most bike couriers. Instead, he had a catlike style of moving, and although he spoke in slang, his voice seemed uncomfortable with the American idiom. Whoever he was, he brought Peter one step closer to getting the spooks off his back. They were probably recording this conversation somewhere. Remembering the big guy who had grabbed him in Central Park helped some of the fear evaporate. That spook could take this messenger without much problem.

If anything, Peter McNamara knew how to hustle a client. *Show strength and confidence, even a touch of arrogance.* He straightened his sky blue tie.

"OK. OK, pal. Enough with the bullshit. I want you to take a message back." He unscrewed the top of a brushed silver pen and scrawled a note of his own: *Set up a meeting now! Something has happened! Others have contacted me! Urgent!*

The messenger took the paper, read it, then nodded understanding and folded it once before putting it into his shoulder bag. "You want the package or not, mister?"

"Yeah. Give me the damned package and go get back on your wheels."

Djahid removed a cream-colored shoebox from the bag, took off the top, and laid it carefully on McNamara's desk. His father had told him to make his own decision after seeing the young man, so Djahid came prepared for any eventuality. That scribbled note and anxious manner were tantamount to a confession from McNamara that he had talked to somebody else about private affairs. That could not be allowed.

The silenced pistol came out of the box smoothly, and Djahid Rebiane whipped McNamara hard twice across the face with it. The broker was on the floor with a crushed nose, and a wide gash along one cheek was pouring blood. Djahid reached back into the box and retrieved an old-fashioned butcher knife with a blade thirteen inches long and honed razor sharp, and a bag of plastic ties.

"Tell me everything that happened," he said after stretching out the broker and securing him to solid points. He moved the knife slowly before Peter's frightened eyes. Then it flashed downward and Djahid began to flay McNamara alive with a blade so sharp that the victim at first did not even understand what was happening. He kept the pistol handy in case the police burst in, but he had seen none outside and figured he had some time yet to spend here.

Rebiane flicked the point around McNamara's left elbow, circled the wrist, and then made a quick, effortless slice down the forearm between the two cuts. He worked two fingers beneath the flap and pulled. The skin of the arm peeled away with a few jerks as the epidermis layer and the underlying stringy, fibrous dermis parted with the fatty subcutis beneath. Djahid held the skin before his victim's face, and that was when Peter McNamara understood the correlation between truth and pain. His screams were muffled by a pillow, which was loosened occasionally so he could speak.

WASHINGTON, D.C.

COMMANDER BENTON FREEDMAN ran his fingers through his hair. He and the master gunny had ridden the Acela Express up to New York, cornered and threatened the young money guy in Central Park, and returned to Washington. Freedman was back in his chair at Task Force Trident the following day, and Peter McNamara was dead at the hands of an unknown killer, actually flayed by someone who knew how to do that sort of thing. It was as if Freedman had made a dot with a pencil only to have someone else erase it.

The NYPD had few leads in the cases of the two stockbrokers who had been violently murdered in the city, but they should uncover the connection soon enough.

Freedman's concern was that Trident's own contact with McNamara might be discovered. He silently cursed himself. Had he been careless in setting up the sting just so he could get out of the office for a change? The quick trip to the *Vagabond* in the Med to update its comm equipment and brief Kyle and Coastie should have been enough for anyone. *No, I had to go to New York, too.* Liz felt that perhaps he had been sloppy, which was something he would not tolerate.

The Lizard moved to the office of General Middleton, sat uninvited, and stared at the large man. "Did you ever see *Jaws*, sir?"

Middleton signed a paper and looked up. "Of course. The great white whale."

Freedman coughed politely into his fist. "That was *Moby Dick*, sir.

This one is a great white shark: Roy Scheider, Richard Dreyfuss, and Robert Shaw as the boat captain, Quint. Spielberg thought about casting Charlton Heston as Police Chief Brody and Lee Marvin as Quint, but I don't think the chemistry would have been the same with those two."

"Do you have a reason for being in my office, Commander? Of course I saw *Jaws,* and it was a fine motion picture. I agree about the casting, but I don't think that's what you really want to talk about."

"No, sir." When his brilliant mind was grinding on a problem, Freedman often had a hard time settling into a single subject, and the general knew that getting to the point might require some time. The naval officer explained the fatal attacks on Mannix Dillon and Peter McNamara in gruesome detail. "It seems likely to me, General, that although our current operation concerning Spain has not been compromised, there is a big shark out there circling our little boat. Like in the movie."

The general gave his communications officer a full stare. "Has the Group of Six broken our security?"

"No. That would be impossible, sir; we're buried much too deep. The danger comes if they can somehow piece together information they have available and make some correct assumptions. We know these people are well funded and can therefore hire competent hackers to poke around in the cloud. They have a high degree of motivation, for that entire Muslim financial gamble is at risk if they do not stop us."

"You think they will move against Trident."

"Yes, sir. Odds are sooner than later. Also, the killings of those two brokers may be the work of the same guy. They have a pro for the wet stuff."

Middleton said, "So do we, Commander Freedman. So do we. And remember that our boat ain't all that little."

NEW YORK

THE FATHER WAS GIFTED with a quietude that accommodated most problems with the knowledge that time and distance would resolve them, no matter what he did. Yasim Rebiane knew that he had no more control over an accidental setback in his plans than he had over a meteorite crashing into a Siberian town. He was a realist because life had made him that way, and he was proud that he had passed that thoughtful manner along to his son.

In Djahid, the elder Rebiane saw many traces of his own father, including the blue-eyed Berber genes of the wrestler-strong body that had been honed as an oil-field engineer who fought his way up to the executive ranks. That strength had somehow skipped Yasim's own generation. The mental agility Djahid was demonstrating in his independent field operations came through Yasim's mother, the grandmother of Djahid. She descended through the *Pied-Noir* European immigrants of Algeria and brought with her a more formal education. She was honest and trusted, which made her prized as a bookkeeper for businesses. Together they survived wars and revolution, and raised and educated Yasim so he could carry the family name higher. He had done the same with his own boy and had faith that his carefully groomed Djahid was ideal for the world of tomorrow. The turmoil of the so-called Arab Spring showed that the Middle East yearned for true leadership, and Djahid would be ready to enter that political arena, handsome and articulate, with college degrees and military training, and the scalp of Spain on his belt. *Who could stand against such a man?*

What he had accomplished with the interrogation of that toothy fool McNamara was proof, and Yasim was pleased. The money transfers would simply be shifted through another country, probably Switzerland, and proceed as usual. He should have done that from the start, because Americans could never be depended upon; they always served base needs of their own before considering their clients, and thought in terms of quarterly profits rather than long-term results that would require years, even decades or centuries. While Yasim had wanted Mannix Dillon and Peter McNamara to proceed quietly, they had been too flashy for their own good. The convenience of having them squarely in New York was far outweighed by their overweening ambitions. As if choosing cheese, he had picked American when he really wanted Swiss.

The Rebianes had spent a full day going through the material that Djahid had taken from the McNamara office and found the only thing of interest on the pair of computers was a newly created folder bearing the label CARLOS BLANCO. In the folder were brief notations confirming the receipt of the funds that had been laundered through another of Yasim's secret accounts, and the resulting transfer to Juan de Lara in Madrid. No information existed that contained references to the meeting between the broker and Yanis.

The man had not been brave under torture. During the private pain session, he admitted that he had been jogging in Central Park when he was accosted by a large, military-looking man, who forced him to sit on a bench beside a black-haired guy who did all of the talking. Neither had identified himself, nor had they displayed any badge or credentials, but they had left McNamara with no doubt that they were from some powerful governmental authority. They now owned him, they said, and a sniper was hiding nearby if Peter tried to make a run for safety.

When Djahid cut some more, Peter was able to give even better descriptions of the men and the meeting. He had been shown photographs of five men and one woman and had identified the familiar face of Mr. Blanco. There was no reason to doubt him. His only order from the men was to contact Carlos Blanco through a false e-mail, he had whimpered. After a little further work by Djahid, some of it purely experimental in nature, McNamara was allowed to die.

The smell of chicken and vegetables cooking in oil wafted from the kitchen, where Djahid was putting together some stir-fry. Yasim moved to the doorway but did not offer to help. "So these people knew about Cristobál Bello in Mallorca and a number of other points, which confirms access to a lot of information. That points to an American agency, for who else has such assets?"

Djahid dripped oil on fresh Italian bread and put it in a toaster oven to brown, then sliced hard-boiled eggs and tomatoes while his father took plates from a wall cabinet and set the table. This was demeaning work, but they had to eat. Over dinner, their talk turned to minor things, and they laughed at the scolding Yasim had received from Mercedes Sarra Bourihane.

"Why do you allow that quarrelsome woman to disrespect you like that, father?"

"We need her right now, just where she is. Keep your eye on the ultimate goal, Djahid. She will be dealt with when she is no longer useful."

As they cleaned up afterward, the father returned to the subject. "I will present this new information to Senator Jordan and pressure him to move faster in identifying the agency behind these developments. Time is important, so tomorrow, I want you to fly to St. Louis."

"And once I am there?"

"Then just wait for my call."

"I can do that," Djahid said with a broad smile.

"I know you can, son."

CAMP LEJEUNE, NORTH CAROLINA

KYLE SWANSON propped his arm on the podium in a pale green conference room and looked over the fourteen warriors of the Marine Special Operations Team, all of whom were watching him just as hard. Tier One types: best of the best. "I am not here to give a speech, so I'll spell it out quick. Who wants a piece of the bastards who murdered our brother Marines and the others in Barcelona?"

There was an immediate stirring in the room. "Hell, yeah." "Ooo-ah." "Semper Fi!" "Damn straight!"

Swanson nodded his approval. "Also right up front is that this is a high-stakes mission, and we will assassinate one of the bankers who paid for the hit, a civilian, on his homeland in Spain. Still interested?"

This was greeted by a round of hoots and curses. It was the kind of thing these operators had been trained to accomplish. If they were in the room, they were already volunteers for the elite force, and all had seen combat. "Another thing. You need to know that we will be going on our own, bare-ass naked, with no inside or outside support team, no Quick Reaction Force, and not a shred of air support."

The team chief, a rangy African American master sergeant named Sam Smith, interrupted with a solemn and deep television announcer voice, "As always, should you or any of your IM Force be caught or killed, the secretary will disavow any knowledge of your actions."

Kyle squashed a sudden burst of laughter. "This is not a Mission Impossible. In fact, I consider it a Mission Very Possible, because we will go in in the dark, do the deed, and get the hell out before anyone even knows we're there. And we are not murdering a civilian but taking out a real terrorist asshole. Since 9/11, they are not allowed to hide behind borders, peacefully lead normal lives, and pretend to be off-limits."

He left the podium and walked among the seated Marines. He knew them all, and they knew him. Smith and some of the others had run black missions with Swanson before. A captain was in command, and Smith was the team chief. A gunnery sergeant headed operations, and another noncom was in charge of communications. Staff sergeants led each tactical element, which included three critical skills operators and a Navy corpsman who trained with them. This small, formidable force could bound into action anywhere, ready to fly on a moment's notice.

Swanson went back to the front. "Through the authority of Task Force Trident, I can order each of you to carry out this mission, and you would not have the right of refusal. However, we don't do that. I don't want anyone along who has any qualms about the job; too much is at stake. If you have doubts, get the hell out of this room right now and keep your mouth shut about what is going to happen."

Smith's deep voice boomed again. "Hey, Shake. You promised not to make a speech. We're all in, OK? So give us the fucking brief."

15

PARIS, FRANCE

LIEUTENANT COLONEL Sybelle Summers of the Marine Corps and Petty Officer Second Class Beth Ledford of the Coast Guard meandered along the Left Bank of the Seine, tourist booklets in hands. Summers was admiring the massive Gothic Notre Dame Cathedral, its impressive history challenged by Gen X skateboarders clattering in the front plaza. Ledford was awed by the herds of artists encamped all along the broad sidewalks, who were casually sketching and painting and displaying their works, a riot of color and form in chalk or pencil or paint—little masterpieces made in minutes. Although wearing casual clothes to blend with the crowds, the two women were doing a slow recon of the busy streets, settling into the attack environment, and developing a cover, for they were not on vacation; they were there to kill Mercedes Sarra Bourihane.

"I wish I knew more about macro-economics," Summers said. "Then I might be able to penetrate that conference."

Coastie tucked a stray lock of yellow hair behind her ear. "It's like the weather, isn't it? Low-pressure front moving in, or high-pressure front moving in, and bad things are going to happen. Stock market up, stock market down, bad things are going to happen."

Sybelle gave a laugh. "You may have it. In two days, our esteemed Ms. Bourihane will be one of the plenary speakers at the Twelfth Annual Conference of the International Society for the Advancement of Economic Theory, and her topic is 'Economics in Modern Transitional Societies.'

Judging by what she is trying to pull off in Spain, bad things are going to happen."

She closed her book and stood in thought looking at the blocky cathedral. "We cannot hit her while she is outside. April in Paris brings too many crowds, and her protective detail will be drawn in tight. The conference itself is out of the picture because we would stand out like sore thumbs."

"Plus there is the minor point of us getting away. Let's go shopping. Maybe we can dream up something while we look at French stuff." Coastie grinned, and they walked away from Notre Dame and its mysteries, took a Metro to the Boulevard Haussmann, and in minutes were deep into the Galeries Lafayette and Printemps. "I don't imagine she would come out here, huh? Too common?"

"Not even," Sybelle replied, stopping before a stunning collection of baubles resting on purple velvet in a window. "This would be too downmarket for her. Our girl is a fashion plate and probably buys her burkas in a designer rag shop along the Avenue Montaigne." She checked the reflection in the window but saw nobody watching them.

They wound through aisles of fashion, touching the fabric, checking prices, wanting to try on clothes but remembering they were on the job, and promising to come back sometime with Lady Pat and her credit cards. "And Bourihane's home in Algeria is out of the question?" Ledford asked again.

"That is probably a fort by now. Her team will be looking for snipers there. We have to take advantage of that."

"I don't get it, Sybelle. This woman is totally against type in the Muslim culture, yet she is successful beyond measure. She never married, refuses to bow down to the men, and although she's somewhat gaudy, in my opinion, they treat her as an equal."

"As long as she can further their ideological goals and make them money, she will be accepted. She started off ahead of the pack, you know, as the sole heiress to a fortune created by her French grandfather and increased by her parents. It is lucky for the Group of Six that she has chosen to remain a Muslim at all. They need her more than she needs them."

Coastie held up a trim white blouse before a mirror. "Makes me look too pale. So she has goals of her own?"

"Probably, but that's not our concern." She handed Ledford a light blue top that picked up the color of her eyes. "Try this one. Commander Freedman is all over her schedule, and we know for certain that she is going to be here in two days. We know where, and when, and why. So that leaves us with coming up with a how."

"Look at the price of this thing! I could buy ten of these tops at Target for less than this." She checked the mirror and felt her wallet getting lighter. "Got to get her alone, and she's never going to be alone."

The dark-haired Summers picked at a rack. "We have an expense account, girl, and nobody cares as long as you don't overdo it. Buy the damned thing, not because you will look great in it, but because we have to blend in with the local fashion set. People in stores are supposed to buy things. We probably will need new shoes, too."

"She has to eat sometime," said Coastie. "She probably won't be alone then, either. Some fancy restaurant instead of room service, surrounded by people. Security in the corners."

Sybelle stopped. "Good idea, and better than our other options right now. Maybe the Liz can find out if she has reservations at some gourmet food cart, or if there's going to be a big dinner at the event. Something will turn up, Coastie. We've just got to keep looking."

"No matter what, a cold front is moving in."

"Got that right."

WASHINGTON, D.C.

THE YEARS in the Congress of the United States had given Senator Jordan Monroe a position of power, which he enjoyed immensely, for he was courted like a prince by lobbyists. This Yasim Rebiane had seemed a likable enough fellow and was a very generous donor, but Monroe would have to put a lot on the line to work with him. Rebiane had made it sound simple enough; he had come across information that the United States had conducted two covert assassinations of innocent civilians in Spain as revenge for the tragedy in Barcelona. That had grabbed Monroe's attention. Was the administration launching its own little war inside a major allied nation?

The accursed *Washington Post* would have a field day if they discovered that story, so a gentle touch was required all around. The White House would not want the exposure, and neither would the senator. Mr. Rebiane, after all, was a Muslim from Algeria and a member of the Group of Six that was trying to steer Spain onto a new economic path, one that would benefit Islam in the long run. The two assassination victims were both members of that group, so a concerned Rebiane, who was also a member, was reaching out to see if he was also targeted for elimination by the Americans. The senator had said the idea was preposterous, and that Rebiane should not worry. Senator Jordan promised to take care of it.

Once back in his office, Monroe instructed his administrative aide to request a background briefing from the Department of Defense concerning what, if any, military actions had stemmed from the Barcelona incident.

The following day, Brigadier General Alfred Coleman of the U.S. Air Force was in a chair facing the senator across a small table that was polished to a high gloss. Handsome, with silvering hair, and totally at ease, Coleman wore an immaculate and tailored blue uniform bedecked with honor ribbons and the wreathed star and silver wings of a command pilot. He had squared off against America's enemies in combat in foreign lands until it was discovered that he was even more valuable in handling the political tempests of Washington, for he was as comfortable at a Georgetown soiree as he was in a cockpit. Old South manners and a laconic speech pattern with a slight accent clung to him like kudzu vines. It was that combination of assets that had drawn Coleman the DOD assignment of paying a friendly, informal visit to Senator Jordan Monroe in an attempt to plumb the lawmaker's Machiavellian mind. Coleman did not really have any new information on Barcelona—a bit more than CNN, Fox, Al Jazeera, and the BBC, but not much. He would go with the flow.

They fenced politely for a few minutes before Senator Monroe began showing irritation. If he asked a question, he wanted an answer, not evasive, politically correct bullshit, which was what he was getting from the one-star whom the Pentagon had dispatched over to him.

"Nothing?" The senator couldn't believe his ears. "American citizens are dead in the rubble of a terrorist attack, and we're doing nothing to pursue them?"

The tall general crossed his legs and folded his hands in his lap. *Stay cool.* "Senator, the internal investigation is being conducted through the State Department. Pentagon involvement in the incident was limited to the six Marines on the interior guard detail."

"And all of them are dead, right?"

Coleman agreed. "Yes, sir, and it is a damned outrage. I repeat, however, our military presence was only a standard package for interior security. The State Department was in charge of exterior protection there through their RSO, the regional security officer of the Diplomatic Security Service, who coordinated with the local police. He died, too."

Jordan recognized a brush-off. "General, you are artfully avoiding my concern, so stop sounding like a public relations flak when I ask again, more directly, What, if anything, is the American military doing to avenge that attack? Are uniformed American troops involved in what appear to be coordinated assassinations by snipers of important Spanish civilians?"

The brigadier general's surprise was evident on his handsome face. He hadn't heard about any special ops doing any such thing, and anyway, he was a pilot, for Chrissakes, not some rat-chewing commando. A briefer is only as good as what he has been told, and Coleman was never told much of anything happening below the public radar. However, the senator's use of the term "uniformed" provided convenient wiggle room. If there was a black op going on in Spain, the shooters sure as hell would not be wearing uniforms. He shook his head. "No, sir. The Pentagon has nothing to do with any reprisals that may or may not be under way, to the best of my knowledge."

The two men stared at each other without expression until the briefer broke the uncomfortable silence, and the southern drawl was grating like sandpaper on Monroe. "As you know, senator, the security situation in global hot spots is very complicated. The State Department uses local cops but also hires private security companies to handle force protection. Then there is the CIA, which fields its own agents and pulls in military help when required. The military chain of command gets murky, for neither State nor the Agency reports to us."

"I do not need to be lectured by you about who does what, General."

"Of course not."

The senator, although ready to pounce with another sharp response, felt the general might just be telling the truth. It might not be military at all. The CIA had talent, money, and manpower to spare, and police usually had excellent snipers. Then there were the mercenaries, who usually came out of elite military units to do the same work for much higher pay from private security companies and were regularly hired for support assignments. "Contractors?" he asked, hunting for the weak link.

"That might be something you can ask State or the CIA about, Senator. I cannot speak for other agencies, sir. Is that all for me today?" The one-star got up at a nod from the great man.

"Yes. Thank you for coming over, General Coleman. I wanted this to be an informal inquiry, but a word of caution: My colleagues on the Armed Forces Committee will be very disappointed if you have not been truthful in this briefing. You would not enjoy being subpoenaed before our full panel. Good day, sir."

The general gave an uneasy laugh. "It was good to see you again, Senator. If I discover any new and relevant information, I will get it to you promptly." As Coleman walked out, beneath the wings and ribbons, his heart was beating like a trip-hammer. His bosses would not be happy that the senator had taken a sudden interest in Barcelona, with the veiled threat of a Senate hearing. The stench of Benghazi and Tehran and various banana republics down south still hung in the institutional memory of Washington, and if Coleman was hauled over the coals by Senator Jordan, he might never get that second star.

The senator went to the sideboard in his office and poured himself a stiff drink, then walked around in silence, lost in thought. The idea floated by Rebiane that the American military was hitting back didn't seem to float very well. The dandified General Coleman obviously didn't have a clue about what was going on, and although the brigadier had been the Pentagon's designated hitter for today's meeting, he did not seem cut out for the heavy lifting of special operations. Some deeper digging would be needed.

A double knock on an inner door was followed by the appearance of his administrative aide, Douglas Jimenez, a shrewd lawyer and an ambitious political viper. "How did the meeting go, Senator?"

"They sent me a pretty-boy public relations type, Doug. He tap-danced his way out of the corner without admitting, denying, or even saying anything. Reminded me a lot of you. Help yourself to a drink."

Jimenez chose Scotch. "Should we reach higher up the food chain? Just the threat of a press conference would shake them up and force a response."

"Good idea, but let's do more homework first. I want you to touch base with some of our friends over at State to see if they know of any armed response on their end. After all, their people got killed, too. And put together some ideas on who else might be responsible. Are we the only ones in the world who are pissed off with what is happening in Spain?"

"State is licking its wounds on this one, Senator. Guaranteeing the protection of every U.S. diplomat and building in the Muslim world is impossible, and anyway, their job is to build diplomatic relations, not to get into the revenge business. I'm pretty sure they are not running anything, much less targeting Spanish civilians."

"Right. I still need to clear them and other possibilities before moving hard on to the CIA, which is more likely to be behind this sort of shit."

"Good point, sir. We don't know for sure if there even *are* any reprisals. Our friend Mr. Rebiane is probably acting on a hunch, that's all."

"Nevertheless, we have to either get him an answer or at least show that we have made a reasonable effort. I want his PAC on board for the next election cycle. So you get over to the State Department, Doug. I've got to get up to the Capitol for a floor vote, then a subcommittee meeting."

"I'll try to have something by the time you get back, sir."

CAMP LEJEUNE,
NORTH CAROLINA

KYLE SWANSON was famished. He had been fueled only by coffee since the long drive down from Washington, and since his arrival at the huge base, he had done a six-kilometer run to stretch out, then spent hours with the guys in the cramped conference room doing initial planning for the Spanish mission. The other members of the special operations team also were ready to call it a day and pick it up again tomorrow. Some had personal things to do, but three joined him for an early dinner at the Staff Noncommissioned Officers Club in Building 825 just as the sun went down and the residents of Tobacco Road wrapped up another day. Everyone in the state was still arguing about whether the impossible three-pointer that had won the NCAA basketball championship for Duke over North Carolina had really been launched before the buzzer.

"Screw basketball," said Staff Sergeant Travis Stone when they had been escorted into the dining room, seated, and given menus. They ordered a cold pitcher of draft beer.

"That is traitor talk and can definitely get you lynched in these parts. Anyway, you don't like basketball because you're so damned short," drawled Master Sergeant Sam Smith. "The refs gave that damned game to Duke. No way that shot was in time. ESPN has it in slow-slow motion."

"You're still mad because you lost money on the game, Sam. I tried to tell you never to bet against Duke in b-ball."

"Don't spat in public," said the fourth member of the group and the only one who was not a Marine. Rick Suarez was a Navy corpsman who trained with the MARSOC team and, in addition to attending to their combat medical needs, also served as its demolition expert. He poured beer into the cold mugs the waitress had placed before them.

The tension that filled the world outside the SNCO Club melted away as the conversation at their table, and at those around them, fell into quiet and polite tones, highlighted by the clink of silverware and some laughs. The rowdy bar time could come later, if they wanted it, but behavior in the club was mandatory on self-control. Kyle ordered a medium-well steak, mashed potatoes with brown gravy, and veggies, with a house salad sprinkled with vinegar and oil to start. Spain would not be mentioned.

"Hey, look. We got a visiting celebrity over there." Suarez motioned toward a table against the far wall where three men were finishing their meal. Two were Marines in uniform, and the other was a civilian in a Texas-cut sports coat over pressed jeans. "It's that TV guy."

"What are the Panthers going to do with their first pick in the draft?" Kyle asked, to steer the conversation onto a new track. He had recognized Ryan Powell right away—former SEAL, author, movie actor, and now host of the popular military television reality show *The Elite*. Also an asshole. "You Carolina guys need help everywhere."

"They ain't my guys. I'm 49ers," replied Stone. "The Panthers will probably try to improve the defensive line, but they really need another pass-catcher for Cam Newton. That man can cold play ball."

The first pitcher of beer was finished, and they got a new one just as the meal was served. As usual, Kyle had praised his New England Patriots and then stopped talking to dig into the feast. Nothing wrong with the world that a juicy steak couldn't cure.

"Excuse me for a moment, guys." The pleasant voice came from the civilian visitor. He was still not thirty years old, had cut the mane of shaggy brown hair to a neat semimilitary style since Swanson had last seen him, and retained the muscle tone of his SEAL days. Polished cowboy boots added another inch to his six-foot-plus height, and he had a silver belt buckle that bore the SEAL emblem in gold. "I just wanted to say hello to Gunnery Sergeant Swanson."

Kyle stared at him coldly, ignoring the fake smile and the extended hand at the end of a thick wrist that carried a heavy black-faced watch that had a timing bezel, a sweep hand, and a lot of small dials. *Gear queer,* Swanson thought. *Out of the military, unable to let it go.* "Mr. Powell," he said in a flat acknowledgement.

"Relax, Gunny. I really want to thank you for helping convince me to leave the Teams and take a new career path. I owe you one."

So full of shit, Kyle thought. The last time, the only time, they had met, Swanson had intentionally forced Petty Officer First Class Ryan Powell into a series of mistakes during a close-quarters battle shootout in the ultrasecret Ghost House that the SEALs had over on the Virginia coast. Although the young warrior had been rated as a Special Warfare Operator and had a sparkling record with SEAL Team Six, he had not been picked for the Osama bin Laden takedown. His boss knew that Powell had family problems, but when it became clear that the fighter also had succumbed to a gambling addiction and was piling up debt, the SEALs grew worried about his overall effectiveness. A lone-buccaneer attitude had muddled his teamwork requirements. The confrontation with Swanson had demonstrated the final proof that Powell had lost his edge. When the SEALs reassigned him into a training position back at Coronado, he quit.

The smile seemed almost genuine. "How are things with Task Force Trident?" Powell asked.

The Marines at Kyle's table stiffened at the mention of the top-secret unit that reported only to the president of the United States. Kyle brushed it off. "Oh, them? It was just an experimental thing back in the day. Never got off the ground."

"So you're not a shooter anymore?"

"Lost my edge, Mr. Powell, just like you. I push a desk in the puzzle palace these days."

The civilian absorbed the insult and nodded as if in understanding. "I'm taking up too much of your time, gentlemen. Gunny, perhaps you could meet me in the bar after you're finished. We can talk about old times. Swap some lies."

"Thanks for dropping by."

"Maybe I can even talk you into being on my show. Congressional Medal of Honor winner and all that."

Kyle turned his attention back to the food and stabbed his knife into the thick steak. "I don't do publicity."

Powell laughed, but it was a chilled sound, and he leaned in, placing his nose close to Kyle's collar and pulling in an exaggerated sniff. "You're still in the game, Swanson. I can smell it on you."

"But you're not. So go away." Kyle put the chunk of meat in his mouth. Delicious.

The TV host looked at the three other Marines at the table. "You guys want to be careful around this guy Swanson. I trusted him once, and it didn't work out so well. Don't make the same mistake."

"Our food is getting cold, sir," said Sam Smith, looking up with a face of marble.

Ryan Powell held up a hand, palm out, apologetic, as he easily slipped back into the smooth TV persona. "You're right. Sorry for the interruption. I hope to catch you all in the bar later and buy a round in appreciation for your service." He spun a white Stetson hat on his finger and walked away, his star power drawing admiring looks from guests at other tables.

Kyle and his friends finished their meal in silence, then ordered coffee.

"Well?" asked Travis Stone. "Y'all have a history. Anything we need to know?" What he was really asking was if Powell was going to screw Kyle over, and if that would jeopardize the Spanish job.

"I knew him for about an hour a few years ago when the SEALs brought me in as an evaluator to test him in a CQD. He was a conceited jerk then, too, although he looked like Captain America and had the record to match. Somewhere along the line, he let his personal life get screwed up, and Team Six was concerned about him. Anyway, long story short, he failed the drill and lost his job. After that, he retired. He blames me."

"Shit, man. Time catches up. It happens to everybody. We can't play war forever."

Rick Suarez chewed his steak, then spoke. "He bounced back OK. Big book and a TV show. He should be kissing your boots in appreciation for the soft landing. Must be making about a coupla million these days."

"What kind of show does he have?" Swanson had never seen it.

"Sort of like *Survivor,* but ain't they all? Only he personally 'leads' teams from different special ops units in running around doing live-fire exercises and attacking pop-up targets and whispering to the cameras. They even—horrors—have to live off the land for a couple of nights. A bug might bite them."

"It's just boom-boom bullshit, but the Pentagon loves the publicity and gives full cooperation. The reality part gives way if you remember that behind the camera are dozens of people who put it all together. Those two uniforms with him tonight are from the public relations shop, probably arranging for some new episode."

"Well, may God bless them all," said Master Sergeant Smith. "My concern is how he knows about Task Force Trident."

Swanson toyed with the coffee spoon. "Don't really know. I would guess that he asked around about me after the SEALs booted him and somebody mentioned it. Maybe somebody needs to remind him that he is still bound by secrecy oaths before he starts blurting out national security information that could jeopardize operations. I'll mention that to General Middleton tomorrow."

"Better yet, say I go beat a reminder into him right now."

Swanson laughed. "That's not worth the effort, Master Sergeant. Better if we let a team from the Naval Criminal Investigative Service deliver the message."

"NCIS has a television show, too. Everybody has a TV show but me."

"Bitch, bitch, bitch," said Kyle. "Let's have another pitcher, then go get some sleep."

* * *

Ryan Powell was at a back table in the bar area of the SNCO Club, chatting up anyone who stopped by, especially those wanting him to autograph his book. The base PR people had ordered two boxes of hardback copies from the publisher, but that was nowhere near enough for the demand that followed his book tour address that afternoon, and the copies had all been sold. A camera crew from a local station had done an interview that appeared on the early evening news. Now people were arriving with copies they had bought off base during the previous months, and Powell signed and signed, loving the glow of attention and trading good-natured SEAL-versus-Marine banter and insults with his fans.

Running into that damned Kyle Swanson in the dining room had been a surprise because Powell thought he had flushed the man out of his system.

"Who do you want me to make this out to?" he asked a female Marine noncom who handed forward a book and commented that she had just loved it.

"Mandie, with an *ie*," she replied. Their eyes locked. Female Marines were a lot cuter than he remembered. This one was standing right there for the asking, if he wanted it, but Powell avoided groupies and one-nighters, not so much because he loved his wife, which he did, but because if the girl somehow created a YouTube scandal, it could end his celebrity gig. He scrawled the autograph, and she moved on.

Swanson was still black ops. Powell knew that in his bones. The Marine was a living reminder that Ryan Powell, star of *The Elite,* was not really part of the brotherhood, and that was a cold fact that time would never change. Gunny Swanson had consigned Captain America to the dust heap of hero has-beens, although Powell was able to capitalize on the past glory.

Another copy of the book was put before him, this one by no less than a full bird colonel looking sharp in his uniform, who announced, "I enjoy your show, Powell. Just sign your name, please, no use messing up the pages with personalization. I tell my men, keep it simple! That's always the best way."

Ryan signed his name and thanked the colonel, thinking the man was overbearing and pompous, but still a fan. Powell got along with everybody these days. The Swanson thing still rankled, like a burr under a blanket, and was an itch that couldn't be scratched. Or could it?

Next up was an eager young sergeant who confided in a low voice that he had signed up to test for the SEALs. Powell complimented him, wished him luck, and ordered one of the public relations types to buy that man a beer. Making friends right and left.

How could he take down Swanson? Another face-to-face showdown was unlikely, and realistically, Powell doubted he was good enough to best the Gunny. Back in the day, when he was running two thousand rounds a day downrange in practice, yes, and he had followed the rules that day in the Ghost House, had done everything right, but had failed because Swanson cheated. That was much too long ago in a business where the edge starts to dull in a day. Maybe *The Elite* could be the answer. Somehow get the Corps to make Swanson go on the show, and embarrass him before a million viewers.

He kept signing and drinking and thinking until the last book was done, and he capped his pen and leaned back while the PR skunks closed it up for him. Pretty Mandie with an *ie* was near the door, watching, and Ryan thought, what the hell, and made a pistol out of his finger and pointed it at her. She smiled back, and a minute later he walked out after her, waving to some of his newest admirers. He put on his big Stetson as he stepped outside, and the fresh air triggered an idea just as Mandie grabbed his sleeve and pulled him into the shadows and stood on her toes to kiss him with a hungry mouth.

Task Force Trident, he thought as they traded tongues. Powell had lots of media pals now, any of whom would love to expose Swanson and his secret team. He would figure out exactly how to do that later, because Mandie was going to demand his full attention.

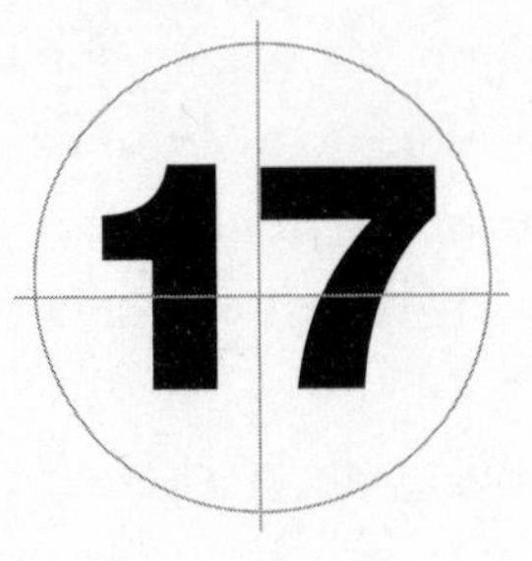

WASHINGTON, D.C.

SENATOR JORDAN MONROE was trying to put a good spin on a bad situation that was getting worse by the minute. For the third time, he explained it all again to Yasim Rebiane, on the other end of the call. The senator was growing weary of the conversation; he had a full calendar today and wanted to clear this problem. "Look, my friend, I had a sit-down with a brigadier general sent over by the Joint Chiefs, and the general assured me that United States military forces are not carrying out any reprisals in Spain over the Barcelona incident. This man sat right here in my office and confirmed that to my face. There was no misunderstanding. He's really plugged in, this general. If he says they are not involved, I believe him."

Rebiane insisted it was a polite brush-off. "Just a one-star, and you think he knows what's really going on? I'm disappointed; I expected better of a United States senator. May I suggest that you put someone who is really in charge—say, one of the Joint Chiefs—under oath before your Armed Services Committee and ask those same questions."

Monroe felt the entire episode was taking too much of his time. "I also reached out to the State Department and the CIA, both of which deny any covert actions, sir. I really want to help, but there is only so much I can do on deep background, calling in favors all over Washington."

"Then what is stopping you from making it official? Call for a hearing. Turn up the pressure." The voice brimmed with contempt.

The senator fidgeted in his big chair. "Now calm down, sir. You have been a major supporter of my campaigns, and I appreciate that and hope it will continue, so I was willing to make some informal inquiries in your behalf. That being said, there is a limit to what you or anyone else can ask of me. I cannot just snap my fingers and hold a hearing without any real evidence of wrongdoing."

Rebiane made an impatient clucking sound. "Is it just a matter of giving you more money?"

"Of course not! No United States senator is for sale." Monroe was growing exasperated.

"Well, that is too bad. Imagine the blowback from Europe when the news breaks that American assassins are running amok, killing important civilians. The president will have to answer some angry calls from other world leaders."

"That is not happening. It is not going to happen. Any such thing would have to be vetted and approved in advance, and it would not be because of policy ramifications. Be reasonable."

"You seem to lack proper motivation, Senator Monroe." Rebiane was silent for a moment before resuming with a changed tone. "I was reluctant to supply this new information for your calculations. Are you before your computer?"

"Yes."

"Go online and type in this address." Rebiane recited a dummy file that he had prepared for just this occasion.

When Jordan Monroe called up the site, he coughed and his throat tightened. It was a photograph of a twelve-year-old girl on a school playground in jeans and a black T-shirt, with long honey-colored hair streaming behind her. "You bastard!" he shouted into the phone.

"That, of course, is little Michelle, your daughter by a campaign volunteer whom you raped after getting drunk at a party. You pay all of the bills and give a stipend to the woman every month. This photo was taken yesterday."

"Don't you dare bring her into this! All I have to do is call a press conference and notify the FBI of this clumsy extortion and bribery attempt, and you will be arrested!" His grip on the telephone was slipping as his hand sweated. His eyes couldn't break away from the photograph of the beautiful child he had never met, joy on her face as she sailed on a swing set. *Michelle.* Monroe knew that if this affair was exposed, there would be a huge personal scandal, and the political fallout would be of nuclear proportions. Nevertheless, he would not back down from this Middle East bully. Persian? Iraqi? What's the difference? "I'm warning you, Rebiane," he hissed. "I have resources that you cannot imagine."

"Why, Senator, I have no intention of ruining your career. You can be useful to me not only now, but again in the future." Yasim allowed himself a smile, knowing that Djahid, who had taken the photograph, had everything in place in St. Louis.

"Then why—"

"Forget about your resources, or going to the press or to the FBI. My foot is on your throat, you arrogant fool. The child and her mother both are already in my custody. Unless you are able to answer my question, I intend to kill them both."

CAMP LEJEUNE, NORTH CAROLINA

Ryan Powell lowered his binos and looked up from the dirt, straight into the television camera, and heaped praise on a Marine squad that was assaulting a ridge with maximum firepower. His words were underscored by the buzz of a Squad Automatic Weapon. The NCO in charge of the attack yelled for cease-fire, and the explosions and gunfire died away, leaving a sheen of gunsmoke hanging in the air. Powell smiled and said, "And that, my friends, is how the Marines do it!"

The director of *The Elite* yelled, "Lunch break. Thirty minutes." The two dozen Marines involved in the exercise for the reality show had earned a treat, and instead of eating military field rations today, they headed toward a pair of waiting gourmet food trucks and the alluring smell of barbecue created by an executive chef. It was cheaper for the production company to hire a top-rate food service than pay overtime to the crew, and there was still another show to finish this afternoon.

Powell slapped a few palms, shook hands, and made his way to his air-conditioned trailer, careful not to mop away the sweat on his face and neck in front of the Marines. With his star power off the set, the boys could enjoy themselves mixing with the crew, particularly the women. Once in the trailer, he stripped away the dirty clothes and took a quick shower, wrapped a towel around his waist, and went into the bedroom, where a shrimp salad and an assortment of cool beverages waited on a table. A change of clothes was on the bed. He had to appear fresh for the next episode, which would involve a new set of Marines plus some armor. A few bites of the salad and some cold water, and he had five minutes left for a nap. His active night with Mandie had taken a toll.

A rap on the door, and a female voice called out, "Telephone call, Mr. Powell. Somebody from Washington."

"Shit," he exclaimed to himself. Probably some asshole general with an idea for a show. Then, to the assistant, "Tell them I'm not available. Take a number."

"Sir, I explained that we're on a working set, but he says he's calling for a senator and that it is urgent to speak with you."

Powell exhaled in defeat. "OK. Bring me the phone." The brunette came in, appreciatively eyeing her muscular boss in the towel, and handed over the phone. "This is Powell," he said.

"Mr. Powell, my name is Douglas Jimenez, and I'm the administrative aide for Senator Jordan Monroe." The aide paused, letting the name sink in. Monroe equaled the Armed Services Committee, which equaled access and funding.

"What can I do for you, sir?" Powell slipped into the humble servant-patriot voice.

"I'll come straight to the point, for your girl told me that you are working. My boss has been tipped off that a covert U.S. operation may be behind the assassinations of two civilian financial figures in Spain. Both were killed by snipers, and while the Pentagon, State, and the Agency deny any involvement, we believe that where there is smoke, there may be fire. Do I have your attention?"

"Yes, sir, you do. How can I help?" An idea was already forming in his mind.

"I was asked to check with people plugged into the special operations community, and rather than deal with the usual chain of command, I decided to start at the top: with Ryan Powell and *The Elite.* You have knowledge on both sides of the spec ops fence, having been an outstanding SEAL yourself, and now doing such outstanding work on the overall military program."

"Well, I'd like to be of assistance, Mr. Jimenez, but I haven't heard anything about any Spanish operation, either from inside or outside of the community. Nothing from the private contractor grapevine, and those guys swap a lot of stories. However . . ." Powell let the intriguing thought dangle. "You said a sniper did the hits?" He had not really been keeping up with the news, but he certainly remembered his evening at the SNCO Club last night, for several reasons. He had a chance here to damage that asshole Swanson. Maybe he could take down the entire organization. *Sweet!*

"However . . . what?" asked Jimenez, whose heartbeat was increasing in anticipation.

"How private is this conversation, sir? I don't want to be called to testify on anything I give you in confidence, since it may be just a hunch on my part." He took a bite of a seasoned french fry.

"The senator will see to it that you have nothing to concern yourself about."

"In that case, there is a very off-the-books unit that would be fully capable of carrying out this sort of thing. Small and lethal and really deep black. I don't know where it stands in the chain of command; it might not be in there at all. I have always considered such an organization to be borderline illegal, a bunch of rogue assassins. Just a possibility, something I heard, you know?"

Jimenez was scribbling notes. "Go ahead, Mr. Powell. The senator would be very appreciative for any insight you may provide. It stays between us, I promise."

"OK. As I understand it, the group goes by the name of Task Force Trident. Like I say, I don't know much about it, other than it exists. The one thing I do know from personal experience is that Trident has a cold-ass killer as its triggerman, a Marine sniper, name of Kyle Swanson." Powell smiled broadly and punched his pillow in delight.

There was a pause in Washington. "Task Force Trident and Kyle Swanson. Strange that we have never heard of them."

"That's the point, sir. Like I said, they are deep in the special ops budget or even somewhere else. This character Swanson fits the profile. He's very good, but he has always been a lone wolf. Rules do not stop him from doing whatever he wants. Matter of fact, I saw him at dinner down here just last night, and he looked as if he was gearing up for a job."

"Well, we find that to be very interesting. We thank you, Mr. Powell. Now that I have these names, I have a starting point. Hey, now, you have a good day."

"Good luck," Powell said and closed the phone. A moment later, a loud, rebel-yell victory war whoop from inside the star's trailer startled those standing nearby outside.

THE PENTAGON

THE IDEA had been sound, but the variables were just too wobbly for the proposed simultaneous assassination plan to work. After spending days trying to pull it all together, the frustrated Lizard finally bit his pen in half in frustration. By lunchtime, he had set up a secure Skype call that would put himself and General Middleton in Washington on the same screen as Sybelle Summers in Paris and Gunny Swanson in North Carolina.

"We know the probable location of Torreblanca, the guy from the Islamic Progress Bank, to a ninety-five percent certainty. He will be in Seville to attend the big April fair. Beyond that, his itinerary has been closed down because of the additional security."

Swanson, in a small communications trailer at Camp Lejeune, replied that his MARSOC team could be in place and ready and just wait for the right moment. Having to wait was not enough of a reason to cancel the operation.

"Kyle, without exact movement times, it is impossible to match him up with the woman in Paris. Mademoiselle Bourihane is just as dicey a target. Her office also has stopped saying when and where she will be during the next couple of weeks, and her earlier public schedule has been changed severely. I doubt if it is any good at all."

The general entwined his fingers as he listened, then chewed a thumbnail. "Too many moving parts," he said.

"Yes, sir," said Commander Freedman. Summers and Swanson could not disagree. If they could not make simultaneous strikes, the second team in action would lose the element of surprise and their target would immediately go to ground.

Typically, Middleton made his decision. "Summers and Coastie have the best chance of a takedown while Bourihane is still in Paris, if they can penetrate the security. What are the chances, Sybelle?"

"Excellent, if we are no longer tied to Kyle's timetable in Seville."

The general agreed. "Do it. And Swanson, stand down your team for now, but keep them handy while we dream up a Plan B. You get back here by tomorrow morning."

Kyle hated to stop something where the momentum was already gathering, but they were right. Too many moving parts had killed many a plan throughout history. It was better to take out one target for sure, but he just wanted it to be *his* target. He saw a little smirk on Sybelle's face. "Sir, we can nail Torreblanca at the fair. No doubt."

"We'll talk about it tomorrow in the office. Don't pout."

There is always a time to shut up when arguing with a general. "Yes, sir. I'll leave this afternoon, soon as I clean up something down here. Liz, would you detail a couple of NCIS agents for my use later today?"

Middleton had considered the conversation over, but his eyes suddenly flashed back to life. “Why the hell do you need NCIS, Gunnery Sergeant Swanson?”

“Nothing important, sir. I’ll explain it all tomorrow morning back at the office.”

18

WILMINGTON, NORTH CAROLINA

FATE. KARMA. LUCK. However he sliced it, Ryan Powell had enjoyed a very good day from start to finish. He returned to his suite at the Hilton Riverside on North Water Street with a bounce in his step and a smile on his face. Done with the Marines at Lejeune, he looked forward to a week in New York to edit the new episode and trek along the meet-and-greet circuit looking for sponsors, then back to L.A. and prep for another segment of *The Elite.* All of that, plus Mandie the night before. The whipped cream on top was this unexpected chance to hand Kyle Swanson and his entire team to the Washington wolves. Whether they were guilty of anything was beside the point. Ryan was still in his TV outfit, sweaty and dirty from playing war, intentionally attracting attention as he casually walked through the lobby.

Powell had developed bad habits since leaving the SEALs, such as dropping his shields when they were no longer needed. While it was true that he was not working on dangerous assignments, the changes had come quickly and without his even realizing it. The stealthy operator who had once been among the best in the business no longer automatically searched the shadows for places where death might lurk, forgot all the protocols for personal security, and abandoned conducting a surveillance detection route, or SDR, to see if he was being followed. He was a civilian now. So although the two men in the black Crown Victoria parked in the first row of the hotel lot stood out as conspicuously as roses in a weed patch, Powell completely missed them.

Kyle Swanson crashed into the door with his shoulder as Powell opened it, powering through the move with linebacker strength, coming from behind when Powell was only halfway through. The heavy slab of wood rammed back so hard against Powell that the doorknob cracked a rib, and then Kyle slammed Powell's left wrist against the sill and broke it with an audible *crack*. Before the stunned man could respond, Swanson grabbed his shirt, swatted him twice with a collapsible steel baton, and threw him stumbling into the room. Powell collapsed with a moan.

The room was illuminated by fuzzy, fading sunlight coming through sheer drapes when he regained his senses a few minutes later. He was in a soft chair facing that window, with no restraints, and a bag of ice was wrapped in a towel around the broken arm. A figure in the other chair was almost invisible in the glare, the digital camo pattern of his BDUs defying definition, but he knew who it was. "Swanson," grunted Powell, rubbing his damaged arm, then touching the swelling above his left eye and breathing in sharply as the broken rib made its presence known. "What the fuck?"

"I wanted your full attention, Powell, so let's get this over with. On your feet and walk to the window. Now!"

Powell grimaced when he moved, but his senses were returning. "I'll kick your ass," he said as he stood up.

Swanson faced him, then slapped Powell hard across the face, spinning him back across the chair. "You weren't good enough back in the day, and you sure as hell aren't good enough now. Get your ass over to the window, bitch." The open-handed palm slap was an intentional insult, but the bravado already had drained out of Powell, and Kyle knew it. "Look down in the parking lot."

The beaten man moved to the window and pushed aside the curtain. Two men in dark suits and sunglasses were staring back up at him. He turned back to Swanson.

"Those are NCIS agents, and if I give the word, they are going to arrest you. For some stupid reason, you have forgotten that you signed secrecy oaths that are to follow you all of your life. We are here to either make you remember that or put you in a dark hole."

"What the hell are you talking about? I'm a civilian now and have freedom of speech. I'm going to have my lawyers all over your butt. Fuck you and the NCIS."

"OK. The third option is that I just shoot you where you stand." Kyle pulled a .45 ACP caliber pistol from his belt and picked a pillow from the chair.

Powell knew the pillow would be an effective silencer, but also knew that Swanson would not hesitate to pull the trigger. Killing an American citizen was a big no-no in the law, but the body would never be found. Special operators have to live by different rules.

"What do you want?"

"You were running your mouth about Task Force Trident in the club last night. That stops right now because it is putting operators at risk. You knew better than that, but you had to show off."

Powell staggered to the bed and sat down, relieved that he wasn't going to be shot. "I didn't mean anything, Swanson. I would never break my oath."

"Bullshit. You did it on purpose. Those NCIS guys are ready to haul your ass away and file charges. I'm ready to put you down for good. To get clear, you swear to shut the hell up, and never again mention Trident to anybody, and forget all about me. We never met. Ever! Is that clear?"

The big man nodded in understanding. "I got it."

"Explain the arm and the bruises."

"Training accident during the show. Shit happens." He shrugged.

"Then I'm gone. You be a good boy and I won't come back."

"I said I got it." Powell waited until Swanson walked out of the door and it clicked to lock behind him, then fell back on the mattress and began to giggle, putting his hand over his mouth to muffle the sound. The spook was a day late and a dollar short. The damage was already done.

Swanson drove back to Washington, hoping the moron would remember this little tune-up so they would not have to go through it again. If there was a next time, Kyle would have no choice but to kill Powell. Some people never learn.

PARIS, FRANCE

THE REAL STRENGTH in having women warriors as members of Task Force Trident was that they possessed an advantage that men would never have, no matter what their training. Their gender alone made them seem less of a threat than a bulky male with a bald head and a Fu Manchu mustache. When eyes roamed over Sybelle Summers or Beth Ledford, the first thing that registered was that they were attractive women, not that they might be a pair of gunslingers.

Sybelle's normally elegant and quiet dark beauty and black hair were disguised on this night beneath a wig of long auburn hair and green contact lenses. She was flashy in a purple knee-length dress that was gathered at the waist and flared from the hips, and she walked with total confidence in medium heels, head high, chin out, a woman used to the model's runway. Any onlooker's first guess would have been that she was in the fashion business.

Coastie's chirpy blue-eyed blonde persona was buried tonight in a brunette hairstyle that matched the dark contacts in her eyes, and she was draped in a pale lemon low-cut creation that clung to her curves. When she smiled, dimples appeared.

The maître d' of the restaurant in the upscale Sixteenth Arrondissement had been alerted that the women were celebrity models, and a private corner table awaited them. Stuffy and officious in his tux and starched shirt, he personally escorted them to their seats through the arched entrance to the dining area, and across the mosaic floor in a roundabout fashion to show them off, then effusively wished them a happy meal while stealing an admiring glance at Beth's chest. Both women put their purses in their laps and adjusted them so their weapons were readily available.

Instead of a surly character with a stained apron, a courteous, middle-aged waiter helped them negotiate the monster menu. He knew that with the average meal running about two hundred euros here, and fashionistas having little regard for prices, the bill for the evening would be large, and his kindness should reap a bounteous tip. One famous designer had signed his Visa bill after adding a gratuity of five thousand dollars. For that kind of money, François worked hard at being nice. He was followed not by a wine steward but by a tea steward, who suggested specific teas for each course. Sybelle and Coastie decided to spare no expense, since they weren't going to be around to pay for it anyway. They spoke accented English with British overtones, but said little that could be heard beyond their table. He couldn't guess their nationalities because models come from everywhere.

"Snails? Is it too late to have the waiter run out and bring us a couple of Happy Meals?" Coastie checked out the dining room guests, then the staff members and anyone in the area. Lowering her voice even more, she said, "Second guy behind the bar is security. He isn't helping the bartender at all."

Sybelle also kept her head on a swivel. Big smile. "I don't see any others. Maybe one will come with her. And look pleasant while you eat your little Escargots à la Bourguignonne. Remember, as they slime down your throat, that François promised they were raised carefully on radishes and spinach, and are delicious in the chef's special garlic and herb butter."

They kept up a quiet conversation about photo shoots and magazines. As mission prep, they had read some gossip and celebrity news. Then they switched to reading and working with their cell phones, almost ignoring each other.

François frowned at that practice as not being worthy of a gourmet meal. Admiration of their beauty was mixed with distaste for their public manners. Beautiful women in that special supermodel world often believed they were entitled to do as they wished, because they were idolized. The cover was perfect for the two striking women, whose eyes reflected the light from the chandelier overhead. He would later recall that the two actually had said very little.

Mercedes Sarra Bourihane arrived quietly in the company of three fellow conference attendees, all older men in rumpled suits who seemed exhausted from their long day of wrangling over global economics. In contrast, Bourihane looked as if she had been at a spa rather than attending a tiresome conference. Her sandy brown hair was in place, and the slight smile was genuine above the understated black designer outfit. They were shown to a table near the middle of the room, not because of their obvious lack of importance but because of its proximity to the protective agent at the bar.

Within minutes, she had settled back in her chair, showing some of her weariness. She had spent a long day trying to convince fellow money experts that a substantial Islamic transfusion of funds to prop up the Spanish economy would benefit everyone involved. It was a hard sell because everyone knew that more than money was on the table. Politics, power, and control were in play, which meant a lot of opponents wanted to stop the Islamic gambit.

"She's alone," Sybelle said. "Maybe one guard was left outside, but the assistant bartender is the only one in with her. You ready?"

"Better than sitting here eating a snail," Coastie replied. She rose from the cushioned banquette and wasted a few moments adjusting the light yellow dress and slinging her beige Gucci bag over a shoulder. Even Bourihane gave the beautiful young brunette an approving look when the girl moved past on her way to the toilet. Beth knew the bar agent had given her a quick once-over, then dismissed her from his thoughts as representing no threat.

The ladies' bathroom was a beautiful place, with long mirrors on one side above a sparkling marble vanity and sinks, and four private compartments with full-length doors on the other. A stand of purple flowers occupied one corner. Beth locked herself into the far stall, removed the little Ruger SR22 pistol from her purse, and screwed a sound suppressor on the end. Putting the pistol on the closed toilet lid, she lifted her skirt and jerked away the tape that secured a spring knife to her inner thigh. Duct tape was marvelous stuff, she thought, and peeling it away didn't hurt nearly as much as a bikini wax. Coastie texted Sybelle that she was ready, then gathered her tools and sat down to wait.

Seven minutes later, Mercedes Bourihane finished her second glass of tea and decided to freshen up before the meal was served. She tapped her lips with a linen napkin, excused herself, and headed for the arched doorway to the restroom. The protecting agent watched but did not leave his post, for he could see that entrance from where he stood, and no one was around her.

Sybelle pushed the SEND button on the cell phone, and a prepared text message lit up on Coastie's screen in the bathroom stall. Summers got up from her table, pausing to brace herself a bit; then she, too, headed for the toilet, bag over her shoulder.

The agent behind the bar thought the redhead might have had too much to drink. He watched her in the mirror. No threat.

Bourihane had opened a door into a little foyer that provided privacy, then pushed through a double inner door just as the brown-haired young woman in the yellow dress was exiting the far stall. The economist decided to use the foremost facility, but as she reached for the knob, she realized the other woman had not gone to the sink and mirror as a normal woman would have done. Instead, she was right beside her.

Sybelle came through the outer door and put her back against it as Coastie raised the pistol, pressed the long silencer against the right side of the target's head, and pulled the trigger three times.

The noise was no louder than a series of coughs as the little .22 caliber bullets bored into the skull and tumbled around in the brain cavity. Bourihane jerked sideways, then slumped down to the floor, leaving a spray of blood on the rich fabric of the compartment door.

The agent had finally realized something was wrong. There were two women in there with the important lady he was guarding, and the redhead that he thought was tipsy actually had not ordered any alcohol, just tea. He jumped over the bar and ran to the arch, drawing his pistol and crashing through the outer door.

Sybelle took a step away from inner double doors, and when the bodyguard surged through, she met his forward momentum with an elbow strike to the bridge of his nose, bone on bone, and he went down hard. "Let's go!"

Coastie paused only long enough to put a bullet in the inattentive guard's head, then stepped over him and followed Summers out. Instead of returning to their table, they went left and through the swinging doors into the kitchen, Busy chefs and workers began to shout as the women headed for the rear entrance. Trailed by shouts, they broke free into the night as fast as they could run in high heels.

A black Land Rover with a CIA driver at the wheel was double-parked beside a line of cars. Primary, secondary, and tertiary escape routes had been planned for them to reach the next vehicle. A shooter was supposed to be in the passenger's seat, but that place was empty. Sybelle yanked open the rear door and jumped inside, using her own pistol to try to cover Coastie, who was climbing in behind her.

The guard posted outside the front door had run inside the restaurant when the shouting started, then chased the two fleeing women through the kitchen. He screamed in French for everybody to stop them, and held his own pistol pointed up until he cleared the back portal. He was in time to see the woman in the yellow dress getting into a big vehicle. He stopped, took a firing stance, and aimed at her back.

Another figure stepped from the shadows thrown by the light coming through the open kitchen door, and the gunman was grabbed by the chin, his head jerked backward as a big knife came in over the shoulder. The unprotected throat was opened almost to the point of decapitation.

Coastie was in the SUV, the door closed behind her, when the unexpected attacker left the new corpse bleeding on the cobbles and calmly got into the front seat. "Hey," said Kyle Swanson. "What's up?"

19

PARIS, FRANCE

THE LAND ROVER sped out of the alley and cut into a light stream of traffic, with all four people inside rocking on the adrenaline pumping in their veins, averting their faces from the prying security cameras that laced the modern city. The driver did not speak as he kept his foot heavy on the accelerator for a half mile, weaving into and out of gaps, then made a sharp left turn into a side street and an immediate right that put them into a quiet area of apartment buildings with a few shops fronting the street. He parked behind a store, out of the sight of passersby and where there were no cameras with unblinking eyes.

"Everybody out," he shouted. "The white Toyota is ours. Swanson, you drive!" The Trident operators abandoned the luxury SUV and jumped into the common sedan, which had a pebble-pitted windshield and had not been washed for weeks. The Agency man popped a thermite grenade into the Land Rover, which he had filled with gasoline at $5.54 per gallon before starting tonight's mission. The incendiary grenade exploded a few seconds later and set off the gas tank, which erupted in an incredible flash of heat with a ball of flames. The intense brew gobbled up the sturdy Land Rover, scorched the area around it, and destroyed all DNA evidence and traces of ownership.

They were out of immediate danger. The wigs came off, and to the surprise of the CIA agent, the redhead had black hair and the brunette transformed into a blonde. Both women put away their pistols to fuss with their hair.

"We weren't expecting you, Kyle," said Coastie, beginning to swipe off the makeup with tissues from the purse. Her voice was steady.

"I landed in Paris just about the same time the two of you entered the restaurant, so our CIA friends let me ride in place of their own shooter since I knew the operation better. How did it go inside?"

Sybelle shrugged her shoulders. "Easier than anticipated. Bourihane had only one security man in the place, and he was lousy. Had to take him down on the way out, too." She smiled at Swanson. "Coastie put one in his head as she stepped over him just after popping the target three times. Lot of damage for a little .22 pistol."

"I want to get out of this damned dress and these heels," Coastie said.

"Go ahead," said the CIA guy. "Don't mind me."

"How much longer until we're out of here?" Sybelle asked.

"Port of Grenelle coming up in about two more miles," the man said. "We have a nice little boat that we use as a floating safe house, so I guess you should keep your clothes on until we're on board. We'll motor up the Seine a ways to a heliport to ferry you all to a private airport. By then you will be all back to normal, and we have passports and visas ready for you to exit the country. Your stuff was brought over from the hotel." He handed over a couple of raincoats and towels. "Meanwhile, you can use these."

Sybelle and Beth struggled into the long garments and resumed attacking the heavy makeup as the Agency representative tried not to stare. With the lights of Paris flashing by, and the distant *whoop-whoop* of police sirens sounding, they went about the business of transforming themselves from glamour girls into shapeless, plain creatures. He didn't really know who these people were, because he had not needed to know. *But damn!* The dark-haired one seemed fearless and in charge, the cute blonde had just cold-popped two people in a fancy restaurant, and the guy driving, well, he hardly broke stride as he ripped off that dude's throat.

"Can I ask a question?"

"No." Sybelle drilled him with piercing eyes. "But thanks for all of your help tonight. You'll never know how happy I was to see that Land Rover waiting outside."

"No problem. My question is, are you married?"

THE SAFE HOUSE was merely a cramped cabin on an ugly aluminum-hulled work barge that had a deck littered with coiled ropes, tools, and machinery. The quirky silhouette was intentional, for a vessel had to be relatively small to navigate the ancient low bridges along the Seine, and similar workboats plied the river at all hours. Below deck, it had two powerful engines for extra strength if needed, watertight compartments, hidden cabinets, and a private room that served a variety of purposes, including interrogations. "Y'all ladies go on down there out of sight while we shove off. Once we get under way, you can come up for air." The CIA man was all business now, peeling off his black leather jacket and putting on a sweater that had been through better days. A billed fisherman's cap covered his head.

Swanson was already in boots and jeans, and by putting on a crewman's sweater, he also disappeared into the commonplace sights of the river.

"We're ready," said the agent. "Cast off the mooring lines."

Swanson freed the ropes that held the little barge to the dock, and the engines surged to life with a low growl. He then stayed busy curling lines and moving tools as the agent fed more throttle and the flat vessel slipped away from the pier. Once under way, Kyle stopped pretending to work and sat on the deck with his back to the cabin. He could see the Eiffel Tower from the river. Sybelle and Coastie joined him in a few minutes, both also in jeans, sweaters, and caps that hid their hair; some grime from the boat streaked their white faces.

"That was almost too easy," Summers commented, knees drawn up to her chest. "Bourihane should have had more security."

"Don't overanalyze it," said Kyle. "Take the gift and say, 'Thank you.' They screwed up. I can guarantee it will only get harder."

"Were they more careless just because she was a woman?" Coastie had wondered about that big gulf that separates the sexes in the Muslim culture.

Would they have acted differently if she had been a man? Beth's mind was untroubled by the sights and sounds of the restroom slaughter; that was already old news to her. Instead, she was puzzling through the job, giving herself an after-action critique and not finding any flaws. By any measure, she believed she had met the high Trident standards. They had trusted her with a lot by letting her take the kill shots instead of giving that assignment to the more experienced Sybelle, and she carried it out. Yet down deep inside, she felt miserable.

Kyle had also been working on what had happened. "Arrogance, maybe. She was in France and not Spain, and moving in public, so they did not consider the actual danger. That's the whole point of our mission, that no terrorist white-collar mastermind is safe, anywhere. No matter what the reason, this was sloppy planning on their part. It won't happen again."

The boat was moving at a cautious waterway speed. Sybelle watched the shoreline and said, "The Paris police are going to try to throw a net over us. I never underestimate the *gendarmes*—they cannot ignore three dead at a fancy bistro and a burned-out SUV and two good-looking suspects. We sold the international supermodels cover pretty well, so it will be difficult to prove we are Americans, but just to be on the safe side, I want to get on that plane and out of France before they can clamp down." She got to her feet and brushed herself off.

"Sounds like a plan," said Kyle. "Where are you going?"

"I want a few words with our cute savior from the CIA."

Coastie looked up in wonder. "You pick the oddest time for romance."

WASHINGTON, D.C.

THE SENATOR had secretaries, assistants, schedulers, aides, and other assorted staff to handle the routine business of his office, such as making telephone calls to get the other party on the line before Jordan Monroe had to pick up the phone himself. It was an etiquette thing. This call, however, he was eager to make himself, and in utmost privacy. He left the office entirely, explaining that he was going to walk over to the U.S. Supreme Court for lunch with his old hunting buddy, Justice Benjamin Rathmann.

Once clear of the Capitol, he slowed his pace and looked around. No journalists had followed him, and to the tourists strolling by, he was just another government worker in a dark suit. During their initial meeting in the limousine, Yasim Rebiane had said that he could be reached through his company's office in Kansas City, which would forward the message, but he also had provided a private direct number. The senator dialed. "This is Monroe," he said when the voice answered.

"Do you have what I need?" Cold.

"Yes. Now let the girls go. If you have harmed them in any way—"

"Just give me the information, Senator, and quit pretending you have control of this situation."

Jordan Monroe moved from the sidewalk onto the new grass and stood rock still. "Are they OK? At least tell me that." He was not used to pleading, and felt tears of helplessness gather in his eyes.

"The information," reminded Yanis Rebiane, with a hint of threat.

A chill tingled down the senator's spine. "All right. There is indeed a secret unit that does conduct operations far outside of other agencies and services. The group is known as Task Force Trident. It supports a very skilled operator named Kyle Swanson, who is an experienced Marine sniper. He once won the Congressional Medal of Honor."

Rebiane thought that might fit the profile. "Who was your source for this?"

The senator was not a reporter and had no problem with giving up the names. "My top aide, Douglas Jimenez, got it through an ex-SEAL named Ryan Powell, who currently has a popular television show and knows the special ops community."

"This is a good starting point, Senator Monroe, but now you have to start digging harder. Use your influence to find out more about both Trident and this Swanson man."

"My girls! Yasim! You promised!"

"Yes. Rest easy. Pretty young Michelle and her mother have not been harmed, but only had to spend the night in a hunting cabin in your state. We are not monsters, Senator. The lodge is an isolated but easily accessible place, with a frequently used road a mile away. They will be free to leave about ten minutes after I make the call. Afterward, you must convince them not to call the police, for they remain hostages. I can reach back for them again whenever I choose. There is no place that they would be really safe, nor is the secret of your relationship."

The senator looked over at the huge white Supreme Court Building and then back to the Capitol. The FBI's Hoover Building was just down the street, and beyond that was the White House itself, while across the Potomac sprawled the Pentagon. He was standing in the center of power of the strongest nation on earth, and he usually could make things happen in this town with a snap of his fingers. He was also helpless, caught in a web he didn't really understand. It was also finally dawning on him that he might be under the control of a terrorist. "I understand," he said softly. "I already have my top man working on it."

The phone clicked off, and the senator put away his own device. He returned to his office, looking glum and ill, as if he had aged ten years in the last half hour. The splendor of the building and this spacious, decorated office suite meant nothing. The receptionist said that several calls had come in while he was gone, but Monroe waved her away as he went into his private chamber and locked the door. Rebiane had him by the balls and would never let go. Julie and Michelle would forever exist as valuable pawns. He was risking ruin no matter what he did, and the only clear way out was to cooperate with Rebiane for the time being and get him to back off. A final solution could come later. In the meantime, the senator would go full throttle after the elusive Task Force Trident.

MISSOURI

YANIS REBIANE was glad to be done with the senator's call, and immediately contacted his son, Djahid, in Missouri to tell him to give the hostages a stern warning to keep quiet, then let them go. "I need you back here right after that, so we will be leaving for home. Check the news from France on your laptop. Mercedes Bourihane has been killed."

Djahid seemed to miss the second part of the comment. "Set them free? Why?"

"If we kill them, we lose them forever. It must be clear to the senator that we can return and take them again at some future date if he disobeys. Free or not, they remain as bargaining chips. Never mind them. We must concentrate on what has happened to Bourihane."

Djahid had locked the woman and the girl in a bedroom at the lodge, and found them huddled together on the bed when he opened the door. He smiled. "You come with me, woman. Leave the child. I will be setting you both free in a few minutes."

Julie Scott felt a surge of relief. The kidnapper had hardly said a word to them since the carjacking, and the lack of information scared them. He had not harmed them physically, just kept them locked in the bedroom, which had an adjoining bath. Before he took Julie from the room, Djahid turned on the television set and tossed Michelle the remote controller. "Watch something."

Then the door was closed and Julie was pushed into the kitchen. Thumping bass notes penetrated the bedroom door as her daughter tuned in MTV and jacked up the sound.

"She is a cute child. It would be a shame if you caused something bad to happen to her."

Julie's brown eyes widened. "What do you mean? What are you going to do?"

"Nothing, probably, if you continue to cooperate. Take off all of your clothes."

"*No!*"

Djahid punched her hard in the stomach, knocking her to the floor. "Don't be difficult. I'm not going to rape you. Now take off your clothes."

Julie stood trembling, gulping for breath. She kicked off her shoes, lifted off her sweater, and stepped out of her jeans. Looking at the man, she asked, "More?"

"Everything." He was leaning against the counter, a new cup of coffee in his hands. A small camera was pointed at her.

Julie summoned her courage and dropped the bra and panties. Her eyes were closed and her fists clenched. She could feel the cool air and embarrassment as fear painted her skin with goosebumps.

"OK. You can get dressed." He had hardly looked at her nakedness.

"Can I ask what that was all about? In fact, what is this entire kidnapping about?" Julie was putting her clothes on in a rush, buttoning and fastening.

Djahid held up his camera, then handed it to her. "Insurance, Ms. Scott. I wanted you to be certain that you understand how serious this is. If you call the police, I will return, and next time, it will not be so easy. Very bad things will happen. You can look at these images of your body anytime you need a reminder. You really need to protect pretty little Michelle from me, and from men that I may use. They are violent in their tastes. By the way, your senator in Washington cannot help. We took you because we needed something from him. So far, he has cooperated."

He put on his jacket and zipped it halfway. "So now I suggest that you leave this place, for there is a gas leak in the basement, and it is going to blow up in ten minutes and burn to the ground. Walk down the driveway and turn left on that unpaved track. A paved road with traffic is a mile away, and if nothing else comes along first, emergency vehicles will be responding to the fire. By the way, the bedroom door is locked. Use that sledgehammer I have left on the table to break it open." He backed out, keeping his eyes fixed on her. "You should have just enough time."

As the door closed, Julie Scott snapped from her trance. She screamed her daughter's name, grabbed the sixteen-pound hammer, and ran for the bedroom. Outside, she heard the sound of a truck rumbling away from the cabin.

ABOARD THE *VAGABOND*

KYLE SWANSON clearly understood that the elimination of Mercedes Sarra Bourihane changed the entire situation. They had bagged the first two members of the Group of Six with precision shots and beneath the dark veil of secrecy, because each of the shady moneymen had accrued numerous enemies and rivals. The Spanish police had been working a very wide spectrum of suspects. They had suspicions, yes, but not evidence to point directly at Americans. The hit on Bourihane in Paris was different. Just as when Julius Caesar crossed the Rubicon River to launch his insurrection against Rome, there would be no turning back now for Task Force Trident. They were committed to wiping out the entire Group of Six as massive payback for the massacre in Barcelona, and the pattern was clear for anyone who looked. Hiding American involvement was going to be more difficult.

Real tests lay ahead. Security rings around the remaining three targets would be tightened, and those principals would never again be as foolish as Bourihane by taking time for unguarded relaxation.

The news of the Bourihane takedown was smeared all over the Internet. Aboard the *Vagabond*, Kyle clicked through the links one by one while a large flat-screen television recessed into the bulkhead showed live stand-up reporting from grim newsies in Paris. Pictures of the victim were shown frequently: a stylish female financier who had engineered billions of dollars in deals around the globe during a meteoric career that had been cut short by murder in a ladies' bathroom. Two bodyguards were also brutally slain, and the suspects were beautiful women.

"Seems you lot have swatted quite the hornet's nest," observed Sir Jeff. "People appear quite upset. Biggest thing in Paris since the unfortunate automobile accident that took our lovely Princess Diana."

"Bourihane was nothing but a killer who wore lipstick," replied Swanson.

"Yes. But she was also an important economist, although her political views were radical Islamist. All geniuses have flaws. The Muslim attempt to take over Spain is an ambitious project, and her brainpower was crucial."

"Lucky for us, the newspeople are interviewing mostly European economists, who are boring. The story doesn't have attention-grabbing names, and the audiences in America will click away from it after two minutes unless it can be carried by the mystery models and rumors of fashion wars. The publicity storm won't last long if it is confined to the BBC and Al Jazeera." Kyle glanced at another story.

Jeff picked a triangle of toast and stuck it into a bowl of spicy artichoke dip. "Interpol won't be distracted, and neither will the French police, nor the Spaniards. Three members of the Group of Six being killed will not be considered a coincidence, and will be laid at America's doorstep no matter what. You can wager that the intelligence services in all of the Muslim nations are paying attention."

Swanson closed the laptop computer. "It doesn't matter. The mission from the start has been to take out six targets. We're halfway there."

"Any worries, Kyle, knowing the desk is stacked against you from here on out?" Jeff crunched the toast thoroughly, then had a sip of wine.

"No. As far as I'm concerned, those next three are already dead."

"Don't forget your basic infantry training, Kyle. You have already taken an important objective, so what still needs to be done? Do you think the other side is just going to sit there and let you roll over them?"

"We have the momentum, Jeff. They can guess, but as of right now they don't know who we are, and have no proof. Therefore, they have no choice but to play defense."

"Do not let your personal feelings for your fallen comrades cloud your tactical mind," Jeff warned. "You are in a holding pattern right now, regrouping and planning another strike. All of the potential targets will be on high alert. Do . . . not . . . rush."

He rose with the help of his polished mahogany cane and hobbled across the room and out the door. "You stay here and think about it. I'm going to join the ladies on deck, where I understand that Coastie is wearing a scandalously tiny bikini."

Swanson took a pull on his beer, kicked back in a soft leather recliner, and closed his eyes and pondered Jeff's caution. The old guy had been through a lot of fights and knew what he was talking about. This mission had reached beyond the anticipated and normal eye-for-an-eye style of retribution on terrorism. In that, Trident had been spectacularly successful. The people who called the signals now found themselves on scope and had every reason to be worried.

Both sides were committed. Swanson and Task Force Trident would remain as invisible as possible and continue the attack, while the Muslim investment schemers would rally their own forces, continue to present innocent faces to the public, and go about their bloody business of taking over a European nation.

Battle was often like a ballet, with moves that had been honed by eons of war and were common to every fight. Prepare your forces, pick your point of attack, capture the objective, and immediately consolidate to meet a counterattack. The enemy would undoubtedly want to respond, but where? Against whom? How? Right now all they had was anger and a faceless enemy, terrorism in reverse. Trident had its shields up. Kyle slipped into a doze with a half-smile on his face.

WASHINGTON, D.C.

BRIGADIER GENERAL Alfred Coleman was back on Capitol Hill because Senator Jordan Monroe had demanded another meeting after Mademoiselle Bourihane was shot. Coleman sent a memo up the chain and received permission to go over and listen to the United States senator. Naturally, the general was to disclose nothing and report back. Wary of the second meeting, the one-star decided to take along a legal adviser from the Air Force Judge Advocate General's Corps. A driver picked up Coleman and Captain Howell Andrews at the Pentagon, and the general briefed the captain as the driver dodged heavy tourist traffic by choosing the Arlington Memorial Bridge. He eventually deposited them at the southwest entrance of the Russell Senate Office Building.

Douglas Jimenez, the senator's chief of staff, was there to meet them on the stone stairs outside, and although he shook hands, his greeting was icy. "Senator Monroe is upset because he believes that you lied to him, General Coleman, and declines to meet with you again personally. So if you would dismiss your driver, we can just talk in the privacy of your car."

General Coleman's normally placid face colored pink at the accusation and the brusque manner of the aide. Being called a liar and told to deal with an underling was a direct affront to his integrity, his rank, and his position, and he would not condone it. "Negative. I think I'll just go back to the Pentagon. Tell your senator that I remain available at his convenience, and in the meantime, you can explain whatever the problem is to Captain Andrews here."

"Very well," said Jimenez, seeing the fury and delighted to know that he had gotten under the general's skin.

Coleman stepped into the vehicle and told the driver to head back to the barn.

"Nobody left here but us chickens, huh, Captain?" Jimenez laughed. "Come on. I'll buy you a coffee and we'll go over this thing lawyer to lawyer. It would eventually come down to us anyway." There was a sidewalk café nearby, and they had beaten the lunch crowd so were able to get a table on the side.

Captain Andrews, a short and stocky man not far beyond his law school years at the University of Arizona and his USAF-JAG training at Maxwell Air Force Base in Alabama, already had the pallor of someone who did too much desk work. He got out a yellow legal pad, on which he had filled several sheets with notes, and clicked open his pen. "General Coleman briefed me on the way over, so I assume this is about the same subject."

"Yeah. Let's make it Howell and Doug informally, since we're probably going to be meeting a lot." Jimenez wanted him at ease. "Last time, my senator directly asked your general if American troops were involved in some reprisals that seem to be going on in retaliation for the Barcelona terrorist incident. Your man said there were none. This latest murder of the woman in Paris knocks that into a cocked hat. Three members of the Group of Six. It's you guys."

Howell flipped back a yellow page and read his scribbles. "The question was clumsily phrased, Doug, and ambiguous. Senator Monroe asked, quote, 'Are uniformed American troops involved in what appear to be coordinated attacks by snipers on important Spanish civilians?' The general said there were not. *Uniformed* was the way out, and he took it. The answer would have been the same anyway, because he really doesn't know about any such operation."

Jimenez chuckled in appreciation. "So he taped the meeting. I imagine that a microphone could be hidden in all of that colorful spaghetti on his chest and never be seen." He opened a window on his iPhone. "Then your general said, and I also quote, "The Pentagon has nothing to do with any reprisals that may or may not be under way.' "

"Everybody records everything." The captain returned the smile. "Makes our jobs easier when we start parsing the language. So let's put our own recording devices on the table today." They both switched on apps on their phones. "What do you want?"

Doug Jimenez leaned forward, his elbows on the table. "It has come to us now from multiple sources that something is indeed going on over there, and that it probably involves the U.S. military. This new assassination of the woman economist in Paris extends the pattern of suspicious deaths of foreign nationals who apparently were directly connected to the

Muslim offer of funds to the Madrid government. The senator is convinced you guys have secret boots on the ground over there, stomping on our alliances and working against our national interest."

"That's a pretty big leap, Doug. I smell a fishing expedition."

"Naw, Howell. We've already got the big fish. It is called Task Force Trident, and contains a shark Marine sniper named Kyle Swanson."

"Never heard of them," Howell Andrews honestly replied as he wrote down the names. "Anyway, what does any of this have to do with anything? We conduct black ops in a lot of places for a lot of reasons, and under a lot of code names."

"Here's Swanson's picture from back when he received the Congressional Medal of Honor. Downloaded it from Google this morning, but there is no background on him, not even a driver's license. Every query is diverted to an ERROR message, and that means to me that his record has been scrubbed." Doug Jimenez paused to drink some of his coffee.

Andrews stopped writing. "Maybe you need to upgrade your telephone?"

"Let me be clear," said Doug. "We're not talking about some drone strike in an isolated Afghan village. This apparently is a rogue operation that endangers global American interests."

"Rogue? You think the military is dodging civilian oversight? Preposterous. We don't work that way. Sounds more like CIA, if it exists at all."

"Remember Marlon Brando's crazy character, the mad Colonel Kurtz in *Apocalypse Now*?" Doug Jimenez looked hard at the young man in the blue uniform and recited a line in his best hissing Brando voice. "We must kill them. We must incinerate them. Pig after pig. Cow after cow. Village after village. Army after army."

"That was just a movie, Doug."

"Iraq and Afghanistan ruined a lot of people, Howell. So let's find out if you've got a new Colonel Kurtz going bananas on you and carrying on his own private war with his own private army. What do we want specifically? Any and all documents pertaining to Task Force Trident, including internal discussions, e-mails and other electronic media records, and the personnel jacket of this guy Swanson. The senator is willing to let the military deal quietly with this out-of-control unit, as long as we have access to ensure there is a thorough investigation."

"So you want us to crack open black operations for you and hand over everything? Get real. That sounds like subpoena talk—produce everything ever said about anything. You are still fishing at a dry hole, Doug."

"It doesn't have to be hostile. Congress has inquisitive powers and can call for a full hearing, but we want to settle this off the record—stop this travesty of justice and save the military from another black eye."

Howell shook his head. "You got nothing. How about a swap? Give me the names of your sources so we can interview them independently while we look into your accusations. Then we can have a level playing field."

"That's not going to happen because of confidentiality, but I'll sweeten the deal. We offer partial immunity to Kyle Swanson if he rolls over on his organization. He could not possibly be doing this on his own."

Captain Andrews folded up his material. "Particularly when the woman in Paris was killed by other women, and Swanson obviously is the wrong gender. I'll take this back to the brass, but our position remains that we don't know what the hell you're talking about. Tell the senator we thank him for the heads-up."

Jimenez tossed a twenty-dollar bill on the table, and they both got ready to leave. "Tell them to put their shoulders to the wheel, Captain Andrews. The clock is ticking."

SEVILLE, SPAIN

DANIEL FERRAN TORREBLANCA let his mind tumble the sharp-edged questions as he sat alone in the office of his crowded home in Seville. The rest of his large family was out enjoying the riotous Feria de Abril, which was where he wanted to be. He glanced at a clock; it was five thirty, and he longed to be at the Plaza de Toros de la Maestranza, shaded about halfway up the stands, watching Pepin Liria cape a bull with nonchalant elegance, even daring to fight on his knees. He would probably be rewarded with an ear today. Instead of being in the Cathedral of Bullfighting with his friends, Torreblanca was isolated with his thoughts, hidden away and praying to Allah that the bullet-resistant glass in his windows worked.

Mercedes had been careless! She was an old hand in the sneaky world of high finance, but she carried on with her life as if a diamond necklace were a suit of armor. She had known that the Spanish proposition was a high-risk operation from the start, and that lives would most certainly be lost, but she acted as if she herself were exempt from any violence just because she always had been before. Even when schemes that were hatched in her air-conditioned offices funneled money to Muslim warlords and resulted in many deaths, she had sailed untouched above the killing fields, shielded by phony accounts, front companies, paperwork, and foreign banks. Her fingerprints were never actually on the killings. This time, she had been wrong about how distance protected her, and now his dear friend Mercedes was dead.

Bourihane had been a valuable piece of the overall strategy to bring down the government of Spain precisely because she embodied the image of a nonthreatening, progressive Muslim woman. She could walk into a boardroom anywhere in Europe, make a sales pitch, and walk out with a multimillion-dollar deal. When she put on her lawyer hat, she was fierce, but that was always tempered by the friendly personality. Mercedes simply would not let people *not* like her.

Anyway, Yasim Rebiane and his son, Djahid, were supposed to be protecting them all throughout the bargaining with the Madrid financiers. That was part of the original plan, and Yasim had vowed that it would be carried out efficiently and quietly. Instead, the fools had launched a preemptive attack on the Americans in Barcelona, allegedly to warn Washington to stay out of the way. In Torreblanca's view, all that did was guarantee more U.S. involvement. This time, Washington was not waiting for permission. There was no actual proof that the Americans were carrying out reprisals, other than the cold bodies of Cristobál Jose Bello, Juan de Lara, and now Mercedes Sarra Bourihane. *Sometimes you do not need proof; you just know.*

Daniel Torreblanca had wanted to ride his black stallion with the silver saddle during the morning parade, but canceled. He could hear the lively music in the distance but doubted he would even go out and wander through the *casetas* tonight to laugh and dance with his wife, drink hard wine, eat delicious tapas, and watch the girls swirl about and dance in rhythm to wild gypsy flamenco guitars. He was scared. The Group of Six had become a kill list, and his name was on it. That had come as a total surprise to them all, and before they could react, the whole operation had been dealt a serious blow and three were dead.

It had seemed so brilliant and easy when they had first gathered at Cristobál's resort home in Mallorca. Yanis was the strategic brain who had gathered them and would plan an extraordinary financial coup. Mercedes was the pleasant face who would work directly with top banking officials throughout Europe and Asia. Torreblanca would choreograph participation from other Islamic banks, while Cristobál would do the same for the pro-Arab banks spread around the world, enlist avaricious and apolitical pension fund managers, and gather back-door contributions from some governments that detected an opportunity to weaken European solidarity. The obese but jolly Juan de Lara was to launder the needed paper trail to show the money was clean, and to handle the media with positive stories about the alternative rescue offer to whip up popular support. All would simultaneously work to loosen the grip of the European Community.

The sixth member stood ready to swoop in like a hawk to close the deals. The inclusion of Marwan Tirad Sobhi in Abu Dhabi had added prestige and international political clout to the venture, not to mention his ability to tap into the vast oil profits around the Persian Gulf. Sobhi's extended family linked him to the royal families in three countries and also to leaders in the tribal and religious movements. He held no official title because he did not need one. Prime ministers and presidents answered when he called.

Torreblanca came out of his reverie when there was a rap on his door and it was opened by a bodyguard. An older woman in party attire came in with a tray of tea and tapas, with slices of cheese and fruit, which she placed on his desk.

"You will not come out to the fair, Daniel? Not at all?" The face of his mother was etched with concern. Her son, so strong and handsome, had always put aside business for the April fair, and he looked so beautiful astride the big horse, like a smiling warrior prince.

"I am bound to this awful machine as if by steel cables, mother." He pushed the computer keyboard away to make room for the tea tray. Smiling, he said, "Look at you in your pretty red dress and with ribbons in your hair. You have to tell me all about it later."

"I am enjoying every minute of it. My four grandchildren are watching after me, and your wife is dancing in a beautiful gypsy costume. Your papa is trying to sample all of the wine. The only thing missing is you."

Torreblanca sipped some tea. "It pains me not to be there, mama, but look at this." He turned the computer screen so that she could see its clutter. "Urgent e-mails from China and Brazil, a Skype conversation with the always nasty Russians, new contracts for confidential agreements that are already two days past deadlines, and reports from Berlin and Cyprus that I must approve."

"All of it, that is just business." She sighed and waved it away with her hand. "You are neglecting your family. And why do we have all of these new bodyguards?"

He stood and stretched. At six foot three, he towered over the woman who had brought him into this world forty years ago. He wrapped her in an affectionate hug while at the same time escorting her from the office. "Those are just some improved security measures for the time being. I am involved with some very sensitive negotiations, and a thief would love to grab this hard drive in my computer and reveal my secrets to our competitors. Now you go out there and thump my kids on the head if they give you any trouble. Take some pictures for me."

The interruption by his mama had been a small welcome break in the strain that was trying to overwhelm him, and the spicy boiled-meat tapa helped clear his head. The absence of half of the Group of Six, and the ways by which they had died, made a lot of the other investors nervous, but Daniel could argue that nothing had really changed. The numbers told their own story, which was one of the many reasons that Torreblanca loved the steady, harsh figures.

Unemployment in Spain continued around 26 percent—meaning more than one out of every four Spaniards had no job—and in the under-twenty-five age range, half could not find work. The nation's debt still hovered at more than 90 percent of its gross national product, with a shrinking budget that was being drained partly by having to prop up the lame economies of its Euro-partners of Cyprus, Ireland, and Greece. Earlier rounds of borrowing from the European Central Bank came with demands for austerity that directed Madrid to slash social programs, health care, and education.

Those belt-tightening measures imposed by the EC were working in his favor. Trust in the government was eroding. An overhaul of labor laws sent rioters into the streets as unproductive Spanish workers tried to protect their minimum twenty-two days of vacation time, plus the fourteen government holidays, at the expense of the poor getting even poorer and more numerous. Tens of thousands of people had been fired, and the real estate crisis still raged. In his view, that was all to the good. As any veteran investor knew, the ideal time to take a gamble was when blood was in the streets.

The numbers on his spreadsheets proved that, without a doubt, the country was still caught in a downward spiral. Spain wanted to borrow more than 200 billion euros for the next year, the equivalent to 266 billion U.S. dollars. Torreblanca reasoned that this situation still presented ample opportunities for all of the participants in the global game of money that had been invented by the Group of Six. If everyone would just stand firm, the potential profits would be enormous.

No one would mention the Group's privately held long-range goal of a new government in Madrid that would use Muslim money and force Spain to introduce Sharia law in some instances of legal and social matters. It was only a first step and would take years to implement, but it was huge. International finance was just another battle front in the war against the nonbelievers. Mercedes would be greatly missed, but even she could be replaced. In Torreblanca's opinion, the six architects of the Spanish takeover were all expendable, just like the brave young desert martyrs fighting giant military tanks with nothing but stones and slingshots.

WASHINGTON, D.C.

"SO WHAT ARE WE GOING to do about this Torreblanca guy?" Kyle Swanson asked. The Trident team was gathered in the Pentagon offices. "He's gone to ground."

Sybelle Summers closed her eyes, lost in thought. "Couldn't be helped," she finally said. "It's important to remember that we got Mercedes Bourihane, the third of the six. With half of them off the board, the rest have to be feeling the heat."

Major General Middleton was not dismayed. The White House had not backed off of the new focus of antiterrorist attacks. "I haven't received any orders to curtail our work. So as far as I'm concerned, the Green Light package is still a go. We could always shift the spotlight and go after the others if this one is too hard to reach."

Swanson disagreed. "We've put in a ton of study and work on this guy already, and the information will go stale if we don't keep on it. Liz? You got anything new on him?"

Commander Freedman flicked his fingers over the screen of his electronic notebook, wiping out some images and calling up others. "Apparently, he hasn't even stuck his head out of doors during the opening events of the festival in Seville, a time when he normally is seen everywhere. It's a big deal. He is operating out of the house for right now, his schedule has been cleared, and more security teams have arrived."

"That was to be expected once he learned of the hit in Paris."

"One strange thing," said the Lizard. "Torreblanca did not hire the new guards himself. They came from a private security company based in Algeria, and the mercs showed up in Seville within hours of the news from Paris."

"Do we know who runs it?" Middleton squinted at him.

"Onworking that, sir. It's a false front. Somebody has to be signing those paychecks."

Swanson exhaled loudly. Mercenaries on the scene would make things tougher. "Coastie and I will go over to Seville right away and do some on-site recon. Torreblanca may be acting like a rabbit in a hole, but he's got to come up for air sometime."

Beth Ledford looked over. "So you think that three deaths aren't enough to send the signal that we're onto their game and get them to quit?"

"There were six dead Marines in Barcelona; I need at least six scalps just to even the score, and I don't believe in a tie."

"Is the big fair still going on?" Her eyes were steady on him.

"Yes. It lasts all week," the Lizard replied.

"Good. We can do the starving artist routine again, Kyle. I can spin it off of some visits to the Museum of Fine Arts there, and nobody questions a girl with big puppy eyes walking around a colorful carnival carrying a sketch pad. It will get us in close. Then Liz can download overheads and his other stuff when we're ready to move."

Kyle was already thinking about the needed hardware. If the other side increased its protective capability, he would also increase his methods to beat them. He had looked forward to doing in this banker with a knife, up close and personal, but now he was leaning the other way, and would put even more distance between himself and the target by delivering a precision, powerful shot over an extreme distance.

NEW YORK

NEARING THE END of another hectic day, activity had slowed down enough at the John F. Kennedy International Airport in New York to allow Air France flight 007 an early pushback from the gate, almost ten minutes ahead of its normal 8:05 P.M. takeoff time. The white, double-deck Airbus A380 taxied out of the parking ramp, moved into final position, and braked for a short time to receive clearance, then the pilot opened the throttles on the four giant engines and the plane thundered down the 10,000-foot-long Runway 13L. The big wings flexed, and it lifted out over water, starting the all-night haul back to Paris, the arrival time almost exactly twelve hours away.

There was some low-level turbulence as the commercial airliner climbed higher, and Yasim Rebiane unconsciously fingered his seat belt in the first-class cabin. Djahid was next to him, unbothered by the chop and watching the mass of lights that was Manhattan fade into the gathering darkness. They had made it safely out of the United States, and Yasim doubted if they would ever return. America had overreacted after 9/11 to the actual security threats it faced at the time, and billions of dollars had been spent since then to give law enforcement and federal intelligence agencies all of the tools they needed, and then even more. With the McNamara incident, it was clear that the U.S. authorities already had a photo of Yasim, and since the country was the most plugged-in and heavily armed society on earth, it was only a matter of time before he triggered some electronic database tripwire they did not even know existed.

FinCEN, the financial crimes enforcement network, was certain to be examining the records of the two murdered New York brokers. Perhaps the woman and girl in Missouri had talked to the police, despite the threats. One of the senator's office workers might have entered something on a computer that could have compromised security. He believed that eventually, the infamous PROMIS network would tie it all together. The Prosecutor's Management Information System was the world's best electronic detective, able to sift through millions of pieces of information ranging from credit card receipts to CIA database notes, and from specific cell phone tower usage to utility bills and fingerprints, eventually finding links and tying the lines of code together enough to provide names and locations. Worse, PROMIS never took a day off, not even a minute. There were no more secrets.

Once it recognized a specific identification, the game was usually over. The FBI's National Crime Information Center (NCIC) network and the National Law Enforcement Telecommunications Systems (NLETS) would kick into real-time response, and when a cop or an agent named a suspect, the system would spit out the entire life story. The identification could be confirmed with a response time of no more than twelve seconds. That was what America did with its own citizens every day, and Yasim mused that there was no telling what was at work trailing a couple of international terrorists like himself and his son.

He could not guess why his picture and name had not been added to the no-fly list, but felt confident that the pursuing agency was not sharing its information as it was supposed to do. If they had stretched their time in country, Yasim and Djahid Rebiane might never have been able to get out. Better to leave now with safe passports before any alerts were issued or facial recognition software made escape impossible.

Senator Monroe did not even know they were gone, and would not be told. He had a private telephone number to call when he got the needed information and also could contact Yasim through the false-front agriculture conglomerate in his state of Missouri. Prior to that, the big man could just sweat with the memory of what had happened to his whore and their bastard love child. Yasim planned to check in with the powerful member of Congress in two days if he had not heard anything more. The threat had worked; at least Rebiane had a scent of the enemy now, where before there was nothing.

Djahid pulled down the plastic shade over the small window, kicked back the seat, doused the overhead light, and closed his eyes, already drifting into sleep. Yasim cast a glance at his son, knowing that the young man had been disappointed at not being given permission to harm and kill either the woman or the girl who had been his prisoners in Missouri. Djahid was a creature of the hunt and yearned for blood to mark his victories, particularly when he worked in the United States. He was obedient only to his father; Yasim could control him, but Djahid was always tugging at the reins. It was just the way he was, the way he had been carefully constructed since boyhood.

The leash would be very briefly removed in France, just a single feeding that might be a prelude to others, depending on what had happened with this one man who had broken secrecy. Djahid would find out and take care of it. Then the two Rebianes would drive out of France all the way down to Seville for an emergency gathering of the remaining members of the Group. Djahid would be in charge of overall security for the unusual gathering, which would keep his mind occupied after Paris. Hired mercenaries were notoriously unreliable, even to the people who paid them, but the Rebianes had long ago established their own Warsaw-based private security company with a roster of rough men who were more interested in women and drink than in ideology. They were a pack of wolves, and only the fear of a bigger wolf kept them in line. Yasim saw that big wolf sleeping soundly in the airline seat beside him. He opened a new book he had purchased before boarding.

THE PENTAGON

Air Force Brigadier General Alfred Coleman had listened carefully to the follow-up telephone call from Captain Howell Andrews, the lawyer he had left to deal with the senator's brusque point man. Coleman was still in a bad mood at being snubbed, left waiting at the curb by the senator, and was in no mood to do any favors. Captain Andrews advised Coleman that it had all the earmarks of a fishing expedition and the senator was trying to put some hard meat on a couple of scraps of information he had picked up. The general complimented the captain on the good job and said he should take the rest of the day off and file a formal report the next day that could be sent up the chain of command. No, don't bother to investigate on your own, Andrews was told. They just needed to prove to the senator, if ever asked, that they were doing something about the guy's repeated request. Take your time, General Coleman said, as long as I have your report by the end of the day tomorrow.

The captain put it out of his mind as he started thinking instead about getting a half day and a whole night free. He called his wife with the good news and told her to find a babysitter so they could go to the steakhouse for dinner and then to a movie, preferably a comedy. On a captain's salary, they could not afford an evening at the Kennedy Center, but they managed to have a great night together all the same. He got up the next morning, went for a three-mile run along the Tidal Basin, showered, dressed, and was at his cubicle in the JAG offices by nine o'clock. He typed up his notes, plus his impressions, listened to the audio recording he had made and wrote some quotes, and then shaped it all into a terse two-page document that included the names of Task Force Trident and Gunnery Sergeant Kyle Swanson of the Marines. He figured that was one page too many. There was nothing there but some implied threats of a congressional hearing.

The captain logged on to a secure server and transmitted his brief report to General Coleman, then left for a quick lunch before moving on to his next case. It was a review of the charges against an AWOL eighteen-year-old airman who ran away from Lackland Air Force Base in San Antonio, Texas, during his second week of basic training. He was homesick for his mother in Minnesota, who loved him, while the snarling sergeants at

Lackland plainly did not. An Air Police investigator arrested him at home within a week of his getting on a bus in San Antonio.

Andrews wanted to knock the charges down enough for the kid to just face an Article 15 hearing, not much more than a verbal spanking, although there would be a lot of shouting about deserting his post in time of war. They could not take away his rank and privileges, because he did not have any. Andrews believed the youngster should just stay behind bars for a few more weeks, then rotate back into a new training squadron to try again, starting in July. Drilling on the concrete formation pads in the wilting heat of a Texas summer was a sweaty business. If the airman acted up again, he would incur some more brig time and be kicked out of the service for being more trouble than he was worth. Not everybody was cut out to be a hero. The captain preferred simple cases with a guaranteed win to delving into some international conspiracy that could sink a career before it even got under way.

The captain's digital report to the general was routed routinely through a Pentagon computer database that was for routine use and not encoded as classified or secret. As soon as the document entered the system, a powerful software program that was a secret military version on the level of PROMIS plucked it from the electronic stack and promptly delivered it to one of the computer monitors on the desk of Navy Commander Benton Freedman in Trident.

No one could possibly keep up with all of the material being swept up every hour by various intelligence services, so the Lizard had implanted key words that would automatically break them out of the nets of the CIA, the FBI, Homeland Security, the National Security Agency, and a few of the other major players, including links overseas. It seemed these days that everybody was being tracked. PROMIS was primarily for use against crooks, while the bigger computer guns were saved for terrorists and military contingencies. Among his trigger words were "Task Force Trident" and the names of everyone on the Trident roster. His goal was to never see any of those terms pop up, and now they were both flashing in highlighted red boxes in one corner, along with an audible alert, a pleasant female voice that repeated, "Commander, please look at this. Urgent. Commander, please look at this. Urgent."

Freeman muttered a rare obscenity—"Heck!"—beneath his breath, chewed on the tooth-cracked cover of a plastic ballpoint pen, and started digging into the databases. He transferred a copy over to another computer and was rewarded with a loud *"Oh shit"* howl from the office of Major General Bradley Middleton. In another moment, the Trident leader was standing behind Freedman.

"OK, Liz. What's going on?"

The general was aware that the big bulk of Master Gunny Dawson had moved in beside him. "Just in case you need a translator with the commander's dialogue, sir," Dawson said.

This time, no translator was needed. Freedman removed the pen from his mouth. "Somebody's cracked us," he said.

SEVILLE, SPAIN

IT LOOKS like a convention of steroid monsters and meth tweakers over there." Kyle Swanson made a quick examination of the Torreblanca home while Beth Ledford drove their little tourist-type rental car through the area. The whitewashed house with the traditional roof of red tiles had been there for several generations, and the landscaping was mature. Thick pomegranate trees provided shade, red carnations were clustered in pots along the balconies, and a garden of shy bluebells outlined the driveway. A shiny black Suburban that had not been there before was now hulking in the driveway, all four doors open and four men standing beside it, hands out from their sides. Another ring of men surrounded them. None were in uniform, but that very difference made them seem alike.

They came in all physical sizes. Most wore black, in varying styles from motorcycle jackets to sports coats. Some were scraped shiny bald while others needed serious trims; some beards, but not all. Tattoos were visible on exposed skin. Wraparound shades, some pushed atop their heads. Some had a military bearing; some appeared indolent and lazy. They seemed to have a problem communicating with each other, indicating that different languages were in play. To Swanson, it all spelled hired guns from out of town.

Coastie turned the corner and headed away from the hacienda at a moderate speed. It was safe to assume their car had been noted, and spotters who were now focused on them would stay locked in until they were gone and presented no threat. Kyle wore a loud Hawaiian shirt, and Beth had a straw hat, so obvious that it was effective, as they hid in plain sight as sightseers. "Were you able to get a count?"

"No. There's a bunch of them on-site and probably more on the way." It puzzled him. "Way too many to just be protecting Mr. Torreblanca."

She steered around another corner to move deeper into the city. "It's going to be tough finding a clear shot with those guys all over the place and so much foliage."

Swanson agreed. "Maybe. The guards don't look like they have worked together before as a unit. If they are having language problems, they may not even know each other. Might provide an opening. We just have to be ready. Park over there."

She pulled the little car into a parallel-parking space in front of a grocery store. Before they got out, she flipped off the hat and picked up a big cloth bag while Kyle dumped the loud Hawaiian shirt that covered a dark T-shirt and pulled on a Boston Red Sox baseball cap. Time for some foot surveillance, food, and music. The sky was as blue as it could be, and children in colorful clothes were out in the streets, ready for another day of the fair.

"You're thinking about something?" she asked as they headed toward the carnival tents.

"Yeah. We need to get a better look at those guards. There's something there that we can use, but I can't put my finger on it."

They did a slow tour of the food tents, bought some hot tapas, split up, reversed their routes, did some unexpected stops and starts, and checked shop windows for reflections as they ran countersurveillance. No one was following, and the crowd was growing thicker for the day's festivities. Riders in brilliant costumes cantered by, including boys prancing along on big horses with girlfriends in rainbows of dresses seated behind the saddles, all moving toward the start of the parade route. Even the most alert guards would be distracted by all of this activity, which was to continue for another few days, Kyle surmised. For a precision shot, though, Kyle and Coastie needed a hide, and so far they had not seen anything that would do.

He had not totally given up on the idea of using the Marines, which would be a good Plan B if the guard teams proved too numerous and any good at all. The Trident team could fly into the Navy base at Rota in the middle of the night, and the aircraft would drive right into a secure hangar. Spanish customs would not see them until the men rolled off the base dressed as civilians. The weapons and gear would follow in other trucks. The footprint would be bigger, but it would be a quiet operation until they attacked the compound in Seville. That had a sense of retribution about it that Kyle liked, because it would be similar to the strike in Barcelona that had started the whole thing. The problem was that such a Plan B would take too long, since the guys were still in North Carolina, and that meant they might have to use Plan C. Only they had no Plan C.

WASHINGTON, D.C.

Senator Monroe believed he had broken through the secrecy wall. Such was the power of a member of the Armed Services Committee. It was almost pitiful to watch generals grovel, anxious for his support when budgets were determined.

That little hard-line talk that his aide, Doug Jimenez, had with the Air Force lawyer had paid dividends. The lawyer's report obviously had reached the attention of higher officers, who decided to show some cooperation instead of stonewalling. As a result, on this bright Friday morning, the senator and his aide were aboard a Whiteside executive helicopter from HMX-1, the same unit that flew *Marine One* for the president. Their pilot was a full colonel and the copilot a female major, both of whom normally served as presidential pilots. They had greeted him with salutes before turning them over to the flight crew that got them settled. The seats were soft. Jimenez had raised an eyebrow of approval once they strapped into the comfortable cushions and the blades began to turn, almost unheard in the soundproofed interior.

The trip would not take long because the helo went over all of the traffic and flew a direct line that would put the two civilians down right where the darkest secrets were kept, in the special militarized part of Virginia Beach that was the home of SEAL Team Six. Instead of being back in Missouri doing some fund-raising, the senator would be in the dust today, wearing blue jeans and a field vest with a lot of pockets instead of a suit and tie, and he would come back with pictures of himself and a lot of grinning SEALs. Great campaign stuff.

The bird settled onto the tarmac of the U.S. Naval Special Warfare Development Group with only a slight bounce as the wheels took the weight. The crew chief told them they could unbuckle, and the copilot stuck her head back into the cabin to say she hoped their trip had been comfortable. The senator thanked her and walked down the stairs, followed by his aide. A very fit naval officer with a lantern jaw presented them with Navy blue baseball caps bearing gold braid and the distinctive SEAL insignia, and their VIP tour began in a camouflaged open-back Humvee.

For the next four hours, including time for lunch with some of the dusty warriors, Senator Monroe and Douglas Jimenez were treated to the best reality show in the military world. Paratroopers poured out of high-flying planes, drifted to earth on silk canopies, and landed standing upright and ready to fight. Other soldiers pitched out of helicopters and slid down long ropes, while still other helos ferried in assault troops with waves of touch-and-go landings. Gunships ripped through the target area with rockets blazing and chain guns roaring, tearing up the dirt. They watched an assault on a mock village, and the takedown of a shooting range target to rescue "hostages" in a close quarters battle drill using real bullets and real people tied to chairs. Everywhere they were taken, there was the snap of gunfire and the thump of explosions, and the escort officer gave a smooth running commentary on what was happening. The obstacle course had the look of a psycho-designed maze of high fences, barbed wire, and mud, but the armed-up troopers charged through it without serious effort, because they faced the same challenges almost every day of their lives.

The visitors were most impressed, but the senator had not lost sight of why they were here, and the escort officer eventually took them away from the live training area to a grassy knoll where several men in uniforms were waiting in a loose circle. One saluted the officer, who returned it, then left them alone.

"Welcome to DEVGRU, Senator. My name is Senior Chief Richard Sheridan of SEAL Team Six. They call me Rockhead," said a compact, muscular man with a layer of gray hair in a buzz cut over a sun-weathered face. He had an automatic AK-47 over his shoulder. They shook hands, and Sheridan motioned to the others, all of whom stood at parade rest, with their hands behind their backs. "Today you were able to witness a solid exercise by units of the U.S. Joint Special Operations Command, and these gentlemen here are senior noncommissioned officers with some of the units involved."

"You put this on just for us?" Doug Jimenez asked. The senator didn't want just a dog-and-pony show.

"No, sir. Not at all. It takes months to schedule these things, so the timing was, shall we say, just convenient."

"How's that?"

Sheridan ignored the question and looked around. "You saw SEALs out there for sure, because this is our surf and turf, but you also had Delta Force, Rangers, Marine Special Operations, Air Commandos, and the Night Stalkers of the 160th Special Operations Aviation Regiment. Even some Brits from the Special Air Service. Cream of the crop, Senator. Best of the best in a live-fire environment. We hope you enjoyed it."

"We have no doubt of their abilities, Senior Chief. You can be proud of them all." The senator looked around and realized there were no officers present.

"Good. Good. Please, call me Rockhead. Now, sir, which of them do you want to kill today?" Rockhead Sheridan unslung the AK-47 and in a smooth motion racked in a round from the banana clip. "Careful with it, sir. It's loaded. There's the safety. Click it off and fire when ready."

"What?"

"We cannot furnish a complete roster, Senator, but maybe you could just point to a couple at random, maybe a helo load, we can line 'em up and you can shoot 'em."

The hard men around them, sweaty in their battle dress uniforms, had not moved but were staring with laser eyes. "You are overstepping your authority, Senior Chief, not to mention being rude. Where are the commanding officers? They are the ones I want to talk to."

"No. Today, you talk to the warfighters, sir. That's us. While you politicians and lawyers make your speeches, we are the people out on the battlefield."

"You set me up!" Anger flared in the senator's voice, and his face was flushed.

"Not at all. We have permission to show you everything we've got, which we did over the last few hours. Then our commanders told us to answer all of your questions as soon as you furnish us with the appropriate documents, subpoenas, letters of authorization, and clearances. Ball's in your court, sir. Hand them over."

Douglas Jimenez interrupted. "We didn't bring any such documentation with us. You know that."

Rockhead scratched an ear. "Well, then, I'd like to say you are among friends, but you really aren't. We can't stand pretentious assholes like you, Doug. You might pressure some young JAG lawyer, but try that shit out here and I will personally kick your ass into last week. You got me? Just stand there and be quiet so the senator can talk."

"I want to see your commander."

"He's not here. Apparently what you do not have is permission from the Armed Services Committee chairman to be poking around in forbidden territory. You remember Operation Neptune Spear?"

"Of course. That was the mission that killed Osama bin Laden."

"Did you know about it before it happened?"

The senator paused. "No. I did not."

"That is because it was *secret*!" Rockhead shouted at the senator, then paused a moment to collect himself. "All this you saw out there today, that's also secret. All of it. Their names are secret, as are their pictures. All of us here work in the utmost secrecy, and now you're trying to get some of us killed. You make up your mind on which ones yet?"

Monroe's fury was growing. "Don't be silly, Senior Chief. I'm not going to kill anybody. How dare you even say such a thing?"

"But you and your boy are shooting off your mouths about secret stuff. We are part of a brotherhood, although we wear different uniforms. You are becoming a threat to our fellow warriors, operators whom we will protect with our own blood if need be."

"You mean Task Force Trident?" It was clear to the senator now that this was a clumsy attempt to muzzle him.

"Task Force Trident doesn't even exist, Senator. It was formed for a one-time mission some years back and then disbanded. Happens all the time in our community, depending on the job." Rockhead never blinked while he lied. "In fact, the Armed Services Committee was notified at the time."

"We were not!"

"It might have been in the small print. Your people might have missed it."

"My information is that Trident still exists today and is conducting an unauthorized military intervention in allied countries." Monroe refused to hold the AK-47, and when Rockhead declined to take it back, he handed it to a shocked Doug Jimenez. A soldier laughed and retrieved the weapon, putting it back on safe. It had never been loaded.

"You've been talking to Ryan Powell, the numb-nuts TV star who was kicked out of the SEALs. Powell will say anything to anybody who will listen, and he has been bragging that he now has a senator in his pocket, owing him favors. I guess that would be you. The man can't keep his mouth shut and blames others for his being booted out of Six when he could no longer measure up."

The senator turned to stare at Jimenez, who seemed stricken. Maybe he could do some horse trading. "I must pursue any report of a rogue military unit that endangers American foreign policy."

"By doing so, you might put at risk special operators on a secret mission that has official governmental approval, which, I might remind you, is more than what you have today. What you are doing is trying to get some of our people killed by exposing them, and we will not cooperate in that, sir, not even a little bit."

"I can subpoena you all."

"If you try, we will smear you all over the press for jeopardizing American troops and putting ongoing secret operations in jeopardy."

The senator and Rockhead stared at each other. "Then at least let me talk to Kyle Swanson."

Rockhead and several of the men around him laughed. "Senator, like Trident, Gunny Swanson doesn't exist either. I even went to his funeral in Arlington some years back."

"Are you bullshitting me, Senior Chief? Is he really dead?"

"Far as I know, sir. Died a hero, too. Got the Medal of Honor."

"Let me talk to him."

"Visit his gravesite at Arlington and talk all you want." Again, chuckles from the other men.

The Navy captain who had been the escort reappeared and told the senator that his helicopter was waiting to return him to Washington.

"I want to see the base commander," Monroe said.

"Sorry, sir, the admiral is gone for the weekend. I will tell him you wish to speak with him first thing upon his return, sometime next week."

"Goddammit," swore the senator. Everyone in the group threw him a perfect salute, without any expression on their faces.

PARIS, FRANCE

HENRI LECROIX stepped in a puddle, lost his balance, bumped off a wall and collapsed on the sidewalk with a splash and an abrupt curse that changed immediately to a laugh. *I am drunk*, he thought happily as he rolled to a knee. He pushed himself upright. The night was cool and rainy, and since he had nothing else to do, he might as well drink. The last bar had thrown him out, but there was always another one ready to accept his money. He did not even mind the light rain, for it refreshed him enough to push on, and he felt like singing, so he did. People avoided the wobbly bearded man with long black hair that was plastered to his wet, dark skin.

Lecroix had been inebriated for almost a week. The binge started when he went on the prowl with two of his friends, who had matched him glass for glass as they talked about the old times as engineers in the Armée de Terre, which taught them all the hazardous trade of being a demolition specialist. After having wasting his early years on the family's dismal farm, Henri had found something he truly enjoyed, was good at, and was paid well to do. Dynamite, TNT, plastique, C-4, Semtex, fuses, and timers were wonderful things. Anybody could blow things up. To do it just right was an art for a special few. He would have continued being a soldier, but his expansive loves of whisky, dope, and women far outshone his love of explosives. The other two men also had been on the demolition squads, and they were able to talk shop and argue in boring detail.

One of his buddies had gone into construction after the army, using his blasting skills to clear old buildings and reshape stubborn rock formations. The other was in a private business that defused old military ordnance from two world wars that still surfaced around France.

"What keeps you busy?" One peered at Lecroix with wet and unsteady eyes. "If you are still able to blow shit up, I can get you a job."

"Got a job," Lecroix declared. "Good work. Pay is outstanding, which is why I'm buying the drinks for you bastards."

The friend laughed. "Doing what? Besides drinking."

They had another round, and Lecroix added it to his credit card. Then he held a finger to his lips to shush them and looked carefully around the bar. They were in a corner, and he lowered his voice. "I'm no terrorist, you know that; could not care less about any religion or politics. But did you hear about what happened in Barcelona?"

There was no reply. The two men looked at him, then at each other, suddenly sobering.

"*Boom!*" said Henri, opening the fingers of his left hand like a flower. "My beautifully timed explosions on the corners pancaked that place right down. *Booosh!* Not many people could do that. They needed an expert, somebody like us." He tapped his thumb on his chest.

One of the astonished friends shoved his chair back, got up, and left the table and the bar, never saying another word or even looking back. Henri smirked and shouted, *"Alors fillette!" You pussy!*

The other called for still another round, eased closer, and said, "Tell me more." Henri had launched his drunk that night. Somehow he awoke the next day in his own bed, groaning in pain from a terrible hangover. With his eyes still closed, he felt for the bottle at his bedside, fished a couple of aspirin tablets out of a packet, and, after rushing to the toilet to vomit, was soon ready to begin the cycle anew.

Such gossip about terrorist activities, even if it was a wild lie, spread quickly in the underworld. Henri's pal told another friend, who spilled it to a traffic cop two days later while trying to talk his way out of a parking violation. The unconfirmed report then worked its way up the investigative chain, and when it jumped into the intelligence realm, alarm bells began to ring. It was the first real break investigators had gotten about the Barcelona attack. Things had moved much faster when an informant passed it along to Yanis Rebiane.

This was a race Rebiane would win.

Henri Lecroix gulped in the fresh wet air. He still had plenty of money. He could get more. He tested to be sure he was steady on his feet before moving toward the lights in the next block that promised more whisky. He was suddenly hungry, too, and wanted some cheese and fresh-baked bread. As he thought of his immediate future, he took no notice of the shape coming directly toward him, someone who did not move to the other side of the street to avoid the drunk. The man's face was down as he struggled to open an umbrella. They were on a collision course.

Djahid Rebiane looked up at the last moment and said, "I warned you about this, Henri." Before Lecroix's befuddled brain could register the danger, Djahid lifted a Heckler & Koch semiautomatic pistol from the folds of the black umbrella, stuck the barrel to the tip of Lecroix's nose, and pulled the trigger until the magazine was empty.

WASHINGTON, D.C.

"I WAS NOT pleased with all of that, Doug. An ugly piece of stonewalling, that's what it was." Senator Monroe shouldered back in the familiar chair at his office, still fuming after their visit to the SEAL base. "They can't treat a United States senator like that."

"But they did, sir. You gave them a chance to come clean about this matter, and they flatly refused." He had been thinking about the next step during the entire helicopter flight back to Washington. They had treated Doug worse than the senator, as if he were unmanly and no more than a speck of dirt. "They have no more chances. Now it's our turn."

"I can't tell our, uh, client that we failed. We have no proof of Trident and Swanson being real, much less being the ones doing the killings in

Europe." The solemn face of Yasim Rebiane rose in his memory. "He is going to call me tomorrow."

Jimenez laughed out loud. "Sir, it's the old thing about how if something walks like a duck and quacks like a duck, chances are it's a duck. It's Trident; no doubt in my mind. Otherwise, why this big show-and-tell by the Pentagon to convince us that it is not? People jumping out of airplanes and shooting guns were interesting to watch, but no answer to our questions. They could have just totally ignored us. All they did was try to bluff us out of the game by saying our inquiry will cost American lives. I call it bullshit."

This was when Monroe liked his young aide best, and why he had hired him in the first place. The younger man was equal parts politically smart and devious, and when things got dicey, Jimenez retreated to the gang culture of his early days in Los Angeles, before his father was killed in a drive-by shooting. He never let an insult stand, nor allowed a challenge to go unanswered. His mother had moved them all the way across the country to Florida to escape the dangers of the street and worked hard to give her son a chance in life. The resulting law school diploma from the University of Florida had not erased the violent memories.

"What do you have in mind?"

Jimenez held up his cell phone. "We're back playing on our home field now, where we have the power to make things happen. Let me make some calls and do some research. I think we may have this dustup in the bag in a couple of hours. Fuck those grunts."

The first problem was the location from which a small Marine unit would stage to reach Spain. Ex-SEAL Ryan Powell had said Swanson was a Marine sniper and had been spotted at Camp Lejeune within the past forty-eight hours. That was the starting point. A private Pentagon source soon explained to Jimenez that a strictly military flight to Europe from Lejeune would most likely launch from Pope Field in Fayetteville, North Carolina. Pope was part of the giant Fort Bragg Army base a little more than 160 miles from Lejeune, and the home of a U.S. Air Force airlift group which specialized in such missions across the pond and could easily take personnel and equipment right past the customs inspectors.

Next, the Air Force helpfully furnished the powerful senator's aide a roster of everyone who worked in air traffic control at Pope, a list of several hundred names. Spain, Task Force Trident, and Kyle Swanson were never mentioned.

Now Doug wanted a vulnerable individual on that roster, and the other government agencies soon cleared most of them as being ridiculously clean of legal or financial trouble. The State Department furnished three names on the list for emergency visas. Jimenez thought Master Sergeant Leftwich, Gary J., was the best shot.

Back to State and the Pentagon. He learned that Leftwich had married a local girl while based at Incerlik Air Base in Turkey. They had transferred back to the States six years ago and had two children. Leftwich and his wife were trying to get a special compassion visa to bring over the wife's elderly mother, who was seriously ill and had no family left to take care of her in Turkey. So far, the request had gotten nowhere because there were so many similar requests and passport demands were so tight.

Jimenez took a break, grabbed a quick meal, and updated the senator that things were looking good. After that, he called Master Sergeant Leftwich at home, identified himself, and had Leftwich call back through the Senate switchboard to confirm his identity. A favor was proposed. "My senator can cut through the paperwork and get that visa for you within a week," Jimenez said. "All we ask in return is that you tell us whether a transport plane from Pope was routed to Spain in the last few days or within the next two. No secret information is involved." Leftwich grabbed the deal and was able to provide the information within thirty minutes: Yes, only one special flight was so designated in that time frame, and the master sergeant provided the tail number.

"Who authorized it?"

The click of computer keys was loud as Jimenez awaited the answer. "It was a JSOC flight, sir. Looks like a squad of Marines from Camp Lejeune. That's all I can tell you without getting into confidential special ops territory."

"My senator and I just spent all day with those guys down at SEAL Team

Six, and I'm following up a matter they asked us to straighten out. It's likely a bureaucratic snafu, but they believe that it might needlessly cost American lives if it remains unsolved. This is a favor for Senior Chief Rockhead Sheridan of Six. I understand your caution, so let me ask just one more question. Was one of the passengers a Gunnery Sergeant Kyle Swanson?"

There was a pause. "Sorry, sir, but that is classified."

Jimenez met that with a pause of his own, then bombed Leftwich. "Very good, Master Sergeant. Thank you for your assistance. Let's hope that U.S. troops don't die because I can't solve a problem for a SEAL master chief. Please send the name of your mother-in-law to me, and I will see what we can do to help her get a passport."

"You told me you could get her into the country!"

"We can. As soon as my question is answered. Also, if you won't give it to me now, Master Sergeant Leftwich, we will subpoena your testimony when this thing blows up, and that will be the end of your career. Now choose: a quiet favor that gets sick old mama-in-law into the U.S. for treatment, or a summons from Congress?"

The keys started clicking again. "Yes, sir. Swanson was listed as team leader."

"Good. Send me her name and all the vitals. She'll be here in two weeks. And thank you for your service."

Senator Monroe was still in his office when Jimenez barged in at eight o'clock with a broad smile. "Got the sonofabitch," he said, giving a concise summary of what had happened.

"Hell of a piece of good work, Doug."

"Hoo-ah," Jimenez replied with a mocking laugh.

SEVILLE, SPAIN

Daniel Ferran Torreblanca felt as if he were locked in a beautiful prison, under house arrest by brusque and impolite guards who ignored his protests. He had no control over them, no matter what he said, and they refused to let him go outside. They answered to Yanis Rebiane, the person atop this so-called security. It wasn't supposed to be this way.

Torreblanca was in charge of the Spanish branch of the Islamic Progress Bank in Saudi Arabia, and a rich and powerful man who enjoyed his freedom, wealth, and luxury. He moved about in limousines and private jets, wore tailored suits, and enjoyed manicures and massages at health spas, playing tennis and golf, and taking joy in his family. His control of massive amounts of money had been a propelling force behind the scheme to destabilize the Spanish government. Islam had been good to him and his family for generations as they melded into the polyglot society. Today, instead of being lionized, he was being treated with no respect by large men who had locked down his home. Other family members could come and go as they pleased, but not him. He was effectively chained by links stronger than steel, at least until Yasim arrived.

He did not even know how many guards there were, but guessed that about twenty professional gunmen were roaming the estate in four groups of five men each, rotating shifts all day and all night. They represented a hodgepodge of countries and apparently did not like each other, probably the result of old nationalist hatreds and professional jealousy. When the mercenaries conversed, he had overheard Polish, German, and Ukranian words and even a smattering of Chilean-flavored Spanish. English, the international language, was a struggle for all of them. Mostly, there were a lot of incomprehensible sounds and sporadic cursing in little arguments. The only things they had in common were that they all wore black, carried weapons, and moved like lumpy shadows with blank eyes in the fading light.

Unable to give them orders, Daniel had wrestled for hours with the question of whether all of this security was even necessary. Torreblanca considered himself to be a law-abiding and generous citizen and a moderate where religion was concerned. He was a Muslim, and his wife had switched to his religion, although her parents remained staunch Roman Catholics. He had stayed distant from the awful depravities of the radicals, and acted as a valuable financial funnel between both worlds. Politics was not his forte, but with the economy of his homeland of Spain collapsing ever more by the week, the banker had agreed to the rescue plan and an escape from the merciless European controls. The revolution was to be carried out in boardrooms and on trading floors, and he wanted to prove to the uneasy citizens that a long-term shift toward Islamic rule did not have to be some bloody coup or an impossible moral burden. Then came Barcelona. Everything changed overnight.

The only member of the Group of Six who even knew the specifics of the terrorist strike in advance had been Yasim. The others had agreed to a controlled action, perhaps a protest riot before the U.S. Embassy and consulates, some flag burning, but Yasim had given the job to his unhinged son, Djahid, who habitually left catastrophe in his wake. The Rebianes had totally misread the situation. Instead of being intimidated, the United States reacted vigorously in the financial realm, throwing up more obstacles to the needed loans, and now blood had begotten blood. He did not need an official notification that the CIA, probably working with the help of Western European nations, was striking back hard.

Three of the Six were gone as if snatched away by some phantom force. The others were in danger. So, yes, Torreblanca knew, the security squads patrolling his grounds and the quiet, beautiful city were needed. The question was whether they were up to the task. He didn't think they were.

WASHINGTON, D.C.

MASTER GUNNY O. O. Dawkins was still in his battle dress camo when he returned to the Pentagon from Virginia and reported to Major General Middleton. He had been among the nameless senior NCOs who had met with Senator Jordan Monroe and his aide after the spec ops demonstration. "He didn't have any authorization of any kind, sir. Other than being a United States senator, he had nothing."

"Being a senator usually is good enough," observed Commander Benton Freedman.

Dawkins gave a lopsided grin. "Rockhead Sheridan chewed him out pretty good, gave him every chance to explain why he was nosing around. The senator and his little-dick assistant should have come prepared to slap some legal action on us from the Armed Services Committee, or the courts, or somebody. It was their golden opportunity. Instead, he just huffed and puffed and we sent him away. Should have seen their faces when Rockhead handed them an AK-47 and told them to shoot some soldiers. Empty, but they didn't know that."

Sybelle Summers, the Trident ops officer, looked over at the hard-faced master gunnery sergeant. "However, he specifically asked about Trident and Kyle."

"Yes, ma'am. That he did."

"Why us?" asked the Lizard, Commander Freedman. "Hundreds of special operators are on the move every day. Why is he digging so hard to get us out of the closet? And how can he be linking us to what's going on with the Group of Six?"

Dawkins spread his hands in an I-don't-know motion.

"Why do politicians do anything?" Middleton asked. "He didn't just dream this thing up out of blue sky. It sounds to me like someone called in a big favor and he is poking around for answers. As an Armed Services member, he knows better than most that special ops work is secret, and that blowing a secret op is a big deal, something that he would not chance unless he had a very good reason to do so. It could backfire on him politically."

The Lizard acted nervous. "Jimenez, that assistant, has been busy. After finding the name and photo of Kyle, he managed to get some low-level Department of Homeland Security hacker with administrator clearance to track Swanson's recent movements. Back when we pulled Kyle out of Germany to go to Spain, he left some electronic footprints in Barcelona when he visited the widow of one of the Marines who was killed. Added to what Ryan Powell gave up, the assumption could be made that he, and we, are involved in the Spanish surgical strikes."

The general sighed. "Thank you, Dr. Spock, for your *Star Wars* logic. It still leaves unanswered the question of why."

"That would be Mr. Spock, sir, the first officer and science officer of the starship *Enterprise.* Dr. Spock was a famous pediatrician. And it's *Star Trek,* not *Star Wars.* You do that on purpose just to see what I will say, don't you, sir?"

"Be quiet. Any suggestions for a next step? I don't want the White House involved." The general looked at the team. "Come on, people. Think."

"A private talk with the senator might help," suggested Summers.

"To scare him? We don't want to be accused of threatening a member of Congress."

"Just the opposite, sir. Let's throw him a bone. See what he wants in an informal session."

"You're not going over to his office, are you?"

"I'm thinking more about his living room, say about oh-dark-thirty." She flashed a wicked smile.

SEVILLE, SPAIN

SWANSON stood before a mirror, hardly looking like his normal self. He wore stiff black leather shoes, black trousers and belt, and a black shirt buttoned to the neck, with no tie. A gold chain dangled loose around his neck. The new black leather sports jacket was still rigid around the shoulders, but a good fit overall. He had not shaved for several days, so there was stubble on his face, and his skin had been darkened with a spray tan.

Attacking someone who never set foot outside of his home was a difficult job, and Trident had supplied a set of CIA operatives for backup. Two field spooks arrived with a minivan filled with toys they would need, and they had pitched in with the high-tech surveillance. There was no longer any need to hold big binoculars for hours on end, because tiny microcameras that never got tired had replaced them, and listening devices could penetrate windows and walls. Even a small drone looked down with infrared eyes on the hacienda grounds from ten thousand feet and fed the images to monitors in the van. A computer program mapped the routes and timing of the guard details.

A third agent worked most days as a commercial makeup artist in Hollywood. In the movie industry, he went by the trendy one-word name Montaigne, but when the CIA needed his talents, he fell back into being plain old Mark Dixon, a former Army Ranger sergeant who could kick butt as well as cut hair.

Dixon had studied the photos of the guards and conducted some personal surveillance before he took Kyle and Coastie out shopping to buy what he called costumes for this one-act play. Back at the hotel, he set to work by trimming Kyle's hair in a choppy way, then dyed it black and brushed it into some spiky peaks cemented in place with sticky goo. Some pieces of rubber and coloring gave Kyle deeper wrinkles around the mouth. The masquerade master had considered contact lenses to continue the dark color scheme, but Kyle refused. He would not chance anything happening to his vision, or the risk of wearing them if there was a fight. When Dixon was done, Kyle turned and looked at the mirror over his shoulder to see the back view.

"You look just like Zombie One," Beth Ledford said, her arms crossed in satisfaction after her own afternoon of preparation. She didn't look much like herself, either.

"I don't know how the Zombies work in these clothes." Swanson's tight jacket had a bulge where the pistol rode in a holster on the right side. Everything about him was meant to be obvious and make him seem like just another flashy Eurocrook.

"It's the intimidation factor," explained Dixon. "All dressed in black, with a big gun and looking mean. Normal people will get out of the way."

"Yeah. But the chain rattles and gets in the way."

"The Zombies like their bling," said Coastie. The hours of surveillance had given names to each of them. The Zombies were mercenaries from the Ukraine who had the overnight shift, with three around the house and two on foot patrol in the surrounding area. Kyle and Coastie and Dixon were betting that Swanson looked enough like a mercenary for a bluff to work.

Coastie was transformed with a long, curly wig, satin black, that fell to her shoulders, and a gypsy dress of green and white. The makeup artist darkened her eyebrows to match the hair and carefully applied mascara and lipstick. She wore low-heeled dancing shoes.

She was delighted with the new personality and preened before the mirror. "Ain't we are a pair, buddy? Beauty and the Beast. I think this is just crazy enough to work. Say something in Ukranian."

"*Mene zavut Karl Vidal.* My name is Karl Vidal."

"That's not going to get you very far." She twirled and the skirts flared.

"All I have to do is get past the first sentence, then switch to grumbles and English."

"Remember, guys, this all holds up for only a few seconds once you are under way. Keep any contact with others to an absolute minimum. I can fool a camera forever, but not a curious human eye." Dixon wiped his hands on a small tower. "You look great. Maestro Montaigne has accomplished another masterpiece."

There was a double knock on the door, and Coastie waited until Swanson and Dixon were both ready with pistols. "Who is it?"

"Calypso," came the challenge code word. The other spooks had arrived.

"Broadway." She gave the answer and unlocked the door.

"Wow. You look great," said the agent they knew as Bob Smith, a genial six-footer with graying hair. "Let's leave your trashy partner and go to the fiesta."

"Sounds like a plan." Coastie stood aside and let him look at Swanson.

"That will do, Gunny. That will do. All you need is garlic and onions on your breath. Good job, Montaigne."

Swanson put away his pistol and took one last look in the mirror. He did not like what he saw, but that was the point. "Anything new on the surveillance?"

"Naw. They just did the shift change, and the Zombies are on deck right on schedule. The foot patrols should start in about five minutes. So, much as I hate to disappoint the lady and miss the music, we better go do our thing."

VIRGINIA BEACH, VIRGINIA

ONE THING that Gary Leftwich loved about his wife, Ayla, was how proud she was to be an American. They had met in an Internet café in Turkey on a quiet night during his tour of duty at Incerlik, when the beautiful young schoolteacher with shining hair had helped the frustrated staff sergeant rescue the crashed chapter of a story he was writing. She loved the creative side of his personality, and he was enchanted from the start. Her name meant "Moonlight." Before his time was done in Turkey, they were married in a base chapel.

In the States, Ayla dove into becoming a citizen with a ferocious intensity and had passed all of the tests with a will not only to succeed but to master the required information. He believed that she knew more about American history than he did, and she cared just as deeply about the country that had adopted her as did her husband, who currently held the rank of master sergeant in the Air Force and worked with secret operations at Fort Bragg.

Leftwich had arrived home tonight with a bouquet of flowers and the good news that a wonderful thing had happened: A powerful man in Washington had promised to break through the red tape of passport controls and bring Ayla's mother over to live with their family so they could care for her and get her well again. In only two weeks!

She brought out some wine, and they were into the second glass when she noticed a bit of worry shadowing his eyes. "What is wrong? You are thinking on something."

Leftwich finished his glass in a gulp. He got a kick out of listening to her accented English, which was too precise to have the sound of a native-born American. The story came spilling out in a rush, and Ayla hung on every fact, her face darkening as the minutes went by and he recounted the call from Doug Jimenez as closely as he could remember.

"Did you do anything wrong, Gary? By talking to this man?"

"No, I don't think so. He was legitimate. The more I think about it, the more I think that he may have not been telling the truth. When I balked—"

"What means 'bawkt'?"

"When I started to question why he wanted some specific information, he turned on me and threatened that your mother would not get the passport after all. Unless I cooperated."

"Did he want secret information?"

"No, it wasn't all that important. Just some routine material about a single flight. He kept telling me how important he was and that this was something—he didn't say what—something he was doing as a favor for the SEALs down in Virginia."

Ayla's dark eyes were reflecting heavy emotional weather inside of her. "Why could this man not just go through regular channels to obtain this valuable information, if he is so powerful?"

"That, my dear, is one of the many things I've been asking myself. It was a strange call."

She poured another glass of wine, took a sip, and set it carefully on the glass-topped coffee table. "I do not like this man, Gary. I do not believe we should trust what he said, for if he lied to you, and you turned over secret information, then our life could be damaged, yes?"

"I could go to prison. Yes."

"Then we must report the contact to your commander. Annem, my mother, will just have to wait a little bit longer. She would insist on it, if she knew what was going on."

They both got up and fell into each other's arms, and Gary ran his fingers through her thick hair and gave her a kiss. "You are right. I was stupid. Look, honey, I have to make another call first, just to confirm something, then I'll contact the duty officer. We will be OK, and so will your mom. I will work something out."

Ayla pushed him back and waved her hands to shoo him away. "Go and do it now, Gary. We are not traitors to our country."

SENIOR CHIEF Richard Sheridan had finished the workday, satisfied that his SEALs were ready for whatever the world might throw at them. Then he signed out and went home to see his real gang—his wife of fifteen years and their four daughters and a bunch of pets. At work, he was the hard-nosed Rockhead, who never cut anyone a break. His training-ground voice could peel paint. At home, he discarded both the uniform and the granite persona and entered a special place where the ladies ruled, and he loved them without reservation. It was pizza night, and when he was cleaned up enough to be deemed acceptable, they all piled into the SUV and headed out to a cheap family-style restaurant where everybody sat at long tables and helped themselves to plates of pizza, salads, and Italian food. He was a happy man until the telephone on his belt buzzed. He looked at his wife, who stared back at him, more than aware that danger might be calling. When he read the number, however, he winked at her. Personal call. Nowhere important was blowing up.

He unfolded the phone as he left the girls and stepped outside for some quiet space beside the beach. "Sheridan," he said.

"Senior Chief Richard Sheridan?" It was a man's voice, crisp but with some stress.

"That's me. Who is this?"

There was an audible sigh. "My name is Gary Leftwich. I'm an Air Force master sergeant over at Pope Field. Your headquarters gave me your private number when I convinced them this was official business. Sorry if I disturbed your evening."

Sheridan kicked at a rock. "OK, Master Sergeant. What's on your mind? How can I help the Air Force tonight?"

Leftwich gave a short laugh. He liked this guy. "I'm calling about your request to Senator Jordan Monroe, Senior Chief."

Rockhead felt something shift in his stomach, and it wasn't pizza. "Let's make it Rockhead and Gary. I haven't asked Monroe for a damned thing. In fact, I have personally told him this very day to go to hell, not in those exact words, of course."

As Leftwich began to lay it out, Rockhead Sheridan staked out a place on a wooden bench away from the crowd. His wife would come looking for him in a little while, and he knew she would understand the sudden change. As if on cue, she came out of the pizza place and brought him a slice of pepperoni and a fresh beer, then left him alone.

Sheridan pushed Leftwich for more details, breathing deeply to calm himself; the senator and his punk assistant had tried to roll a couple of patriots with a bizarre carrot-and-stick approach. Bad mistake. Instead of being a weak link, Leftwich and his wife were strong and determined to right the wrong.

"OK, Gary. I think I've got it all now. The next steps are easy. This is a national security matter for real, and some shit is going to hit the fan. You and your wife don't have to worry. You are in the clear. You were jobbed by a big-time liar, but you picked up the smell and reported it to me almost immediately. Hell, before it's done, you may get a commendation. Those bastards."

"Good to hear that, Senior Chief."

Rockhead could almost envision the man's relief. "I want you to keep it under wraps for now. Don't file an official report, because we don't know the reach of these people. I'm going to holler up the special ops stovepipe and make this information known to those who count in the Pentagon, the State Department, on Capitol Hill, and in the White House."

"Jesus Christ," breathed Gary Leftwich.

"Yeah. Him, too," Sheridan said. "One last thing. We have to get your mother-in-law out of harm's way so she can't be used to punish you. Once I get this rolling, she will be protected by the Turkish police until State can hustle her onto a plane to Virginia. That's a SEAL promise."

"I owe you big, Rockhead."

"Bullfeathers. Your nation owes you, Master Sergeant Leftwich, and I'm buying the beer next time up in Fayetteville. I want to meet your family."

Senior Chief Rockhead Sheridan folded his phone and drained the bottle, then walked back to the smell of pizza and good times. His wife smiled, and he winked. Family first; calls later.

WASHINGTON, D.C.

THE LIZARD was running on caffeine and curiosity as he rippled through his humming network and the lights from multiple screens bathed his glasses in flashes of different colors. The Seville op was under way, and the new information from the SEALs in Virginia Beach had changed the situation with the senator from a bothersome bit of Capitol Hill chatter to outright treasonable offenses. Freedman's machines had snared the National Security Agency's latest alert that the tagged words of "Task Force Trident" and "Kyle Swanson" had again shown up in telephonic communications.

It was like backtracking a trail of crumbs deep into a loaf of bread. First, the words had popped up in a call that was identified as being between this television action hero named Ryan Powell and Douglas Jimenez, the administrative aide for Senator Jordan Monroe. Soon thereafter, a JAG legal officer named Captain Howell Andrews had drafted a memo about his meeting with that same assistant and sent it up the chain of command to Brigadier General Alfred Coleman of the Pentagon's Congressional Relations Office. The reaction ball began to roll. Now the SEALs raised a new red flag, saying Jimenez had tricked an air traffic controller down at Pope Field, and almost immediately these new mentions had fallen on the NSA Big Ears. Big Brother was indeed listening, and had been for quite some time.

He was about to text General Middleton when the general, Lieutenant Colonel Summers, and Master Gunny Dawkins all returned to the Trident offices after an early dinner. Commander Freedman had settled for a cold turkey and cheese sandwich, unwilling to leave his electronic world because of his total fascination with the quick-moving events. He was ready with an updated report by the time the others walked in, and put it up on the big screen, his palms wrapped around a cup of coffee and his foot tapping fast with joy as he waited for Middleton to go ballistic.

"A goddamn United States senator spilled this information? Who the hell did he call?"

"Don't know that, sir. Only that it was someone in France. Whoever it was probably used a burn phone and tossed it when he was done. The cell tower triangulations pinned down the number on this end with great accuracy, and the number belongs to Senator Monroe of Missouri."

The general rubbed his wrinkled brow. "Anything unusual in Spain?" They all had been expecting only to oversee that operation tonight.

"No, sir. They remain right on schedule."

Dawkins was on his feet, pacing, then pounded his big right fist into his left palm. His face was angry. "We've got to stop it, sir. Bottom line is that our team is now compromised."

Sybelle Summers disagreed. "I don't see that. If Liz just picked up this information, no one could possibly be in Seville right now to block them."

"We cannot be certain. Whoever he called in France may have some immediate way to warn the target or to intervene. We know they have guards on the premises, and they have radio communication. A warning may have gone out, or be on the way. We must consider that our own people are in danger."

"Our people usually go dark on comms once things are under way, right?" Freedman looked at the experts, and they nodded confirmation. "We may not be able to reverse course now, even if we wanted to."

The general agreed with Dawkins. Middleton would not chance letting his team walk into a trap. "We have to try. The guards and even the local cops may have been alerted. Freedman, get on the horn and tell them to abort. If they don't answer, try something else, go directly through CIA. Bring them home, like right now."

He swung around to face Sybelle. "Summers, you get in touch with our friend David Hunt at the FBI. I want the pair of you to meet me in the office of the chief of staff at the White House. Brief him in the car on the way over, and I'll arrange for the Secret Service to clear you through the East Executive Drive gate. Double-Oh and Commander Freedman can continue trying to stop the Seville operation. Go, people. The clock is ticking."

"The president's chief of staff, sir? What about the Joint Chiefs?" Sybelle asked.

The general walked over to the windows that looked down on the memorial park outside the Pentagon. He had a hard time believing that a senator in good repute would sell out to murderers such as the kind who struck on 9/11 and violently ushered America into the Age of Terrorism. "In due course. Right now, we have to go all the way to the top."

SEVILLE, SPAIN

THE TEAM had terminated outside communication five minutes earlier, when Zombie One left the hacienda grounds for the long trudge up to the crest of the hill, a walk that he made every hour. The dark van was parked near the top.

Beth Ledford had begun walking downhill on the sidewalk, measuring her steps so that she and the Zombie would pass each other at the vehicle. "They're both on the way," said the CIA man in back, watching his two cameras and the overhead drone feed.

Swanson just sat there, trying to stay calm. Coastie, Mark Dixon, and Bob Smith would handle the takedown while the third spook stayed on the surveillance electronics inside. He was in the streetside passenger seat to avoid the fight, because he could not afford an errant gush of blood spoiling his makeup.

Spain was six hours ahead of Washington time, so since it was two o'clock in the morning in Seville, it was eight the previous night back in

D.C. He knew the Tridents were in the office back there, nervously awaiting word from the strike team. So far, so good; the assault team went black on comms except among themselves.

Through the front window, he watched Coastie walking in her fancy dress, her hips making the big skirt fan side to side. That made him think of some other women, and he banished them from his mind. Torreblanca had a wife down there with him, and her mother and father, and their children. There was always the chance of collateral damage. He knew that. Innocent people die in combat all the time. His job was to go in and kill the guy and get out clean, without awakening anyone else in the house. But what if one of the kids was still up, or if the mother was watching a movie, and what if Torreblanca and his wife were making love? *What if* a hundred things? Coastie was a lot closer, and she had a flirtatious smile that was directed down the sidewalk at someone moving toward her. In the big side mirror, he saw the shape of the Zombie lumbering forward.

Swanson took a few deep breaths. He could not control everything. All he could do was his job. *Do not rush. Slow is smooth and smooth is fast, and stop beating yourself up over things that have not happened!* With that, he wiped his mind clean as Coastie, the little Spanish temptress in the lacy gypsy dress, sauntered past.

Zombie One had been watching his shoes as he went one step after the other up the sloped sidewalk. He knew the route by heart. All the way to the top, where the fountain was, check that area on both sides for thirty minutes, then return in time for a brief break, and do it all again. Any sniper would have to have a hide up high, and he was familiar with all of the possible spots along this route. He was tired. He had drunk too much raw wine that afternoon, and although the noise of the fiesta had calmed a great deal, the Spaniards partied late. He still heard music and shouts and the *clack* of flamenco castanets. He was passing a line of parked vehicles. When he lifted his eyes, there was a beautiful young woman almost right in front of him. Dark hair, dark eyes, beautiful body beneath a fancy frock, and apparently a little drunk.

She locked eyes with him and missed a step, falling forward. Zombie One leaned over to catch her. Coastie knocked his hand aside and dropped all the way for a single-leg takedown as Mark Dixon rolled from beneath the van and piled on before the guy could even react. Bob Smith was right there, his right hand tight around the rubberized hammer grip of a mountain climber's ice ax. He grabbed a handful of the Zombie's hair to steady his target, then drove with a powerful swing that buried the steel point deep through the guard's skull. Smith had to twist to yank the curved blade free from the tight bone, and it exited with a gush of blood and thick brain matter. Then he struck again with a wide swipe into the exposed temple.

Kyle Swanson opened his door and stepped carefully onto the sidewalk and around the tangle of bodies, then walked away, slowly assuming the shambling, disinterested gait of the dead guard. In the dim light, they would have seemed identical.

Behind him, the team worked quickly to finish with the lifeless body, first pulling a thick plastic bag down over the bleeding head wound, then stretching the corpse out flat and rolling it into a body bag. With the corpse wrapped up, all three of them lifted the Zombie into the rear of the van, where it was pushed to one side like a rug and almost immediately forgotten. It would be dumped on the way out.

"No reaction below, and no witnesses around here. We're good," said the spook on the cameras. "Swanson's on his way."

"My dress is ruined," said Coastie, looking at the stains. She pulled a curtain across the space behind the seat for some privacy and wrestled her way out of the clothes, stripping down to a sports bra and running shorts. A black sweater, jeans, socks, and sneaks were on the floor at her feet. "OK, Mark. I'm ready now. Get up here and rake this goop off my face."

Dixon slid into the driver's seat and went to work with creams and towels to clean her up, pretending not to see the tears forming in her eyes. She dabbed them, but in a low voice told him, "That was horrible." She yanked off the long-haired wig and replaced it with a black combat beanie.

"Up close, it always is," the former Ranger said in a comforting tone.

"Just let it go, Beth. We're still on a mission. These tears are just a normal reaction. No prob."

"I know." She sniffed and wiped her nose, then was out of the van door again, climbing the ladder attached to the back. Up top, she gave a kick to a rolled sleeping bag and sprawled out on her stomach to face the hacienda some 250 meters away. From a cushioned box, she removed an M-40A3 sniper rifle and adjusted the cheek piece and the recoil pad to her comfort. She slid an AN/PVS-10 nightscope onto the rail, and added a clip of M-118LR rounds, working the bolt to put one of the 7.62 mm bullets into the chamber. When she finished adjusting the weapon, the nightscope illuminated the target area, and she swept it back and forth.

If things went sour, Coastie would give precision covering fire to Kyle. This was better, and she was back in her zone as the familiar weight and smells of the big weapon helped clear her mind about the savage death of the Zombie. She concentrated as never before, remembering the lessons of controlled breathing and almost hearing Kyle's advice on the practice range. Her heart rate slowed and her vision sharpened, and she listened to the night and the faraway music and shouts of people still out having a good time. She touched a little microphone attached to the earbud. "Ready upstairs," she reported.

"Ready down," came a flat voice from within the van.

Smith was now at the wheel. "Ready front."

Swanson, who had a similar bud in his ear for internal communication within the strike team, acknowledged, "I'm gone."

A few minutes later, he plodded by the van at the same lethargic pace, eyes down at the sidewalk and not giving any sign that he even saw the vehicle. The broad sidewalk seemed like a shimmering thin tightrope in the sparse moonlight, and every step had to be exact to get him where he needed to go. A long stiletto blade, razor sharp on both sides, was in a leather case attached beneath his left forearm by a simple strap of Velcro. The pistol was in his belt and the silencer in a pocket. Halfway between the van and the hacienda, he clicked the transmit button on his radio twice, the signal to ask if everything was clear. He heard two clicks in response from his partners. *Go.*

The drone was in the air at only five thousand feet, flying lazy loops over the house, and its infrared cameras had identified the positions of the remaining guards. Zombie Two, as usual, was also on countersniper patrol about a mile away on a different patch of high ground, and was therefore not a factor. Zombies Three and Four were in static positions at the front and rear, and Five, the team leader, roamed the grounds. All was quiet, and the protectees were asleep, which made it harder for guards on such routine duty to stay awake, much less keep sharp.

The specter that was Kyle Swanson reached the edge of the grounds, walking in the deep darkness of the big pomegranate trees and putting on a pair of soft black gloves. He tightened the cylindrical sound suppressor onto the barrel of his pistol. He pressed the transmit button only long enough to say, "Location Zombie Five."

The van observer who was flying the drone had seen the flare of a cigarette lighter and whispered, "Z's Five and Four are in back. Just lit up smokes."

Kyle moved forward. That bored pair would be back there swapping lies for a while. Good luck improves any plan. Swanson kept his face tilted down to further hide his features as he approached the front plaza, where the guard designated as Zombie Three was leaning back with his chair propped against the wall, hands behind his head beside the entry. Zombie Three saw exactly what he expected to see: the dark shape and general appearance of Zombie One, back early from his patrol. The man grunted. Kyle grunted. The garden was redolent with the scent of flowers.

Swanson covered the distance in three quick strides, pinned the man's neck in his left hand, and used his right to stuff the pistol against the heart of the seated guard. He fired twice. The noise was quashed by the sound suppressor. The body bucked on the impact of the big slugs, but Kyle held him in place. Had stealth and time not been factors, he would have also delivered a head shot. He looked into the dim eyes. This guy was dead.

Kyle left the body balanced on the chair, so a quick look from a distance would give the impression that the man was asleep, which would also explain why he would not answer a call. That would buy a little time. Every second mattered now.

He keyed the mike. "Zombies Four and Five?"

"No change."

The front door was made of huge planks of oak that had darkened over many years and were held together by forged bolts. Heavy hinges of black iron attached it to the stone house. There was at least a 50 percent chance that it was unlocked, since the guards on exterior security might need to get inside in a hurry. The people inside were considered secure because the mercenaries with guns were outside. Swanson let out a long breath and softly depressed the large lever handle. It went down smoothly, and the giant door gave way with an easy push. He was inside in a single step.

27

BETHESDA, MARYLAND

THE UPSCALE condo was less space than Douglas Jimenez wanted, and the payment plus homeowner fees was a little more than he could afford. It was located in a maze of such homes that were the nests of many Capitol Hill worker bees that had latched onto the properties before the real estate crash, eager to get a toehold in the prestigious, prosperous community. Then the "no money down" American dream became the "no money in the bank" nightmare.

Since most of the homeowners in this clutch of Washington commuters worked in some shape or form for the government, there was no real concern about losing their jobs. Even in crisis, the government still rolled out the paychecks. If one lived somewhat frugally, one could almost pretend the outside market forces were not taking a toll on one personally. The project developers had gone bankrupt, and with that promised assistance gone, the homeowner association's finances were getting rocky, and as its rules were unbending, maintenance fees kept rising. The administrative aides of members of Congress and young financial magicians and health care specialists and naval officers did not cut their own grass or shovel snow off the steps; that was why illegal immigrants were invented and unofficially sanctioned.

Jimenez lived well when he was at work on the government dime, but when he was paying his personal expenses, he had become much more careful. His credit cards were almost maxed out, and the interest was eating him alive. Since he expected the monthly HOA cost would soon be increased by at least another hundred dollars a month per household, he had to cut back on something. Dumping the Beemer, which cost five hundred dollars per month to lease, and riding public transit instead was a horrible possibility. He had to stay dressed properly, which meant the clothing and cleaning bills had to stay in the budget. The financial magazines were telling him to save, save, save and invest at a modest 8 percent annual gain so as to be a multimillionaire by retirement, and then not outlive his money. Where was he going to find an 8 percent annual gain when the banks were offering less than half of 1 percent? That was assuming he had any money to invest, which he did not. Maybe he had enough clout now to get a K Street lobbying job. Fat chance of that happening, he thought as he puttered around his kitchen.

As a sacrifice to reality, on the evening after pulling off the biggest backroom coup of his professional political career, he was celebrating by himself at home, cooking a hamburger with sautéed onions and a slice of cheese, accompanied by a bottle of Coors Light beer. The meal would cost twenty dollars, plus tip, at any saloon between the District and Bethesda, except for Mickey D's and BK, and he wasn't desperate enough to eat at either of those places. Yet.

The melodic chime of the doorbell broke his dour reverie. It was not unusual in this complex, which contained many singles of both sexes, for a party to crank up on the spur of the moment. The old saying that misery enjoys company was never truer than these days around the Beltway, and anyone showing up with a six-pack or a bottle of wine was welcome. Things would grow from there when the tweets and texts alerted everybody else in the block. He wiped his hands on a cloth towel and walked quickly across the carpet, just as the doorbell dinged again. Impatient. "Yeah! I'm coming," he called and opened up.

"Mr. Douglas Jimenez?" Two men in neat suits were on his doorstep. The one in front held a little leather case flipped open to show a bright shield with an eagle on top, and the ID card with his picture and the big letters FBI printed in blue. He had neat black hair and friendless blue eyes that almost matched his shirt. "I'm Special Agent Lassiter, and this is Special Agent Martin."

"Uh," Jimenez said. His lawyer Spidey sense had immediately snapped to alert. *Say nothing. Do not let them inside.* "Yeah. That's me. What's this all about?"

Lassiter pushed him backward hard, with both hands, and Doug was flung sprawling across the foyer. Feeling as if his chest had been crushed when he bounced on the floor, he gasped for breath. Both agents were now inside, and Martin closed the door.

"Douglas Jimenez, you are under arrest for violations of the National Security and Official Secrets Act." They flipped him over like a rag doll and cuffed him, ratcheting the steel bracelets tight.

Douglas caught his breath. "Hey! What are you doing?"

"We're taking your sorry ass into custody. Isn't that sort of obvious?" Martin, a large man with a boxer's bent nose, smiled as he said it.

"Like hell you are. I know my rights!" He tried to sit up, but Lassiter kicked him hard in the ribs with a steel-toed shoe and Doug crumpled back to the floor.

"You have the right for me not to shoot you in the fuckin' head right now. Beyond that, you don't have any that I can think of. The act is pretty generous in how we deal with security issues. We may Miranda you at some later time, if you're lucky and not considered an enemy combatant."

The National Security and Official Secrets Act had updated the old Patriot Act, stripping out some of the unworkable parts but adding stern new ones. It had been passed by Congress after years and years of leaks of vital government information that aided enemies and rivals of the United States. Modeled on the old British Official Secrets Act, the NSOS left very few avenues of legal defense. The American Civil Liberties Union and defense lawyers howled, claiming it was merely antiwhistle-blower legislation. American voters weary of bootleg lone-wolf terrorist strikes had gone along with the idea that people who sign the governmental pledge of keeping secrets and protecting the country should do that, and keep their mouths shut.

"That's crazy! What's the exact charge?"

"Good question. Why don't you just think of this as being taken into protective custody so that some future cellmate with body tats and a permanent hard-on doesn't learn that you're a traitor."

"Do you know who I am? I work for Senator Jordan Monroe!" Jimenez's voice was breaking in fright. His mind was bending under the weight of the unnamed charges. The NSOS was a mean motherfucker of a law.

Martin strolled to the stove and turned the fire out beneath the cooking hamburger. "Not any longer."

"I want to call a lawyer."

"I would imagine that you do. Sorry, but no. Anyway, you're a lawyer yourself. So am I. Lots of lawyers around this town. You want anything else?" Lassiter and Martin each grabbed an arm and pulled Jimenez to his feet.

"I'm willing to make a deal."

"That's where things really get interesting. You don't have anything we want, Dougie-boy. Not a damned thing. You broke the wrong law, so now out we go, and quiet or loud makes no difference to us."

"I'll yell my head off and my neighbors will see. They'll report what you're doing." The steel cuffs were so tight that they were cutting off the blood circulation in his wrists.

"If you try that, an official answer is already in place: that you are a dirty old man and a child molester, as well as a spy. Child pornography will be found on your hard drive. We give the news to a local channel and supply a picture of you in chains. The traitor stuff will come out later, if necessary."

"That's illegal!"

"No, it's not." Lassiter yanked him forward. "Move it, Doug. Time for you to do the perp walk."

SEVILLE, SPAIN

THE MAN IN BLACK slid the lock home on the thick front door, creating a barrier that he could control. The bad guys could not use it, and Swanson's prey was now trapped, although he could leave when he wished. He paused and breathed in the strange surroundings, letting his eyes adjust to the dim light.

The spacious entry hall had a tiled floor that he moved across carefully. Kids lived here, which meant something could be underfoot at almost any step. Toe, then heel, five steps, and he was in the living room, where a single night-light plugged into a wall gave some illumination. Silence enveloped him. He pulled the little light from the electrical socket.

The dining room was long, with a large table and numerous chairs, reminding him of the old Zorro movies he had seen about the lavish lifestyles of Spanish grandees. The kitchen would be in back, maybe an office. The surveillance had determined that the household help lived elsewhere, but if the mother and father of Mrs. Torreblanca actually owned this place, it made sense that they would have the master bedroom.

Slowly prowling the ground floor, he found them, snoring lumps beneath the covers, in a comfortable bedroom downstairs. The older couple no longer wanted to handle the stairs on a daily basis. He closed the door silently and let them be.

Wide stairs along one wall led up to the other sleeping quarters, and he rested a hand on the metal railing, putting the weight of his feet at the ends of the wooden steps to prevent squeaks. Another hallway was at the top, with multiple doors and more decorative tile squares on the floor. He wanted more time for recon, but did not have it. Those guys in back would not smoke forever.

Regular doors at the far end and a double door filling an arch on the left. Another night-light in a bathroom next to the main bedroom. *The kids are down there, so my target is in here.* Kyle took a deep breath and put pressure on the lever, and again a door swung open without a sound. He did not close it all the way because he would not be here long.

The knife came out as he moved to the bed. The dark hair of the wife was spread on the pillow, and her face appeared relaxed in sleep. Torreblanca was on his back with his eyes closed, breathing in steady rhythm. Both arms were beneath the covers. Swanson studied the scene a few seconds to figure out the best way to kill him without awakening her and decided to slide the point in at the Adam's apple and straight into the brain so it would not be trapped by bones, then yank it out and slash the big veins pumping in the exposed neck. When the blade was entering the skin, he would clamp a hand over the man's mouth, and he had to gamble that the struggle would be short and without a scream, a movement that the sleeping wife might just believe was her husband turning over to adjust positions. Swanson gave some thought to climbing on the bed, a knee on each side of the victim to pin him down. He gauged the time he had left. *Should be enough.*

A light flashed on behind him and caught Swanson completely off guard, freezing him in place. The strip of brightness flooded through the six inches where he had left the door ajar and spread to the rest of the room. Easy footsteps in the hall. Kyle faded back against the wall beside the door to adjust to the changing situation, holding the knife a bit higher, ready to make an offensive lunge. The people on the bed did not move. The steps were not those of anyone wearing heavy boots. Then the bathroom door was pulled shut and Kyle relaxed a bit. What could be more common than a child going to the bathroom in the middle of the night? Normal, familiar family noises would not alert anyone. He waited, knife in hand, for the child to finish peeing and go back to bed.

"ABORT!" The sudden voice in his earpiece sounded like a shout. "*Bounty Hunter, abort!*"

The target was in a deep sleep on a bed six feet away. A kid was in the bathroom. Armed guards were outside, and the call meant for him to terminate the mission immediately and get out. His mind whirled as he sorted through the situation and reordered his priorities, but he forced himself to remain calm. Panic would be fatal.

The abort order carried the highest priority. No other information came with it. The team was supposed to be dark with all communication for this part of the mission, so someone obviously had some important information that he did not. Standing alone in enemy territory was no option, as was speculating about what was happening outside. A soldier, no matter how well prepared, can see only a short distance beyond the rim of his helmet. His knowledge was limited. Were police on the way? Had a new load of Zombies showed up unexpectedly? Was the team outside in danger, which would limit his escape chances? The possibilities were endless, and he was wasting valuable seconds thinking about them. An abort order was always rock solid. Something bad had happened, and it meant the operator must stop whatever he was doing and get out as fast as possible. Explanations could wait.

Kyle stared at the inert figure of Daniel Ferran Torreblanca lying quietly beside his wife. There was no sympathy for the man, because Swanson considered him as only another terrorist. It would be so easy to take a few steps forward, slice his throat, and haul ass down the stairs. Then the toilet flushed in the adjacent bathroom, and the kid was back in the puzzle.

Swanson slipped the blade back in its sheath and moved out of the bedroom. In a few seconds, the bathroom door opened and a boy of about eight came out, his black hair mussed and his eyes puffy with sleep. Swanson was at the top of the steps, with his cell phone out, and snapped a picture of the little guy before the boy even knew he was there.

The flash startled the child, stopping him as if he had hit a wall. Stars and colors caused by the flash danced before his eyes until he blinked and rubbed them away; then he saw the big man on the steps, but he looked like all of the guards who had been around the house for the last few days. The man smiled and put his hand to his lips. *Shhhh.*

Swanson knew the boy would bolt at any moment and cry out for his parents, so he kept his presence as nonthreatening as possible and placed the cell phone on the tiled floor without approaching the kid. "Give this to your papa," he said softly.

Then he backed down two steps, turned, and headed for the front door, pulling his pistol as he went.

"Zombie coming around the east side, heading toward the front," warned the CIA man on the drone. The op was blown. Kyle twisted the lock and pulled the door in toward him. Behind him, the little boy finally came to his senses and screamed with a wail that pierced the entire house.

The Zombie moving to the front heard the child scream and ripped his pistol free as he broke into a run just as Kyle dashed out the door. Coastie fired, and her M-40A3 cracked like thunder in the stillness of Seville, and the Zombie was blown backward by a bullet that tore into his chest, through his heart, and out of his back. The man collapsed as another rifle bullet tore into his head.

"Zombie in back is on the move," the van surveillance reported. "He has a bigger weapon, holding with two hands."

"I'm coming toward you," Kyle responded, puffing in exertion. He could see the van about two hundred yards away, uphill, and pounded toward it.

"I see you. Backing up to get closer," said the driver.

"Don't move the vehicle," countered a female voice. Coastie did not want to ruin her aim points. "I'm locked in at this distance. Hold in place a few more seconds."

The remaining Zombie had sought cover as he arrived at the front and his partners did not respond on the radio. He raised the AK-47 above a concrete wall that lined a flower bed and opened up with a long spray of automatic fire in the direction of the threat.

Swanson had covered fifty yards, and his lungs were burning. The Zombie's bullets were wild and zinging off the stones, not even near, but a bouncing bullet was unpredictable. He kept going. Another ten yards, but the van seemed no closer.

The Zombie saw the lifeless bodies of his two comrades in front of the hacienda. Lights were being turned on in every room inside; then great floodlights directed outward from the house were activated and wiped away the darkness.

"Damn!" Coastie yanked her eye away from the night scope when those big lights were caught by it and amplified in intensity. Her entire view had gone white in an instant. "I can't see!" Temporarily blinded, she let touch become her primary sense, dropped the M-40, and grabbed her alternate weapon, an M-16 with an ACOG day scope that was already registered for the same distance. Ledford had been reluctant to carry backup weapons on such assignments, but she could almost hear Kyle barking at her back on the range: "Prior planning prevents piss-poor performance."

The Zombie had slapped a fresh thirty-round magazine into his AK and crept to a new location, feeling more confident by the sudden break in incoming fire. He heard the roar of a vehicle engine and the steps of a man running away. *Were they gone?*

Swanson was winded after running a hundred yards flat-out uphill but kept his legs chugging forward, his balance wobbling from the strain. The van was moving in reverse, coming back for him, and he jumped out of the street to the sidewalk, but tripped on the high curb and fell.

The Zombie popped up to aim and saw the man fall. He brought the wooden stock of the AK-47 to his cheek. At this range, he couldn't miss with a full magazine. He would take out the guy on the ground first and then chew the van to pieces.

The boxy vehicle slid to a stop with its side door already open, and Kyle scrambled toward an outstretched hand just as a rip of bullets nicked along the sidewalk behind him. The instant that the van momentarily halted, Coastie fired directly at the flashes erupting only a hundred yards away. Her second bullet nailed the Zombie in the face and dropped him.

"You got him, Coastie!" shouted the drone man. "Get back in!"

She handed down her rifles and sleeping bag, then jumped to the ground and vaulted into the van. Wiping her eyes, she complained, "I still can't see." The vehicle lunged forward.

"Now," said Kyle. "Somebody please tell me what just happened."

28

NEW YORK AND WASHINGTON, D.C.

MRS. MARY MONROE was in her early forties, in her prime, and she owed it all to her loving husband, Senator Jordan Monroe. It was very sad that they could not stand being in each other's lives for too long at any one time. She still liked him very much, just not in that way, so they had developed a comfortable relationship of living apart and getting together on occasional weekends. Neither wanted a divorce.

Mary was eleven years younger and a political asset to the senator in Washington with her beauty and grace. That standing was fueled by his growing power within the military, which had led to her being hired by a defense contractor as a vice president with unspecified duties and a middle-six-figure salary, plus generous benefits in New York. In the old union days, it would have been called a "no-show" job. A fair trade for everybody involved, she thought.

"I love you, Jordan," she cooed into the little telephone. "Do you want to come up this weekend? We could catch a play, and I'll take you to a decent restaurant."

"Love to, hon, but I can't. Three fund-raisers and two churches back home. Want to come along for the BBQ and some hymns?" The senator had his eyes closed, single malt Scotch in hand, and was sprawled on his sofa. It was dark both inside and outside of his apartment in the Watergate. "Been a helluva day."

She checked the antique clock on an oak bookshelf. Fifteen more minutes before Richard showed up for their date to see Rossini's *Moses in*

Egypt at the City Center. Rural Missouri and endless miles between the ditches and drippy BBQ and uncomfortable pews and grip-and-grins sounded awful. It made her wince just to think about it. "Then how about just the two of us spending the weekend in bed?" she countered with a purr. "I can still make a mean omelet."

"That's more like it," he said with a short laugh. They might not be together often, but Mary was still the woman in his life. Mistresses came and went. She had made a deal to campaign in Missouri with him four weekends every year, and this one was not on the calendar. "Really. Let's do it soon. I miss you."

She looked at the skyline, where the neon and traffic of Manhattan were calling for Mary Monroe to come out and play. With the flick of a fingernail, she adjusted an eyebrow. The blue dress clung to her figure, and the jewelry accented it. "Me, too," she admitted. "I'm going to the opera tonight."

"Girlfriend or boyfriend?"

"Half and half: Richard."

That brought a loud guffaw from the senator. Richard was an artistic director from the West Village and her squire on speed-dial when she needed an escort. He was a good guy, as was his life partner, Phil, the backup escort. Both men looked great in tuxedos. "Have a good time, honey."

"I will. You stay out of trouble down there."

"You know me. Always one step ahead of the alligators. Talk to you later."

"Bye. Try to have fun in Missouri." Mary hung up. She would go to the opera and the reception with Richard, but probably would not come home with him. Jordan wouldn't care, just as she didn't care whom he slept with as long as it was discreet. It was not important, and was part of their deal.

He tossed the phone aside and exhaled a long, tired breath. It was rare that he had an evening to call his own, but barring some end-of-the-world cataclysm, the senator planned to do some serious nothing tonight. He struggled out of the big sofa, picked up the remote, and started the hidden Bose sound system. Kat Edmonson's silky jazz voice over a background piano softened the room. From the fridge, he snared a cold German brew, then snapped off the kitchen light as he went to his bedroom. The clothes came off leisurely and were scattered without thought. In the bathroom, the Jacuzzi tub filled, and steam clouded from the surface of the bubbling water.

Naked, he eased into the hot pool and slid down, resting his head on the sloping end. He placed a folded washcloth across his eyes, took a sip of beer, and felt the problems of his world lose some weight. He had called the Arab guy, Rebiane, and passed along the desired information, and that should be the last of him. By Monday, Doug would have dreamed up some way to tip the authorities about the extortionist while keeping Julie Scott and Michelle safe from being kidnapped again. He knew that the next time, they wouldn't be returned, and that scared him. Well, Douglas was a very clever boy. He would think of something.

The bath bubbled and whirred, and Senator Jordan Monroe hovered on the edge of sleep. Then the bubbles stopped.

"Hello."

Monroe snatched the wet cloth from his eyes. A woman in black jeans and sweater was seated with her legs crossed on a little chair, staring at him. He blinked and she came into sharper focus, although the lights in the bathroom had been switched off and there was only the background light from the bedroom. She had dark hair. Against one cheek, she rested a big pistol.

"What? Who?" he sputtered.

Sybelle Summers kept her voice low and even and threatening. "You have been asking a lot of questions about Task Force Trident, Senator Monroe. Well, here I am."

The senator caught his breath and tried to assert his authority, demanding, "How the hell did you get in?"

"It's what I do," she said. "People have been breaking into the Watergate since 1972, back in the Nixon years. It isn't exactly rocket science."

He gripped the green beer bottle tightly and saw her adjust the pistol in response. A thin red laser beam darted out, and she pointed it at his groin. "Don't even think about throwing that bottle. I came only to talk, so be a good boy and I won't have to shoot you."

"This is absurd. Why would you shoot me?"

"That's another thing I do."

"I'm a United States senator." Bluster.

"I'm an executioner." Total calm. "I kill high-value targets who are enemies of my country. People like you."

He stirred as if about to get up. "You're crazy. Don't you know that I will call the police as soon as you leave?"

Summers ignored him and put a boot on the side of the tub. The red dot danced along his bare chest. "Not if you're dead. Why are you asking about Trident?"

"I'm not telling you anything, Ms. Whoever You Are. Get the fuck out of here right now, or I will have your damned head on a plate. I'm not afraid of you."

"Why are you asking about Kyle Swanson?"

"None of your business, bitch. Leave now. Send this Gunny Swanson by to see me. Maybe I'll be willing to talk with him, face-to-face."

"He's dead, Senator. You wouldn't enjoy that at all." Sybelle got to her feet, the gun hand steady, the red beam traveling up and down his body. "You're going to have a dreadful home accident getting out of the tub. Maybe you grabbed for the towel rack and missed, and cracked your skull open on this nice tile floor. Stand up."

"Like hell I will!"

He could see her better now, and she still wore that curious smile. "Well, a suicide in the tub would work, too. So depressed over your treason that you shoot yourself in the head; the blood will be contained and easily washed away. Electrocution is also possible." She cocked her head to one side and listened to a voice in a small earbud. "How long?" she asked, talking into a small microphone. "OK. I'll be done by then."

The senator suddenly realized this woman was not bluffing. She was willing to kill him right in the bathroom. The color dropped from his face. "Who *are* you?"

"A kindly night visitor with a warning. You're on our map now, and that is never a good place to be, because you can't get off of it." She put away her weapon. "I am an omen of bad things yet to come for you tonight, Senator Monroe. I will let myself out, but remember that we can reach you anytime we need to. Run, and I will find you. Try to expose us, and I will kill you. Right now, I advise you to dry off and get dressed. Two FBI agents have unknowingly saved your life with a nick-of-time arrival, just like in the movies. They apparently are here to take you over to the White House."

Then she was gone, disappearing into the darkness of the apartment, somehow leaving without a sound. The senator stayed in the water, gulping air in fright.

ABU DHABI,
UNITED ARAB EMIRATES

RECEIVING A TELEPHONE CALL in the early morning hours never troubled billionaire financier Sheikh Marwan Tirad Sobhi, who only slept an average of four hours a night anyway, with a one-hour rest after lunch. Business was always being done somewhere in the world, and his skill at timing when a deal needed to close for the best price and advantage was widely known, thanks to a *Fortune* magazine profile six months ago. This was no ordinary call, and that made him instantly alert. On the other end of the conversation, in Seville, Daniel Torreblanca of the Islamic Progress Bank and the Group of Six was falling apart.

"They almost killed me tonight, Sheikh. The killer came right into my house! He took a picture of my child!" There were loud voices in the background, children and women crying and men shouting.

Interesting, the sheikh thought. "How are you still alive?"

Torreblanca coughed. "I don't know and I don't care. Four of the private guards, some of Rebiane's best men, were slaughtered outside. The rest are all around us now, when it's too late. They are useless morons." His voice dropped softer. "The police are also investigating. I wanted to call and let you know what happened."

For Sobhi, several decisions needed to be made, and the first was easy. "Then our meeting at your place in Seville tomorrow evening is obviously not going to happen. Rebiane and his gorilla boy are probably on the way, but you can inform them that I will not come to an unsecure location. Add that I am once again disappointed with both of them."

The man in Spain understood. "I cannot blame you. I would do the same in your shoes." There was an uncomfortable pause. "Marwan, he took a picture of my son, right outside my bedroom door! A man must protect his family."

The sheikh knew Torreblanca was under incredible stress. "That is true, my friend. Are you going to continue the Spain project?"

Another pause. "I regret that I cannot do that, Sheikh. Three of our friends have already fallen, and I was obviously the next target. I will tell Rebiane when he arrives that a replacement is needed for me, at least to give me some distance from the publicity. My bank's directors will react strongly tomorrow when they learn that I am in real danger and the bank's reputation might be tarnished. I doubt if they will continue to support the Spain plan. I can't tell you how sorry I am."

"This is not your fault, Daniel. Look, my friend, business deals fall through all the time for thousands of different reasons. I thought this project might have been overly ambitious from the start. Conquering Spain for Islam remains a noble cause, and we should continue to support it in the future. But we could have helped our faith there without bringing down this backlash of revenge on ourselves. The Rebianes mishandled it."

The sheikh wanted to get off the telephone and contact his own security chief. Torreblanca had been spared, but that did not mean Marwan Tirad Sobhi was no longer a target. It was time for a vacation. "So I also am out of the plan. We are bankers and financial experts, Daniel, not street-slum fighters. We will live to give battle another day, in our own way."

"Then the money pipeline will close on your end as well?"

"Yes. I am happy that you survived, my friend. Now take your family on a holiday while I leak to the financial press that the Group of Six has ceased to exist, and its offer to help the Spaniards recover from their recession is withdrawn. That should remove the threat to our lives."

"Barcelona."

"Probably. Djahid Rebiane could have just worked in the background and let Spain endure its riots. The nation is still rotting from the inside and not going to get any better for at least a decade. There was no need to goad the Americans with such a violent attack when simple bribes probably would have worked to advance the cause."

Torreblanca had already settled down. "Yanis will be furious."

"Tell him that his old-style terrorism is nothing but a pinprick to Americans anymore. They are a tough people. Look at how they reacted to the Boston Marathon and other strikes; instead of being fearful, they are rising in wrath, and the Congress passed that new NSOS Act that tightens the security net even more. All Djahid and Yanis accomplished was to alter the way in which Washington responds. They did not go after the actual perpetrators of the crime in Barcelona, but immediately came instead after *us*, the sponsor! It took years for them to track Osama bin Laden to the ends of the earth, but we were placed in the crosshairs in a matter of days. No amount of protection is good enough to stop them if they want to eliminate someone."

"We probably need to prove that we are no longer involved, Sheikh. They may not accept our words and back-channel signals."

Sheikh Marwan Tirad Sobhi agreed. "I concur. Let us feed them something valuable. Like Djahid, the Barcelona butcher."

"Yasim, too?"

"If necessary. Probably."

WASHINGTON, D.C.

SENATOR MONROE tried to rebuild some confidence as he lurched from the tub, dried, and hurriedly dressed, fumbling with his shirt buttons and belt buckle and getting the tie on crooked, shaky from the encounter with the assassin. By the time the FBI agents knocked on his door, he was able to demand that they call for the police to search the entire Watergate complex and arrest the woman who had broken into his apartment and threatened him. The agents shrugged their shoulders, replied they had seen no one when they approached his door, and then politely put him under semiarrest and took away his cell phone. There were no handcuffs, just a strongly worded request from the president of the United States to come and visit on a matter of national urgency. On the drive over, he tried the "I'm a Senator" gambit, proclaiming that he was a member of the legislative, not the executive, branch, and not under their jurisdiction. The agent riding shotgun choked on a quick laugh and acknowledged being aware that the senator was one-hundredth of one-half of one-third of the federal government.

Even in the middle of the night, they would not take the chance of some television news reporter or freelance paparazzi being around when Senator Jordan Monroe was delivered to the secret meeting. A black stretch limousine with blinking red and blue lights showed up and stopped at the White House main gate as a diversion to draw the attention of any passersby gawking at 1600 Pennsylvania Avenue NW. The only person in it was the driver. Meanwhile, an unremarkable sedan slid quietly to a stop across the street before the green canopy that extended out from the singular row of town houses at 1651–1653 Pennsylvania, where the FBI agents turned Monroe over to a pair of uniformed Secret Service officers who hustled him into Blair House, the guest home used by ranking diplomatic visitors. No civilians were waiting inside to greet him, and the white-shirted officers would not speak as they escorted him down to the tunnel complex that worms throughout the executive grounds and nearby federal buildings.

The senator heard only the *whoosh* of air-conditioning fans and the click of the heels on his own shoes and those of the Secret Service guides who sandwiched him, one in front and one behind, pistols riding on their hips. He felt claustrophobic, then sweaty, as their steps clicked closer to the off-limits underground section of the White House. Closed and secure doors led away to God alone knew where. Monroe guessed they had crossed beneath Pennsylvania Avenue and must be approaching an elevator to go up again. He sent a silent prayer to let the whole thing collapse on him, for he already felt dead and buried, dreading what might be waiting. Instead, the tunnel split at a Y, and the guards walked him to a door guarded by two Marines in dress blues with sidearms, and another Secret Service agent at a small desk who demanded his identification.

Cleared and searched, less than thirty seconds later, Jordan Monroe stepped into the conference room of the Deep Underground Command Center. Elsewhere in the DUCC, experts and technicians monitored the world, ever vigilant and ready to give the national leadership whatever was needed to fight a global war. At one end of a long table sat the president, and along the sides were the directors of the CIA and the FBI and the chairman of the Joint Chiefs, plus a two-star Marine general, the Speaker of the House of Representatives, and the minority leader of the Senate, both of whom were members of his own political party. They all glared at him with a mixture of anger, distaste, and disappointment as the big door hissed closed and automatically sealed.

The president pointed to a chair and broke the silence. "Have a seat,

Senator Monroe. We have some things to discuss." *Senator Monroe, and not Jordan?*

Monroe settled into the cushioned chair and folded his hands on the table, as if trying to gain some traction to keep from spinning out of control. *This has to be about Trident.* "Should I have an attorney present?"

"Has he been charged with anything?" asked the Senate minority leader.

The FBI director, looking as friendly as a shark, replied in the negative. "No lawyer is necessary at this point, under the terms of the NSOS Act."

"I believe you are familiar with almost everyone around this table," said the president in his usual flat voice. "The one you do not know is Major General Bradley Middleton. General, please go ahead."

The general was muscular and large, a few inches over six feet, with close-cropped brown hair and fiery eyes beneath menacing brows. He wore two silver stars but none of the usual rows of honor ribbons and other military hardware on his green tunic, making it impossible to see where he had been or what he had done. "Senator Monroe, I am the commander of Task Force Trident, which is an ultra-top-secret unit for special operations. At least it was until you came snooping around and opened your big mouth to the wrong people. Because of you and your aide, a clandestine foreign operation against terrorists who murdered Americans was compromised tonight, and five U.S. agents were placed in extraordinary danger. The mission had to be aborted prior to completion . . . because you, sir, blew the operation and have exposed our group. They escaped by the skin of their teeth."

Monroe gathered himself for a retort, but Congresswoman Sylvia Clark, his old friend who was currently Speaker of the House, interrupted. "Don't try to deny it, Jordan. Please. I've heard the recordings and read the reports. Your aide Doug Jimenez has been arrested."

The president's voice turned glacial, and his eyes were unblinking. "Senator, it looks as if you have done great damage to the security of this nation. Task Force Trident has been in operation for many years, under the tight and direct control of the Oval Office through two presidencies, men from both political parties. It is assigned to do things that need to be done far off the books and out of sight, but cannot be handled through the usual chain of command. General Middleton reports directly to me."

The senator was nervous. "Those Trident people sent one of their assassins to kill me tonight, right before the FBI got to my place." He could still feel that little red laser dot tracking around his body, and his pulse raced. Monroe realized that he was trapped; he was the only fly on a web full of spiders.

Middleton shook his head. "Negative, sir. That operator came to give you a personal demonstration of our capabilities. There was no actual danger or threat to you. If she had wanted to kill you, you would be dead. You brought on that little visit by giving secret information to your friend Yasim Rebiane, who has been classified as an enemy of the United States and is among the sponsors of the deadly attack on our consulate in Barcelona. In fact, we believe he was the mastermind behind it." Middleton paused and pointed his finger across at the senator. "I think you deserve the death penalty, but you will just end up in some country-club prison somewhere instead of in an orange jumpsuit with a black bag over your head at Gitmo."

The president turned to the FBI director. "Do you have enough to charge the senator with a federal crime?"

"Yes, sir. There are multiple NSOS violations and some other things."

That was delivered without hesitation, and Monroe felt his bowels clench. Violation of the National Security and Official Secrets Act carried brutal penalties. It wouldn't be a white-collar prison at all. A lonely little cell in a Supermax loomed.

The president rose and leaned on the table to stare unwaveringly at Monroe. "Seldom in my administration have I been as disturbed as I am right now, Senator. You broke your oath to protect this nation. You have disgraced your high office and have turned against the citizens of your state. You have collaborated with terrorists, and I, like General Middleton, am highly tempted to slap your ass into Guantánamo with our other enemies. Do not expect any mercy or intervention from me." The president was wearing a light tan jacket with the seal of office sewn over the heart. He zipped it closed, then addressed them all. "Don't get up. I'm going back to my quarters and try to get some sleep. You guys work this out, and I will support whatever punishment you decide. At minimum, he must resign his office immediately, and any charges will be kept in strictest privacy. I hate leaked secrets."

"I'm not a traitor, Mr. President! I was forced to do this! I'll give the FBI everything I know! I . . . I had no choice!" Tears were painting wet paths down the senator's cheeks as the president walked away, and the door opened, then closed behind him with finality.

Jordan Monroe surged to his feet, light-headed and disoriented, and gulped a great breath, and his left arm involuntarily tightened as the incredible stress of what had just happened descended on him with full force. Everything he had worked so hard to get was being snatched away from him; his position, power, money, his arrogance and status, could not shield him from becoming a common prisoner and the terrible fate sure to await him behind bars. His friends and colleagues would call him a terrorist, and Mary would abandon him. Doug Jimenez, who knew everything, would testify against him to save his own skin. The press would be devastating. It was over.

Before anyone at the table could move, the blood drained from the face of Senator Jordan Monroe and he grappled at his chest as if trying to tear away his shirt. Then a great pain crushed him as the heart attack took hold. He fell back into the chair and toppled to the floor.

ABOARD THE *VAGABOND*

SWANSON HELD a cold beer as he leaned against the rail at the sharp bow of the great white yacht, which rode gently as it maneuvered into open water. The Rock of Gibraltar dominated the starboard view, while across the strait lay the edge of the African continent. The wind was strong in his face, and the sun was up behind them. Seated beside him in a deck chair was Lady Pat, working on a Bloody Mary and smoking a thin cigar.

"Our Miss Coastie Ledford is interfering with the operation of this boat," she complained. "The crewmen cannot do their work properly because they all have lust in their hearts. Can you please make her wear more clothes?"

"You make her! Even God doesn't have that power," he said. "You should have seen her all dolled up as a gypsy prostitute. That was right before she started killing people."

Pat laughed. "I love that girl. She's like a spirited and beautiful Thoroughbred running free. Even the other women in the crew like her."

"They are not lusting?"

"I exaggerate. Jeff loves her. I love her. Why don't you love her?"

"Jesus. Not that again." He tipped back his bottle. "You're still trying to get me married."

Pat turned her head and blew out a stream of cigar smoke that trailed back in the wind. "It must happen sometime, Kyle. It is nature."

"Lecture forty-two," he said. "I've heard it before, Pat. Coastie is my partner, and I trust her with my life. When things got hairy last night, I felt better knowing that she was out there covering me with a big rifle. That innocent-looking little girl took out two bad guys with hellacious shots while being shot at herself. Cinderella is a stone killer. It ain't exactly the material for a storybook romance."

"All stories are different." Lady Pat stretched her legs out and studied her sandals. "That aside, it's time for you to give up the Marine Corps and get to work with Jeff running the business. We're tired of waiting."

"Not yet."

"Your luck is going to run out sometime, Kyle. You can't go on doing this forever."

He winced inwardly, recalling how luck had played such a big role in the botched attack on Torreblanca.

"And you're going to get killed in some no-name place, which will ruin my whole day because I'll have to plan your funeral, and you will leave me and my husband without grandchildren. Right ungrateful bastard, you are."

"Ahoy there on the bow!" Sir Geoffrey Cornwell called. "Avast and belay the tops'ls. Mizzen up the taffrail!" He was in his wheelchair, laughing and being rolled forward by Coastie, who wore a short Japanese-style robe with the belt loose over a red bikini. Her blond hair was in a ponytail, and her smile beamed.

Pat waved and lowered her voice. "This is so frustrating. You know that girl could fall in love with you, and you do nothing. You can be such a fool, Kyle Swanson."

General Middleton's planed face was on one of the flat-screens in the *Vagabond* communication center, patched in from Washington. "Son-of-a-bitching senator had a heart attack on us. Keeled over, plop, right there at the table."

"Lot of that happens when people talk to you, sir," Kyle responded. He and Coastie and Jeff were gathered in the sleek room. They had listened with rapt attention as the general related the conspiracy involving Senator Jordan Monroe, and the strange follow-up.

"Is he dead?"

"He's not getting off that easy," the general snorted. "Monroe is being given the absolute best of medical care at Walter Reed. We intend to keep him alive, even if he only has the brain of a carrot."

Coastie joined in. "It's hard to believe that a United States senator would sell us out."

"We cannot change that, Ledford. He did what he did. Claims he was forced to give up the information to Yanis Rebiane, but who knows? Main thing for right now is that we got you people out in time. The Lizard tells me that Seville is now crawling with cops and private security guards."

"General Middleton, if I may?" Cornwell was quiet but insistent.

"Of course, sir."

"You do want to turn the senator, don't you?"

Middleton smirked. "As usual, you are ahead of the rest of us, Sir Jeff. Yes, we want to make him a double agent to feed disinformation back to the bad guys. I promised that if he refuses, he could look forward to another little visit from Sybelle, who by the way, scared the hell out of him."

"Yay, girlfriend," Coastie chirped.

The general explained that the senator's administrative aide, Douglas Jimenez, was also in custody and had already flipped. He would put Monroe's office on the standard routine for a senator recovering from a medical emergency so the terrorists would not become suspicious. Information would flow.

"Sounds good. Then we track 'em down and kill 'em."

"Close, Gunny Swanson." Middleton folded his big hands on the desk. "We let them do the tracking this time and let them come to us. We will dangle you and Coastie out there as bait."

"Whoa." Swanson was surprised with the idea. "Why include her?"

Beth Ledford laughed. "You may not be enough by yourself, while I'm irresistible. I'm in."

SEVILLE, SPAIN

"YOU ARE A COWARD!" Yasim Rebiane whispered hoarsely, drawing not anger but only a derisive laugh from Daniel Ferran Torreblanca.

"Perhaps. That is a childish remark and makes no difference. What matters is that I am a vice president of the Islamic Progress Bank of Saudi Arabia, and as such I am confirming what you were told earlier today by our friend Marwan in Abu Dhabi. We are terminating the Spanish plan." Torreblanca had composed himself quite a bit in the hours since being awakened by his child's scream and the firefight. "It is over, Yasim."

They were seated at a round table draped with white linen in the pleasant inner courtyard of the exquisite Hotel Alfonso XIII. The other member of their group was Rebiane's son, Djahid, who seemed disinterested in the conversation. It was one o'clock in the afternoon, a few minutes after the San Fernando Restaurant had opened for lunch, so the coffee was fresh and strong.

The paid security teams had all retreated to their rented rooms around town as police took over the protection and investigation duties. Television cameras were staked out along the fashionable street at the house as workmen repaired the hacienda after the blazing gunfight. Fresh flowers were being planted, bodies were hauled away, and bullet gouges were plastered over.

Rebiane, Torreblanca, and the sheikh had originally planned to meet at the private residence, but the hacienda was being investigated by the police as a crime scene. Marwan had canceled his trip entirely. That left the Rebianes and Torreblanca to rendezvous in the Santa Cruz district hotel.

"You are being foolish, Daniel. We can still do this. Reconsider, and don't back out now that we are so close to success." Yasim fought to remain calm when what he really wanted to do was stick a knife in the banker's eye. "Look around you here. Look at this place; it is a Moorish palace! The roots of Islam are deep here in Seville."

"Look even closer, Yasim, and you will see how those roots are today a hybrid that blends the artistry of Castile and Andalusia. Seville is what the Americans would call a melting pot of culture."

"The American assassins are going to be eliminated. We are getting closer to them, and soon there will be riots in cities throughout the world."

"I think not. It seems the rest of the world believes Washington is just rubbing out some more terrorists, after they were provoked and attacked first. The cities of Europe are not exactly brimming these days with pro-Islamic pride, you realize."

Rebiane tapped the little coffee cup with a fingertip as he thought. There was nothing he could offer to make up for the security breach last night. The promise to protect the Group members was a shambles, and if Torreblanca could not believe his family could be protected, he would not do anything.

Yanis glanced over at his dreamy-eyed son, who was watching the courtyard's tiled fountain and listening to it burble. The conversation with Marwan had been brusque and ill-humored. *Another coward!* This was the problem with making important decisions by committee and trying to run a war of ideals with men and women whose vision was so limited by money. Sitting at that little table, Rebiane vowed never to make that mistake again.

"Did you bring the assassin's telephone?" he asked, changing the subject.

Daniel reached into a side pocket of his suit as he nodded. "I did not mention it to the police. Their investigators are questioning my entire family, so if my boy says anything, I will have to lie and say it was lost during all of the confusion." The man scrolled the screen, placed the cell phone on the tablecloth, and pushed it across. "That is the picture of a scared little boy. My son."

Yasim thought the child seemed more befuddled by sleep than actually frightened. He turned it toward Djahid, who ignored it. "This is a common make and model. It would be clean and untraceable. May I keep it?"

"No." Torreblanca's eyes were sharp and dark. "I will hold this little phone in my shirt pocket, next to my heart. If nothing else, that picture will always remind me of the consequences of making rash decisions."

Djahid finally stirred. "You are refusing a polite request from my father?"

The banker did not flinch from the menacing look and replied in an easy voice. "I do not work for your father, Djahid. I owe him nothing, and I am not afraid of you. Both of you are responsible for Barcelona, for bringing the roof down on our heads and for ruining months of hard work."

The younger man's eyes glittered. "You should be very afraid of me."

Torreblanca folded his napkin and let it fall to the floor, the signal for two men and one woman to step from their hiding places nearby and converge on the table, their hands on or near pistols in hidden holsters. "Your imported thugs failed to protect me last night, Djahid. They were all big and dressed in black and ultimately worthless, which is why four of them were killed. As you see, I now have a new security team, all from the CNP, which has assigned them to me during this dangerous time."

Both Yasim and Djahid blinked. The Cuerpo Nacional de Policía was the hammer for the Ministry of the Interior. Among its duties was combatting terrorism. "This is madness, Daniel," Yasim sputtered. "What will you tell them?"

The new guards were in a semicircle about ten feet from the table. "I will tell them the truth, my friends. I was a member of the Group of

Six and trying to help Spain resolve its financial difficulties. Unknown forces, probably Americans, targeted us all, and despite having professional security teams, a massacre took place at my home last night."

Yasim lowered his voice. "What will you tell them about us?"

"Nothing they do not already know. That you are also one of the Six, and we were previously scheduled to have this meeting this morning. And that our offer to lend Madrid a helping hand is being rescinded because of this upsurge in American terrorist activity that has killed three of our partners, all innocent civilians."

"So we just crawl away with our tails between our legs?" Djahid was on alert now, his eyes on the gun hands of the lurking police guards.

"Yes. That would be my advice." Torreblanca was glad this was over. He was certain that Washington was behind the attacks, and the new American policy of holding the high-ranking people responsible for terrorism was frightening. They would never stop. Torreblanca brushed unseen crumbs from his jacket and stood. "Good-bye, Yasim. If you come up with more ideas in the future, please do not contact me."

The police guards closed around the banker and escorted him from the hotel.

SPRINGFIELD, VIRGINIA

SOUTHWEST of Washington, just outside the I-495 Capital Beltway, Douglas Jimenez sat alone in a bare room, eating scrambled eggs and a blueberry muffin with coffee. His hands were no longer bound, and his feet were also free.

The arresting agent who had removed the restraints had warned, "We will allow you to be comfortable because you are too much of a bureaucratic weenie to try to escape, and my orders are to double-tap you in the head with a pair of nines if you get rowdy."

Douglas knew the agent was right; he wasn't going anywhere and had no intention of getting into a physical brawl that he could not possibly win. Hell, he doubted if he could even give the guy a black eye. His karate training was of zero help. He nibbled at the cheesy eggs sprinkled with tangy red pepper while the man talked.

"I'm with the government, and I'm here to help," the man joked with a deadpan look. He was of medium size, had an angular face and neatly trimmed hair going gray, and wore a dark suit, a white shirt, and a patterned tie. When he hung up the coat, Doug saw the badge and pistol clipped to the belt. He pulled a chair up to the table and powered up a laptop.

"What about my rights?" Jimenez asked with a listless voice. "No matter what you think, I am still an American citizen, with constitutional protections."

"Yes, you are, Douglas. I am absolutely certain that when the process goes forward, all charges brought against you will be dropped because we overstepped our authority. Some judge will be shocked, just *shocked*, at how you were treated. No lawyer, no Miranda warning or that sort of thing. By then, you will be of no further use to us anyway, so we will apologize and cut you loose."

"I could sue your asses off."

"Feel free to do so. It would be interesting. Imagine the case file: *Traitor and Child Porn Monster Douglas Jimenez v. The United States of America*. The minute you file the first piece of paper, we will have lawyers and investigators all over you. Do you really want to be audited by the IRS for the rest of your life? To be followed by cops forever? Stop with the impossible dreams and let's get down to business. Eat the muffin. It's good. Came from Starbucks."

The unidentified agent worked the keyboard briefly, and a picture popped up, sharp and clear. "Oh, my, Dougie. Look at this. Your senator has had a heart attack. This is a live feed from his room at Walter Reed."

Senator Jordan Monroe was beneath hospital sheets, hooked to a rack of IVs and monitors, with a ventilator down his throat. His eyes were closed, the chest and stomach rose with regular breathing, and he looked like a shriveled old man.

"Did you do this?"

"Nope. That was all his own doing. Too much barbecue and sugar over a long life of overindulging himself and creating stress."

"Is he going to pull through?"

"The doctors give him a good chance. He's under arrest, but we hope he does."

That threw Jimenez off balance. "Why? Monroe was the one making me do this stuff. Just let the bastard die."

The man went silent for a few minutes, putting on glasses to read from the folders. "We need him alive, Doug. He is of no use to us as a corpse. And here's the surprise: We need you, too. These folders contain your get-out-of-jail-free card. Would you be interested in getting your life back?"

Doug straightened in his chair, crossed his arms, and nodded. "Hell, yes."

"You two losers form the only direct contact we have to the people behind the terrorist bombing in Barcelona," the man explained. "Consider yourself to be part of a bridge between us and the bad guys, Douglas. Our intelligence units will feed specific information for you and the senator to pass along."

Jimenez said, "Fine, but as far as I knew, it was another rich campaign cash cow."

"Quit lying. You knew Yasim Rebiane was a member of the Group of Six that was trying to overthrow the Spanish government. They planned, paid for, and carried out Barcelona, which killed a bunch of Americans."

Jimenez struggled with the big picture. Morality had never been his strong suit. "I never talked to the man."

"That is immaterial. You will, if you want to get your life back."

Jimenez leaned forward, interested, sensing opportunity.

"Are you are willing to help by taking charge of the senator's office as if nothing has changed?"

"Will that make these charges go away?"

"You haven't been charged with anything yet, remember? After this is over, you'll never work in this town again, and you'll lose all of your security clearances, but there will be no criminal charges. We will expunge the record, give you a wad of cash, and help you set up a law practice in some faraway city under a new name."

"If I don't help, I'm fucked."

"Really and truly."

"Brilliant. I'll do it."

ABOARD THE *VAGABOND*

"WHAT IS NEXT in your training cycle, dear?" Lady Pat sat still, facing a mirror, as Beth Ledford brushed the older woman's hair with lazy strokes.

"They're going to teach me to fly a helicopter," Beth replied. "The Army school at Fort Rucker, Alabama. Trident likes to move me through the different branches of the service, but I'm still a Coastie."

"They believe in you. So do Jeff and I."

Coastie stopped for a moment, put her hands on Pat's shoulders, and smiled at her in the mirror. "Thanks. It means a lot. I can see why Kyle loves you guys. People like us need a place to decompress after a dirty mission; a home away from home."

"I have been doing that for a long time, dear. When Jeff was with the SAS, he also brought his lads home on occasion to give them downtime. Your feelings are not unique in the company of warriors I have known."

Beth tried a little grin, but failed. "But mine *are* unique, Pat. I'm a woman, and you know that it's different." She continued brushing the hair. "Every springtime, like right now, I start getting all maternal and want to hug a fuzzy baby chick or buy a kitten. Then I realize that I can't even take care of a potted plant. I really love Mickey, and I don't want that to fade because of the miles and time between us. Sex? What's that? A man might be able to walk away from feelings, but women remember."

Pat reached back and closed her fingers over the brush hand and found it trembling. Tears welled within her. Beth was finally breaking through her tough-girl shell, and her natural breeziness was gone. Lady

Patricia got up and locked the stateroom door for privacy, then returned to where Beth had plopped down on the green sofa and wrapped her arms around her and hugged the girl close, saying nothing. Coastie started crying so hard that she shook and developed hiccups.

Pat thought of how Special Forces could take kids out of high school, with a minimum of training and no worldly experience, and in a few years cram them full of college-level or advanced-degree knowledge in things ranging from ballistics to meteorology to electronics to aviation to medicine and teach them how to kill other people in a dozen ways without flinching. She had been expecting Coastie's tears for some time. The emotional dam burst and the internal agony came flooding out. Pat had played this same role over the years with Jeff, and with Kyle, too, and with others, even Sybelle Summers. It came with the territory . . . but Beth was so different, on so many levels. She was a savant with a firearm, but that prodigious talent had led her to a dangerous crossroads. Her choice would affect the rest of her life, but she would never be the same once the decision was made.

"I don't know if I can take this much longer," Coastie sobbed. "I'm not normal, Pat! Normal people can't do what I do. I've turned into a monster, a point-and-shoot mutant toy for the government. I don't have any close friends my age, I don't have any social life, and since Mom passed away last year, all of my family is dead. When I get Facebook pictures of my high school classmates getting married and having babies, I want to scream."

Beth put her hands up and squeezed her temples as if she had a migraine headache or wanted to tear out her hair. "I'm not really *me;* I'm just a freak with a gun."

"Umm," soothed Pat. *Let her talk.*

"I can't keep it inside any longer. My supergirl act is just that . . . *an act.* My professional competence is at a peak while my personal confidence has collapsed to below zero. Some of the things I have seen and done are beyond the bounds of sanity. I kill people, Pat, just take their lives and erase them from the world. Worst of all, I'm beginning to enjoy it!" There was another hard, shaking burst of weeping.

Lady Patricia Cornwell was concerned. She went and got them both shots of whisky. "Have you seen a doctor or confided in a psychiatrist?"

Beth shook her head. "I was afraid if I told anybody at all, I would be kicked out of Trident. General Middleton would never let this pass. I shouldn't even be telling you."

"Kyle doesn't know about it? Sybelle?"

"No. At least not yet. But it's always there now, Pat, like a curtain over my entire life."

Pat paused and let some silence pass. "How about Mickey?"

"Absolutely not. How could anybody as sweet as my Mickey love an emotional cripple like me?"

Pat finished off her drink. "I'm the only person who knows? You poor thing. It is too heavy a load to carry by yourself, Beth. You have done nothing wrong, and you are not the only Special Forces operator to be caught in such a tangle."

Coastie fetched another round of Scotch, this time in a glass with ice for herself. "I want to be normal again." She mopped her nose and eyes with a tissue. "I guess I have to make some big choices, huh?"

"I'm afraid so. Time will help, and some psychotherapy, and definitely love." She caught Coastie's hands in her own. "You have to go and tell Mickey everything. My guess is he will be your strongest ally. And you do have to decide whether you want to continue this peculiar, but very important, life."

"I'm a mess."

Lady Pat held on to her. "Well, just think about attending your twenty-fifth high school reunion, when they ask what you have been up to."

That brought a sudden little laugh. "I guess I could do a strafing run on that little bitch Shauna, my archenemy mean girl since the ninth grade, as a show-and-tell."

"Now that would add a little sparkle to the event, although it probably would be somewhat ill-advised. What you cannot tell them, of course, is that you have been protecting all of those dear mommies and daddies and babies by putting your life on the line every damned day."

"At least it's not boring." Beth rubbed her eyes with the sides of her hands.

Lady Patricia Cornwell pushed her back and gripped her shoulders. "No. Boring, it is not. You were wrong in not telling Trident right away. They are also your family, Coastie, every one of them. And you cannot go back into the field on another mission, with mixed feelings that would endanger your partner."

"I know. I would never do that to Kyle. Never."

Pat pressed an intercom button, and Swanson answered from his room. "Kyle. Get your butt down here to the bar. Beth wants to tell you something."

SEVILLE, SPAIN

SIX MARINES had been murdered in Barcelona. Gunnery Sergeant Kyle Swanson had escorted their bodies back to the United States, and subsequently was tasked with going after the Group of Six, the money people who sponsored the massacre. Three of the scheming financiers had since forfeited their lives: Cristobál Jose Bello in Mallorca, Juan de Lara in Madrid, and Mercedes Sarra Bourihane in Paris. Their outrageous scheme to turn Spain into an Islamic state lay in ashes. Then Swanson was told the mission was both successful and over, and he was ordered to walk away.

Swanson felt unfulfilled. What about the other three schemers? Why should Daniel Ferran Torreblanca, who had been so close to death beneath Kyle's knife, still be alive and safe in Seville? Or the wealthy Marwan Tirad Sobhi isolated by his money in Abu Dhabi? Or the mysterious and dangerous Yanis Rebiane? It was clear to Swanson that the overall mission had never been an eye-for-an-eye exchange at all, and just ironic that the numbers worked out that way. Instead, it had a larger purpose, a ruthless method to squash the money ring supporting the radical political cause.

When the Group of Six conspiracy fell apart, Kyle, Trident, and their CIA helpers got pats on the back, and everybody got a week's leave.

He had hardly been surprised by Coastie's confession about having doubts about their work, and had helped Pat settle her down by recounting his own periodic hallucinations involving the character he called the

Boatman. They had had similar conversations before. "You're my partner, Coastie. I trusted you yesterday, I trust you today, and I will trust you tomorrow," he told her. "If we had to go right now, I would want you with me."

"I might not be strong enough, Kyle. I might not . . ."

"Quiet down," he said and gave her a hug. "You're not crazy. You're just a regular member of Task Force Trident, a place where we all have nightmares or risk having a mental meltdown and disconnecting entirely from the world. We go out and do a dirty job in order to stop bad guys from doing horrible things."

They all agreed to let her take some more time to think about the situation, and she remained with Pat and Jeff on the boat to play tourist along the Spanish coast.

Kyle decided on a more private holiday. They would rendezvous back in Washington in eight days, where Beth would be dispatched to go play with helicopters, getting her out of harm's way for a while. Kyle made her promise to tell General Middleton and the other Tridents about her confused feelings during the stopover. In his opinion, she would be crazy if she didn't have such doubts about killing human beings, because that would mean she was just a plain vanilla psychopath.

Meanwhile, things were slowing down in Spain as the Islamic offer was removed from the table to ease some of the overall tensions. It would not be long before some new assignment took its place for Trident. Swanson did not mind it. It was part of the game. For him, the War on Terror never ceased, and his skill set was always in demand somewhere. It should have been enough just to know that he had been instrumental in foiling an international plot, and yet he had the nagging feeling that he had not done enough, that his buddy Gunny Mike Dodge deserved a better send-off. Swanson could not turn off the unanswered questions.

Who had planned the tactics of the Barcelona strike? Who gathered the terrorist muscle? Who was the on-site commander of the hit team? That had all been pushed aside in the haste to rupture the financial pipeline that threatened to destabilize Madrid. As soon as the word came down from Trident that the main job was over, and he should take a week off, Kyle decided to spend his vacation time trying to find that missing combat leader. It was unlikely that a man who had committed such an atrocity had gone underground. Like Kyle, he would feel an important job had been left undone.

THE SUN felt warm and good on Swanson's torso as he lay on a deck chair beside the sparkling swimming pool of a luxury hotel, with dark sunglasses letting him watch others without moving his head. Squealing children splashed in the shallow end with brightly colored rubber rings and floats. Teenagers were showing off: the boys extravagant with their swagger; the sleek girls acting cool and ignoring them. Men and women of all ages came and went while Swanson baked silently and let his thoughts roam.

He had told the Lizard he was going surfing in California during the break, then made a first-class reservation to fly all the way to Los Angeles, en route to his beach house, from which he could easily bounce back to D.C. after a week of relaxing. After picking up his ticket at the airport counter without checking any luggage, Kyle went downstairs, rented a car from Hertz, and drove away. He bought a throwaway cell phone and some minutes, which left him off the grid and on his own for a while.

He dozed and rested in the sunshine. After a shower and a shave, he would get down to business. Swanson was back in Seville.

A hotel concierge sees many things, but he had not judged this one correctly. The hard man's gray-green eyes contrasted with an already tanned face that was slightly rosy from a morning in the sunshine. The brown hair had been trimmed that morning. He wore a white hotel robe over his swim trunks, with a white towel flung over a shoulder, and he was as lean as a whippet at about five feet nine and about 175 pounds. Mr. Swanson looked more like a mixed martial arts fighter than a businessman. The memory bank of the concierge recalled that the guest was executive vice president of a firm called Excalibur Enterprises, based in London.

"Good afternoon, Mr. Swanson. How may I help?

The man leaned casually on the front edge of the concierge's desk, silently invading the polite space. "I would like the telephone number of a discreet escort service."

The concierge had such a list, for such a request was not uncommon from tourists and visitors. "Of course, sir. Do you wish me to make the appointment?"

"My Spanish is not so good, so yes, it would be better if you made the arrangements."

Then came the jolt. He wanted a male escort who was physically fit, handsome, and neat in appearance and spoke American-style English. The concierge acknowledged. A *tryst?* No matter. Still, it rankled the concierge that his observation skills had erred; he liked to know what his guests needed even before they did. To ask directly if the escort should be homosexual would be impolite. He would discuss that with the agency, who would probably have someone of multiple sexual abilities.

"Do you wish the escort to come to the hotel?"

"No," said the guest. "I will meet him in two hours at El Serranito on Ronda de Triana."

Swanson was paying cash, with generous tips, for everything during this off-the-record visit.

"Very good, sir. Anything else?"

"No. Thank you." The man in the robe walked away as if he did not have a care in the world.

Once back in his room, Swanson cleaned up and changed clothes. At the hotel-furnished computer that was secured to a small desk, he used fake identification to make a reservation for the 3:30 P.M. nonstop flight from Seville to Lisbon. Overnight in Portugal, then the long jump to California. He sent an e-mail to the front desk asking them to prepare his bill, and another to the real estate manager in Venice saying to prepare the house for his arrival.

* * *

THE VIBRATING BUZZ of the cellular telephone in his shirt pocket startled Daniel Torreblanca. He was at his desk, alone in the big office, working hard while the others took a siesta. A lot of legitimate business had been pushed to the side while he had been with the Group of Six, and his employers at the Islamic Progress Bank, who had supported the Spanish expedition, now wanted him to get on with other projects. The business world had already moved on, with or without the revolution.

He flipped open the phone, and the screen shot of his son flashed on. "Hello?"

"This is the guy who was in your house recently. The one who left you this phone." Kyle Swanson kept his voice even and unthreatening, as if talking with a friend at a bar.

An icy fear spread alongside a bolt of anger in Torreblanca, and he fought the urge to dash upstairs and count the sleeping family members. "You bastard. You murdered my friends."

"You murdered mine, too. But you are off the list now. I was at your bedside with a knife and intended to slit your throat when your boy decided to go to the bathroom. Bad timing for me, good for you. The child saved your life. I did not harm your family and left you sleeping there so your son would not see your bloody body. You are no longer in any danger. That part is over."

"Then what do you want?" The banker spat the words with genuine hatred.

"A few minutes of your time."

"Do you think that I would expose myself to you again? You are mad! Whoever you are, you are still a killer."

Kyle remained unflustered. "I'm thinking of an exchange of information. Tell you what, Señor Torreblanca. We can meet in a public place. I will be waiting at an outside table at El Serranito on Ronda de Triana in one hour. I will be unarmed. You can have your bodyguards check it out first; then they can set up a close perimeter. I want a promise of safe conduct out."

"My bodyguards are members of the Spanish National Police. Why should I not just turn you over to them?"

"Because if they try to capture me, things will get ugly in a hurry, I will get away, and you go back on my list. All I am asking is ten minutes. Then you will never see me again."

"And what is this information you have to exchange?"

"Show up and find out."

Torreblanca hesitated as his mind raced through possibilities. A part of him wanted to meet this assassin, for one could never tell if such an asset would be useful in the future. The police guards would be on hand, so he would be reasonably safe. How could this man believe that he could escape a trap? The banker shut down that line of thought. He was no detective, but he had some close at hand.

"One hour at El Serranito and safe passage," he confirmed and hung up. Torreblanca rose from his desk and went to find one of the bodyguards. Here was a chance to get even and have the authorities arrest the deadly invader.

Kyle Swanson folded his phone and placed it carefully on a table inside a small café directly across the street from El Serranito. Before him sat the empty plate of tapas he had eaten for lunch and a glass of red wine. Through the large glass window, he had watched a man in a monochrome blue suit, with a silver shirt open at the neck enough to show a gold necklace, arrive and sit down at a sidewalk table outside El Serranito. He was a tall kid, obviously a gym rat, good-looking with thick black hair, and carried the reptilian look of a hooker ready to relieve a client of several hundred euros.

Swanson figured the cops would descend in about fifteen minutes to put the place under surveillance. They probably would not grab the guy outright until the banker arrived and made contact. With everything in order, he finished off the wine, put down some bills, walked to his car, and drove away. He had no intention of waiting around to be picked up by police. This scheduled meeting was only a diversion to focus attention here and slacken the protection at the hacienda. Kyle had no information to give Torreblanca in a tabletop deal anyway, but the financier could tell him about the leader of the pack.

* * *

He parked the little gray sedan on the same street they had used for the van stakeout, upslope from the front garden of Torreblanca's home and facing down. Swanson pushed back the seat and adjusted the mirrors to give him sight lines all around, then settled down for what he expected to be a short wait.

The damage had already been almost totally repaired, and the shaded garden was abloom again with fresh blue plants. An old gardener poked around the thick hedges up on the hillside. Swanson mentally compared it all with what he had encountered in Barcelona, where the remains of the consulate were only a twisted steel skeleton supporting slabs of burned concrete tilted into a huge deep crater with steep walls and littered with still-smoking debris and emergency crews digging frantically for survivors by the time he had arrived several hours after the blast. The image of body parts and bones could not have been sharper. That was why General Middleton had made him go there and retrieve the Marines. This had not been some abstract assignment for him after that; it was personal.

Swanson controlled his breathing, willing himself to remain calm and watch the front door. He had no illusions about the guilt of this enemy. Daniel Ferran Torreblanca did not deserve to live. That knife thrust would have been so easy! Today, though, Swanson just wanted to sneak in and force him to talk. After that, well, he would just wait and see. Kyle caught the scent of old, angry smoke from Barcelona mixing on the air with the morning flowers of Seville and slumped down further, until he was looking through the round steering wheel and the seat hid his head.

The San Pablo Airport lay thirty minutes away on the A-4 motorway, and he had factored in extra time for the ticketing and security check. With the sky clear and blue, there should be no weather delay. An hour to get from here to there, through the gate, and out of Seville seemed doable. The fallback would be to dump his car at the airport long-term lot, rent a new one, and drive to Lisbon, about 195 miles away.

Kyle snapped back to reality when a bald, burly man in a suit appeared in the front door, walked out slowly, and stopped, taking his time to look all around. His gaze swept right over Kyle without pausing. Swanson thought, *Stupid. Where are your binos, cop? Do you think your job is supposed to be easy or that you have Superman vision?* The guards were police officers, not soldiers, and trained to protect by defense, not by offense. The policeman raised a handheld radio and spoke into it.

A long black SUV emerged from behind the house and followed the drive to park beside the patio so the driver's side was away from the house. The tinted windows were dark squares. Kyle figured the cops at the café had reported they had established a perimeter and it was safe to bring in the principal for the contact. A woman officer emerged next and walked in quick strides to the front passenger side, opened the door, and climbed in beside the driver.

Swanson had observed that most rich people liked to ride behind the driver in such vehicles, a little automatic establishment of privacy because it was harder for the driver to observe them in the rearview mirror. The big man opened the door behind the driver, gave a final look around the grounds, and called back to the house.

The tall Daniel Torreblanca stepped onto the patio and paused uncertainly at the door, long enough for Swanson to see the bulk of an armored vest beneath the long white shirt that hung over his trousers and buttoned at the wrists. He walked out of the shadows and around the front bumper of the large vehicle. The banker was three steps away from the door when the shot rang out as clear as a banshee wailing over someone who is about to die.

The first bullet flew true and took him in the right side, which was unprotected by the ceramic safety plates. Torreblanca stumbled back against the SUV fender and spent the last moments of his life grabbing for support on the slick black paint as the tumbling high-velocity round scrambled his internal organs all the way through his heart before exiting at a downward angle. A second shot went into his face.

Kyle lurched upright behind the steering wheel. *Holy shit!* The gunshots had come from his left, near the hedges. He looked over and saw the old gardener sprawled on the ground and scrambling to hide behind his plastic cart, away from the hedgerow. That's where the sniper was.

Down the street, the stunned guards were frozen in place like cartoon characters glued on a bloody page. The police had anticipated possible trouble at the café, not here at the house. The big man dove over the body of the already dead Torreblanca; then the woman was out and around the SUV with her pistol drawn, pausing to look down at the victim. The driver threw open his door and jumped out and covered the right flank, nine-to-noon, while the woman swept over the twelve-to-three sector.

All of them backed away from the assassination site, pulling the corpse with them, until they vanished through the doorway. There had been no more follow-up shots. All they saw of possible interest was a lone car parked up the street.

Kyle could not stay where he was parked. He started the engine and let the vehicle coast forward in neutral to avoid any sudden movement that might draw police attention and gunfire. Cops would be all over this area in a minute, and he did not want to have to answer any questions.

NEW YORK

HOURS LATER, when Swanson was standing in the customs line at Terminal Four of the Kennedy Airport, he still had not untangled what had happened at the Torreblanca hacienda back in Seville. Perhaps a deep thinker like Sun Tzu or Nostradamus might have come up with an idea, but Swanson doubted if either had a lot to say about what happens when you do everything right and the grenade still explodes in your hands. Swanson shuffled with the line of passengers as it edged forward, intentionally trying to look very American with a maroon golf shirt hanging outside of his worn jeans. He could have used other credentials and breezed through the security barrier, but he wanted to take the slower road, hoping an answer would come to him. The line for citizens returning home from abroad was shorter than the one for foreign nationals, so he would be clear soon enough anyway.

He had tried to keep the moving parts of his little plan in Seville to a minimum: draw away the cops with a crude deception, then break into Torreblanca's house for a private chat when the Spaniard returned. All plans, however, are as fragile as Venetian glass. Somebody else obviously had another plan, and that shattered his own with an unexpected volley of gunfire. Kyle was not saddened by the death of the banker, but now thought himself naive for not considering that there might be competition in the sticky world of terrorism.

During the flight back across the Atlantic, Swanson had replayed the scene a hundred times, trying to remember anything he might have ignored at the time because he had been so focused on that front door. Kyle recalled hearing the muffled bark of a suppressed rifle off to his left, and had turned that way in time to see a small fluff of dust rise above the decorative bushes on the hillside. That was the result of the muzzle blast jarring the ground immediately in front of the gun barrel. The sniper had not used a mat to keep down the dirt, either counting on the bushes to do that or not being professional enough to think of doing so. The only person in view when Kyle had parked was the old man in long-sleeved green overalls who had been lazily working the landscape. Rake and shovel handles stuck out of his rolling plastic trash can. That guy had dived to the grass when the sniper fired, a normal reaction. Running away from the sound would have been even more normal, but he did not do that. Was he ducking to hide from the cops? Kyle considered there was a strong possibility that he was working with the shooter as the lookout. The rifle could be stashed in the cart and hidden beneath plastic. That made sense; they were a team.

Kyle moved forward again in the long trek to the customs agent, getting near the counter where weary travelers were being scrutinized by officers who were as alert as the police roaming nearby. He had never gotten used to seeing cops with automatic weapons inside an American airport. Swanson exhaled a full breath and readied his passport and entry declaration form.

What about the timing? How could the sniper have known Torreblanca was going to come outside at that moment? Was it Kyle's plan that had drawn him out? Or maybe there had been another ruse he knew nothing about. Coincidence or just Murphy's Law at work, proving once again that whatever can go wrong, will go wrong, and at the worst possible time. He had seen that happen before in other places, and had no answers then either.

Then he was at the counter, handing over the documents while being eyeballed by the officer and video cameras. She was a curly-haired woman with brown eyes and thin lips that needed new lipstick. Her attitude was professional, not bored, and she studied the papers and the computer panel that crunched the information. The eyebrows rose as she read the unusual data on her screen, then settled into place as she smoothly handed back his passport. "Welcome home, sir," she said. "And thank you for your service."

Swanson walked through the portal and was only fifteen minutes from downtown Manhattan. He knew the interlude would not last long as soon as his name and number hit the electronic grid, so he had not even bothered checking the connecting flight to Los Angeles.

Reluctantly and because he could not put off the inevitable any longer, he powered up his cell phone, fully expecting what was waiting. Under MISSED CALLS were a dozen text messages from Lieutenant Colonel Sybelle Summers. The first had been a polite inquiry about his location, but her choice of words had changed remarkably when there were no replies, and the last bluntly ordered him to put his ass on a plane and get to Washington, like right now.

THE PENTAGON

"TELL ME you didn't do this."

"I didn't do it, sir."

"Did you?"

"No. I just went there to try to talk to him about the Barcelona raid. I thought that I had everything under control."

"And then it went all FUBAR."

"Fucked up beyond all recognition does pretty well describe it, sir."

"Weird," said General Brad Middleton.

"Very," echoed Sybelle Summers.

"We were killing these people. Then we stop and somebody else starts," observed Commander Benton Freedman. "That is indeed strange."

"Another dog in the hunt," said Master Gunny O. O. Dawkins, his forearms folded across his big chest and his boots crossed at the ankle. He looked comfortable, like a rhino after a good meal.

Middleton had not been angry, only perplexed. "You did not disobey orders, did you? I forgot the precise wording."

Swanson shook his head and lied. "No, sir. This was a last-minute thing. I really was going to California, then thought, what the hell. With the heat off, Torreblanca might be curious enough to meet me in person. I hoped to get intelligence on the tactical commander in Barcelona."

"I don't like you going off our grid. Disappearing like that. Don't do it again."

"Sorry, sir. Of course not. Are you through chewing me out now? Can we get on to other things?"

"Yeah." The general got up and refilled his coffee cup. "Put your thinking caps on, boys and girls, and let's comb through this Barcelona thing step by step again. Lizard, crank up your machines. The answer on who led the attack team is right under our noses. Got to be."

"Hey, everybody!" Coastie came in and grabbed a chair. She had been back in Washington for a day and had already checked in with Trident. "Sorry to be late. Kyle, did you try to take down Torreblanca without me?" Her brightness had returned to full glow.

"What's got you so happy?" Kyle asked.

"Oh, nothing. It's just nice to be home."

Nice to be home? Kyle looked over at Sybelle, who winked at him.

The entire group worked the rest of the day, dissecting the attack and follow-up with the Group of Six and coming up with more questions than answers. That someone had overheard Kyle's call to Torreblanca and timed his own plan to match was impossible. Timing alone would have ruled it out, since Kyle had left only a narrow window of minutes for someone to snatch the information and get into position for the shot.

Benton Freedman tapped his keyboard to call up the reports of the Spanish police, who had found a shooter's position in a narrow trench that had been dug beneath the bushes on the hillside. No brass or other data, no fingerprints, just a hole in the ground and crushed dirt and leaves. "The gardener that you saw had the right tools, so it could easily have been prepared in advance." The Lizard made a note. "A prepared hide."

"I think they also had time to make a ghillie suit, using the exact foliage from his surroundings. He would have been impossible to see," said Swanson. "I didn't ping on the danger until after he fired, and still never actually saw him."

"Any best guess on what kind of weapon was used?"

The Lizard studied the cop report. "Police say they were 7.62 rounds. Fits a lot of rifles."

"AK-47? Plenty of those around," Coastie suggested, fully engrossed in the topic.

"Too much of a precision shot for an AK," said O. O. Dawkins. "They are more for spray-and-pray attacks, not drilling somebody at long range."

"I could do it. Kyle could do it," she challenged him.

There it is again, thought Kyle, smiling inside. That confidence was back.

"I'm not talking about you two space aliens," drawled O. O. Dawkins. "I'm talking about a regular humanoid with basic military skills."

Kyle made his own guess. "A Dragunov with a scope is easy enough to get, if they didn't already have one. Not great, but dependable. Most likely the cops also have found a nice little tunnel trimmed out through the brush, straight toward the target area." He remembered the actual sound of the shots.

They talked for a while about the remaining two live members from the Group of Six and agreed that they were now targets for the mysterious shooter. Both men would realize that and have increased their own protective measures.

"OK, everybody go on home and get some rest," Middleton said. "I'll see you back here tomorrow morning. Meanwhile, I will confirm for the president that we were not involved in this latest shoot, although Swanson was sitting right there and watched it. From what we know, the police have not pinned this on an American, because Swanson only spoke to Torreblanca. Maybe the escort service guy can be traced, but that proves nothing. However, you can bet the president is going to keep us in stand-down rather than risk further exposure."

Nobody moved. "We need a goddam break," the general grumbled. Then he added in a softer tone, "Beth, I wish you would have spoken up sooner about what was going through your head."

"I was afraid that if you knew, you would throw me out of Trident." She locked her blue eyes on him.

"Never happen, and you should know that. We would have helped. We *want* to help. Everyone in our line of work must deal with the demons. We have medical experts who see this all the time."

"I realize that now, sir, but so many emotions are involved, and I was scared. Being able to work with Trident is the best thing I have ever done."

"So you're good?"

"Good to go."

Middleton pushed away from his desk. "Let me know if you want anything. I hope you let us set you up to see a doctor and talk it out. Don't you ever forget, Coastie, we didn't pick you for Trident out of thin air, and nobody gets into our little club unless we want them. You are one of us. We need you and respect you and trust you. Whatever decisions you make, we will be there for you."

ABU DHABI,
UNITED ARAB EMIRATES

THIS HAD TO STOP. Marwan Tirad Sobhi was getting calls and electronic messages that were bringing him to the surface as surely as a steel hook hauling up a sailfish. The sailfish might not want to go up, but did not have that option. Even the media was awakening to the story, with Al Jazeera, the BBC, and the Spanish press leading the charge. The American press ignored the murders because they happened abroad and there was little sign of U.S. involvement, but conspiracy rumors were bouncing all over the Internet.

"Another member of the controversial Group of Six has been assassinated," intoned a blank-faced news reader from London. "The murder of

Daniel Ferran Torreblanca in Seville yesterday has brought to four the number of Islamic-connected financiers who have died in an unexplained series of recent attacks in Spain and France. The Group of Six were creators of a multibillion-euro package of bailout loans designed to assist the Spanish government's economic rescue efforts. That offer was withdrawn earlier this week, following the third murder, that of Mercedes Bourihane in Paris. Police said their investigations were continuing." When the reader took a breath to start another story, Sobhi muted the sound.

He was not taking any calls from the press. Publicity was no friend of a man who made his fortune in the shadows and the corridors of real power. His barrier of aides told almost everyone that he was in conference and could not be disturbed, and they took messages from well-wishers who hoped he was safe. The banker personally contacted leaders throughout the region. They wanted to know more about the killings, but he had little to give them.

There was only one call that Sobhi really wanted to receive, and it had not come. Yasim Rebiane had telephoned him right after the morning meeting with Torreblanca, outraged at the decision to halt the Spanish episode. He described with cold fury how Torreblanca had also insulted him in public. Since then, nothing.

Sobhi was certain in his soul that Djahid Rebiane, not any American, had pulled the trigger on Daniel. It was not for some overarching financial scheme or a change in government, but for old-fashioned revenge. The father had coated the bullets with his poison of hatred, and the son delivered the final message. Sobhi was just as certain that Djahid would do the same to him, if given the opportunity.

Heavily lined curtains were drawn across the windows of his office to prevent anyone from seeing inside, and the sheikh's security people had been put on a higher alert. The police had been asked to participate and they had stationed uniformed men at the doors of the office building and sent marked patrol cars to cruise the streets around his location in Abu Dhabi. When the influential financier grew tired of waiting for Yasim to call, he summoned one of his assistants, a smooth fellow from the

United States who had read his law at Yale University, and told him to pack a bag and get to the airport, where a private plane would be waiting. He would leave soon for Cairo.

WASHINGTON, D.C.

IT WAS DIFFERENT THIS TIME. *Kyle Swanson had been to this place many times before, when the black water of the imaginary swept by with unrelenting force, conquering everything with its roaring tide and hauling the booty to hell. Sound asleep and dreaming, his body felt nailed to the spot on a narrow bloodred beach at the border of a stinking marsh. This was the domain of the Boatman, Charon, the skinny, frightening figure in black rags that waved like pirates' flags, who seemingly could visit Kyle's dreams at will to taunt him about the many deaths on his account. The Boatman's job was to ferry souls into the underworld, but over the years of nightmares, he had mellowed enough to communicate in rhyme and riddle. Swanson really hated the Boatman.*

Yet there he stood once again in his long skiff, idle in the storm, facing Kyle. The steering oar was under one arm, and his eyes glowed. The ruined skull face smiled, and the voice inside Swanson's head said, "My boat is already full tonight, but I can always make room for you."

"Why am I here? I'm not killing anyone." He saw the dead bodies of Cristobál Jose Bello, Juan de Lara, Mercedes Sarra Bourihane, and Daniel Ferran Torreblanca all seated neatly along the benches. "I only did two of those. The woman and that guy in back aren't mine."

A discordant thunder of laughter bellowed from the Boatman. "That doesn't matter tonight. Don't you see?" He waved his ragged sleeve. "Look and see."

"See what? I see you and some corpses, all of you on the way to the nine circles of hell. Big deal. I've seen it before." Kyle put his hands up to shield his face from the tremendous amount of heat searing the water. That was a difference this time. The Styx normally was black and cold and evil, but to-

night it was alive with rolling waves of intense flames that torched the dead bodies in the boat and caused them to scream over the hissing din.

The Boatman was motionless, watching him. His rags caught and burned brightly, but the demon was unaffected. Swanson felt his own flesh start to blister, and he thrashed for freedom. At the far end of the marsh was a little sign in the air, a single green word: EXIT.

"Ha. Now you see, so now you know. Farewell." He spun the oar a little, and the burning hulk moved off along its boiling path, trailing the first screams of the souls heading to everlasting punishment and maybe eventually to Satan himself, who was trapped in the middle of hell, from where even he was unable to escape.

A horn sounded inside his head and Kyle jerked awake, soaked with sweat, swatting at his arms, smelling the stench. He realized that he was not on fire, and he saw rain falling against the windows. Swanson hurried to his balcony, threw open the door, and stepped into the spring shower to wash away the dream. Then he held his arms above his head like a boxer dancing after winning a fight. He saw—*he knew*—just as the Boatman promised.

33

VENICE, ITALY

THE LITTLE SIDEWALK CAFÉ, shaded by old cypress trees and climbing bundles of oleander, was located three bridges away from the Piazza San Marco. The distance was just enough to deter tourists who did not like to walk. Yanis and Djahid Rebiane shared a table at the edge of the stone street, near some gigantic potted plants. The only other customers were a young couple at a table beside a weather-beaten statue. The paving stones were still wet from the previous night's high-tide flood, and almost everyone in the city wore rubber boots to work that morning, changing into regular shoes once at their offices. Both father and son were booted as they sipped tiny cups of *espresso con panna*, double shots of caffeine topped with whipped cream.

"I have been considering ways that we may have our revenge on that pig Marwan Sobhi." Djahid's manner was casual and quiet, appropriate for the morning, but his father knew he was wound tightly.

My son is mentally unstable, he thought, not for the first time. "Good. I agree." Yanis spooned up the thick cream and tasted it while the puttering motor of a passing water bus echoed in the courtyard. "For now, Djahid, we must be careful until we determine what the police and intelligence agencies are doing. Our sources remain active and will stay in contact."

"I am not afraid." Spoken with the bravado of a careless warrior.

The father gave a rueful shake of his head. "I am afraid enough for both of us. Things went well for us in Seville because of a mixture of preparation and surprise and good fortune. After I telephoned Torreblanca with the fake warning, it was obvious that he would be coming out quickly. I just did not expect him to do so immediately. It was fortunate that we had built that sniper's hole for you during the night so that you were in position and ready. There was no time to spare."

Following the morning murder in Spain, they had been able to board an international flight without a problem, and it took them directly to Marco Polo Airport in Venice. They used trains and a private water taxi to reach their hotel by nightfall. Less than twenty-four hours after the assassination of Torreblanca, the Rebianes were more than a thousand miles away, in another country, sipping coffee, just two of the some two hundred thousand visitors who would enter Venice that day.

Djahid pulled up the collar of his light jacket, for the day was still cool and a strong wind stirred the greenery. "How long must we wait, father?"

"As long as it takes, my boy. This is not over. Marwan will tire of the tight protection soon enough. Having to employ guards in plain view is bad for business, for they are a sign of fear. Marwan loves his freedom of movement too much to sustain a long siege."

Djahid raised his cup, licked off some foam, and drank the strong coffee. "What if he acts against us?"

The elder Rebiane was certain that would not happen. He held too much evidence of Marwan's years of corrupt practices, and it was all safely hidden. The scale was in a precarious balance between them, and if neither side moved, it would stay that way. Sheikh Marwan Tirad Sobhi, the shrewd billionaire businessman, would understand the same thing. There was nothing personal in the dispute between the two old acquaintances; this was just business, and time would heal the wound, and life would go on for both of them. In fact, he planned to telephone the sheikh in about a week to be certain both of them were on the same page. He did not plan to tell Djahid about the call, because he would not understand settling of differences without spilling blood. Yasim did not want Sobhi as an enemy. The man had too many resources.

"If he tries anything, then you will kill him," Yasim said, and his son smiled, content for the time being.

WASHINGTON, D.C.

THE MORNING BRIEFING in General Middleton's office did not add much to their base of knowledge, at least during the first hour. The killer who had taken the life of the last Spaniard still had not surfaced in the Lizard's international law enforcement databases, so they chewed around the edges of what they knew some more, getting nowhere slowly.

Swanson chose his words carefully when he told them about something he had realized subconsciously late last night, not wanting to mention the Boatman, his own private specter, to the group, who would think he was nuts. "The thought came to me while I was taking a shower," he said. "I do some of my best thinking in the shower."

"Were you showering alone?" Coastie needled.

He flashed a look to shut her up, then continued. "The First Amendment guarantees us the right of free speech, but it is a limited right; that means you can't shout 'fire' in a crowded theater. I was thinking about how Torreblanca came charging out of his house so fast. I had given him plenty of time to meet me at the café, and the cops were already there. His movement seemed rushed and awkward from where I was in my car. For the sake of this argument, let's suppose he was not coming to see me at all, but was reacting to something entirely different, something more urgent."

Double-Oh was nodding his head, getting the picture straight, thinking tactics. "Maybe somebody was saying his kids were in danger, or another attack was coming his way, to draw him into running."

Kyle had closed his eyes and leaned his head back, trying to get it straight himself. "I had called the private number of the cell phone that I left behind, so the rest of his lines were open."

"You think somebody else called him between the time that you did and the time you got to the house?" Sybelle frowned. "I don't like it, Kyle. We don't do coincidences."

Middleton carelessly sloshed another mug of dark coffee. "No, we don't. But strange shit can happen at any time. Carry on, Gunny Swanson."

"I think he got an emergency call, sir, just like Double-Oh says. And just like anybody sitting in a dark theater munching popcorn and someone yells *'fire,'* he reacted immediately by heading for the green exit sign, to clear out of there as fast as possible."

"Right into the kill zone," said Coastie. "Wow. What a slick move."

Middleton said, "Maybe. That would explain the how." He went back to his big desk. "Still leaves the big question of who, as in who done it, and why?"

They all fell silent for a while, mulling the possibilities in a groupthink of veteran special operators who didn't always need words to communicate. Commander Freedman screwed up his lips, blinked a few times, then spoke. "We have been saying this sniper is a mystery man. Since we are opening up to coincidences, try this: That was the second time our people had been chased away from that hacienda because of a botched operation."

Coastie picked at her fingernail. "First time was when we got the call to abort the mission because our identity had been compromised. Now Kyle has to egress because the cops were about to swarm down on the place following the murder. Same force behind both the leak and the hit?"

Silence again. Kyle said, "It fits. So the dance started with Senator Jordan giving up my name and that of Trident to Yasim Rebiane. And Rebiane is someone to whom Torreblanca would listen in an emergency. He could have made the call in Seville."

They went silent for a minute. Double-Oh asked, "How is that old bastard Monroe, anyway?"

"He's sucking oxygen and morphine in the ICU at Walter Reed, with the FBI parked at his door but not allowed to question him right now. Stable condition, but it could still go either way. Quadruple bypass surgery tomorrow morning." The Lizard had checked his laptop computer. "No help to us."

General Middleton interrupted. "Maybe the senator doesn't have to talk. The Feebs are trying to figure out how to use him anyway, maybe through his administrative aide, the little rat they have in custody as an accomplice."

"Where is he?" asked Swanson.

"Some safe house, probably. Why?"

"Maybe I should talk to him personally. Give him some encouragement to help. Like you said, sir, we need a break."

DOUGLAS JIMENEZ stared across the small table at the meanest-looking man he had ever seen. An open set of handcuffs lay between them, reflecting the fluorescent lights of the tight interview room. There was nothing and no one else in the room, which was bare of shelves and the usual cop junk like dusty computer screens and file boxes. Two blue plastic chairs and one small table on an easy-clean floor. Nothing else, not even a pinhole camera, microphone, recording device, or the obligatory one-way mirror. He had grown used to the austere surroundings of police work in the past few days, but this was extreme.

"Put these on me," the stranger ordered with the tight-lipped grin and the hungry gray-green eyes of a predator who has found easy prey. He wore faded jeans and a loose sports shirt that showed strong muscles in the forearms. "Nice and tight. I want you to feel safe."

"No." Doug held up his hands as if surrendering, trying to make peace. "That won't be necessary. I'm good. Who are you?"

Without another word, the stranger put both hands on his side of the table and violently shoved it into Jimenez so hard that it knocked away the lawyer's breath and toppled him backward out of the chair. He gasped like a fish on a rock as a broken rib radiated a sharp sting in his chest, and his vision reddened.

By the time Doug was able to catch some breathable air again, the man was back in his chair, the table was back in place, and one of the handcuffs was dangling from the stranger's right wrist. "Get back in your chair and sit back down. Now do my other wrist."

Doug struggled up, grabbing the injured and throbbing area, which only made it hurt more. "Goddamn, man, you broke my rib!"

"I used measured and minimal force. It should be just a contusion. Hurts about the same but is not broken. Doesn't matter anyway. Now, if you please, hook me up." The man held out his arms, and Doug reluctantly locked the other cuff in place. Then they both settled back.

It happened instantly. The stranger lunged across the table and looped the handcuffs behind Jimenez's neck and yanked him forward and smashed his own forehead on Doug's exposed nose, which gave way with a snap from the bone-on-bone strike. Pain flooded through Jimenez, the sharpest he had ever felt in his life, and blood poured out of the broken nose, coating his mouth and chin. Without releasing Doug's neck, the man whipped around the table and got behind him, so that the steel handcuffs twisted and became a noose, and then he kicked the plastic chair from beneath Jimenez. It went clattering across the room and bounced off a wall. He let the victim sag downward, pulled by his own weight. Doug's fingers clawed helplessly at the chain that was crushing his throat.

He was allowed to sink all the way to the floor before the man knelt beside him, maintaining enough of a grip with the cuffs to choke off the air, and Douglas Jimenez's eyes bugged from his head as he passed out, certain the last thing he would ever see was the gray-green eyes that were studying him as if he were nothing more than a dust bunny beneath a bed. The last words he heard were, "My name is Gunnery Sergeant Kyle Swanson, you shitbird, and I hear you have been looking for me."

Jimenez slowly regained consciousness on the floor as the room swirled and he gagged. Blood was caked on his hands and had formed a stiff mask on his face and coated his tongue and blocked his nose. He was on his side, so the puke and blood spilled out of his mouth instead of clogging his throat. He was hurt, but he was alive, and heaving to get some air into his starved lungs.

"Get up. You're not hurt." The sharp voice was accompanied by the vise grip of a strong hand that lifted him by the collar, then gave a rough shove to put him back in the chair, and he was back at the table, everything in place again. Swanson moved around to his own chair, fished a key from his pocket, and unlocked the cuffs, putting them once again on the slick table surface.

"That little demonstration was necessary to prove a point without wasting a lot of time. If I can come this close to killing you so easily while in restraints, imagine what I might do with no cuffs on. Back in the day, I learned hand-to-hand combat from a little instructor who really knew his stuff. He was so small, like an elf or something, and looked totally out of place among us badass Marines sitting around him. When he asked for his first volunteer, I made the mistake of standing forward. He whipped my ass for about fifteen seconds, leaving me on the dirt in much the same shape that you are in right now. After that, I became a believer and his best student, and have gone through a lot of even better instructors since then. In other words, I can always find you and kill you in a hundred different ways even before needing to reach a gun. And I can make it pretty painful, you fucking terrorist wannabe."

Jimenez glared blearily at Swanson. "I understand, Gunny. I'm not a terrorist. I have been cooperating to the best of my ability."

Swanson stood and checked his shirt to be certain that it had no bloodstains, then took it off and set it aside. The muscles on his torso stood out in sharp definition. "It would be best if you continue to do so." He balled up his fist and struck Jimenez squarely on the mouth, splitting the lower lip in another shock of pain and sending out another big splash of blood.

"Get it through your thick head that you *are* a terrorist, asshole! Just because you wore a coat and tie and worked on the Hill doesn't make you any different from some raghead on a donkey packed with explosives. You were helping a guy that put six of my fellow Marines in coffins. You revealed classified information that has put more special operators, including me, in danger, and you fucked up a sensitive operation. So I'm giving you a little look into our world."

"Stop! Please stop. Why are you doing this to me? You don't need to beat me up. I'm already helping clear up this mess. Anyway, you are violating my rights as an American citizen!"

A quick twist of the right ear, with Kyle digging his fingernails into the soft flesh, brought another yelp, and Swanson was in his face again. "You don't like me, do you? You want to hurt me like I'm hurting you, but you're too much of a pussy to even try."

"No! Owwww!"

Another twist on the opposite ear, and a spark of anger flared deep within Douglas Jimenez, the part of his mind from the street days reacting. Swanson caught the flicker, and it earned a hard slap that spilled Jimenez from the chair again.

"You don't like me, Doug, and I don't care. In fact, I want you to hate me, to think about me all the time, knowing I'm likely to keep coming back and hurting you on my days off when I have nothing better to do. Fucking piece of horse crap."

Jimenez, on the floor, kicked out, and Swanson stomped on the extended ankle and heard it crack. Jimenez curled into the fetal position, crying and holding his leg. "The only way you can stop me is to kill me, asshole, and you can't do that by yourself. You need big-league help." Swanson walked away and leaned against the smooth wall. A splatter of blood had crossed his chest.

"Here is your only way out. You are going to be asked pretty soon to call the terrorist that your boss had talked to earlier. You will have to do the sales job of your life, because I want him to break cover and try to take me down. Who knows, you and your terrorist buddy might even get lucky. Then I won't be able to slap you around anymore."

Swanson stepped easily across the floor with a leopardlike economy of movement, grabbed Jimenez by the lapels of the orange jail suit, and slammed him against the wall, raising him up on his toes and pressing a knee into his groin. "I want you to hate me as much as I hate you, you little prick. I can see it happening already back there deep in your eyes, the way your mind is shifting from outright groveling fear to a hope of some revenge. You want somebody to bring me down. This is your only chance."

Jimenez spat a gob of blood and mucus on the floor. He had been brutally handled, but that part was over. His ankle and nose were broken, but not his brain. He wiped his face with a sleeve. "Don't you ever hit me again," he warned, and Swanson laughed at him.

Kyle walked to the door, putting on his shirt, certain that the attitude adjustment had been successful.

Doug stared with fury at the man who walked out of the room. Jimenez had always prided himself on his gift of gab; he could talk his way out of tight places, peddle backroom deals for votes, and even make people donate cash to candidates they really did not like. When it came to making deals, he was in his element. So he would make that call to whoever it was, and do his best to paint a target on the back of that fucking Swanson.

CAIRO, EGYPT

ONE CROWD was gathering in Mostafa Mahmoud Square, unrolling its banners beneath cloudless skies and handing out ink-smeared antigovernment leaflets, getting into the spirit of the day's demonstration aimed at forcing the Muslim Brotherhood out of political power. Another crowd, supporting the Brotherhood government, was assembling at the same time in the Sayyida Zeinab area near Garden City. It was nine o'clock in the morning, and by noon the battle would be joined once again in Tahrir Square. It happened frequently, and today showed no indication of any change from the usual useless oratorical thunder from the loudspeakers and a few cracked heads. President Hosni Mubarak had been ousted early in 2011, and Egypt still had not settled into a long-range government. Revolution was still in the air. Both sides remained stridently anti-American.

McKay Bannermann used extreme caution in threading his way from his hotel to the United States Embassy, and he was pleased that the taunting protesters who usually loitered around the area were gone to their respective camps for the demonstrations. At the embassy gate, he put aside the burgundy red German *Reisepass* he was carrying in his hand and retrieved his blue American passport. He was a dual citizen, with a parent from each nation. Bannermann was an attorney who had been in private practice in Abu Dhabi for many years, but his only real client was Marwan Tirad Sobhi and the billionaire's myriad interests.

Once past the exterior guards, he avoided the lines of people who were there on regular embassy business and spoke to a young man in a blue blazer and tan slacks, the so-called cultural attaché who had been expecting him. In less than ten minutes, Bannermann was easing his soft bulk into a chair across from a resident agent of the Central Intelligence Agency. The faux diplomat had perfect black hair and a square jaw, and Bannermann was delighted to see the Yale diploma on the office wall. Since he had one of those himself, that got them off to a good start, mutually loathing the Harvard Crimson.

In his unexpectedly high-pitched voice, the attorney said, "My client sent me to pass along a piece of vital intelligence information to you. I will be brief."

"I'm listening, Mr. Bannermann."

"Ordinarily, I would invoke client-attorney privilege, but in this case, my client has authorized the release of his name. He is Marwan Tirad Sobhi. You probably knew that before I sat down here."

CIA did not react other than with the bland offer, "Would you like a drink?"

Bannerman waved it away. "As you are also aware, the sheikh was a member of the ill-fated Group of Six that attempted to give the Spanish government a different option during its economic crisis."

"They tried to buy a way in for the Muslims."

Bannerman ignored the jibe. "A series of deadly murders decimated the Group after the American Consulate in Barcelona was attacked."

CIA pursed his lips as if in thought. "Is that right?"

The lawyer was just as relaxed, for he was only a messenger. He opened his briefcase and removed a note. On it was written the names of Djahid and Yanis Rebiane. He gave it to the CIA agent. "These are the two men who were directly responsible for Barcelona, and they acted without the authorization from the others in the Group. Djahid is a very dangerous man and actually led the ground attack. Yasim, his father, planned it. It is probable that they also killed Mr. Torreblanca when he canceled the Spanish project."

The CIA man realized Yanis Rebiane was one of the two remaining members of the Group of Six, and he had vanished. Marwan Sobhi was giving them both up, which indicated the Rebianes perhaps did murder Torreblanca and the sheikh did not want to become another notch on the gun of Djahid. "How solid is this, McKay? Do you have photos of these two?"

The attorney gave a lopsided smile. "Extremely solid. The sheikh would not be at all displeased if Yasim and his son, who is truly a mad dog, encountered some unfortunate luck, and the sooner the better. I've never seen a picture of Djahid Rebiane. You should have many of Yasim."

"Does your man know where they are?" He was not ready to bet a lot of chips on Sobhi's word. The CIA had taken a serious black eye from a similar walk-in kook called "Curveball" during the run-up to Iraq. The more information that could be gleaned, the better.

"Unfortunately, no. If you give me a number, I will notify you immediately should we hear anything new."

"That's not going to be good enough, McKay. No matter what the movies say, we don't have electronic trackers on everybody in the world. We need to get these mutts out in the open."

"I will take that request back with me. Perhaps the sheikh can reach out to friends for assistance." He picked up his briefcase, ready to leave, but the Agency man had one more question.

"So what does your guy want in exchange for us getting the Rebianes off his back? Nothing comes free from a lawyer." CIA was willing to give up a few bricks of cash, but Marwan Sobhi was already richer than the average American teenaged dot.com gazillionaire, so that wouldn't be effective.

"Why, nothing at all!" The lawyer protested as if shocked at the very idea of doing something like this with a price tag attached. "He always stands ready to help his American friends."

Neither of them believed that for a moment. This was a situation of convenience. The sheikh was adroitly recruiting the Americans to stab his former friend Yanis Rebiane in the back before this Djahid Rebiane muscle could silence Sobhi. It was the worst kind of deal in the Middle

East: a favor owed, to be collected at some future date. CIA took it in a heartbeat.

ANNANDALE, VIRGINIA

DOUGLAS JIMENEZ rubbed his sore face. For what he had endured, there was little external damage. The Feebs had asked no questions about the private session with Swanson, but gave him two mild painkillers that also contained a special brew of a relaxant that took off just enough of an edge to keep him under control while leaving him wide awake. He had no idea how long he had been in custody.

Senator Jordan, according to the FBI agents, was still in the intensive care unit at Walter Reed Hospital. His physical condition should have been improving, but the man seemed to have lost his will to live. The hospital reported two flatline incidents the night before that required the crash carts to pull him back from the brink, only to have the doctors discover an unexpected buildup of fluid in the lungs. They said his condition was critical, and he was being sustained by machines that breathed for him, pumped nutrients directly into his veins, and evacuated his bladder and bowels. Adding to the misery were drug-induced hallucinations that made him mumble and thrash. When the senator's wife had come down from New York to see her hospitalized husband, she had been informed that he was a suspect in a national security matter and was taken in for some questioning herself. She returned to Manhattan as soon as possible. His mistress and their daughter stayed away, hating him for putting them in grave danger because of one of his schemes. Once one of the most powerful men in Washington, Monroe now faced eternity all alone, and nobody cared.

That included Doug Jimenez, who had hooked his own career wagon to the senator's rising star, only to have it turn out to be nothing but a piece of falling space junk. His own dreams had evaporated, and he just wanted this whole thing to be done, so he could get the hell out of Washington and never talk to another politician or cop or Swanson as long as he lived. The best way out—the only way—was the deal offered by the FBI. As a lawyer, he bargained for a while, jacking up the payout to $250,000, then looked over the fine print closely and signed his name. He imagined his future shingle hanging on a little office somewhere in Oregon, where he would conduct a practice based on a low-profile lawyer's best friends: WILLS & TRUSTS & PERSONAL INJURY. Anything else would have dire consequences.

After that, they became best friends, Doug and his agents. They let him walk around in the daylight, then they served him a good lunch, let him watch a little TV, take a shower, and put on fresh clothes, and gave him plenty of easy time to climb back into his skin after the harrowing experience. He was shocked to find that he had been in custody for less than forty-eight hours.

When they gave him a script to follow for his talk with Yanis Rebiane, Jimenez read it and exclaimed, "Who the hell is Catherine Elizabeth Ledford?"

"You don't need to know that," said the agent. "Just spill her name along with Swanson's. Call her Beth."

"I'm getting fucked over by you guys for disclosing Swanson as a so-called secret special operator, and now you want me to give away both him and another one? That ain't hardly fair."

The agent cocked a dark eyebrow. "Life ain't fair, Dougie. You have to give Rebiane something he does not already have, and that is confirmation of Kyle's position, and the additional prize of Beth Ledford. No sweat, pal. It's all part of the plan."

"God. A government plan. What could go wrong?" he whispered to himself, exasperated, then began to edit the script down to a couple of main talking points, arguing that he had to sound extemporaneous. Any script would sound stilted and false. "I did this bullshit for a living, man," he protested to the agents. "I have to be offhand to make it believable. He has to believe that I'm legit before he buys anything from me. It's Telemarketing 101."

"OK, then. Let's do it," said the agent. Recorders were in place, as were tracking devices, and Doug held a familiar private cell phone. His own. The agents went into an adjacent room, able to communicate on a computer screen that Jimenez could read. No outside noise could distract the parties involved. "Dial the number. Make this dude a believer, Dougie."

There was the flutter of an international ringtone, then a second one, and Yanis Rebiane recognized the calling number. "Senator Monroe," he said smoothly.

"No, sir. This is Doug Jimenez, Senator Monroe's chief of staff. I am afraid that I have bad news. The senator has been hospitalized with a heart attack. The doctors say he will live but is in for a long recovery. I spoke to him in the intensive care unit, and he said that you and I need to talk."

"I don't know you." Yanis did not hang up. Anyone tracking the call could only discover that the phone was somewhere in the busiest part of Venice, the popular area around Piazza San Marco and the majestic St. Mark's Basilica. Thousands of tourists were milling about, and cruise ships disgorged more by the hour. He would give this man a minute, no more.

"But I know you, Mr. Rebiane. The senator has taken me into his confidence since I had been doing the legwork for him on some, uh, military matters that you discussed."

"What are you talking about, Mr. Jimenez? I am just a contributor to the senator's campaigns. We have met exactly one time, and it concerned agricultural issues in Missouri. I regret his illness, but I know nothing about anything to do with the military."

Doug sighed enough to be heard on the phone. "Let us just say that our interests are exactly the same, sir, and I will be running the senator's office during his absence. It is important for constituents like yourself to understand that anything he could do for you, I can do instead, everything but vote."

Rebiane still had not hung up, so Doug felt he was almost home. "For instance, I can confirm now that as the senator advised earlier, the commodities trader Kyle Swanson is indeed the man handling the operations for Trident Manufacturing, including its international work in Spain."

"I suspected that already, Mr. Jimenez. So it is not information that my business would find useful."

A brief message came up on the computer screen: HE IS IN ITALY. Doug silently raised his fist in anticipated victory, and the agents silently applauded behind the glass window to encourage him. *Now. Ring the bell.*

"I also have the name of his partner. Would that be of interest?"

There was a dramatic pause in the conversation as Rebiane found a pen and a piece of paper. "Yes. Very much."

"Surprisingly for that line of work, it is a woman. Catherine Elizabeth Ledford. She goes by the name of Beth." The computer screen put up a new word, VENICE.

Rebiane scribbled the name. "Do you know where I can find them? Where are they?"

"I can probably obtain the location, sir." *Make him want it. Ask for money. Make a deal.* "It may be an expensive and time-consuming endeavor, however. They will not be listed in any, uh"—*pause, struggle for an appropriate word*—"conventional databanks, like a telephone book or *Who's Who in America.*"

Small laugh. "I see. That can be arranged. I appreciate your call, Mr. Jimenez. It was timely because this number will no longer be in service after today, so I shall have someone contact you at your office soon."

"That works. Good to speak with you, sir."

"Please give the senator my best wishes for a speedy recovery." He hung up and stepped between two shops to join the mingling customers along the covered stone walkway of the Rialto Bridge, from which he tossed his phone into the Grand Canal.

WASHINGTON, D.C.

A WEEK PASSED following the Jimenez call to Rebiane in Venice, then another, and no one showed up at the senator's office to meet with the aide. There were no telephone calls, no contact at all. Meanwhile, the senator was being kept alive at the hospital by machines, because letting him die was out of the question if Doug Jimenez was to maintain legitimate importance. The FBI covered both of them night and day, but it appeared that the bad guys were not going to step forward.

Rebiane had been traced to Venice but had vanished again. There was no point in sending a Trident team to the water-laced city if there was no target there. The Rebianes could still be there, or they could have left by train, plane, or boat after the call. As days passed without further contact, the suspects could be anywhere in the world.

Swanson padded along the Rock Creek path at a comfortable pace, trying to fit things together, and was drawing a blank. The sheikh in Abu Dhabi who had given up the identities of Yanis and Djahid Rebiane to the CIA in Egypt became a dry well as far as further information. Agency watchers reported that Marwan Sobhi had even reduced his security presence, moved about freely, and was maintaining a normal schedule. To Kyle, that indicated Sobhi no longer felt afraid, which led to the conclusion that a deal had been struck between the final two members of the infamous Group of Six: You don't bother me, and I won't bother you.

One sure thing was that Task Force Trident was done with the Spain operation. It had been a political and diplomatic scandal waiting to happen if they had been caught shooting Spanish civilians. Four of the Group of Six paymasters had been killed, one not by Trident hands, and now with summer approaching, the rioters in Madrid would have better weather in which to argue about many other things. Their livelihood trumped any other concerns.

Kyle had done the best that he could do for Mike Dodge, but the helium was obviously leaking out of the balloon, and the operation was fizzling to an incomplete conclusion.

As Swanson's thoughts drifted, he found himself watching the water in the big rowdy creek as it poured over huge boulders and rushed along its shaded corridor in one of the most beautiful settings around the District. It was also among the most polluted and bacteria-ridden brooks in the nation, taking in metropolitan sewage overflows and other repugnant matter. Like so much else in Washington, what looked serene and trouble-free could kill you. He loped along, one foot in front of another in easy strides, rolling off six kilometers and deciding that would not be enough today. He had started on the neat stones near his Georgetown apartment, then hit the Rock Creek Trail, and now swung off onto the well-kept C&O Canal path and headed south into wilderness, letting the workout smooth out his frustration.

We're not going to find these Rebiane guys if they don't come out of hiding, he thought. Terrorism elsewhere had not come to a stop just because this evil pair had returned to the shadows. Iraq was a bombing range for warring religious sects. Afghanistan was like supergum stuck to Uncle Sam's boots. American troops were still dying over there, and Kyle thought he probably should go back to MARSOC for a period of active duty gun work. He doubted if Middleton would approve that.

He was sweating harder, feeling the sun on his back and shoulders. The next Green Light package could come down at any moment, and there had been some chatter about a new warlord in Africa that was stoking his army of kids with dope, giving them machetes, and turning them loose in harmless villages to chop wildly and yell "God is great!" The reality was that as the harsh spotlight that had been on the Rebianes dimmed, the FBI and the CIA would slide the matter down to a lesser importance as newer cases came in.

In his logical mind, where he tried to think like the enemy, Swanson still thought they had presented a gift that the killers would not pass up. This was a rare chance for them to bring down the pair of American special operators who had wrecked their dreams of a new caliphate anchored in Spain. It was a matter of pride. Then again, maybe they weren't as good as originally thought and did not have the ability to track Coastie and Kyle into a kill zone. A deal-sweetener might be needed. He thought, *Come to us, guys. Take your best shot. Let's finish this.*

The cell phone clipped to his running shorts began to chime, and he trotted to the shade of a grove of trees, catching his breath as he flipped it open. The digital ID showed that Beth Ledford was calling from Mexico. "Yo," he said.

"Kyle!" Coastie was screaming, laughing, and crying all at the same time. Drunk? In trouble? Had they gotten to her?

"What? What's wrong?" He went from casual to business in a heartbeat.

"Nothing's wrong. Absolutely nothing! Mickey and I are going to get married!"

WASHINGTON, D.C.

SHE MET with General Middleton a few days after returning from Mexico to turn in her resignation papers. "I am happy for you, Petty Officer Ledford," he said, sounding as if he had a rock in his throat. "May your marriage to Captain Castillo be as happy as mine."

"Thank you, sir. It wasn't an easy choice for me. I just could not be Mickey's wife and run with Trident at the same time. A bihemispherical global relationship can't work. I had to choose."

"Understood. Well, I will put through the papers with a glowing recommendation for your personnel jacket, which will remain top secret. You've been a hell of an operator, and your shooting talent is incredible."

"I plan to be a hell of a Mrs. Castillo, too."

"It will take a few weeks for this separation work to clear the paper-pushers, Ledford, because you are still under deep cover. Unfortunately, that means that you can't send out engraved invitations and put your name out in public."

"Yes, sir. Mickey and I talked about that. He will stay in the service, but Beth Ledford will just vanish. Since we will get married down in Mexico, where I'm unknown, I will start using my first name and become Catherine Castillo. The Lizard says he can work with State and CIA to line up my new identity with a passport, driver's license, and some other papers in that name to get me out of the memory banks here. Then I'll slow down my life."

The general had his hands on his hips, watching her closely. So much talent in such a little package. She was good people. "You gave us three good years, Coastie. I couldn't ask for any more. Thanks for a job well done."

"Thank you for giving me the chance and believing in me, General."

ANOTHER MONTH EXPIRED, and on the final night of Ledford's military career the team met for a good-bye dinner and drinks in a Georgetown pub. The Rebianes still had not raised their heads.

Middleton, Summers, Freedman, Dawkins, and Swanson raised shot glasses brimming with good tequila and chanted a loud toast, "To Coastie!" They knocked them back, slapping the little glasses back on the bar for refills. Beth Ledford raised a glass of her own and countertoasted, "Right back at you!"

They were around a tall table in the bar area, with a piano playing show tunes in the background, waiting for the karaoke to begin at ten o'clock. Each wore casual civilian clothes, and Coastie looked radiant in her tight jeans and a trendy green cotton top from her recent shopping jaunt in Paris. Despite the celebratory mood, the Tridents were also glum: Losing Coastie back to the world, even in a wedding to a guy they all liked, was almost as bad as losing her in action. Either way, the lively spirit that she brought to her job was going to be missed. That was military life, and the machine would move on, no matter how individuals stepped off the train.

"Don't you think being a June bride at a resort is kind of a cliché?" Master Gunny O. O. Dawkins called across the table. "How about you jumping out of a plane and saying the vows on the way down? Make it memorable."

"Oliver," she replied, using his hated first name for emphasis. She no longer had to call anybody by their ranks. "That is, like, so stupid. Anyway, the wedding is in July, not June." They talked a while about unusual weddings, and after a few more drinks, the music changed, a microphone was brought out and a spotlight came on, and the karaoke began. Benton Freedman got up and started a country song with a surprisingly smooth baritone. Sybelle darted up next to him to make it a duet, an unlikely Willie and Waylon, and they breezed through "Mama, Don't Let Your Babies Grow Up to Be Cowboys."

Kyle Swanson sat back in the slender chair with a boozy grin on his face and a small hole in his heart as he listened to them croon about smoky old pool rooms, faded jeans, warm puppies, and clear mountain mornings; his life. He had talked with Lady Pat and Sir Jeff earlier in the day, and they wanted to pay for the entire wedding, anything Coastie wanted. Then Pat berated him. "You let a real winner get away this time, Kyle. This is all on you. All you had to do was show your feelings, just for a moment. A real smile would have done it. You can be such a shit sometimes. You are a hateful and disappointing boy, and I will never have grandchildren."

Mickey Castillo was a good friend. He and Coastie would be good for each other. Kyle understood her, though, understood her better than anybody else, probably. They had communicated without speaking during the long hours together on watch, as they had done in Seville. He trusted her with his life; she trusted him. He was the best sniper around; she had the potential to become just as good. She was beautiful and young and full of life, but she wanted more than he could ever give. Why start, why give hope when there was none?

"What?" snarled Dawkins. "You look like a tank just ran over your kitten."

"Fuck you and have another drink," Swanson snapped back. He realized his face was giving away some feeling. Not allowed.

Coastie spun around at the growl from Double-Oh and caught Kyle's somber look; she registered shock but recovered quickly, her cheeks flushed red. She bit her lip slightly, that unconscious little thing she did when nervous, one of those things that nobody else ever noticed. She leaned close and grabbed his arm and looked deep into his soul. "Hey. Still BFF, right?"

She had declared them to be best friends forever after their first mission together, infiltrating and taking down a terrorist fortress in Pakistan. He eased his hand over hers. "Yep. BFF, partner. Till the wheels fall off the wagon."

The song had reached the part about always being alone, even with someone you love. "Did you know the Liz could sing like that?" Coastie asked, trying desperately to change the subject and talk about anything other than what they were both really thinking at that moment.

Kyle raised his beer bottle to the sweet face. Could have been worse. Willie also sang "Blue Eyes Crying in the Rain." He couldn't take that one right now. He would later remember this moment as the instant that he dropped his self-pity and hatched the idea. She would never be his girlfriend, his lover, or his wife, but she was his field partner, and a damned good one.

"Hey, Cinderella," he called over to her, suddenly excited as the song ended and Sybelle and Liz rejoined them. "Sorry, but your pumpkin is going to be a bit late tonight." Kyle motioned for them all to lean in close over the table. "We can use this wedding to get to the Rebianes, if Coastie agrees to stay on the payroll just a little longer."

She flared, as he knew she would. "I'm not postponing my wedding, Kyle. Forget it. Don't start being a jerk."

"Just the opposite. We *want* it to go ahead on schedule. The thing that may have been keeping the Rebianes from making a move is they are not sophisticated enough to track us down in the United States. We overestimated their ability once we wrecked their network. The wedding is a chance for us to guarantee that both of us will be in the same spot, on the same day, at the same time. It's an assassin's dream!"

"You want to turn her wedding into a shooting gallery?" Even Sybelle was stunned, and her cheeks grew rosy with indignation.

"I want to turn it into a trap."

"That's too harsh, Kyle," the Lizard said. "Even for us."

All eyes swung to Coastie, who took a sip of beer as she thought it over. She rubbed a rim of suds from her upper lip. "I kinda like it," she said. "One last job. A day to remember."

"You're both insane," Brad Middleton said. "Let's do it."

CONSTANTINE, ALGERIA

HOME. SAFE. Yanis Rebiane had exchanged one city of bridges, Venice, for another, although the bridges that spanned the Rhumel River and the deep ravine of Constantine dwarfed the little footpaths of the Italian tourist town. He had been born on this mountain plateau, and he was safe because he was a good friend of the president of Algeria, who, although elected to office, ran the country like a dictator. Enemies of Islam never had an easy time here.

Yanis and Djahid had left Venice not long after he had thrown the cell phone into the water. International law enforcement would have used the telephone signal to at least put some agents on the ground, although any search would be fruitless. They could search every gondola and never find a trace, and now even that tenuous chance had evaporated. The police had nothing. If they wanted to try this fortress, well, let them come.

He had been certain from the moment he began talking with the senator's aide that it was a setup. Making the deal for the secret information had been too easy. Everybody bargains, but the abrupt young man had been too nervous by far. It would have been foolish to buy into his game.

The fact that Senator Monroe had a heart attack was not a concern. If he died, whatever he knew would not matter. Even if he lived, Yanis would never contact him again. Plus, the Spanish operation had collapsed totally, leaving only a tenuous peace with the sheikh. The senator's usefulness was done, but Yanis would never forget what had happened with Marwan; he would get even someday, but for now, it was time to move on.

"The major thing the fellow gave up was proof that the United States was behind the response to our victory in Barcelona," he said. "Why else would anyone in Washington have pursued us?"

Djahid was also happy to be back in the home near the cliffs. He let his bare feet grope the softness of the large Berber rug that had been woven by some unknown women in the Sahara more than a hundred years ago. He wore torn jeans and a favorite black T-shirt bearing the logo of a German beer company. "Are you going to need me around for safety now that we're back?"

His father drank mint tea from a glass with a gilt border and tried a cookie made with rosewater. The weather was just beginning to feel like summer on the plateau, and he was also in casual clothes. "No one is coming after us."

"Are we going after them? To follow up those names the caller gave? I really want to kill those two people."

The cookie tasted somewhat bitter. He put it down and tried another, which had a sweet lemony taste and was better. "Of course, sometime in the future, but on a timetable of our own making. Right now they are expecting a strike. Let things go calm for a while and Americans always lose interest. This Task Force Trident is obviously a secret military organization, so information on its personnel will be classified, but they had to be born somewhere, educated somewhere, and have lived somewhere before they went into the military. We can spend some time and money to hire computer hackers and private detectives to work on the records. They eventually will turn up a mention somewhere; there is always a hole in a cover story."

"So I can go hunting for a while, and you can call me when they are found? Don't leave me out of this, father. They must be mine." Djahid loved Africa for many reasons, because he could hunt without repercussions. The feeling of such freedom filled his soul. Conflict and war had watered the sand and jungles of the dark continent forever, and his services as a mercenary were always in high demand. All he had to do was put out the word that he was back in the game, and he would have all the work he could handle. His quarry was never lions and elephants, which he considered little more than livestock. Djahid hunted humans.

Yanis knew he was setting a killer free to roam, but understood that the boy needed it, and rationalized that the bloodletting would help him stay sharp. Who knew what the future held?

"The Americans are too pushy, as always. They want this thing done and that thing done in such a hurry, stumbling toward a finish line that is not really there." He watched through the big window as a flock of birds burst from the crowded pines and eucalyptus, dotting the cloudless sky. "We think in terms of centuries, so take your time. I will summon you when an opportunity arises."

FROM THE *GAZETTE*

***Local target-shooting** legend Catherine Elizabeth Ledford, daughter of the late Stephen and Margaret Ledford, will be married next month to Captain Miguel Francisco Castillo of the Mexican Marine Corps.*

The Gazette *followed the many exploits of the little sharpshooter from the time she won a turkey shoot when she was only eight years old, in competition with hunters from all over the county. Other publications and television shows also ran profile pieces on the "Kossuth County Annie Oakley."*

"Beth is amazing with firearms," remembers Deputy Sheriff Bill Turner, who attended school with Ms. Ledford and received a formal invitation to the wedding. "She was hands down the best shot I ever saw, and I have seen plenty. Throw a quarter in the air at fifty yards and she can nail it on the fly and give you change. You can't teach that. Great family, too."

Her brother was the well-known Dr. Joey Ledford, who was killed in Pakistan several years ago while leading a medical relief mission.

Her mother and father owned Ledford Dairy Products near Algona. As Beth's reputation spread from winning competitions, they became wary of the impact that national publicity was having on their young daughter, so they put a stop to public exhibitions. Instead, they hired coaches to prepare her to compete for a spot on the Olympic Shooting Team. "That was absolutely the right thing to do," said Deputy Turner. "TV today would have eaten that kid alive."

Upon her father's death, Beth joined the United States Coast Guard, which trained her to become a sniper. She and Captain Castillo met in the course of their duties. The ceremony will be held in the groom's hometown of Mazatlán in Mexico.

Bill Turner said the new couple's military background will be on full review at the wedding, according to a personal note she sent along with the invitation: Her boss, U.S. Marine Major General Bradley Middleton, will give her away; her co-worker Marine Lieutenant Colonel Sybelle Summers will be her maid of honor, and a combined honor guard of Marines from the United States and Mexico will include their mutual friend Gunnery Sergeant Kyle Swanson, a holder of the Congressional Medal of Honor.

The Gazette *and all of Kossuth County wishes happiness to*

Captain Castillo and Beth, our hometown girl who grew up to serve her country so well.

The wire services picked up the story in abbreviated form, along with area television news programs, and inevitably it was filed on the Internet. The Lizard planted similar wedding news in other media.

WASHINGTON, D.C.

JORDAN MONROE died during the day shift at Walter Reed, despite heroic efforts of medical personnel and exotic machines to keep him breathing. He had withered away in the bed and was down to only a hundred pounds, not much more than skin over a skeleton, and the physical body finally just could not sustain the punishment. He never regained consciousness from the coma that followed his heart attack, and with one final lurch and a deep exhalation of breath that sounded like a prolonged burp, the senior senator from Missouri died.

"So what do we do now?" Douglas Jimenez was locked in the senator's private office with his usual FBI special agents, Jim Lassiter and Ron Martin. "The governor will be appointing an interim senator to serve out the term, and he will bring in his own staff."

Martin appeared comfortable, leaning back and eating a bag of M&M chocolate pellets. Lassiter still had the wicked grin that was his trademark. "Don't need you anymore, Dougie, that's for sure. Monroe is dead, and there goes your clout. The bad guys haven't made contact with you since we started the game, so they probably are not going to."

"Can you phrase that another way, Jim? It sounds like you're going to kill me."

"You watch too much television. Most often, we don't kill people who have helped us, and you played your part."

Jimenez remained very still, wary of a trick. "You mean I'm out of this mess?"

"Yep. We came to tell you the good news personally. It was a good idea, but the terrorists apparently were spooked by Monroe's heart attack and decided to fold their tents. We want you to handle the funeral arrangements and volunteer to stay on until the new appointment is made."

"Then," added Martin, crunching a cheekful of candy, "you get out of this fucking town. Go away and never come back. We have neither forgotten nor forgiven that you are a traitor, but a deal is a deal."

"You good with that, Dougie? We all clear?" He handed over a business card bearing the name of a woman in the U.S. Marshals Service. "Here's the person taking over now. Call her and she will help you move on the quiet. They are the professionals at this sort of relocation. You will not be in protective custody."

"What about my start-over money?"

"She will cut you a check."

They both stood up. Martin wadded up the empty yellow wrapper and flipped it onto the big desk. "I wish you only bad luck in the future, Jimenez." The two agents left the ornate office without shaking hands or looking back.

AFRICA

THE MESSAGE FROM FATHER had arrived three days ago, while Djahid Rebiane was working in the Sudan with a splinter group within the Sudanese Revolutionary Front, the latest political force in that sad country. The undisciplined men and boys were supplied with Russian arms and trained by foreign mercenaries like himself. Sudan, South Sudan, and the Sudanese Revolutionary Front and its politics were equally meaningless to Djahid; he was only there for the buzz.

An entire village was in flames, and the government rescue unit had been ripped apart in an ambush that Djahid had directed on that sweltering July morning. He had been behind a .50 caliber machine gun mounted on a battered Toyota pickup, the normal cheap striking arm of any African guerrilla movement, and had his shirt off and a bandanna around his head in the heat, screaming with delight as he laid down a hurricane of big bullets that devastated his targets, which was anybody and anything he didn't recognize as an ally. Civil war was wonderful.

He returned to base camp with the smell of roasting flesh still clinging to his nostrils. Djahid found a burly young black man waiting, having come all the way from Khartoum to hand over a phone and say there was a video message on it. Djahid poured a bucket of water over his head and wiped his face clear of most of the dust, then walked into the jungle until he was alone. He turned on the phone and called up the video message.

A picture of his father appeared, and Djahid was pleased that he looked well. The voice message was brief. "Greetings, my son. Your holiday is over. Get to Mexico City as soon as possible, and more details will be waiting at the Four Seasons. A suite is booked there under the German alias. Our patience has paid off."

Djahid walked back and threw the telephone into a campfire and stayed to watch it burn. He had been in the bush almost a month and was ready for something new. The raids and training illiterate children as fighters were getting tiresome, almost routine. He yearned for a clean bed, fresh food, and new challenges, and his father was indicating that something important was waiting in Mexico. It must be the Americans. Finally, time to settle things with them.

He left for Khartoum the next morning, clean-shaven and looking like the man in his German passport, Hans Böhm, a weathered freelance magazine photojournalist.

The next leg of the trip took him from Khartoum to the rancid capital of Lagos, where there was not a blip of alert as he passed through the laughable security checks of the steamy Murtala Muhammed International Airport. His biggest concern had been facial recognition software, but not even the air-conditioning worked well, much less any sophisticated computer software that might combat terrorists. Terrorists had little to fear from Nigerian authorities. With his fake passport and a few well-placed bribes that were openly expected, he elbowed through the swarm of passengers in the departures terminal, knocked over a clumsy pickpocket, and settled down in the private lounge to await the Arik Air flight to Johannesburg. He had no luggage, since it probably would have been looted anyway, and he would buy what he needed as he went along, including some camera gear.

Because he had been cleared in Lagos, he was considered in-transit in Joburg and did not have to go through customs, as long as he did not leave the security bubble during the layover. South African authorities were far more efficient and dangerous to him than those in Lagos, so he waited for a few hours, reading, until he could board a Lufthansa Dreamliner flight. It took him directly to Caracas, Venezuela, another democratic republic that terrorists did not fear. From there, it was simple to get to Mexico City and the next message.

ABOARD THE *VAGABOND*

"NO! WE WILL NOT postpone our wedding again. We already pushed it back to August instead of July. I put off my resignation. Enough is enough." Coastie's arms were crossed, the big eyes defiant. Seated at her side, Mickey Castillo, the silent type, agreed. "No," he said.

Lady Pat and Sir Jeff had brought their luxury yacht to Mexico for the nuptials, and they were all on an afternoon cruise. Pat put a hand on the shoulder of her husband in his wheelchair. "Told you so." She took a sip of her drink.

Carlos and Alita Castillo, the parents of the groom, had never seen anything like this. They were enjoying the hospitality aboard an elegant vessel that rode so easily on the warm waters of the Gulf of Mexico, but were totally confused and somewhat afraid of what was going on around them. Their son's wedding was going to include women and men with guns.

They knew Mickey was in military special operations with the Infantería de Marina, but he had only last night revealed that their future daughter-in-law was an elite American military operative whose resignation would become effective the day after the wedding. The little blonde had given them a dazzling smile in confirmation. Carlos and Alita could not believe it; such a sweet and pretty girl? "I'm not going to do that any-more . . . after this," she said. "I promise. I love your son, and making him happy is going to be my full-time job."

Aboard the white yacht, they had met the rest of what she called her "other family," a unit called Task Force Trident. There was a friendly two-star U.S. Marine general with cropped dark hair and a thick mustache, and another huge man with the unusual name of Double-Oh Dawkins, who had a rank they did not understand. The impressive woman officer in the American Marines was Sybelle Summers, a lieutenant colonel, and an officer in the U.S. Navy who wore thick glasses was Commander Benton Freedman. The quietest man was Kyle Swanson, who had shadows in his sharp eyes. Then there was the British couple that owned the yacht, Sir Geoffrey Cornwell and his wife, Lady Patricia. Seeing them all together, and feeling their combined strength, the Castillos understood that for her to have been working with these people, she must have been just as Mickey described.

For reasons they did not understand, they called Freedman "Liz" and Beth "Coastie." She was not cowed when some of the men suggested putting off the wedding that was inexorably rushing toward them all. Her refusal had been firm. The marriage was going forward on schedule.

The gruff general spoke. "Coastie, we have not received any information that our quarry is on the way. I just wanted you and the captain to consider giving it a little more time, just another four weeks."

Mickey, holding Coastie's hand, objected. "We are ready now. It is better to force their hand rather than let them have second thoughts. We control the time and place for the fight if they choose to try a hit."

Lady Pat moved over and leaned back against the railing alongside Alita Castillo, who had been bewildered by the idea that the wedding was also a careful trap to try to snare a couple of murdering terrorists. The entire rear deck was shaded by an awning. "I agree with Beth. The planning has been a staggering load for the event organizers, who have it all timed to the minute. Everything is ready, including a beautiful bride with a beautiful gown and a handsome groom who will be in uniform with medals and gold braid. We can't just call it off."

Kyle Swanson cleared his throat. "Zero security problem," he said. "We're ready."

"Let them come. We are not going to live our lives in fear of some crazy terrorists," Beth snapped.

Sybelle said, "Beth and Mickey deserve the wedding they want. Nothing has happened since the last action in Seville. The CIA tracked them to Algeria, and snippets of intelligence put them in Yasim's home village of Constantine. He is unreachable there. The dangerous one, Djahid, dropped off the map entirely. Best guess is he is the one who will take the shots." Summers resumed thinking about how hot she was going to look in that maid-of-honor frock.

Double-Oh felt like he was the father of Beth Ledford, and by God, he wanted to give her what she wanted and keep her safe. He remained a rock of silent resolve; nobody was going to hurt these kids if he had anything to do with it. The Lizard also was quiet in a chair, thinking about the electronic net he had thrown over the event.

Sir Jeff wheeled over to Beth and took her free hand. "So we stay on schedule, and you two concern yourselves only with that wonderful half of this event. The other stuff is covered by professionals. Normal life must go on, despite the actions of a few mad criminal bastards. Their sort will always be with us. The whole Trident team is here, plus our friends in the Mexican Marines and the police. We could not ask for more."

Jeff twirled the chair around. "Look, my friends. We're gathered to celebrate a wedding. Now. More champagne!"

MEXICO CITY, MEXICO

DJAHID REBIANE, alias journalist Hans Böhm, had a small Federal Express package waiting for him at the front desk when he checked into the Four

Seasons Hotel in the Paseo de la Reforma district. The clerk made small talk while the guest completed the forms and handed over his passport and told her he was exhausted and in dire need of a cheeseburger, fries, and sleep. A warm shower, room service, and a bed, and then tomorrow, he said, he would be ready to start work. The assignment was for *National Geographic*.

The room was elegant with an understated light green decor, and Djahid had not been lying to the clerk; he really did want a bath, burger, and bed. The package could wait until he was fresh enough to give it his full attention. He called room service and not only ordered the meal for now but preordered breakfast for tomorrow morning, along with a full kit of shaving and dental care gear. He put his clothes in a bag to be cleaned and laundered and returned by 6:00 A.M. Then he turned the air conditioner to maximum strength and the shower to medium warm. Djahid was sprawled on the king-sized bed in the white hotel robe and almost snoring before the cheeseburger arrived.

He awoke the next morning to a polite knock at his door for the breakfast and clothing delivery, and it took him a moment to remember where he was. Mexico City. Hans Böhm. A new day, a new mission, something that didn't require chasing runaway children through the African bush. The coffee, cereal, fruit, and a sweet Danish stepped him back into the here and now, and when he was done, he flopped back on the bed, adjusted some pillows, and opened the FedEx package.

Another throwaway cell phone was inside, along with an envelope. Djahid chuckled at the reliable delivery method; in this high-tech world, sometimes the low-tech methods of the past were better. He powered it up.

His father appeared again, still looking well, but very somber. "My son. May the blessings of Allah be upon you forever. You had asked when we would strike at our real enemies, the two American spies, and I urged caution. While you were hunting in Africa, the simplest of things breached their secrecy. In the accompanying material, you will find details of a wedding that will take place in the resort city of Mazatlán."

Djahid paused the video to look briefly through the documents. Reports in the American media had been found, and they opened new frontiers for the private investigators. Where there was once blank canvas, now there was a gallery of details.

Back on the telephone message, father said, "That man who called pretending to be offering details for sale after the senator's heart attack—the senator died, by the way—gave us two names, and both will be at this wedding. From the phrasing, I think that perhaps other members of their secret team also will attend, as bonus opportunities. These are the people responsible for wrecking our grand scheme to advance the cause of Allah and Islam in Spain. I want you to kill them. Make the Christian crusaders feel the penalty for challenging the Prophet, blessed be his name. With your attack, you will reach into their secret world and yank out their black hearts."

And I will probably die in the process. Fucking suicide mission, thought Djahid.

As if reading his mind, the recorded voice of his father continued. "This will be a very dangerous assignment, my son. You are the only person I know who can carry it out with even a chance of escape. I leave all of the planning to you. I have no wish for you to be martyred, and I want you back home safely to grow into an even greater man than you already are. If you are called by Allah, then the name of Djahid Rebiane will ring out from paradise for a thousand years. Good luck, my boy. Kill them all."

Djahid dropped the phone onto the papers and sat for a while with his head propped back against his interlaced hands. It took some time to brush away the philosophical cobwebs until he came down to the nugget he wanted. *This Marine Kyle Swanson was their best operator, and he even won their highest military honor. I'm the best on my side of the street. I can take him. I know I can. Then I can take out the woman Ledford and probably a few more agents, too. My name will indeed live forever.*

MAZATLÁN, MEXICO

THERE WOULD BE NO danger coming from the west, unless a frogman came rising out of the Gulf of California, which Kyle Swanson thought pretty unlikely. A motorboat sped by offshore pulling a colorful parachute and its screaming paragliding tourist dangling below. Girls in bikinis walked in the surf, and guys played with Frisbees.

He and O. O. Dawkins were making still another antiterrorist patrol around the lavish waterfront hotel at which Beth and Mickey would say their vows in less than twenty-four hours. All they saw was people having fun in the big hotel pools and with normal beach activities. Also deterring any problem from the west would be the anchored presence of the huge *Vagabond* just off the Playa Olas Altas. Sir Jeff only hired ex-military for his crew, and they would remain at discreet combat alert during the event, with two long guns manned and ready with former SAS shooters.

Beaches stretched north and south, and there was no easy attack route from either of those directions. It would take too long over open ground. The lushness of Deer Island was too far away for consideration.

"Our general does not seem pleased with his new assignment," said Dawkins, with a careful study out over the rhythmic waves that came in to smoothly tattoo the beach. "Getting a third star and being deputy national security adviser to the president seems like a pretty big plum."

Swanson did a slow 180, looking for places where death might hide. Not the beaches. No way. Having the wedding out in the open actually was much better from a security standpoint than being in the middle of an urban environment with a multitude of hiding places. Urban combat is always a bitch. "He's going to miss Task Force Trident."

"Aren't we all? I mean, this is our last tango as a Trident team. Been a good run, though."

"It's the only call, Double-Oh. Our cover has been totally blown thanks to that fool Senator Monroe and his aide. The White House and the Pentagon had no choice."

"All those balconies up there scare me," said Dawkins, crossing his arms and scowling at the layer cake of receding patios on the gleaming white hotel that guaranteed every occupant an ocean view. "A good gun in any one of those hundreds of rooms could take a shot."

"The Mexican cops and Mickey's boys are going to do a full sweep, every room, tomorrow morning, and no fresh check-ins will be allowed for two hours before the ceremony." A web of scaffolding was being erected between the hotel and the white gazebo where a justice of the peace would stand with the bride and groom. Police would patrol each floor of the hotel. Metal detectors would sweep each guest at the entrance to the protected compound.

"What about Sybelle?"

"What about me? Come on, guys, we are ready to do the rehearsal." She wore a loose sundress that the breeze pressed against her legs and a big straw hat.

"You like our new jobs?"

"Same as the old job, just with a new address. Word is around that I requested a field command with MARSOC but was handed a desk job. Glass-ceiling shit, you know?"

"Maybe you really should spend the rest of your life signing papers on transfers."

"No way, Master Gunny Dawkins." She punched him on one of his big arms. "Anyway, on paper, you're going to grow old doing ceremonial parades at the Marine Barracks before retiring to chase fish in North Carolina."

"Ouch. Officer-on-enlisted-man brutality. Kyle, you saw her. I'm going to sue."

"I can still smack you whenever I want. You will never even see the Marine barracks, because you have an office right next to mine." She thrust her chin toward the building. "All those windows give an attacker a chance."

Swanson shrugged. "We've done about everything we can on that, Sybelle. Just time to roll the dice and see what happens. Nobody knows if there is really going to be an attack."

"This is what we do, remember? Worry and fight," Sybelle said. They started the walk back. "Actually we have a sweet deal, since the National Security Agency is giving us a whole corner of their new building at Quantico. On paper, the Lizard is moving deep into the National Security Agency. In reality, he will be right there with us, and have legitimate access to all of the NSA stuff rather than having to steal it. The only remaining question is you, Kyle. You decided?" They headed toward the pavilion overlooking the largest pool, where the rest of the wedding party was gathering, everybody in casual clothes meant for the tropical weather.

They waved to Hans Böhm, the friendly German photojournalist from *National Geographic*, who was drinking a beer at the gazebo alongside his sexy assistant while joking with Lady Patricia and Sir Jeff. He had been around for a few days and had freely handed out business cards. A phone call to his assignment editor at the magazine headquarters in Washington confirmed that he was in Mexico to photograph the famed cliff divers of Mazatlán. He was a tanned and rugged guy, and in the bar he had regaled them with outrageous stories of his last assignment in Africa, where, the German complained, nothing "verked," and even the lions were lazy. The magazine editor asked if Hans was drunk and bothering people, and Kyle had replied that he seemed to be sober. At that, the editor had snorted and asked if he had hired a local beauty to be his assistant. Kyle confirmed that that had happened; the gorgeous girl carried the camera bag and the lights, and Hans carried a beer.

When they hung up, the man who had answered the call, and truly was a magazine editor, immediately sent a coded message to Yanis Rebiane in Algeria to confirm that Djahid was where he needed to be.

Hans Böhm had asked permission to take some shots of the wedding rehearsal against the setting sun and the palm trees, talking about a special lighting angle from the sun being gold from the heavens, and how he hated Photoshop colors, and both Mickey and Beth agreed. They had hired a local company for the big event, but having some informal shots done by a *National Geo* expert was an unexpected treat. The girl assistant was trying to set up a tripod but didn't know how, and Hans went over to help her.

As they approached the others, Kyle explained to Sybelle and Double-Oh that his adoptive parents, both Jeff and Pat, were pressuring him to make the jump into the business and that the CIA was eager to get his counterterrorism skill set under its wing.

"Your cover with us will be fine, Kyle. First, we bring you back from the dead zone officially because it's no secret anymore that you are alive. So you work under your real name from now on, as a senior instructor at the Quantico Scout/Sniper School. Under this new setup, you can train openly between missions." Sybelle was looking at him curiously.

"Maybe you can help Lieutenant Colonel Summers sign papers," Dawkins mumbled. "The only thing that really changes is our name. Our team won't have one anymore. All part of the happy NSA family, but darker than dark. It works."

"That's the part I don't like," said Kyle. "I really enjoy having two hundred thousand other Marines covering my ass when I am on a mission. Can't ever trust the spooks."

"You're pretty smart for a little guy," Double-Oh said. "The jarheads will still be there. Only now we have a three-star general running interference for us, not some peewee two-star."

"Same song, different verse. We change the letterhead on the stationery and keep on doing what we do best," said Sybelle. "What about leaving for the civilian side, Kyle?"

"Not ready for that."

* * *

COASTIE AND MICKEY, his parents, Sir Jeff and Lady Pat, and General Middleton, who would walk her down the aisle, were huddled with the justice of the peace who would perform the ceremony. He was a chubby man who had done hundreds and had a friendly, open face. His job today was like that of a stage manager, making sure that everyone knew exactly what to do, where to stand, and what to say. There were bound to be a few mistakes due to nerves tomorrow, but this exercise would prevent chaos, unless a bridesmaid fell into the pool or something equally as unfortunate happened. His couples liked knowing everything was under control. He was unaware of the threat.

The largest pool had been made off-limits to the other guests for an hour to accomodate the walkthrough, and everyone took their places. Coastie had four bridesmaids, and Mickey's four closest pals were his groomsmen. Tomorrow they would all be in gowns and tuxedoes, but tonight it was just shorts, shirts, and sandals.

Hans came up carrying a Canon EOS and a 75-300 mm zoom lens and started to snap from the far side of the pool. A smaller iPhone 5 hung around his neck.

Sybelle joined the wedding party while Double-Oh and Swanson moved to where the Lizard stood with three members of the Mexican naval *fuerzas especiales*—Marine Special Forces—already strapped up with their ceremonial swords. The six men would raise their blades to form an arch of steel under which the newlyweds would pass. They, too, needed a couple of practice tries, since the swords with long blades were seldom used. They were strictly for show and, except for the points, weren't even sharp.

Swanson had never liked the swords and remembered cursing the hours he spent learning the drill for something so useless. Nevertheless, he put on the belt and scabbard, and the unit formed its lines. They could be outside of the gazebo while the justice of the peace ran the interior practice.

On emerging from the tent, the bride and groom would find Dawkins, the tallest man there, on their left. Beside him was one of the Mexican spec ops veterans, Jorge Alvarez, a grizzled older sergeant who had helped train Mickey when he was just a pup. Then came Kyle, at the end of the file.

On their right would be Sergeant Francisco Lopez, Commander Freedman, and Lieutenant Dante Gonzalez, the unit commander.

"Let's try it," said Gonzalez. "Draw!" Six hands wrapped around the grips of the swords. "Swords!"

The blades flashed from the scabbards on command and were rested erect against the men's right shoulders. "Present," Gonzalez ordered. "Swords!"

They went up at 45-degree angles, three on each side of the exit lane. Then the men broke into laughter because the arch was so ragged. They might as well have been a bunch of amateurs playacting *Game of Thrones* warriors.

"Oh, yes! That is *gut*! Please do it again. Look how they sparkle in this sun! We must catch the light," cried Hans Böhm. He hurried closer and handed off the big Canon to the trailing assistant and started working with the iPhone 5.

Gonzalez did not care about the light, but his swordsmen had looked like crap. They needed work. "Let's do it again before we hurt ourselves," he joked, returning his blade to the sheath. The others did the same, without formal command. They ran the drill again, crisper this time, and with Hans kneeling at the very end of the arch, which would frame the shot. The officer in charge was to his immediate left, and Swanson was near his right elbow.

Djahid Rebiane moved away, back to the girl holding the bag, and fiddled with some more equipment. Not yet. The whore Ledford would come out in a minute, and she would have to pass directly in front of Kyle Swanson. At that spot, he would attack, push Swanson into her, and take them both in no more than ten seconds. With Allah's will and a couple of tear gas grenades, the confusion would be so great that he would escape through the gawking and startled tourists to a jet ski that was waiting at the water's edge.

His secondary escape route would be the nearby service door to the hotel, which he had unlocked and propped open with a twig. Third choice was straight into the lobby and out the other side. There was no fourth choice, because if none of the other three worked, he would already be dead. He had spent a lot of time watching the security preparations around the hotel and knew they were expecting the hit tomorrow, actually during the ceremony. Djahid had come to the party early.

The honor guard did its practice again, but Djahid was ignoring them, facing the other way and pretending to be photographing something else. He chatted with his assistant while he casually unzipped the long side compartment on his battered black leather camera case. "Stay very close to me now," he told the girl.

THERE WAS NOISE beneath the trellised gazebo as the justice of the peace finished his stage directions.

"This is the part where you get to kiss the bride," he told Mickey, who did exactly that to a chorus of whoops from the others. "Then you depart back through the entryway and beneath those swords. Be careful out there with the pool. I don't want to lose my bride and groom before the ceremony!"

They turned, and Coastie hooked her arm through Mickey's. Then they paused. Outside, Dante Gonzalez said, "Let's get it right this time, guys." He gave the orders and the six blades came out, this time with precision, pointed outward and upward, the extensions of strong and rigid arms.

The German photographer was back on his knee, directly in the path of the departing couple. "Come to me now," he called. "Do not look at my camera. Oh, so pretty!"

They exited the gazebo and moved beneath the first swords. Hans got to his feet and backed away, as if pacing them, and worked the little iPhone 5 at different angles. "Quickly, now," he said and motioned to his assistant as he stepped aside to clear the way, ending in a position just behind and to the left of Kyle Swanson.

Coastie was radiant, Swanson thought. He imagined her in that fancy bridal gown tomorrow and wondered if she could be any more beautiful.

The German pushed the iPhone camera into the big bag and with the same motion slipped his hand into the long side pocket and gripped an Israeli-made Dustar combat knife. With his left hand, he quickly lifted out two ball-shaped tear gas grenades and slipped them into his vest. Then Hans Böhm ceased to exist.

Djahid Rebiane sprang forward, with the black seven-inch steel blade rising for an overhand attack toward the neck of the unsuspecting Kyle Swanson, three steps away. He had nothing to lose but his life.

Mickey and Beth were directly beneath the last pair of swords when Lieutenant Dante Gonzalez, facing Swanson, saw the unexpected charge. His own arm was still straight out in proper position and he was blocked from intercepting the danger, but his dark eyes widened in surprise. Beth had stolen a glance at Kyle, and her mouth opened to form a shout of warning. The German was the terrorist! He had a knife and was a step away from plunging it down into Swanson's totally unprotected neck with an overhand stab-and-rip move that would tear into the muscles and arteries and the throat. The blow did not have to be precise, for Swanson would bleed out even if he survived the initial strike.

The inner workings of Kyle's mind processed the information in a fraction of a second: Gonzalez's big eyes, and now the Lizard's, too, Beth inhaling to scream, and a sudden footstep and a disturbance of the zone of air behind him. He bent slightly forward to change his position, sweeping the blade of his sword down and behind Beth as he moved, as if chopping a loaf of bread.

While doing so, he also spun to the left and saw a figure almost on top of him with the black blade of a big knife coming down. Swanson's left hand shot up to parry the blow, but he only managed to shield himself, and Rebiane drove the point down hard, ripping down the left forearm from the wrist to the elbow as easily as a razor cutting paper.

Kyle didn't even feel it, because his eyes and brain had fully adjusted in that instant to what was happening. He grabbed the other man's passing wrist. *The German.*

Completing his turn and rising from the low point of the crouch, Kyle twisted his sword and thrust upward with the etched twenty-nine-inch blade. He rammed hard and the point impaled Djahid in the soft skin just beneath the chin. For a second, they stood locked in a motionless tableau, with Djahid's knife-hand wrist trapped by Swanson's left hand and unable to either withdraw or push forward. Djahid had his own left hand on the curved basket grip at the bottom of Swanson's big saber, pushing down while Kyle pushed up with all of his strength.

This was the assassin Swanson had known he would have to kill sooner or later, the crushing hammer of the Islamic terrorist movement in Spain. The guy who had killed Mike Dodge.

Djahid's eyes reflected pain and unexpected fear as he realized that his strength was not enough this time, and that this fight, his mission, and his life were all over. They were almost nose to nose, and he stared with cold hate into the gray-green eyes and found Swanson staring back with equal hatred. Then Kyle found a final burst of strength, rose to his toes to gain more leverage, and tore through the attacker's last defense. The silver blade of the sword went up hard, through the palate, then the soft tissue of the brain, and finally punctured out of the skull from the inside. The point emerged bloody and rose even higher as Kyle finished the thrust until the hilt of his sword stopped against the chin of Djahid Rebiane. Swanson held the impaled man there for a moment, then let Djahid drop, writhing and gagging on his own blood.

Beth grabbed Kyle and made him sit down while Mickey peeled off his blue T-shirt and pressed the cloth hard against the bleeding arm wound. Dawkins knelt beside the body of Djahid, with the sword through its head, as it twitched a final few times; then he looked over at Kyle and said, "The guy seems to be very, very dead. You hurt?"

"He just scratched me. Couple of stitches maybe," Kyle said, although his head was starting to swim from the loss of blood. The pain he had ignored during the fight was hitting now, and he winced against it. "My sword is all screwed up, though."

Beth laid Kyle's head on her lap and stroked his hair as he closed his eyes, drifting away as unconsciousness overtook him. Tears coursed down her face as she looked at the bloody mess of his left hand and arm, then the sleeping face of the man in her arms. "We'll have everything all cleaned up for you, Kyle, and get you fixed up, too. A few stitches. That's all. You've got a wedding tomorrow."

Epilogue

MAZATLÁN, MEXICO

"NO. Of course we are not going to postpone the wedding. Why should we?" Beth Ledford said in a kind voice, shaking her head. She and Mickey Castillo, accompanied by Lady Pat, had taken his parents up to their hotel suite to calm them down with stiff shots of tequila and soft words. Carlos and Alita Castillo had never seen anything like what they had just witnessed. The image of the shining sword poking out through the man's head would be impossible to forget, but Miguel and his bride-to-be and Pat seemed unfazed, on the verge of smiling. They took turns cleaning up in the bathroom of the suite while simultaneously tending to the shocked parents.

"But what happened down there . . ."

"Mama Alita, that's all over now." Beth hugged the small woman tightly. "This was actually a good thing. We were worried that an attack might happen tomorrow during the ceremony. I did not really want to wear body armor beneath my gown."

Mickey handed his father a drink. "That was a very bad man, Mama. Remember the terrorist attack recently on the American Consulate in Barcelona? This was the man who led it. He was a cold, professional murderer, and there is no real estimate of the number of people he slaughtered during his wretched life."

"You were expecting it? That's awful." Alita's shock was giving way. "Hans seemed to be such a friendly person."

Lady Pat leaned toward them, elbows on knees. "His real name was Djahid Rebiane, and his deadly skill was proven today by how close he came to success. He was trying to kill both Kyle and Beth and anyone else that got in the way. Good riddance to him."

"We have been hunting him for months," Beth declared flatly. "He was a devil."

Carlos looked over at Mickey. "This is the kind of thing you do in the Special Forces." It was a statement, not really a question.

"When we must," his son responded. "Not so often at our own weddings. In this instance, we had to choose the time and place and let the terrorists come to us. It worked."

"Kyle certainly handled himself well. It was all over in a split second. I hope he is not seriously injured. So much blood."

Lady Pat finally gave a smile that seemed to lighten the mood. "Kyle has been doing this sort of thing for a long time, Carlos. The terrorist had the advantage but never had a chance. Mickey, Beth, Sybelle, Double-Oh—all of them—would have put him down. To get to you and me, the bad guys have to go through people like them, and just knowing that lets me sleep well and feel safe. You can, too. Kyle will be back in a few hours, all stitched up and ready to go."

THERE WAS NO DEEP POLICE INVESTIGATION, because the police had been part of the security arrangements from the start. An inspector arranged for the removal of the body to the morgue, oversaw collection of the evidence, and declared himself satisfied with the statements of the Mexican Marines who witnessed the attack.

The hotel staff moved portable screens around the gazebo and pool and began an emergency cleanup operation as soon as the police gave permission. A mop-and-bucket brigade, veterans of cleaning up extraordinary messes, was paid extra to get this scene back to normal as fast as possible. All traces of Djahid Rebiane disappeared within two hours; then the crew moved up to do the dead man's room so that it could be rented out again tomorrow. The suicide last year of a rock star had been messier than this.

Commander Freedman, the Lizard, notified the CIA that afternoon, and the Agency passed the signal over to the U.S. Embassy in Istanbul. Attorney McKay Bannermann was contacted in Abu Dhabi and informed that Djahid Rebiane had been killed in a terrorist incident in Mexico. Bannermann personally told Marwan Tirad Sobhi that Yasim Rebiane had lost his vicious son and protector, so the shield had been lowered. The delicate balance in the rivalry had shifted, and Sobhi thought it would be best to take advantage of his opponent's unexpected vulnerability. Foreigners might have difficulty reaching deep into Algeria, but the sheikh knew other Algerians who could.

Washington and the White House received the briefing with great relief. The Barcelona episode had been fully avenged, and a new mark had been set in how to deal with such incidents in the future. The risk had been high, but the payoff was worth it. From now on, the men and women who sponsored terrorism had to believe that they were also putting their own lives on the line by making such decisions.

The political fallout turned out to be negligible, for everyone set aside any thought of gaining a voting advantage. Both Republicans and Democrats had been involved in the shadowy foray along the blurry line that separates national security and personal freedoms, and recognized it as political nitroglycerin. Neither wanted the story to continue. It would only get in the way. If it had to be done over, the same decisions probably would be made.

GUNNERY SERGEANT KYLE SWANSON had to stay in the hospital overnight while doctors stitched up his wounds, and they released him the next morning with great reluctance. There was a lot of outside pressure on the administrators, and the patient was very uncooperative and loud, although he had been sedated for the work on his arm and hand. He was expected to recover fully, the doctors admitted, but they insisted that anyone with such injuries should remain under medical care for several days. Bandaged up and with his left arm in a sling, he was virtually kidnapped that morning by a gang of dangerous-looking individuals.

"He's in no condition to do the sword drill," Sir Jeff observed back at the hotel as the others worked to get the wobbly Kyle into his dress blues. "He is liable to stab someone else."

"No problem," said General Middleton. "I'll take his place in the line, and he can escort Coastie down the aisle."

"If he doesn't fall over."

"I can do it," said Swanson. "Gimme my sword."

"You could not even pull it out of the scabbard, you doofus. In fact, not going to let you have one today." O. O. Dawkins held Swanson beneath the arms while Freedman steered the jacket on.

"He's zonked," said Double-Oh. "Maybe we should just let him sleep it off."

"Coastie's getting married! And I'm not going to be dead anymore! How cool is that?" Kyle announced to them all just before Middleton rubbed his face and head hard with a cold towel containing cubes of ice. He started to hum a tune that Jeff recognized from *My Fair Lady*: "I'm getting married in the morning . . ."

In thirty minutes, he was ready. Buttons and shoes were shined, belt and gloves snow white, and ribbons all arranged, despite the arm being in a sling. He felt great.

As the others took their places, he was able to stand alone, and Beth Ledford stepped into the waiting room, wearing a Dior gown. She locked him with a big smile. "You're beautiful," Kyle said.

"So are you," she replied, taking him by the arm and moving to the entranceway that would lead them to the altar just as the music began. The justice of the peace was waiting at the far end.

It was debated later at the reception about who was steadying who while they walked down the aisle, because Coastie was gripping Kyle's arm so tightly. Then he handed her off to Mickey Castillo and sat down in the front corner of the left first row on the bride's side. Pat and Jeff were next to him. The Castillos were across the aisle.

The music eased to a stop, and Kyle Swanson sat there with a goofy smile of total satisfaction on his face as he watched the bride and groom say their vows.